A Pair Like No Otha'

ALSO BY HUNTER HAYES

Shoe's on the Otha' Foot

Hunter Hayes

A Pair Like No Otha'

AVON BOOKS
An Imprint of HarperCollins*Publishers*

HarperCollins books may be purchased for educational, business, or sales promotional use. For information please write: Special Markets Department, HarperCollins Publishers Inc., 10 East 53rd Street, New York, NY 10022.

FIRST EDITION

Designed by Richard Oriolo

Printed on acid-free paper

LIBRARY OF CONGRESS CATALOGING-IN-PUBLICATION DATA

Hayes, Hunter.
A pair like no otha' / by Hunter Hayes.— 1st ed.
p. cm.
ISBN 0-380-81485-4 (alk. paper)
1. African American prisoners—Fiction. 2. Ex-prisoners—Fiction.
3. Friendship—Fiction. I. Title.

PS3558.A8313 P35 2002
813'.54—dc21
2002024231

02 03 04 05 06 RRD/WB 10 9 8 7 6 5 4 3

Acknowledgments

Whew! First, thank you God for bringing me to the point of publication, yet again. Thanks to my mom, Shirley, who encouraged me and never once tired of listening to me agonize about my book drama. I love you, and know that you're my morning glory, too. Thanks to my dad, up in heaven, I hope I'm making you proud. Thanks to my niece, Brandi, for turning out to be the intelligent, beautiful, and the gifted young lady that you are. You keep me hip and in on all the latest trends. I love you. Thanks to my agent, Denise "No-Nonsense" Stinson, for everything, book-related and not, including finding my new church home, CCC East. Thanks to my editor, Carrie Feron, you've helped to drive me professionally, more than you'll ever know.

I can't forget to give a shout out to the usual suspects who have a sister's back. Believe it or not, here's the shortened version: aunts: Evelinia, Bertha, and Barbara; uncles: Jerome, Jamesie, and John; Grandad Henry; my cousins Michelle, Monica, Scheria, Renee, Tony, Flora, Juanita, T.T., Junior, Junie, Izaire, Kerima, Adaya, Arkia, and Eric; Paul; my aunt Sandy; (of course) Glenn; Brenda Loran; my new stepdad Clarence; Janice P. Berry (my on-the-down-low publicist); Craig; Mr. Jackie Wilson; Tracy Robinson; my other cousin Michelle; Etty; Cutey; Nyoka; Latrice; Stephanie; Anette; Sis Tracy Greene; Jeeba; Gully; Al; Son; Mike; Denise; my cousin Kim; Charles; Kimberla Lawson Roby, my own personal mentor; Jacquie-Bamberg Moore, author of *All I Need*; Tonia; Wendy; Robin; Carol; Johanne; Beverly; Patty; Ayanna; Ramona; Marquita; Mama Joyce; the website creator of all creators, Deborah Maisonet of Webfully Yours. And thanks to my readers, and to all who contributed to the craft of the written word. Oh, and much thanks to my fifth-grade teacher, Stan Collymore, who made me read the *New York Times* in front of the class every day. It paid off.

ON LOCKDOWN

by Shemone Waters

Slam. The cell door closes, and so does what appears to be a chapter of your life. So what possible reason would any sane woman have for getting involved with someone on the other side of the law? According to the Bureau of Justice statistics, the prison population in the United States alone is projected to peak at an astounding two million inmates. It kind of probes one to ask the question, Is that where all the men are? Well, for some, the answer is a strong yes, and are they getting their man! It's a different lifestyle altogether, and the usual rituals of courtship don't apply. Case in point, instead of asking their mate if they're in the mood to eat out or in, they're asking if their name is approved on the visitors' list. Will that be a contact visit in the same room at the same table, or a noncontact visit over a telephone through a glass window? So much for romance. For these folks, love is . . . contributing to the commissary fund, and love is . . . being satisfied with communicating the majority of your most intimate feelings through the mail. Let's just hope that you have a steady ink supply . . .

1

Love Jones

"I'm horny for you."

Shemone nodded, and heaved a heavy, high sigh. "You're so vulgar."

"Yeah I am, but you love me for it."

"Now who said anything about love?" Shemone asked into the phone as she stretched out, lying back across the length of her queen-size metal-framed bed. "We're just good friends, Darnell."

"Me." He paused, then said, "I'm saying somethin' about it. I think I'm in love with you, baby-girl."

"Even from behind iron bars?"

"That's right," he answered coolly, using two singled words.

Surprising how talk with him made something inside of her stir. It was almost open-mike poetic when Darnell spoke, like a well-rehearsed rap song, in the way that he rarely ever missed a beat. She, on the other hand, wasn't as quick, or nearly as close to being so sure about the subject of love, or loving him, anyway. He was nothing but a friend, one for whom she held a special fondness for. That was her final answer, and it was the one she planned on sticking to. "Hmm," she managed to murmur. "Funny how I can't seem to fathom that."

"Fathom?" Darnell questioned; sometimes her wide vocabulary span threw him. He'd always admired her book smarts back when they were in high school. She'd been the first one frowning if she got anything less than an A on class exams. Shit. He'd been glad just to pass a class, period.

"It means 'to comprehend,' Darnell," Shemone answered, cutting him off abruptly.

"Yeah, well, Miss Fa-thom, you'll see soon enough for yourself. There's nothing to get to the bottom of but the truth," Darnell replied confidently.

The banter of another voice sounded off loudly in the background. Someone was cursing aloud, nonstop.

The voice was so loud that Shemone's tone of voice became irate. "Darnell, you'll have to speak up. I can't hear you over other people's voices. Isn't there a guard or somebody around?" she asked him. She thought for a moment. Never had she visited a real-life jail before, and never did she care to. But if it was anything like the penal-system documentaries, or the *Oz*-like television dramas she'd tuned in and seen, there would be guards. Armed ones.

The main source of the noise, another inmate, interrupted the conversation again.

Shemone heard the male voice coming through her end of the phone as he spoke to Darnell. It was almost as if she'd been there in Pennington herself, minus the visual.

"Man, how long you gonna be on that phone with all of that la-la shit? You're not the only one in here that gotta make calls, you know," the male inmate said to Darnell.

Darnell turned around to face the voice, his own hardened like steel, as he held the phone away and spoke. "I'm gonna be on for as long as I can." He gave the guy a threatening look with his eyes. "Now, is that gonna be a problem for you?"

The inmate raised his arms in defeat knowingly, once he'd recognized who he was talking to. If memory served him correctly, this was Darnell, from cell block H. Word on the inside was that this man had never lost a fight, and he wasn't about to risk being added to his undefeated-title list. "Whatever, then—man, it's cool. A brother can wait," the inmate casually replied, strolling off down the corridor. Sarcastically, he sang, "La, la, la la la, la, la, la la."

Darnell didn't direct his gaze from the man until he was out of sight, making sure to remember his face. One could never be too careful in the pen. "Bunch of clowns up in here, I swear," Darnell said in an agitated tone. He held the phone back up to his ear, speaking once again into the receiver. "Anyway, I'm sorry for that. Now back to what we were saying . . ."

Shemone had to admit to herself that she found his take-charge demeanor to be, well . . . attractive. In the one year that they had been communicating on the phone, she'd learned plenty. Darnell often captivated her by sharing detailed stories of his street adventures before he'd gotten locked up. Once, he'd told her how he'd paid police officers off, on the spot, to look the other way. According to him, it was the drug bust that never happened. What did happen was the big-time $5,000 payoff of cash that the two officers had each received from him. It was exciting tales like that one that kept drawing Shemone into his world, as each take was often better than the one before. Separating fact from fiction, though, had become really easy. The fact was, she had an actual "bad boy" friend who served so many good purposes in her life.

Darnell was the constant who never seemed to tire of listening to her gripe about what was going on with her life. From the mundane to the insane, she could always depend on him for an ear, some laughter, and even a bit of harmless flirting, which wasn't a new concept, by the way. Darnell never thought that any of the guys she'd dated during their old school days had been good enough for her. It was as if she'd found her high school friend all over again. She'd grown used to speaking with him on a regular basis, and looked forward to his calls. Lucky her. She knew Darnell wanted more than friendship just by the way he'd go on. But she was outspoken, and knew when to tell him when he was pushing the envelope. It didn't stop him from trying, and it didn't stop her from being just a friend to him. That's just the way things were. "Yes, I'm still here," she told Darnell, reassuring him that she was still on the telephone line. Darnell certainly was no slouch. It was apparent to her that he'd earned the respect of the other inmates since getting locked down in the Pennington correctional facility. She also had to admit that she hoped he wasn't going to resume that I-love-you conversation. Attraction was one thing, but acting on it was another thing altogether. Fortunately for her, he moved on to another subject.

"I got the picture you sent," he told her.

"Did you?" A slight smile made its way across her face. It was just the response she'd anticipated, having sent the best shot out of the bunch of twenty-four film exposures. A lady had to look her best, she remembered thinking before stuffing the photo into its envelope. She was clad in funky jeanlike black leather pants, a sexy charcoal-gray V-necked sweater, and matching wedge-heeled suede ankle boots.

"I added it to my collection," Darnell replied.

Goodness. Shemone thought for a second. And what collection did he have? She had sent him only two other pictures. One of the two of them in a group, as friends, that had been taken when they were teenagers, one other recent photo, and now this one. Yes, she concluded, that would make it a collection all right.

"I used to have them lined up across the wall . . . but I took them down after all the guys started coming in my cell, peeping all wide-eyed at you. I'd be talking to them, but they'd be looking up at you," Darnell joked. "Nobody's gonna notice you like that but me. I put you in a scrapbook I made in shop," he said, looking at the photo once again. "Baby-girl, that new hair color is you. What's the name of it again?"

"Red sienna, I'm a redhead now," Shemone replied sharply. "I don't know why I send you pictures, anyway."

"Damn, a brown woman who's a redhead," Darnell quickly

answered, totally ignoring the I-don't-know-why-I-send-you-pictures comment she'd just made.

"Yes, you'd be surprised by what they can do with colors when they match it with the right shade."

"I'm saying, it looks right on you," Darnell said. "Red is definitely your color. It goes with that honey complexion of yours. What, you take that picture in a hotel or something?" he asked her.

"No, that's my bedroom," she answered plainly. The photo he was referring to was of her sitting in a chair, in her bedroom. Not on the bed, and not in nightwear. The point being that it wasn't one of those suggestive poses, it was nothing like that.

There was a slight pause on the other end of the line.

"Your whole bedroom is done up in off-white, huh?" Darnell asked.

"Mm-hmm, you know I like nice things," Shemone said in a matter-of-fact tone of voice. At least he should have known she liked nice things by now, as much as they told each other. Darnell knew more about her personal life than almost anybody else. He knew that she aspired to making the most out of her career in writing. He knew about the strained relationship she'd had with her mother, he knew that she was practicing celibacy. . . . Well, that was one she wished she'd kept to herself. But it wasn't as if it was a news-breaking story. It was hard to find a good man nowadays, and until she did, she was holding on to her stuff. Darnell was constantly telling her what a strong woman she was for all that she was doing to better herself. Shemone's thoughts wandered back to the here-and-now. She picked up where he'd left off, her all-off-white bedroom.

"Yeah, well, it must be hell trying to keep that sucker clean," Darnell said.

"Not really, since it's just me here. Although sometimes I do splurge, and have a lady come in to tidy up. I'm nothing but an absolute neat freak anyway," she told him, glancing around her spotless bedroom.

"Oh," Darnell said in a somewhat uncertain tone. He'd learned something new about Shemone yet again. The thought of having someone in to clean the house had never occurred to him. His mama was the only one who "tidied up," as she called it, where he was from. His ego kicked back in as he tinkered with the insides of an electrical component he was working on. "Better be just you there," he playfully threatened.

"You're fixing something while I'm talking to you, aren't you?" Shemone asked him. She detected that Darnell was preoccupied. Shemone had encouraged him to take up an electrical training course a few months ago, and now all he wanted to do was fix everything he could get his two hands on. He'd told her that he'd agreed to the course only to help pass the time, but it seemed to her that he really enjoyed it.

"Yeah, I'm just fine-tuning up my portable CD player. I think one of the circuits might have gone out on me," he explained as he snapped the cover back on. He watched as the tiny red power light lit up, and heard the music as it blared from the oversize headphones that went with it. Satisfied, Darnell switched the power back off.

"You're allowed to have a CD player in your cell?" Shemone asked him in a startled voice. She'd never heard any kind of music in the background before. He had a lot going on. A confrontation with another inmate, fixing a CD player, and holding a conversation with her. Darnell was a multitasker and didn't even know it, she thought to herself.

Darnell chuckled. "Yeah, radios, electric shavers, even TVs. As long as there are earplugs," he informed her. "There's a big book, the Jack L. Marcus catalog, that I order from."

"I had no idea," Shemone confessed. Darnell was living with all the conveniences of the outside world, only on the inside, in a room with bars. "You know, that sounded like a threat you gave me a little earlier. What if it isn't only me here at my place?" Shemone playfully asked, going back to the subject he'd brought up. She knew better, but part of her wanted to know where he was going with it. If she had to set him straight again, she sure would, she told herself.

"That's why I'm calling you, baby-girl. I've got good news. I wanted it to be a surprise, but I just can't hold it in anymore. Guess who's coming home?" Darnell announced happily. "Me, I'm coming home, baby-girl. Shemone, you hear me?"

There was a click on the end of the phone line when an automated female voice interrupted, "Zero minutes left."

"I'm about to get cut off. Shemone, you there? Did you hear me? I said I'm about to get cut off—"

"I heard you, Darnell," she suddenly answered. "You're coming home. . . . When?"

The phone fell dead silent.

Shemone just couldn't believe it. Out of all the times she'd thought about Darnell actually coming home, she'd never dreamed it would be so soon. Three years seemed to have flown by, Shemone thought. Well, the year had flown by. Darnell had already served two years on his sentence before they'd started to keep in touch.

It was ironic, how she and he found had each other again in the first place. It hadn't been long ago. Shemone had been over at Beatrice's house when it had all happened. Beatrice had since legally changed her name to Ohija. The reason for the name change, Shemone couldn't quite remember. She'd have to check with her to be reminded.

Shemone didn't have to be reminded of April 16 of 2001 though. Clearly, it was only a year ago. Ohija's name was still Beatrice then, and a hysterical Darnell had just called over to the house from jail. The story had made front-page news. Beatrice's cousin Terrance, an exceptional pro ballplayer on the rise, had just been killed in a bizarre car accident. Terrance had gotten behind the wheel of his car drunk, as a result of a heated argument he'd had that night with his girlfriend, and now he was gone.

Terrance, Darnell, Shemone, and Beatrice, known back then as the Final Four, had been best friends since high school, where they'd all first met. Shemone had conjured up the name Final Four before they'd graduated. As far as they all were concerned, there were four of them in the group, and their friendship was final and forever.

Shemone soon realized, though, that people grew up, and that they did different things. That came to be fact, once they'd all actually graduated from Monroe High. Each one of them had taken a different path. Shemone went off to Virginia to Hampton University to study for a career in journalism, and fate rewarded her with a salaried writing position with the same magazine that she had interned for. Terrance headed straight to St. John's on a basketball scholarship, and time and effort eventually took him to the pros, playing for the Miami Heat. Ohija took another route. She stayed home, saved money, and attended a community college part-time. After majoring in business administration and obtaining her degree, she landed a steady city job doing the nine to five. And when that hadn't satisfied her appetite for success, Ohija had become the proprietor of her own clothing boutique, Shades. Darnell had stayed home in Harlem, too, opting not to do the school thing at all. He had set out to let the world know that college wasn't for everybody, and that he could still be a success, as long as he remained true to his music. He'd planned on being the next Quincy Jones. But the music couldn't have made him that quickly. In town one minute, and out of town the next, driving a shiny brand-new black-on-black Jeep Grand Cherokee around, and sporting only the latest clothing, or so Shemone had heard. It all made perfect sense. But all of a sudden, Darnell wasn't doing so great. He'd been arrested, and was serving a sentence on a three- to five-year drug charge.

When a highly upset Darnell got word of the accident involving Terrance, he had still been locked up in prison. Beatrice couldn't be of much comfort to him, having to be strong for herself and her family. She could barely get out the broken words to tell him the sordid details of what had happened; Shemone bravely took the phone away to finish for her.

"Why?" Darnell wanted to know. "Terrance was a good person! He was playing pro for the Miami Heat! I just saw him take a game! Five rebounds and four assists. Terrance can't be gone! It just ain't fair!" Dar-

nell had angrily said. His voice had quivered, and all he'd wanted was to know why.

Shemone had done her best to comfort Darnell, even if it was just over the phone. She reminisced with him about the great times they'd all shared together, and how those memories could never be taken away. Finally calming him, she convinced him that Terrance was in a better place, and that all they could do was to keep living and pass those memories on. They'd have to be the ones to set the example of never getting behind the wheel when drunk. She'd also offered him her home telephone number, and told him to call . . . if he ever needed somebody to talk to. After all, she was Darnell's friend, too, even if she hadn't spoken to or seen him in, what? Practically a total of nine whole years.

Now this, she thought to herself. He was coming home. It wasn't as if he was in jail for murder or anything. He was in on a misdemeanor charge, a victim of being in the wrong place at the wrong time. Unfortunately, he had gotten caught. Hopefully, he'd learned his lesson. She knew the kind person Darnell was at heart, and that was really all that mattered. He was still savvy, that was for sure. They'd had countless in-depth telephone conversations, and Darnell had a strong opinion about everything, which included politics, religion, and even entertainment. Darnell was a solid listener, too. Shemone felt free enough to dream aloud with him when it came to many of her story ideas. Nothing was ever too off-the-wall for him. And when Darnell spoke, he was always complimentary and funny, just like he'd always been back in Monroe High.

Shemone was feeling nostalgic, with all that was going on with Darnell, and from everything positive she'd wanted to remember from the past. She went into the living room and walked over to the huge mahogany Asian-inspired armoire that stood against her exposed red-brick wall. She looked around, then took a hand-embroidered antique footstool from out of its corner. Standing on top of it, she pulled down a big navy book with gold-embossed words that read "Monroe High

School Class of '92." Shemone blew the dust from the top of its vinyl cover, and took it over to the couch. It was still in prime condition after almost nine years. She flipped through the pages, reading the inscriptions that her fellow classmates had written. "Let's keep in touch, see you at the top, and stay as sweet as you are." Those were among the many kind words that her classmates had scribbled across its pages. Shemone wondered to herself what had become of them. She giggled at a corny picture of herself, and at the caption printed below it. "Shemone Waters, Most Likely to Succeed."

Her hair sure was a mess back then, with that jet-black homemade Asian bob style. She just had to have herself some bangs. She giggled again. Shemone couldn't remember the last time her hair had been that color, or that long. With little effort, she ran her fingers through her new short, curly do, making light of the difference in her appearance. It was simple, it was chic, and, best of all, it was low maintenance. On the same page, a few spaces over, was Ohija, a.k.a. Beatrice, wearing thick brown-framed bifocal glasses and a deep-finger-waved hairdo. Shemone laughed aloud. It was a fortunate thing that she didn't choose her friends based on how they looked. Ohija sure was a sight! Terrance had it going on back then, though, with his fine self. He was all maple-looking, with a shaped-up shiny blowout. Shemone couldn't help but wonder what Darnell, the last of the Final Four friends, looked like now. Flipping ahead a few pages led her right to the old version of him, page fourteen. "Darnell Williams." She had to confess that, like Terrance, Darnell did have it going on, too. All toffee-looking. Low fade. Slim goody-goody. Great teeth. Dark eyebrows and lashes that any woman would kill for.

Odds were ten to one that he still looked good. But so what? Shemone thought to herself. Darnell wouldn't be the first or the last attractive male friend she had. There wasn't a doubt in her mind. Of course she'd be there for him once he was released. . . . Male friends. They were the best ones to have, anyway. They weren't always trying to put her business out there with all that drama. Shit, she was working on being totally focused and established. Holding it down as the permanent trendy-relationship columnist for *Sister Soul Magazine* was a nice start. With her skills and insight, one day she'd probably be running it. Diversity was key, Shemone thought, so in addition to her columnist job, Shemone freelanced on the side for a number of other magazines, writing tiny snippets to full-page articles on everything from A to Z. And speaking of alphabets, *S* was the one to go with, because it was just total satisfaction living on the Upper West Side, in a prewar building with shiny hardwood floors, high ceilings, and original crown moldings. And thanks to rent stabilization, and a hookup from a friend of a friend, there was little to complain about. Not even parking in the city, because she usually managed to keep a spot. The car might not be a new Mitsubishi Montero SUV, but it was all hers, and in prime 1999 condition. That was a gift she'd given herself a year ago, after cashing in on some major stock investments she'd made, all at the tender age of twenty-seven, and single.

Single was nowhere near taboo. Especially when there were no obligations, and nobody to have to answer to. Short on companionship? Not a problem. All she had to do was phone up one of her many male friends. She wasn't sleeping with any of them, and they knew this because she'd let them know it. Upfront. Shemone often questioned whether the men she dealt with stuck around in her life for the quality of time spent with her, or just the challenge of getting her into bed. Whatever the case was, celibacy was the route she'd chosen for herself, for going on an entire year. Celibacy allowed her to center more on herself, and not on someone else.

She was through with any man who wanted to play house without the commitment. Those were the same men who wanted keys. As far as she was concerned, there was only one person who was going to have a set to her place, and that was her. After all, she was the one paying the bills, and single is as single does.

Unlike most clueless people, Shemone herself had a well-thought-out ten-year plan. Marriage wasn't until she hit thirty, so she figured she could just date around until she met "the right one." He'd be a successful person of equal, if not better, footing than she had on the career path. He'd be educated, a looker, and funny as all hell, but amazingly he wouldn't be perfect, because no one was. Most important, he'd make her feel appreciated, and be her man.

Shemone continued to look through her yearbook, browsing back and forth, looking at the pictures. In the gym and outside class, at the auditorium, and splashing around in the swimming pool. She looked to the right, she looked to the left, but for some odd reason, she found herself turning back to that page with that boy on it. Page fourteen. Yes, the one with the boy with the low fade, the toffee-colored one, with the name Darnell Williams printed underneath. Her Final Four friend was coming home.

2

Strange Encounters

Hey, sistah-girl."

"Hey, Bea . . . ," Shemone replied, greeting her best friend as she opened her front door Saturday afternoon.

"Not Bea, not Beatrice," she answered, flailing her hands around. "My new name is Ohija. O-hi-ja," she clearly pronounced again, with a smile. "The more you say it, the more you'll get used to it, girl."

"Oh, yes, that's right," Shemone replied, taking Ohija's coat, which was already off and pushed in her direction. Knowing her friend, Beatrice had probably removed it once she hit the lobby of her building. It suddenly dawned on her why Beatrice, now renamed Ohija, had legally changed her name only weeks ago. She'd mentioned something about wanting to be renewed. "Renewed." Shemone couldn't figure out what was so wrong with the old Beatrice.

But she would be a friend to her regardless of who she was, or at least who she thought she was. "Nice coat, girl . . . Is it new in the shop?" Shemone asked, changing the subject.

"It is—thanks," Ohija replied. She made her way toward the bedroom.

Freshly twisted blond locks and a light-caramel face whizzed by. Shemone followed.

"It's kente inspired. You like the print? I special-ordered a handful of them from the African-American Festival. You missed it, girl! It was out of this world. I found a new sistah there who could twist the heck out of some hair! I had her redo mine. See how long they're getting?" Ohija shook her head wildly in demonstration, similar to the way Tina Turner did onstage. "And the smell is to die for, smells like—nature!" She sauntered over to Shemone's dresser, where rows of her favorite perfumes were neatly lined up. After opening a bottle of Shemone's latest purchase, she gave it a generous whiff. "Whooo!" Ohija exclaimed, putting her index finger underneath her nose. "That's strong! You really should consider using oils. They're much better for you, they last longer, and they don't cost nearly half as much as those designer brands."

"Yes, I suppose I could try out an oil," Shemone answered, putting Ohija's coat on a hanger and away in the hall closet.

"I am so beat, girl," Ohija told her. "My head is spinning. Stress! Do you mind if I take a load off?"

"No, I don't mind at all. Go ahead, girl," Shemone answered. When she returned to the room, she found Ohija sitting in the middle of her bed, barefoot, with both legs crossed in the lotus position, often used in meditation. A single thick-tube vanilla-scented candle burned on the top of her dresser. Where had it come from? It wasn't one she owned. As if the sight of her best friend sitting on her bed, and the burning candle, wasn't enough, Ohija had begun to chant aloud: "Ommmm . . . Ommmm . . . Ommmm."

Shemone stood speechless at the door's entrance. She wasn't sure whether she should interrupt or not.

"Ommmm . . . Ommmm . . . Ommmm," Ohija kept repeating, her eyes completely shut. Shemone thought there was no telling how long this chanting session with Ohija would last. Several minutes later, Shemone walked away, using the time to load the leftover breakfast dishes into the dishwasher and clean out the bathtub. And when she returned, it was still going on.

"Ommmm . . . Ommmm." Ohija repeated to herself, after what seemed to be close to thirty minutes, she emerged from out of the bedroom looking all at peace and shit.

"Shemone, girl, I feel like a new woman. I so needed that," her friend announced.

Shemone looked up to answer, "That's real terrific, girl." She sat on the couch thumbing through a clothing catalog. "What exactly was all that, anyway?"

Ohija grinned proudly and took a seat next to her friend. Groups of silver bangles, and her slightly pudgy body, shook as she did. She was comfortably dressed in baggy maroon-colored pants and a black turtleneck. "It's called meditation, girl. It's good for you. I started it about a week ago. It does wonders for the soul. It raises your kundalini."

"My kunta what?" Shemone giggled.

"Kundalini, it's an energy, it's like the center of your positivity."

"Okay—go, Ohija!" she joked. She wasn't poking fun, but she also wasn't surprised. Ohija was always looking for ways to improve herself. She'd always been that kind of I-can-do-anything person, and so far it was working. Ohija was already her own boss, being the CEO and entrepreneur of the Shades Clothing Boutique. She'd gone to school and put the degree she'd earned in business administration to work for herself, leaving behind the humdrum routine of her former predictable city job. Why certainly, Shemone thought to herself, her friend's methods were to be admired.

"So how's life treating you on the Upper West Side?" Ohija asked.

"Life is sweet," Shemone casually answered as she put the catalog down. "Girl—guess who's coming out?"

"Who? Don't tell me, it's your gay friend Adina? The one who's twenty years old and still hasn't told her parents that all she thinks about is the licky-licky?"

"No—not Adina, girl." Shemone chuckled. "She'll probably never let that cat out of the bag. You want something to snack on?" she offered, about to get up and go into the kitchen.

"No, but speaking of snacks—don't you move, I've got just the thing," she quickly told her. "It's something new in my bag that I want you to try. Tell me if you like it."

Shemone twisted her nose up almost immediately. "Ohija, I am not taste-testing any of your new concoctions!" she joked.

"No, girl—it really is tasty," Ohija told her as she reached into her butter-soft brown leather knapsack, whipping out a clear Baggie of tan nuggets. "Try it, it's nature's candy, carob candy."

Shemone nodded a defiant no thanks for the second time. "Not today, you won't!" That Ohija, she thought. Last time she had her drinking soy milk from out of a camouflaged container in her fridge. Needless to say, the soy milk had made her sick to her stomach for that day and half of the one after.

"Suit yourself, then," Ohija said, letting her friend off the hook. "You just don't know what you're missing!" she said, unsealing the Baggie and helping herself to some. "So finish. Tell me—tell me, who is coming out?"

"Would you believe me if I told you it was Darnell?"

"Stop!" Ohija gasped. "The same Darnell Williams of our own Final Four?"

"The one and only," Shemone replied.

"That's terrific!" Ohija beamed, at the thought of Darnell getting out of jail. The guilty part of her felt a huge sense of relief. She hadn't bothered to keep up with him and his whereabouts since before he'd gotten locked up. She'd been way too busy doing the just-graduated-from-college and work thing. Now that he was being released, she'd have a second chance to be there for him. Darnell would have a better chance of making it on the outside with a strong support system of friends who cared about him. "So when's he coming home?" she asked.

"I'm not sure, we kind of got cut off," Shemone replied.

"Wait a minute, you've been talking to him on the phone like that?" Ohija popped a few more pieces of the carob sweets into her mouth, chewing and talking, talking and chewing. "You didn't tell me that, Ms. Shemone! Just how long were you gonna wait before letting me in on your little secret?" she joked.

"It's not even that serious," Shemone answered in a sistah-girl tone. Ohija knew that she and Darnell spoke, she just didn't know how often. And it was very often. Shemone picked up the catalog again, eyeing the front of it as if seeing it for the first time.

"Lies!" Ohija blurted out.

"Wha—at?" Shemone asked innocently.

"Lies! Look at you, you're all fidgety. I don't know how much you talk to Mr. Darnell, and I don't know what kind of sweet nothings he's been saying over the phone to you, but you definitely have caught some kind of feelings!"

"Ohija, please!" Shemone answered playfully. "I've been talking to him for almost a year now, since Terrance passed. It's been difficult for him, like it's been for both of us. I've just been trying to be there as a friend."

Ohija gave Shemone a cynical look, and a smile. Regardless of what she had just heard, doubt was written all over her friend's face, in capital, bold lettering.

"It's just talk," Shemone said in a convincing tone of voice. "He's locked up! It's not like I've gone to see him, and you know that I don't give any man money."

Shemone sounded impressive, but Ohija still wasn't totally convinced. She probed further. "Okay, so then you won't mind if I give you a little test?" Ohija asked before getting up to go into the kitchen. "What do you have in that glorious fridge of yours to drink, girl?"

"There's soda, juice, milk—take your pick," Shemone yelled out.

"Oh, that's right, go on, I forgot you've got everything, with your bourgeoisie self!" Ohija joked from the kitchen.

"I am not bourgeois!" Shemone yelled back from the living room. "Is it bourgeois to shop for what you need at the supermarket?" Shemone asked. Ohija's comments weren't offensive to her. In fact, Ohija called her bourgeois on a regular basis. They joked about it all the time, and if working hard to get the finer things in life was called bourgeois, then she was.

"So the test. Will you take it, then?" Ohija yelled out. Shemone heard the sound of the ice machine as it went off. "Of course, I have nothing to hide."

"There are three questions. You can just answer yes or no," Ohija told her. She came back into the room with two cups filled with fruit juice and ice.

"Okay, go ahead already. Let's get this over with." Shemone turned around on the sofa to both face and humor her friend. This is going be a piece of cake, she thought to herself.

"One," Ohija asked, "have you ever received a letter from him from jail that has hearts or has been signed with 'Love,' or 'Thinking of you'?"

Shemone hesitated, then answered slowly, "Yes." Darnell had written her some letters, and though they were never explicit, he always signed them "With love, Darnell." But that didn't mean anything; she loved Ohija, too.

"Two, have you ever sent him any pictures of yourself? Whatcha say, girl?" Ohija loudly teased.

Shemone nodded yes. "A few pictures, and so what? Darnell wanted to know what I looked like now. It's been nearly a decade!"

"No need for the extra info!" Ohija chuckled. "Please just answer the questions."

Shemone wanted to scream.

"Last and final question . . . Does he say intimate things to you when you speak?"

Okay, well, there was no denying that. Shemone thought to herself that she couldn't control everything that came out of the man's mouth. "Yes! Yes! Yes! Okay?" Shemone reluctantly replied.

Both of them fell out laughing on the area rug.

"See I told you! You two are an item," Ohija announced after they'd stopped laughing.

"It's a dumb test, with no meaning," Shemone answered. "Darnell and I have been friends for the longest, and I just won't throw that away." Shemone continued to speak as if she were on trial, "He's not even my type, girl, and you know that. Ohija, he's a statistic, with nothing to offer me." Then she logically added, "He can only hold me down."

Ohija laughed aloud. "You plan on punishing him for making a mistake? We both know that Darnell is a good-hearted person."

"And just how well do you know Darnell, Ohija?" Shemone asked. "I mean, you were here in New York with him while you were in school and working. What was he like when I was away?"

"I really didn't see him much myself," she replied. "I told you that I was busy with the work/school thing. I mean, I knew him like a brother when we were younger, but I can't say much about him now." There was a look of regret on Ohija's face. "You know how it is. We didn't really keep in touch like that after high school. I suppose we just grew apart. I'd see him every once in a while. He'd always ask me if the family needed anything."

"And you said?" Shemone asked.

"I said that we were doing okay, which we were," Ohija plainly answered.

"So your refusal of his money, it didn't have anything to do with his lifestyle?" Shemone asked.

"Not really, and I did know that he was into that fast life. You know—drugs and stuff like that," Ohija replied, quickly scrunching up her nose.

Shemone cut right to the chase. "Well, it doesn't make a difference either way what he was up to then or now when it comes to the area of romance. I'm just hoping that he'll change his lifestyle. I care about him, but there's absolutely no room for a Darnell in my ten-year plan. He's not even in the running," Shemone told her, sucking on a piece of crushed ice.

"I know, I know," Ohija mocked. "When you're thirty . . . Mr. Professional . . . educated . . . blah, blah, blah. You know, Shemone, everyone isn't lucky in that way. Take my husband, for instance. Raymond's a forty-five-year-old garbageman. Do you think I planned on marrying an old garbageman?"

Shemone laughed, "Girl, you're too much!"

"I'm serious," Ohija said. "But he's good to me. He'll rub my feet in a minute if I tell him I've had a hard day at work, he cooks, and he brings home his paycheck each and every week. He's all the man I need and I wouldn't trade Ray for anything in the world. We've got two strong, solid years going, and I'm hoping for many more!"

"I understand your point," Shemone said. "But that was the course of life that you chose to take, period. You didn't have to marry him. You didn't even have to date him."

"No—but I'm glad that I did." Ohija got up from the floor where she sat. She took a look at her watch. "Girl, I've got to go! I'm meeting the hubby for dinner at six o'clock. See, that's part of what I'm talking about. It's a joy. I can't wait to get home for dessert. Big momma's gonna put it on him tonight!" Ohija said as she gathered up her bag.

Shemone went off to get her coat, laughing, and nodding her head. "Ohija, you're something else!" When she returned, she helped her on with her coat.

"Thanks, and thanks for lending me the space to get my meditation on, girl," Ohija told her. "Speaking of space, I was thinking that maybe we could get some hiking in over the weekend!"

"Hiking? Now whatever would give you the idea that I'd want to go hiking?"

"Why ever not?" Ohija turned around to ask with a grin, going out the apartment door, toward the elevator. She gave her friend a big hug. "You only live once." The elevator chimed, indicating that it was on the floor.

"Can I think about it?"

"Just give me the word," Ohija said, hurrying inside the elevator, catching it just before its doors closed.

"I'll call you," Shemone said as she thought, mmph mmph mmph. That Ohija never missed out on anything. Not even an elevator.

Shemone took a look around her apartment. Everything was in its place, looking like something from out of an issue of *Metro Homes* . . . except for the couch. Shemone walked over to it, and fluffed up the huge throw pillows that added to its deep olive-green velvet decor. Did Ohija leave that candle burning? She hoped she did. Shemone went inside her bedroom to check. Yeah, it was still burning. The sweet scent of vanilla still wafted through the room with what must have been part of that kundalini positivity that her friend had left behind. Shemone went over to her CD player, and slipped on a little bit of jazz, the sounds of George Howard. Her head moved as the aroma overcame her. She did a rhythmic hip-and-shoulder dance around the room. She stopped short, just in front of the mirror of her bureau. At twenty-seven, she still had the body of an eighteen-year-old. Her Tae-Bo tape kept her stomach flat and her waist small. The booty was still big, though. There was no getting rid of that. Her mother, and her mother's mother, had passed it right on down to her, through the generations. Her breasts were another matter. It seemed as if she was always trying to push them up or together. Thank goodness for push-up bras and something to work with. Clad in an orange sweatshirt, faded blue jeans, and sneakers, she decided that she would get out of her clean-the-house clothes and into something a bit more comfortable for lounging at home.

Shemone went into her bureau and took out a pair of navy satin pajamas. She walked into her purple-and-white-checked designer bathroom, and turned the showerhead on full blast. She allowed the temperature to get just right before stepping out of her clothes and into the stall. She lathered her loofah up to its full capacity, then ran it along her body in straight, even lines. That reminded her to shave her legs and under her arms. Still not quite finished, she shampooed and conditioned her curly red hair, then thoroughly rinsed the soap and shampoo off her body and hair before stepping out. Shemone toweled herself off and applied ginger-scented body oil. She brushed her teeth and flossed before putting on the pajamas that hung on the hook behind the bathroom door.

Feeling totally comfortable, Shemone set out to do a little work. She shut off her CD player and went over to her computer. She sat down and switched the PC on, humming the previous tune from the CD as the computer booted up. She swiveled around in her leather desk chair, and went directly to a piece she'd been working on for *Sister Soul Magazine*. She was trying something new. A reader and aspiring new writer had sent her a true story on an experience that she'd had with a male friend. Shemone thought that it would be a terrific idea to submit it for publication along with her advice and personalized comments on the piece. She'd entitled it "Boyfriend," and it was about women who dated their male best friends. It would help to give the sister and herself exposure at the same time.

BOYFRIEND

by Cassandra Wright and Shemone Waters

"Me? What am I doing? I'm working on a magazine article," I'd said as I spoke calmly into the headset of my cordless telephone receiver. It sounded good enough to me. A response was what I wanted to evoke.

"Oh really?" he'd asked with interest. "What's it about?"

"It's about friends who date friends," I'd quickly answered. "I'm totally against it. What's your take on it?" There. I'd said it. After months of agonizing, I'd finally figured out how to let one of my best male friends know that I was interested in something more than . . . a friendship. Not just sexual, but something meaningful. And why not? It wasn't as if we were strangers. I'd known this friend for seven years. We'd attended the same college, and I knew practically everything there was to know about him. Back in those days, I'd had a crush on him because of the way he looked. Like brown heaven. But it was

more than that now, so much more. Throughout the years I'd gotten to discover that he had an intellect, a sense of humor, a direction, and a wonderful job anchored down. Now add being well-mannered and respectful to the list. Damn, he's everything that a woman would want in a man. Frankly, I hadn't found one like him on my own, although I had tried. So I decided to empower myself and take a chance on the four-letter word we all call love. He was at work, so at first he put me on hold. I could respect his professionalism. I added that to the asset list, too, before he resumed our conversation.

"I think it can be a good thing," he'd answered, "because you know what you're getting. You pretty much know how the person is, and if they're a cheater or not."

This was a good sign, a very good sign, I thought. He thought that dating a friend was a good thing, and he wasn't big into cheating. Why, certainly, I was ahead of the game. "I don't know," I'd said, not wanting to be obvious. I continued to play devil's advocate. "It could ruin everything," I'd said.

"But maybe not." He put me on hold one more time.

Then a coworker of his gets on the phone. "Tonia, I'm Tracy. I just wanted to say that yes, it can work out. I married my best friend. It was the best thing I could ever have done," she added.

It was all the confirmation a single, black sistah would ever need, and I was smiling from ear to ear. Things were going just as I had planned. It was almost too good to be true.

Dear "Tonia": Well, there you go, the secret to finding a worthy relationship is Darnell. . . .

Darnell? What was his ass doing in her article? Shemone blew out a slow rush of air, and quit typing. She saved and closed the file, drawing a blank, unsure of how to finish the ending. She'd run smack-dab into the huge brick wall of writer's block. It was fortunate that her editor, Jackie, had given her a little over two weeks to turn it in. Besides that, she had a host of other smaller projects to edit. At least she still had four days to go on this one. Shemone double-checked her desk calendar to make sure, then got up to go into the kitchen. There was some leftover pad thai shrimp in the refrigerator from the night before that she could microwave. It was a day old, which made it taste even better. The mix of peanuts and spices had had a chance to blend in perfectly. Just then the telephone rang. She glanced at the wall clock, which read 7:30 P.M., thinking it was Darnell. This was around the time he'd usually phone. At first she was going to let her machine pick up and screen, but out of anticipation, she personally answered it. If it was him, she wanted to know exactly when it was that he was coming home, since they had gotten cut off the last time. "Hello," she said into the phone.

"Hey, Shemone, I finally caught you at home. If I didn't know any better, I'd think you were trying to dodge me," the voice said.

Damn, she thought to herself. It was Keith. She should have screened the call.

3

Ain't No Mountain High

It had been only a week, and surely, the word was "crazy": C-R-A-Z-Y. Ohija had said to give her the word about going hiking, and that was it. Shemone didn't know how, and she didn't know why, but she was on her way to Pennsylvania, near the Delaware Water Gap, as if having subjected herself to a conversation with Keith Jenkins when she didn't really want to wasn't enough. So be it, she thought to herself; she still hadn't heard anything from Darnell. It just wasn't like him to not stay in touch. He hadn't phoned, he hadn't written, and, quite frankly, she was growing tired of worrying, of trying to figure out what had happened with him. She had other things to preoccupy her time with, like climbing mountains with Ohija.

Ohija took her cue. "I tell you, you're gonna love this," she said as she pulled up into the parking lot for the Appalachian Trail.

Shemone grinned nervously. "Are you sure that you know what you're doing?"

"Well, it has been a while, but the hubby and I used to come up here quite often." Ohija shut her eyes for a moment. "The peacefulness out here just can't be compared," she said. And just that quickly, Ohija was out of the car and around back, opening the trunk.

Shemone followed. She'd decided that she was going to make the most of her first hiking experience ever. She grabbed her red knapsack. Her bag paled in comparison to Ohija's deluxe, jumbo yellow knapsack. "Just what do you have in that thing, anyway?" she asked.

"Me? Oh, everything, girl—everything we could ever need." Ohija took a can from it, then sprayed insect repellant over her arms, neck, and hands. "Have some?"

"I suppose I should," Shemone answered, thinking how about unprepared she was as she sprayed.

The two strapped their packs onto their backs and set off up the trail.

Ohija took in a strong breath of air. "You smell that? You can just swallow up the mountains and greenery up here."

Shemone took a sniff, too. "Yes, it does smell nice and outdoorsy," she agreed. The weather was a comfortable eighty degrees, with low humidity.

They stopped at a sign that led to the entrance of the hike. Ohija explained, "We have three choices. We can take the white trail, which is the easiest, the blue trail, which is moderate, or the green trail, which is the most challenging of them all. What's it gonna be?" she asked.

"Let's go for the big challenge," Shemone answered. "If we're gonna do it, we might as well make it worth our while." She asked herself, How hard could it be? So far, things had been relatively simple. The ground beneath them was pebbled, and they were going across the cutest little wooden bridges. They weren't alone. Two other women were on the trail ahead of them. Shemone wondered why the women were moving so slowly. They were moving as if they were going for a stroll in the park. This was supposed to be a hike, not a stroll. It made her want to pep up the pace. Shemone brought her legs up and breathed, legs up, and breathed. Full strides, arms swinging.

"Now you're moving, girl!" Ohija said, becoming amped by her friend's sudden new optimism.

They moved ahead of the two other sistahs.

After five minutes of the pace she was keeping up, Shemone started to slow down, breathing heavily along the way as the ground beneath them changed from tiny pebbled to a medium rocky. "This hiking stuff is no joke," Shemone told Ohija as she stopped to put both hands on her hips.

"Yes, I know," Ohijah replied. "You really do have to pace yourself. The air does get thinner. Don't worry, you'll get it. It just takes a little adjusting, that's all."

One half hour and a large step-on boulder trek later made Shemone want to adjust her ass back down that mountain. But refusing to complain, she kept up with Ohija, who herself was starting to look kind of worn.

"Water break?" Ohija stopped to finally ask.

"Yes, please," Shemone panted.

Ohija took her bottled water out, guzzling close to half of its contents.

Shemone pulled out her water, and took only a baby sip.

"What's the matter?" Ohija asked.

Shemone sighed. "It's not cold."

Ohija giggled. "City people."

They resumed the hike, walking around huge rocks and entire fallen trees. Shemone still didn't complain. She even alternated taking the lead and following the trail of the green-painted surfaces.

"You know, they say there's a lake at the end of this trail," Ohija told Shemone.

"Really? A lake?" Shemone envisioned taking her socks off and putting her feet in the water. Lunch and the lake. Her honey turkey with Swiss on rye, rippled potato chips, and even, yes, that damn warm water was sure gonna taste good. Yes, that would be her new motivation. Lunch and the lake. It was just what she needed to put that pep back in her step.

"I knew that lake info would help to get you going, girl! You know, the last time I was here, a deer crossed right in front of me."

"Get outta here!" Shemone replied.

"No—and there are bears up here, too."

"Bears? Okay, now, Bambi I can deal with, but I sure hope that we don't have any run-ins with old Smokey, or I'll have to take off like wildfire and leave you behind, girl!"

They laughed and laughed until their stomachs hurt, realizing that laughing was taking away some of the energy they would need to continue the hike.

It wasn't ten minutes before Shemone was at it again, about ready to call it quits. "Are we almost there? Are we almost to the lake? I don't know how much farther I can go. I'm all sweaty and tired," Shemone finally told Ohija.

"Look up there," Ohija said, pointing. "I think that we're almost there."

If Shemone had had more energy, she'd have run up and pushed her. "You mean to tell me that you've never been to the top before?"

"No, I never have. Every time Ray and I come out, it's to enjoy the surroundings," Ohija explained. "Today, with us, it's different. We're two sistahs on a mission. But we've got to be close. It looks like there's an opening up ahead. It's probably some kind of clearing."

"I don't know, Ohija, this mountain is getting really steep and rocky. I'm surprised I haven't twisted my ankle off yet," Shemone replied.

"Yeah, I should have told you to wear boots instead of sneakers for better support. Come on, we can do it," Ohija replied.

Shemone knew in advance that there wasn't going to be a next time. She had already planned to chalk this one up as an experience. She threw herself down on a rock to sit and take a breather.

Ohija must have realized that Shemone wasn't right behind her because she stopped. She looked down at her, smiling.

"You go on without me," Shemone puffed, as if it were her last breath. "I can meet you there, at the lake."

"Oh, no." Ohija motioned with her hand. "We're going to the lake at the same time, together. I'll just wait." And that she did, right over Shemone. Ohija literally just stood there.

"Can you please sit down?" Shemone asked. The best advantage was that her wide friend was blocking out the hot sun and shading her.

"Why?" Ohija asked. "I told you I'd wait. I don't mind."

"I know, but you're making me nervous. It's just too much pressure," Shemone replied.

Ohija chuckled and took a seat on the rock next to Shemone. A slight breeze blew for the first time. "Now I'm not gonna want to get back up."

"Yes you will. Let's just take a minute to enjoy that peacefulness you were telling me about," Shemone replied.

Ohija nodded in quiet agreement.

As Shemone sat there, she thought about how thankful and blessed she was to be where she was in her life. She thought about all the material things she had acquired, and the people she'd known, one of them being Darnell. Thoughts of his arrival were with her, even on a mountaintop. "Well, let's go," Shemone said, getting up and telling Ohija this, thinking that it was time to look forward to something besides Darnell coming home.

Ohija joined her, and the two were continuing, trudging up farther, all the way to the top of the mountain, when she saw something. "Shemone, we're here, it's the lake!"

"It is the lake!" Shemone repeated. She and Ohija grabbed each other and began jumping up and down.

The lake was a sight to be seen. It stretched for what looked to be a mile, and tiny frogs and sun perch darted across its still waters. A large "No Swimming" sign nailed on a wide tree hung nearby.

"No swimming, but it's still beautiful," Shemone said.

"It sure is; how about some lunch?" Ohija asked her.

"Yes, I think that lunch at the lake would suit me fine."

Ohija and Shemone gobbled down their sandwiches and chips, and drank all of their water. Two other hikers had made it up. They looked equally as pleased to be at the lake. They took pictures of the scenery.

"You ready to head back down?" Ohija asked.

"I guess—what's the rush?"

"That little frog keeps staring at me."

Shemone laughed; it was her turn to say it: "city people."

After hanging out for a few more minutes by the lake, the two ventured back down the mountain, choosing to take the easier, white trail back down.

"Whoever said this was the easier trail is a liar," Shemone said as she stepped and bounced down the rocky ground.

"I guess they mean it's not so around and around."

"A person could still break their neck, and my feet are killing me."

"We'll be down in no time," Ohija answered.

"That sounds so familiar," Shemone replied with a grin.

After close to an hour of walking on the white trail, the sounds of laughter and running water were heard in the distance.

"You hear that?" Shemone asked.

"Yes, it sounds like a camp. We must be close to the end."

"You know what? You keep saying that, and we always have to go farther."

Ohija sprinted up ahead, determined to find the source of the noise.

"Uno, dos, tres!" the children yelled. From the side of the mountain, kids could be seen wading and splashing in water that ran down from its source onto rocks. "Those kids are having fun," Ohija told Shemone, who had only just arrived from the mountainside.

"That water looks sooo inviting," Shemone said.

"And from what I remember, it's drinkable and cold."

"Seriously? That rock water?"

"Girl, it's better than any bottled water you can buy from the store," Ohija told her.

"Wish we could get down there," Shemone said.

"And rain on those campers' parade? No, it's too steep," Ohija replied. "Besides, there will be more water, don't worry."

"You mean we're not close to the end?" Shemone asked with a frown.

"Almost." Ohija wasn't lying this time. There was water all right. Clear, fresh, delicious water, and a rocky path had led them straight to it.

"Oooh, it's cold," Shemone said, cupping her hands full, drinking from the side, where it ran down. She inhaled. "It's refreshing, too."

"Didn't I tell you so? Wanna go for a dip?"

Shemone looked at her friend as it she'd gone mad. "How? I don't have a bathing suit."

"Sure you do. Haven't you ever heard of a bra and panties?" Ohija asked.

"Absolutely not," Shemone answered quickly at the thought of being half naked in the mountains. "Someone might see us."

"Like who? Down here is pretty much covered by the rocks," Ohijah said, and with that, she started peeling off her clothes. She stripped down to nothing but her beige bra and panty set. She made her way into the cool water. "This green algae stuff on the rocks is slippery, so be careful. But it is nice." Ohija turned around to look back at her friend. "What are you waiting for?"

Shemone looked up and around to make sure that no one was lurking. "I hope you know that this is my best Christian Dior set that I'm about to go splashing around in." She removed her pants and shirt and reluctantly went in to join Ohija.

"Oh, girl, live just a little bit. Step outside your character just for a minute and lose control," Ohija said, splashing cold water Shemone's way.

"Watch it, girl, or I'll make you hit your head on a rock!" Shemone joked, doing the same back to Ohija in retaliation. The water's effects proved to be very rejuvenating. They both stayed in there for nearly an hour.

Back on the trail, and close to the end, Shemone spotted deer in the distance. "Ohija, check it out, three deer!"

"They're so cute," Ohija said as she looked on with Shemone.

"Aren't they?" Shemone agreed. The deer were a medium-caramel shade, with the softest teardrop-shaped eyes. It looked like they were a family: the father, the mother, and the baby deer.

Ohija made a high-pitched noise from the inside of her throat. Just about ready to dash off, the deer stopped, frozen in their tracks, to look back at them.

"Where did you learn to do deer calls?" Shemone asked.

"I didn't, it's just the sound I thought a deer would respond to," she said. Ohija made the call again, and the deer looked.

Well, hot damn, it worked, Shemone thought.

Fifteen minutes after the deer sighting was, finally, the end of the trail. The ground underneath changed back to small pebbles and they were going back over those cute little wooden bridges, back to the parking lot where the car was parked.

Shemone took a gander at herself in the car window; she looked a sight. She wasn't the same clean, backpacked individual she had first set out as. She was an accomplished hiker who had earned a new title with real sweat, almost on the verge of real tears. She had a newfound experience under her belt. Shemone smiled at herself before opening the car door. It felt satisfying, and her experience would make an interesting article. Shemone looked over at her best friend, who was already seated behind the wheel looking satisfied. She looked that way all the time. Now Shemone knew why a little better.

4

Homebody

Shemone rolled over in her bed on Monday. Every muscle in her body ached from her hiking adventure the day before, even her head. Reaching over for her clock on the nightstand, Shemone read 1 P.M. Just great, I've slept the entire morning away, she thought to herself. Being a freelance writer had its advantages, but snoozing all day wasn't one that Shemone liked to indulge in. She was an early riser, and completed more in a morning than most people who worked a regular nine to five did in a full day. Mornings usually began for her at 8 A.M. with a workout and a light breakfast before a review of the day's work ahead. But not today. Today her head felt like it wanted to explode. Shemone eased over to the side of the bed and sat on its edge. Her answering machine blinked a bright digital 2. Ignoring her messages for now, she managed to pull herself up and into the bathroom. Well, at least she looked well rested, she thought as she glanced at her reflection. Shemone turned the faucet on and splashed cold water on her face and brushed her teeth. Then, opening the medicine cabinet, she took down a bottle of aspirin. She popped two of the capsules into her mouth, then chased them down with water. The phone had begun to ring in the next room. Not feeling like sprinting to answer it, she continued to let it ring. The answering machine sounded off, revealing who the caller was.

"Yo, Shemone, pick up. Shemone, pick up, it's Darnell. Shemone, pick up. Well, this is, like, my third time calling. I guess you're not—"

Shemone thought to herself as she hurried into the kitchen to get the phone before he had a chance to hang up. At least she knew who the other two messages were from, and finally, she'd find out when Darnell was being released. Surprisingly, her heartbeat quickened, but one would never know it by her cool-cucumber tone. "Well, hello to you, too, stranger," she abruptly said.

"Oh, good, you are home, baby-girl," Darnell said. "You're the stranger, I've been ringing your phone off the hook. What, you just getting in?" he asked. His tone came very close to being a hostile one.

"No, I was knocked out, really. Ohija and I went hiking yesterday. It must have taken a bigger toll on me than I thought," Shemone answered. She laughed to herself. Not at her reply, but because she'd found herself actually explaining her whereabouts to this man. This man/best friend of hers. Oh, she'd slipped up all right, but she was about to fix that. "Not like it's any of your business," she made sure to add.

"True—true," Darnell replied. He was quickly reminded of what a strong personality Shemone had. For him, it was a natural aphrodisiac. "What would you say if I told you that I was in your area?"

"In my area?" Shemone repeated after him. Instantly, she felt out of sorts. She hadn't expected him to be anywhere close by before she'd had the chance to properly prepare herself. Her place had to be tidied, she wasn't dressed . . . and there was nothing to offer him to snack on. All perfectly valid excuses for not entertaining friends in her book. Her temples throbbed. The aspirin hadn't quite kicked in, especially not after having heard this new revelation. Shemone answered Darnell's original question as best she could. The what-would-you-say-if-I-was-in-your-area question. "I'd tell you that's nice, Darnell, and go on with my day." What am I supposed to say? she thought to herself. Oh, let me do a cartwheel? Come on by anytime, without any notice?

"Oh, come on, baby-girl, aren't you even a little bit anxious to see me? It's been, like, what, nine, ten years?" he said. There was a brief silence on the line. "I'm anxious to see you."

"You would be," Shemone said in a joking tone, "you just got out of jail."

"Oh, now, you know that you didn't even have to go there," Darnell replied playfully. "You're aware that I could have went and had my pick to go and see anyone, don't you? I'm putting you first," Darnell told her. He wanted her to feel like the special person that he thought she was.

"I should be so honored," Shemone replied sarcastically. Right then, humor was all that she had to go on without giving the actual no answer that she wanted to give.

"C'mon, I want to see you," he urged. "We can even make it a short visit if you want, seeing as how I caught you off guard and everything."

Shemone tapped her perfectly French-manicured nails on the kitchen counter and high sighed. She wanted Darnell to know just how inconvenient this moment was for her. This was nowhere near her norm.

"Please . . . ," Darnell asked, no, make that begged.

"Where are you, exactly? Are you really outside my residence?"

"Oh word? Your residence? Do your thing, girl." Darnell chuckled. "No, for real, I'm not outside your residence," he said as he put emphasis on the word "residence." "I'm just clowning. I'm on my cell phone, around the way in my old neighborhood."

What a relief, Shemone thought. She was off the hook. He really wasn't outside her house. "So we can make this reunion another time, then?" she asked him.

"No, I could never joke about wanting to see you. I just figured I'd call first." Darnell added, "To be on the safe side, you know."

Shemone finally decided to just give in. "All right, Mr. Darnell, you can stop by, but give me an hour. Building 224, on 106th Street and Manhattan Avenue, apartment 4B."

"Don't bother to go and get yourself all prettied up for me, you know. I'll take you just the way you are," Darnell kidded.

She'd sensed that he was kidding, but wanted him to be certain that she wasn't. "Now, you know it's not like that, so don't start. If you're looking for something more than my friendship, we can cancel this reunion of sorts right now," Shemone said in an agitated voice. "I mean, maybe you do need to go and see somebody else," she added. She was out to let him know that she wasn't the prize in anybody's Cracker Jack box. The bigger picture here was that they were old friends. They'd confided in each other about everything, and the flirting that they sometimes did with each other was completely innocent.

"There's no need to cancel or nothing like that, baby-girl. It's not like I'm expecting anything from you," he assured her. "I just miss you, that's all. So can I come by and see my friend now?" Darnell asked her.

"Sure you can," Shemone replied, feeling better about his upcoming visit. She felt more at ease now that he knew where she stood. She hoped she hadn't gone too far, but she also knew that she wouldn't have been herself if she hadn't laid the words out on the line.

"You've got parking, right?" he asked.

"You're driving? You just got released from jail and you've got a cell phone and a car already?"

"Is that a crime?"

"Time will tell," Shemone answered back with a chuckle.

"You're going to stop with the jail jokes. I'm on my way," Darnell said, and with that he hung up, no good-bye or anything.

Hmph. Shemone felt a quick chill go through her body. It had to be those aspirin kicking in.

Shemone put the final touches in place in preparation for Darnell's arrival. She'd straightened up the apartment, which really didn't need much straightening, and was all set for her guest. She dressed casually, in a two-piece gray cotton Adidas workout outfit and white sneakers. She took out a few menus just in case they decided to order something in, but doubted that he'd be staying that long. Darnell probably had a host of other people he'd want to see now that he was out of jail. Just then, the intercom buzzed. On it was the familiar voice of Darnell Williams, and he was on his way up to see her.

Darnell was exiting the elevator, walking toward her only seconds later, as Shemone held her apartment door open. And what a walk it was. A kind of coordinated side-to-side action that only he could get away with. She was just praying that her mouth didn't let on how excited her eyes were. After all of those years, she knew that he would still be attractive, but, my oh my, she thought to herself. Shemone paced herself before she spoke. "Darnell."

"Shemone," he said in an identical tone, with a big smile. He was being cute in the way that he was saying her name, as official as the way that she had just said his. "Can a brother at least get a hug?"

Shemone surrendered, making her body move forward into his arms. She gave him a tense smile and a cordial embrace that kept two inches of space between them, then pulled herself away from him while she could still muster the strength to do so. As far as her emotions meter was concerned, she was feeling uncomfortable. She thought, It sure doesn't feel like friends. "Step inside," she told him. She was certain that after they'd talked, that's when it would feel more, more like friends.

"I like," Darnell said as he entered her apartment and looked around. He was impressed with all that Shemone had done with the space she had. It was lived in, with a style that was all hers. "It does look like a hotel up in here. Do I get the tour?"

"Promise not to rob me?" Shemone joked.

Darnell grabbed her up in a playful headlock.

It was kind of like what he would do when they were teenagers, but now he was a little stronger. Definitely more defined, body wise, Shemone thought to herself. She chuckled loudly as he held her. "Stop!" She laughed. "Okay, no more jail jokes! I promise!"

Darnell released her from his grip. "Okay now," he said, smiling. "Remember your promise."

"Okay, follow me," Shemone said, trying to be serious again. She couldn't believe that after all of these years, and all of the numerous phone calls in the last year, this man was actually in her house. Thinking back, it seemed that Darnell would never be released from jail. Safely in the past, it gave her the permission she'd needed to harmlessly flirt with him at those times when he'd needed more than a friend. She'd answered all sorts of personal questions, like what her idea of romance was, and would listen to him brag about his talents, both in and out of the bedroom, without prompting him to move on to another subject. Truth be told, she did find it to be interesting, to know that part of Darnell, because they'd never "gone there." In short, she grew to learn more about him than ever before. What was most important now, though, was that Darnell had made it through his sentence, and that they'd managed to keep their friendship intact all of this time. They'd been there for each other. Shemone continued with her apartment tour. "This is, of course, the living room, this is the kitchen, the bathroom, the guest room, and this is the master bedroom."

"Master bedroom, huh?" Darnell smiled. "That means your bedroom, right?" he asked her as he looked around. He was thinking what a classy woman Shemone Waters was. Everything in her apartment stood for the kind of woman she represented—her lamps, her photos, her curtains, just everything.

"Right, my bedroom," she answered curtly, getting them both out of that particular room as quickly as she could. Any day now, friendship feelings, Shemone thought to herself. She led Darnell back out into the living room. "I took down our old school album. I was looking through it a couple of weeks ago," she told him. Everything that they might need was within arm's reach. Shemone intended on keeping this social call as short, and as sweet, as possible.

"Man, it's been a long time," Darnell said as he took a seat on the sofa. "How's Bea? I mean—"

"Ohija," they both said at the same time.

Shemone had long since told Darnell about the name change.

"That girl is full of surprises. I can't wait to see her," Darnell told her, thinking about the last time that he had.

The big man on the street, that was him. At that time, way before Terrance had gotten killed, the drug game had Darnell pulling in more money than he could count. He never had a problem with spending it, though. Darnell had become known for his weekly shopping sprees, and was a regular customer at many of the urban retail stores in the uptown area. On the day that he'd run into Ohija, he'd been looking exceptional, dressed to the nines, in everything spanking new from head to toe. Shit, he was feeling like he was on top of the world, and in his mind, any friend of his should be, too. It was out of sheer courtesy that Darnell had asked if she and her family needed anything. Ohija politely had said no, that they were all right. It came off as strange to him, because right after that, she was saying something about not being able to afford to stay and talk long. She didn't want to be late for her nine to five.

He hadn't seen her since. That was six years ago. It was clear to him that she didn't want anything to do with him and the way he was getting his money back then, regardless of whether she needed it or not. Although Ohija never actually admitted it, her face told the full story. The way she was looking at him, and his car, and the way she rushed away from him so quickly, as if he had a contagious disease or something.

It was a day that Darnell had tried to forget for a long time, and when he'd gotten caught, he'd had nothing but time to think about it. Sure, he'd wanted to write Ohija letters thousands of times, but he just didn't think that his lifestyle was anything worth writing home about. He even thought about telling Shemone and making something happen, but he never did. Now that he was out, there was no excuse. Hopefully, he thought to himself, they could go on with their friendship, and catch up on all of the time they'd lost doing their own thing.

"I know Ohija can't wait to see you, too," Shemone told him.

"She's doing very well. I told you that she's married, and that she has her own clothing boutique, right?"

"Yeah, yeah, that's good. She's doing all right for herself then," Darnell replied. Even if he had gotten an invitation, he wouldn't have been able to make her wedding. Not from behind bars, anyway. But Darnell was glad to hear that life was still going on for Ohija, and for everybody else while he'd been away.

The album stayed in between Shemone and Darnell as they looked through pictures, reminiscing and laughing at their old school chums. It was as if they were revisiting their past.

"No! Look at me!" Darnell yelled. He slid down off the couch from laughing so hard at the way he looked in one of the photos.

"What?" Shemone said to him. "You didn't look that bad. Some of those people really looked wild back then."

Darnell lifted himself back up, and took his seat on the sofa again. He silently grinned, continuing to look down at the pictures. He hadn't acknowledged Shemone's comment. Or maybe it was that he hadn't heard her.

Shemone couldn't help but look over at Darnell, who was still looking down at those pictures. Nope. Darnell didn't look bad at all back then. He sure as hell was finer now. Still the toffee man. Long, silky eyelashes. His body was more chiseled from working out. His new low haircut complemented the shape of his smooth face and structured chin, and he wore the sexiest diamond stud, pierced through one ear.

Darnell suddenly looked up. He was looking over at her looking at him and not the pictures. They split a closed-mouth smile between them.

"You hungry?" Shemone asked. She felt the need to break their gaze, not to mention all of the sexual tension that had been steadily building, at least on her part, anyway. So far, Darnell had kept to his word. He wasn't acting like he was expecting anything from her.

Darnell already knew from their telephone conversations that Shemone wasn't comfortable in the kitchen, but decided to go there anyway, just to be funny. "Why, you cook? You know a brother would be real open for a home-cooked meal."

"No, I was talking about ordering a pizza. You better go see your mama about all that home-cooking business," Shemone replied with a smile.

"Why you always gotta be so sarcastic?" he asked her. It was like a double-edged sword dealing with that sharp tongue of hers. Darnell loved her sassy spirit, but not when it was targeted at him.

"I don't know, I suppose that's just the way I am," Shemone replied, easily switching subjects. "How is Ms. Williams doing anyway?" Shemone asked him. She remembered his mother fondly from their teenage days. Anytime the Final Four crew had a meeting, they'd agree to meet at Darnell's house. His mother always had food ready. And when Ms. Williams cooked, she cooked full-course meals with all the fixings. Smothered chicken, seasoned mustard greens, sweet corn bread, and macaroni and cheese. Yum. Just the thought of Darnell's mother's cooking made her hungry.

"She's okay," Darnell answered. "I mentioned that I was coming over here to see you. She said for me to give you my best."

"Your best or hers?" Shemone asked. Her eyebrows arched up in a sisterly way.

"Yeah, I meant her best." Darnell smiled. "Pizza will work for me just fine. Make that pepperoni and extra cheese on mine." Darnell took out a thick roll of bills. He peeled off a crisp twenty.

"That's okay, next time, I've got this one. You're my guest, remember?" Shemone told him, pushing his hand away. She gave the order taker at the restaurant all the information he needed, then hung up the phone.

"You paying, it's like one of those feminist, women's independence things, right?" Darnell turned to her and asked. He was still holding the bill in his hand as if she was about to change her mind about wanting to pay. Not having to pay had never happened to him with any woman before. Never.

"No, it's just like I said, you're my guest." Shemone added

abruptly, "Nothing more." She wanted to ask him where he had gotten that big wad of money, but decided to wait for a better time.

After the pizza arrived, Shemone and Darnell sat at the counter eating and drinking the frozen drinks that she'd whipped up in the blender. Shemone made sure to go light on the alcohol content so that she could steer clear of the naughty thoughts she was beginning to have about Darnell. A year of celibacy was a long time for a girl to wait for some, even if it was by choice.

"So talk to me. How's your job going these days?" Darnell asked her between bites of stringy pizza. "But first, you got any hot sauce?"

"Tell me you're not going to put hot sauce on your pizza," Shemone answered.

"Yeah, okay, then I won't tell you, but I am, if you have any. Do you or don't you? I like hot sauce on everything," Darnell replied. He seductively licked his lips one time.

Shemone smiled at his play on words. "I'll see," she said, going into the kitchen. After pushing several other assorted bottles aside, she grabbed the bottle of hot sauce from the back of her cabinet. He likes hot sauce on everything, she thought to herself. He was ready to go there, too, right along with her, licking his lips at her the way he had. She thought again, ordering her common sense to take hold. It was better to not even go there.

Shemone returned and handed Darnell the bottle. She couldn't believe what she was seeing.

Darnell shook what must have been twenty drops of sauce onto his single slice of pizza, then continued talking. "So? You were about to tell me about your job. What's the latest and greatest you've been working on?" Darnell asked. He loved to hear about Shemone's articles. It was always interesting to hear about the many people and topics she was writing about.

Shemone swallowed hard. It felt like a piece of dough was lodged in her throat, but it really wasn't. She'd never lied to Darnell before, and wasn't about to start, even though she wanted to. "I'm working on a story about . . . friends who date friends," she told him.

Darnell chuckled, took a bite of his pizza, then a gulp of the icy mixture from his glass. It was a minute before he replied. "That's something, baby-girl," was what he told her.

And just when it seemed that he was going to expand on this, and give his take on things, Shemone broke in. She decided that she was going to be the one asking the questions. Darnell was the best listener, but it was what she might have said to him regarding the friendship–dating topic. If they continued on this subject, she'd probably wind up saying something foolish like, "Do me, baby." "I'd much rather hear about you," she told him, changing subjects. "Darnell, why don't you tell me about what you plan on doing with yourself now that you're home." She took a cool sip from her frozen piña-colada after asking a hot question.

"Well, right now, I'm looking into really doing the right thing with my life," Darnell answered matter-of-factly. "I just need to make sure that I know what that is," he said. "I'd like to take things one day at a time, you know what I mean?" he asked her.

"Mm-hmm, okay," Shemone responded. She'd made him a promise not to make any more of those jail jokes. But it was time to be serious and direct. "Nothing to do with drugs is it, Darnell?" she asked.

"No, baby-girl." Darnell chewed a mouthful and kept talking. She could see bits of cheese and tomato as he spoke. "I'm not trying to go back that route, for real. There wasn't much right about selling drugs for a living. I'm looking into getting into being an electrician, or something along those lines." He added, "I also wanted to tell you thanks."

"Thanks for what?" Shemone asked him.

"For just helping me to see what I didn't. I'm glad that you talked me into taking that electrical basics class. You knew that I liked to fix things," he told her, smiling.

"You're very welcome, Darnell, you know that as a friend I care about what you do," Shemone pointed out to him.

Darnell washed the food down with more of the frozen piña-colada. "No you don't. If it was just as a friend, you wouldn't have to keep saying it. It's more," he told her as he took another bite of what would be his second slice of pizza. He said it easily, as if he was telling her what the weather forecast for the day was.

Shemone didn't reply. Why did she have to throw in that as a friend part? she thought. Was she just trying to unconvince herself that she'd felt more for Darnell all along? The walls felt like they were closing in on her. She cleared her throat, suddenly feeling the need to leave the room. "Excuse me," she said as she got up from the stool. "I'll be right back."

"Take your time," Darnell said casually as he continued eating, fully enjoying his meal. It had been a while since he'd had real, fresh Italian pizza, unlike the frozen kind he was used to in Pennington. Even pizza made him feel grateful for all of the things that were still at home.

Shemone went into the bathroom and brushed her teeth, as she routinely tried to do after every meal. While her head was down and she was guiding the toothbrush along her teeth, she was thinking. She was thinking that this was the very first time she'd seen this man friend of hers newly released from jail. He looked better than ever, still had a great personality and a witty sense of humor, and was positive about getting himself into something morally right and legal job wise. He was not going back to the drug lifestyle that had gotten him into the trouble he'd just gotten out of. But yes, he just got out of jail, he just got out of jail, Shemone. He just got out of jail, and . . . on top of that, he's your friend. When she looked up at herself in the mirror, she saw Darnell's reflection standing behind her, and she wasn't even startled.

"I'm right, ain't I?" Darnell asked. He stood at the door's entrance with his arms folded across his chest, and his head was tilted slightly to one side.

"Right about what? Darnell, this visit is over," Shemone said, wiping her face with a towel from the rack. She pushed past him. He couldn't make her admit to him what she was feeling, although he did try. He was on her tracks like a steady row of cars during peak rush hour.

"Shemone, you do know, admit it. You feel something more for me than friendship. It's been more than just a year of phone calls," he said.

"You're getting crazy," she told him.

"Maybe, but I doubt it," Darnell replied. "It's cool, I'm leaving now. Okay?"

"Okay." Shemone answered back, thinking that his decision was for the best.

"We both got other things to do, I feel you. Do I get a kiss goodbye?" he asked in a soft tone of voice, smiling.

This man was something else. "What? I'll hold the door open for you, that's about it," Shemone replied. She went over, and held it open.

Darnell walked past, as close to Shemone as he could get to her on his way out. He brushed by so close that she could hear him breathe. He leaned in purposefully for a kiss. Gently, lingering with soft lips, sweetly and ever so slightly, Darnell placed one right on her forehead.

"Good night, baby-girl. Call you?"

"You'd better," Shemone said, lightening up now that he was on his way out the door. "We've been staying in contact with each other, haven't we?"

Darnell smiled, and handed her a piece of paper with his cell number written on it. "That's right, we have been."

Shemone closed the door behind him and came to the conclusion that no, it definitely didn't feel like just friendship.

5

Joint Ventures

So the deadline date has moved up to tomorrow, then?" Shemone asked early Wednesday morning, pushing her square tortoiseshell frames onto her nose. She rolled her chair in closer, sitting at the full-length mahogany desk in her home office/bedroom. "Fine. You'll have the 'Boyfriend' piece by tomorrow." Her silence caused the person on the other end of the telephone line to squeak. Shemone responded, "I said you'll have the piece, Jackie. Have I ever disappointed you? Okay then." Shemone's call waiting beeped. "Jackie, I've got another call coming in, I'll be in touch."

She clicked over. "Good morning—oh, hi, Mark," she said when the caller identified himself. Mark was her financial advisor, the advisor she'd decided to get when she'd realized that her annual salary was going up. She needed help in keeping her personal books together and handling her business. Already she had established a SEP, or self-employed retirement fund, as it was called. She owned shares in several mutual funds, and as of recently, was looking to dabble in some more lucrative individual stock investments. "Talk to me. How much money have you made me today?" Shemone kidded with her advisor.

It was force of habit, and having Mark was like having a second mother, the way he always made sure of this and that. He never hesitated to point out where he thought she could use improvement financially. It was because of him that she had taken the leap into expanding her portfolio, because she wasn't getting any younger. The day would eventually come when she'd want to retire and live comfortably. With six round figures in mind, it was Mark who'd convinced her to keep her eye on that prize. His payoff was 15 percent, but Shemone did feel comfortable in calling him a friend. In the past three years that she had known him, he had yet to steer her wrong.

"Mo money, mo money. How are you, Shemone?"

"Fabulous as usual, and you?"

"Just trying to make it, just trying to make it," Mark replied in an upbeat tone. "Quick question. Have you sent in the payment for your SEP account?" he asked.

"I'm on it, Mark. Writing the check out as we speak," Shemone said, whipping out her checkbook, making sure to note the payment on her register. Shemone knew that it was wise to have an advisor, but better to always first be your own.

"That's my girl," Mark replied. "I'll give you a ring to confirm when I receive the check."

"Sounds like a plan," Shemone said, and with that hung up the phone. What a day, she thought to herself. She'd have to get to work on completing that "Boyfriend" piece for *Sister Soul*. She'd already put together a pitch for another article on women in abusive relationships, hit the post office to check the PO box, run to the bank to make a deposit, and made and received numerous business-related phone calls. Shemone took off her reading glasses and rubbed her eyes. She glanced at her perfectly made-up bed. Jumping in the middle of it for a quick snooze was tempting, but she knew she couldn't allow herself to give in to that one. Just then the telephone rang. It was the articles editor over at *McCall's* magazine.

"Hey, Shemone, its Martha."

"Hey, Martha, what's new?" Shemone grabbed the banana on her desk and began to peel it.

"Not much, just wanted to make sure that you got that story ready to E-mail over to me for the A.M."

"I sure do," Shemone said as she took another bite of her banana. She opened her planner, quickly flipping to the page that confirmed that the next day was her story due date. Wisely, she'd completed it the day before. "It's as good as sent," Shemone replied, taking cover behind her sparkling reputation. She hadn't missed a deadline, ever, and didn't intend to. Soon it would be time for her to move toward the next level of her writing career, and she wanted to be fully up for the challenge.

"I knew I could count on you. Thanks, Shemone," Martha said before she hung up.

Shemone thought to herself, Get to work on the "Boyfriend" article. Right. The telephone hadn't been down for five seconds before it was ringing again. It was days like this when she wanted to throw the damn thing straight out the window. "Yes," Shemone answered in an agitated tone of voice. It was way past business hours and the need for formalities. She didn't care who it was, she had a story to finish.

"Okay, well, that's quite a greeting," Ohija told her.

"Oh, I'm sorry, girl," Shemone apologized. "I'm under deadline."

"Say no more. Just calling to check on you. Kind of an I'm alive, you're alive call since I haven't spoken to you since our hiking trip."

"Oh, girl, I'm fine otherwise. Darnell's home," Shemone announced. "He came over for a visit."

"What . . . at your place? Girl, our Final Four Darnell? You'd better speak on it! What happened?"

Shemone laughed. "Girl, you know I want to, but I just can't, any day but today. I've just got to get this story out. I haven't really eaten, I'm already beat, and the clock is still ticking. I'll catch you up later, for sure."

"Okay, do what you gotta do then. Order in some Chinese or something. I don't need you to be passing out in front of that keyboard!" Ohija replied.

"I will—later, girl."

"Peace!" Ohija said, hanging up.

There was no time to order in. Shemone gobbled down the rest of her banana, and got to checking her facts on the Internet, in newspaper clippings, and in other articles. Her desk was soon covered with reference papers. She could barely see her keyboard underneath. With the keyboard cleared off, she was inspired to get to typing. Shemone wasn't the best typist, but she got the job done. Three revisions later left Shemone spell-checking and then finally saving. She quickly sent the "Boyfriend" story via E-mail to Jackie that same evening, hours ahead of when she'd promised it. Image was everything, and if Jackie saw that she had sent the story in early, that would be a plus. She'd done it. Shemone spun around in the chair and threw the papers that covered her desk in the air. "You go, girl!" she said aloud to herself.

Shemone shut the PC off, showered, and changed into her sleepwear. She was still hungry, so she checked the refrigerator. The banana wasn't quite making it. She took out a piece of week-old pizza from the freezer. It was from the same pizza that she'd shared with Darnell. She closed the door and wrote on her memo pad in bold black lettering, "GO SHOPPING." After heating and downing her slice with a glass of white wine, she did that thing she wanted to do. She dove into that bed to get some sleep and messed up those pretty white custom-embroidered sheets.

Sleep eventually led her to dreaming, giving her the freedom to relish in nothing but thoughts of Darnell and the gentle kiss that he'd sweetly planted on her forehead. Only, in the dream it hadn't stopped there. There were other places he was placing those soft lips of his. Her candy-sweet dream quickly turned into a nightmare when her alarm went off, instantly awakening her. She jumped up, shut off the alarm clock, and sighed. She thought to herself that he could have at least called. Shemone missed talking to him on the phone like she used to. It had become a ritual just hearing his voice, updating him on her life's events or lack thereof. It was peculiar to her. Now that Darnell was out of jail, live and in person, it was becoming a whole different sort of ball game between them, friends or no friends.

6

INTERIOR MOTIVES

I'm glad that you agreed to meet me for dinner, Shemone."

"I'm glad, too," Shemone answered. Well, actually, she wasn't that glad to be in the company of Keith Jenkins, a week later, in the Shark Bar Restaurant. It wasn't exactly her idea of a perfect Saturday-night date. He was relentless, and wouldn't stop calling until she'd agreed to do dinner with him. So she did dinner with him. It was a free meal. Shemone's eyes scanned the room. There were certainly a lot of good-looking brothers in the house tonight. Shark's was the place to be. Once you laid your credentials on the line, you could get your soul food on, and partake of some friendly conversation with someone else who, potentially, was somewhere near or above your financial level. Credentials questions ran down something like: Where did you go to college? What was your major? Where do you live? And the occasional What do you drive? Given the right response to those questions determined automatic inclusion into the buppy club, making you an immediate prospect. But tonight there was no need to bother. Tonight Shemone was dining with the same man she knew she should have screened the call for: Keith Jenkins.

Keith Jenkins attended Princeton University, had majored in business administration and earned his B.A., and soon-to-be master's. He was currently employed at Sumner Financial, heading up the team in the MIS division. If his life sounded like a want ad, it was because it probably was. He was just so boring. Now Shemone knew that she wasn't exactly Ms. Excitement herself, but she wasn't a stiff either. She glanced across the candlelit table at Keith. His tie, his canary-yellow necktie, was sooo tight, his blue Brooks Brothers shirt, and black wing-tipped shoes, sooo typical.

Keith took her glance for something that it wasn't. He grinned over at her and extended his hand.

Shemone ignored him, creating a barrier between them by eyeing the wine list. She toyed with the idea of getting stinking drunk, even though she wasn't a heavy drinker. "I think I'm going to have a cosmopolitan," she told him.

"Whatever you want, Shemone, go ahead and order whatever you like," he replied. Keith filled his empty hand with the menu as a substitute after realizing that Shemone wasn't going to give him her hand.

Whatever she wanted. Whatever she wanted. She could pay for her own dinner. It was always whatever she wanted. She had slept with him once, a year ago, in her pre-celibacy days, and that had left him hungry for more. It was no biggie. Missionary style, she had barely wriggled. With one push of her pelvis he was done, and after that sexual experience, so was she. The relationship had been platonic ever since. Keith had only served as a distraction. The timing seemed on point tonight. All she had to do was get that roughrider

Darnell off her mind. It was enough that he was in her dreams. She hadn't seen or heard from him in close to two weeks, Shemone thought to herself. Maybe she should forgo the whole celibacy thing and give into Keith tonight just to get some that was, at the very least, familiar. She looked across at him. Or then again, maybe not. He was grinning at her in that stupid, dumbfounded way again.

"Good evening, and welcome to the Shark Bar. I'm Kayla," the shapely waitress said. Her hair was slicked back into a ponytail, and her voice sounded like she should be doing voice-overs somewhere. "Would you guys like to start off with something to drink before you order?" she asked.

"Yes, I'll have a cosmopolitan," Shemone said hastily. She couldn't wait to wrap her mouth around that glass of liquor.

"And you, sir?" she asked.

"Give me a martini, please," Keith replied.

Shemone wondered if Keith would venture out by living a little on the edge. Would he at least try to get a glance at the waitress's butt as she walked away to the bar to get the drinks? No, he sure didn't.

They ordered their meals a drink and a half later. Shemone got the blackened catfish with baked macaroni and cheese and sweet-candied yams. Keith ordered the smothered chicken and grits. Well, at least the food was worth the trip out that night. She could always count on that. Shemone took another opportunity to scan the room for men. Knowing it was wrong didn't matter. It wasn't like predictable Keith would have said anything anyway.

A group of guys entered the restaurant. They caught Shemone's attention because the whole group of men, quite frankly, had it going on. Celebrity types, athletes, and high rollers often dined at Shark's on a regular basis, and it helped to pay attention. Most of the guys who had just come in were dressed denim-down fashionable. Fubu, Sean John, and Phat Farm labels adorned their shirts, pants, and caps.

There was this one, though, who caught Shemone's eye in particular. Darnell. Her heart almost stopped beating when she saw him. "Keith—I'm gonna go to the ladies' room, why don't you take care of the check?" Shemone suggested, wanting at first to make a quick getaway. But why? she asked herself. She was hardly on a date. Darnell had come in with a group of all guys, so it was apparent that he wasn't on a date either. Neutral territory. Keith was just a friend. Darnell was just a friend. It was just plain senseless to run out now. She did have to use the bathroom, and after that she would want to leave.

"But I'm not done—" Keith looked up to tell her.

"Then get it to go," Shemone spat back. "I said I'm ready."

Keith turned around, puzzled, but began to take out his wallet anyway.

A line of women formed along the wall, also waiting to get into the ladies' room. Just as Shemone changed her mind, and was about to turn and walk away, Darnell approached, on his way to her. He was already up in her face. She was getting the opportunity to eye him at a close range, and he looked enticing in all that dark denim and Timberland boots.

"What you doing hanging out? No fairy-tale stories to write tonight?" he asked her.

"It's a free country, and I'm entitled to a day off, aren't I?" Shemone replied.

Darnell chuckled, flashing that perfect smile of his.

Since they'd been younger, he'd never liked sweets. It had paid off, big time, Shemone thought to herself. His smile made it easy to forget to ask him the important question of why he hadn't called her in the past two weeks.

"'Aren't I?'" he playfully mocked. "You so proper. You've always got a answer for everything, don't you?" Darnell asked, giving Shemone the once-over for himself. "You look nice," he told her. But then, she always did. To him, Shemone had always been a diva in the making. She'd always been the one to start the trends. This was the same girl who'd introduced Gucci bags to Monroe High.

Shemone wore a crimson-red halter dress with stiletto square-toed shoes and a matching clutch bag. "Thank you," she replied, taking the compliment.

"Who you here with?" Darnell asked, looking directly at her.

And just as she was about to switch her plan and say that she was there by herself, and that she didn't need anybody to have dinner with, here came good ol' Keith.

"Sweetheart, you ready?"

"Sweetheart?" Darnell repeated with a quick chuckle. "This your date, Shemone? Are you with money?" he asked.

"I . . ." Shemone faltered, at a loss for words. It took everything she had to complete her sentence and come clean. "Yes, Darnell, I'm with money, also known as Keith Jenkins, on a date. Keith, this is an old friend of mine, Darnell Williams."

"Good to meet you, man," Darnell said, giving Keith a firm slap of the hand. Darnell wasn't bothered, not after sizing up his competition, he damn well wasn't.

Keith hadn't done the urban hand-slap thing in a while. He laughed off his awkwardness, but managed to get through it. Corporate America only called for the traditional handshake when greeting someone.

"Well, we'd better get going," Shemone said, tucking her bag underneath her arm. She felt a little out of sorts, and needed to hurry home to think about why.

"Darnell?" a loud voice from nowhere suddenly asked. The entire restaurant must have heard.

Darnell turned around to see who it was. A female, one of the women from his old neighborhood, who had been trying to get him into bed at a time when he wasn't interested.

"It's me, Hope," she said. "Boy, when did you get home?" She gave Darnell a full body hug.

Shemone watched as the young woman held on to Darnell for dear life. Her body pressed firmly into his. Forget what she was doing, what on earth was she wearing? Shemone thought to herself. First, her hair was unbe-weaveably long, and she must have robbed a bank vault with all that trump jewelry she had on. There was a ring on every one of her fingers, bracelets galore, and a gaudy gold necklace with a huge heart pendant made up of what Shemone guessed was supposed to be diamonds. This woman was dressed in a short black spandex number with her belly and back showing, and her breasts were all out and standing at attention.

The Hope woman ran her hand up one of Darnell's muscular-looking arms. "You look so good, boo, I might have to buy you a drink tonight. Who you here with?" she asked, stepping back, working her neck in that sistah-girl kind of way.

Darnell grinned. He was eating up all the attention that Hope had to give. "Tonight, out hanging with the fellas, but I'm saying, you women want equal rights and independence all the time, right? I am feeling a little thirsty," Darnell answered, smiling. He looked over at Shemone after he'd spoken.

Hope laughed.

Darnell laughed.

Even Keith laughed.

But Shemone didn't find anything to be funny at all. He was actually enjoying how this little scene was playing itself out. She thought to herself that he had a little Hope to go on now. It was crazy for her to have made such a big deal about someone who didn't think of her as anything more than a friend. Somebody who was openly flirting, right in front of her face. It really was time to make an exit. She spoke as if on cue. "All right, Darnell, we're going to go. I'll see you around sometime," Shemone told him.

"Okay, Shemone," he answered, using his eyes. "Make sure you call me," he added.

The Hope girl stared over at Shemone and rolled her eyes.

Shemone got her back just by coyly replying, "I will." She and Darnell could still talk on the phone all they wanted, she told herself.

Keith was still clueless, but not that clueless. She'd noticed that he was checking out Hope on the sly. Shemone started to suggest that he slip Hope one of his business cards. *She* sure wasn't going home with him.

* * *

Shemone let herself into her apartment and went to the fridge. She poured herself a cold glass of ginger ale and turned on the TV. It looked like a movie was just about to come on. She checked her machine for messages. There were five.

"Greetings, Shemone, it's Ohija calling to finish getting that info you promised. Call me, girl."

"Hi, this is Jackie. Just wanted to call you and tell you that I love the article! Keep up the excellent work!"

"Shemone, it's your mother, Ruth. Kindly return the call when you get in from wherever you might be."

"What's up, Shemone? Uh, I'm still at Shark's." There was a pause, but Shemone could hear the familiar sounds of the restaurant in the background. "I just wanted to let you know that, uh, I was thinking about you."

"Shemone, it's me, Darnell, again. I just wanted to make sure that you had my cell number. It's 917-555-6686. Call me. It doesn't matter what time."

Shemone lay back on her bed with a smile of satisfaction. Ohija and her mother she'd call tomorrow, for sure. . . . Darnell was a different story; she felt the urge to call him that same night, especially since he'd phoned her already and wasn't too busy being entertained by Miss Hope. For most of her life she'd planned . . . and this was just one phone call, after all.

7

Animal Attraction

"Man, I'm telling you, she's not trying to have nothing to do with me," Darnell told his best friend, Pop, later on that same evening back at Shark's. "She's just not feeling me like that. I'm a thug, and she's bourgeois." He rested his elbow on the bar, and nodded. "She's just too damn high post for me." Then he added, "And I feel that pressure. You should see her house and everything." Darnell continued with a voice-and-hand emphasis, "It's laid. A brother's just not sure he can compete with all that, but I'm trying. It damn near killed me not to call her up on the phone after I first saw her two weeks ago. I thought that if I didn't call her, she'd call me, or at least want to. But she didn't. I'm just so used to having her there for me, you know?"

"Give her time, man, she'll come around," Pop replied. "You've got a lot to offer, D., just handle your business, that's all." Pop's eyes surveyed the women around them at the bar. There was a lot to take in. Women surrounded the two where they sat. Nothing but tube tops, glossy lipstick, and tight dresses. Pop's sight was telescopic. His motto was that there was no harm in looking. Shit. Sometimes he even went so far as to flirt a bit. Most women couldn't resist a bald brown head with a little meat on him, much like himself. His given name was Aloysius. A real gentleman's name, but everyone called him Pop for short. It wasn't as if he wasn't a gentleman. Pop had nothing but respect for his. He had a girl at home and he wasn't trying to mess that up for anything. But hell, he thought, it still didn't hurt to look.

"Excuse me, what cologne is that you're wearing?" a pretty curly-haired sistah approached Pop and asked.

Pop thought to himself that it was that charm thing. Act laid back and the women come to you. He didn't even have cologne on, just plain soap and water. Cologne was for those pretty-Ricky types, anyway. It was probably the brother in the blue Brooks Brothers shirt next to him. "Oh, you smell it way over there? I hope I didn't offend you, miss," Pop answered with a smile.

The young sistah laughed, coming in closer to him. "I'm Stacey. You by yourself?" she asked. She had a tongue piercing, a silver metal ball right in the center, and she wanted Pop to see it.

"Nah, boo—I'm waiting for my girl, but if I wasn't, you'd better believe I'd be talking to you," Pop told her. The one dimple on his right cheek showed through.

"We can finish this conversation another time. I could give you my number," she offered.

"Thanks, boo, but I'ma have to pass tonight. I'll see you, though," Pop told her coolly, without hurting her feelings.

"Okay then," the sistah said, making sure that Pop got a view of her backside as she walked away. "What's your name?"

"Pop, boo, my name is Pop." Pop turned back around to the bar. See D.? Pop thought. Case in point. Now if I was up to no good, I would have had me some of that. But I know a good woman when I see her, and I got one. Pop wanted Darnell to know that the world had changed. It wasn't safe to sleep around with a string of pretty women anymore. It paid to have one solid, strong sistah in your corner. Someone who was completely down for you. What his friend Darnell really needed, in his opinion, was stability. "Shemone's not gonna make it easy," he went on to explain. "It's her job to be difficult, but when you get in with her, you're set. Man, my socks are white, and my T-shirts are crisp," Pop joked. "I don't mean that it will be her job to do your laundry, man, but you'll be taken care of. And you'll take care of her, too, of course," Pop added as he playfully nudged his friend.

Darnell took another sip of his drink. He hoped Pop was right, for the same reason that he hadn't gone off with Hope. He just needed confirmation that yes, it was more than just a year of phone calls. Just then his cell phone rang.

"Hello, Darnell?" Shemone said into the phone.

"Hey—surprise, surprise," Darnell replied in a truly surprised tone of voice.

"You still over at the Shark Bar?"

"Yeah. Why, you trying to come meet me for a drink?"

"Not exactly," Shemone answered. She didn't *exactly* know how her fingers had successfully managed to dial him in the first place.

"You up for some company, then?" he took a chance and asked her.

It was late. She knew that she shouldn't have phoned Darnell but she had. Now that she knew for certain that he wasn't with the Hope girl, what was wrong with a little dialogue between two old friends? Besides, she'd had plenty of late-night socializing with her female friends before. "Sure, I'm up for a little company," she told him.

"You ditch brotha-man with the tight tie?"

Shemone giggled. "Yes, but only if you ditched your groupie."

"You started," Darnell replied. "Anyway, at least mine wasn't a date."

"Believe me, mine wasn't either."

"I'm on my way," he said, and with that he hung up. "Yo, you won't guess who that was," Darnell said with a smile.

"By the look of that happy expression on your face, it's gotta be Shemone or Jennifer Lopez," Pop kidded.

"Is it that easy to tell?" Darnell asked Pop.

"Easier," Pop said with a chuckle.

* * *

"That was quick," Shemone said as she opened her front door at twelve-thirty.

"Well, there's not exactly much traffic at this hour," Darnell told her with a smile.

"That is true," Shemone answered. "Come in." She had changed from her sexy dress into one of her casual shirtdresses and pink fuzzy slippers. It felt comfortable. Oddly, as comfortable as it felt to have invited Darnell over to her place at such a late hour.

"Can I take my jacket off?" Darnell asked.

"I don't see why not," Shemone replied. She thought to herself that taking a jacket off couldn't do too much damage.

"Nice outfit," he said as he took a seat on the sofa.

"Very funny," Shemone said back to him.

"So what made you call me? I wasn't expecting to hear from you," Darnell said as he ran his hand sexily over his head. He did that quite often, and Shemone liked it, she liked it a lot.

"Does there have to be a reason? I just wanted to, that's all." Truth be told, there was a zone there that went beyond the days of being one in the group of the Final Four teenage best friends. Darnell was a man now, with a different experience under his belt. It was one that she wasn't used to being exposed to, and when they were together, she felt brand new. So that was it. Curiosity.

It dawned on Darnell, like destiny, as he sat there and thought to himself that there'd been something between them since the first time he'd visited her house, and yeah, even before that, from the first time they'd spoken to each other on the phone. This person who he'd left as a teenage girl was a sexy, smart woman who was bringing out something in him that made him feel brand new. Kind of as if he could forget about his fast-life past and move forward with nothing in the way to stop him. This was the first time Darnell had ever been up for a change in his life, and seeing Shemone made coming out of jail worth it. Sure, she was putting up some walls, but once he overcame those walls, there was no telling what good things would be in store for him. So that was it. Curiosity. Pop might have had something with what he'd said. Maybe he did have a chance. "I'm glad that I heard from you tonight," Darnell told her. He glanced at Shemone and smiled knowingly.

"Would you like a drink or something?" she asked him.

"Nah, I'm all right, thanks." Darnell looked at the colorful painting that hung on the wall. He stared at it for a while. "That's a nice picture you got. If you look real close, it kinda looks like a sunset and clouds."

Shemone gazed at it. "You know what? In all the time that I've had that painting, I've never seen that until now. But you're right, it sort of does." Shemone added, "Hmph, it cost me enough. It's a genuine Pelle collectors' original."

Darnell continued looking at the picture. He didn't care who it was by, or how much it had cost. It looked like a sunset and clouds.

"You want to watch some TV or hear some music? I've got some nice jazz CDs," Shemone told Darnell. The excessive quiet in the room was creating a nervous energy on her part. Not to mention the way Darnell was looking, all streety and fine. Her thoughts were becoming floaty, they were slowly but surely taking a backseat to her overpowering physical emotions.

"No, no TV, no music. I like it this way. It helps me to think better," Darnell told her.

"Ooh-kay," Shemone replied, looking down at her manicure. Tomorrow she'd get her nails redone.

"Mmph," Darnell mumbled, thinking just a little bit more.

"Mmph what?" Shemone asked him.

"Oh, I was just thinking. I was just thinking that sometimes you just gotta make moves on instinct."

"That depends on what we're talking about," Shemone replied. She knew what he was talking about, all right. Darnell had picked up the loud message in the room full of quiet.

He edged over to Shemone on the sofa, leaned in, and began to plant soft, dry kisses around the outer area of her mouth.

Shemone's eyes were still open, but she wasn't resisting, either. This time, it wasn't a dream. Darnell was kissing her in a seductive sequence that magnetically led his juicy lips to hers. Was she about to be seduced? Shemone made a tiny moan. He was making her feel all warm and gushy inside. *Dayummnnn,* she thought. *It's been so long.*

Slowly, Darnell used his mouth to suck on her lower lip.

Hungry to feel his tongue, Shemone probed his with hers. Darnell made her even more anxious by not totally giving in, but sucking on her top lip in calculated rhythmic motions. Then, finally submitting, Darnell surrendered his tongue to hers, with hands of his hands that traveled to unbutton the first button on her shirtdress.

"Darnell, no—we can't," Shemone stopped to tell him.

"We can't, or you just don't want to?" he asked, his face was so close to hers that she thought she'd melt.

As much as she wanted to, it all seemed like too much, too soon. "I mean both." Shemone stood up and forced herself to reply. She refastened the one button that Darnell had managed to undo. "We don't need to get physically involved. We've already got a good thing going. Why don't we just leave it at that?" Shemone sat back down next to him on the couch and continued, "Hasn't it crossed your mind that us sleeping together could ruin the friendship that we've been building on for years?"

Darnell met her gaze and spoke. "Hasn't it crossed your mind that us taking things to another level could make our friendship even better? Some of the best relationships start from friendships, Shemone."

Shemone stood up again and nodded her head, thinking that Darnell's response was a typical man answer. Of course, sex always makes everything better, she thought to herself. "Mmph," she said.

"It's something to think about, right?" Darnell asked her. It wasn't long ago that he'd mumbled mmph himself. For him, the outcome was about making moves on instinct.

Shemone was still standing. Her celibate body was on a four-alarm fire for this particular man. For every reason that she could come up with for why to sleep with him, there was a not. Then something happened while she was still thinking, still trying to sort out her thoughts.

Darnell came up behind her and gently nuzzled her on the back of her neck. His breath was as warm as she was.

"Stop thinking so fucking much," he said, turning her toward him, then silencing her with a kiss as she tried to speak.

"But I'm not that kind—" Shemone weakly attempted to muffle out to him. Really, it wasn't that huge of an attempt. She did want him with all that was everything at that moment.

Darnell momentarily ceased their kiss, making things right by adding the magic word, "please." He looked her directly in the eyes and said, "Baby-girl, please, stop thinking so fucking much." He didn't want Shemone to think that he was treating her as less than the real woman that she was. His voice was commanding, but not forceful.

Shemone thought to herself, He better had said please.

No one talked to her like that, no one. It felt exhilarating and amazing in the way that she'd given him permission to take charge by kissing her yet again. She was about to speak once more to tell him how turned on she was feeling, but Darnell wasn't even having that.

"Shush . . . ," Darnell repeated in soft whispers between kisses.

He was holding on to her like he never wanted to let go, and it made her feel safe, just being with him. His words were hard, but his touch was the opposite. It was soft, loving, and, thank goodness . . . not rushed, like she'd imagined it might have been since it had been so long for her, and for him. Darnell pulled her gently onto the floor.

Shemone stayed silent, letting him take over. She allowed him to unbutton her shirtdress completely. Underneath, she wore a leopard lycra thong and matching bra. Darnell mouthed her breasts over her bra, then worked his way downward. He held her panties over to one side as he teased her welcoming center with his tongue. Then, in one motion, he slid her panties all the way down to handle all of his business. And just when she thought she couldn't take any more, he'd stepped out of his jeans, down to his boxers. Shemone looked up at him and the bulge that protruded behind those tiny yellow smiley faces. Someone was playing peekaboo, and Yes, Shemone thought to herself, real men did wear boxers. His chest was broad and smooth.

He gyrated as he laid his body on top of hers so that she could get a feel for him. She was getting a good feel. He slowly rolled off her, removed her bra, then used his tongue like a paintbrush, flicking at her now fully exposed brown nipples. Then Darnell moved on to her shoulders and arms. He made a trail that didn't end until he'd raised one hand at a time. He was tasting each and every finger of hers, and reigniting the passion that made her all woman.

"Are you ready?" Darnell asked her. "I'll only do this if you're sure you want to. We can stop here," he told her. He honestly hadn't planned to go as far as they had. Not the full-nakedness thing. It was only supposed to be a little foreplay, but damn. A man just couldn't help himself from wanting to be next to her. The thing was, by the same token, he wanted her to know that he respected her, too. Darnell was prepared to shut everything down if she said no to outright making love with him.

Shemone didn't mince words when she replied. Her answer came across loud and clear. "Yes, I'm positive. Let's do this," she said. The drought was over. Shemone brought both of her legs up, and planted her feet firmly on the floor.

Darnell gently lowered his body in between her legs. With thrusts that started out as gentle, he sped up the movements in his hips, making each one count more than the one before. He was going at it so good that Shemone wanted to call out his name without his having to ask. Just then he stopped. He just stopped. Open-eyed, and open-mouthed, Shemone looked into Darnell's eyes and asked, "What's wrong?"

Darnell answered her. "You feel me? You feel me throbbing? That's how much, and how long, I've wanted you," he told her. His whole body glistened with sweat.

Yes. Shemone felt him throbbing. The throbbing was slow, her heartbeat was fast. Darnell went back at it until Shemone exploded. Damn. It felt like every day was Christmas. Darnell blissfully exploded right after her, around three years' worth. He kissed Shemone on the mouth, held her, then snuggled up next to her, real close, on the floor.

"We weren't supposed to do that, you know," Shemone said as she stared at the ceiling. The thinking, planning thoughts were trying to enter her head again.

"So you wanna take it back?"

"Darnell, that's not funny."

"And I'm not laughing, Shemone. Why do you have to question shit so much? It felt right regardless, didn't it?" Darnell asked her.

Shemone nodded yes, then rested her head on his chest. She listened to his heart beating, and took comfort in its strength at a time when she felt at her weakest.

"Knowing you, you probably want to know, now what? because it happened so soon. Just leave things alone. Now I'm about to ask you something, it's my turn," Darnell said as he ran his fingers across the top of her head.

"Go on, ask."

"You mind if I go in the bedroom, up off of this hard-ass wood floor?" he said.

"No," she answered back. She watched him get up and then smirked. It was just like Darnell to end a conversation on a high note. And it didn't hurt watching him walk away, either. His behind was a beautiful thing. It was rounded and not too tight. She pulled down the throw from the couch, and wrapped it around her as she lay on the floor knowing that what she really wanted was but a few feet away. She looked over at his clothes strewn about. His boots, his shirt, and his silver watch, which was on the table. Shemone got up from the floor and took herself into the bedroom. Darnell lay on his stomach in the middle of the bed, wrapped up in the sheets and lightly snoring. Shemone couldn't help but smile. She'd hardly put it on him the way she'd really wanted to. She walked over to the bed, and told him, "Darnell, move over."

8

News Flash

Hey, girl—what brings you by?" Ohija asked cheerily on Wednesday morning. Chimes sounded as Shemone walked through the door of her clothing shop.

"Just dropped in for a life update, girl," Shemone cheerily replied.

"Well, well, well, correct me if I'm wrong, stranger, but I haven't seen you for over two weeks, right?" Ohija asked with a smirk.

"Correct, this would be my official over-two-weeks life update." Shemone went on to say, "You know, I missed you, girl. I've just been so preoccupied, with getting caught up with work and all." Shemone was smiling.

"You make your story deadline?" Ohija asked her.

"I sure did, as always," she proudly answered.

"That's my girl. Hold on and I'm all yours," Ohija replied as she rearranged colorful pieces of clothing on a rack.

Shemone made herself busy around the store. Ohija had made a few changes since the last time she'd been there. The walls had been newly sponge-painted with flat coats of terra-cotta, orange, and brown. It opened up the space and gave it an Afrocentric feel that she liked. Large potted plants in huge straw baskets were placed about the store and pieces of Africa-inspired fabric were framed and on the walls. "Did this just come in? This is gorgeous!" Shemone exclaimed as she picked up the mid-length black mohair tube dress decorated with cowrie shells.

"Yeah, I just got that in last week," Ohija answered.

"Can't leave this one, and the store looks great," Shemone told her at the cash register. She was surprised that the boutique was empty. There was usually always someone inside, shopping. Ohija must have read her mind.

"Thanks, girl—I'm a little behind today. I wasn't feeling so great this morning, kinda got a late start." The hangers clinked as she slid them across the bar. Ohija added, "I just got here myself a little while ago."

"Really? You're okay, right?" Shemone asked.

"Yeah, I'm sure it's just a bug. I'll be fine. My health acts up at this time of the year, every year, without fail. It's nothing that a little echinacea can't cure."

"Okay now," Shemone answered. Ohija and her herbal remedies, she thought to herself. "Echinacea, that helps with colds, doesn't it?"

"Somebody's been doing their homework," Ohija said in an impressed tone of voice. She grabbed two bar stools from the back, one for herself and one for Shemone. "So?"

Shemone prepared herself. She was really about to let Ohija in on her true life update. "So, Darnell's home. He's been by my place twice." Shemone swallowed, then said, "And he slept over the second time."

"You're kidding me!" Ohija said. "Well, he left that part out!" she exclaimed. All she could do was to be glad that two of her closest friends had found something special in each other beyond friendship. Now all they had to do was make it last, the same as she and her husband, Ray, were doing.

"You spoke to him?" Shemone asked, uncertain of just how much Darnell had filled Ohija in on.

"No, I wish. No one was at home, but he left a message on the answering machine letting me know that he's home, and that he misses me, and can't wait to see me. Do you know Darnell still calls me his little sis? Wait until he gets a gander, and finds out that there's nothing little about me." Ohija chuckled. "Now, back to you. A sleepover, huh?"

Shemone smiled. "Ohija, everything is just happening so fast. Darnell literally just got out of jail weeks ago," she told her.

"So no more drug sales for him for certain?" Ohija asked.

"That's what he says," Shemone replied. "And I think that I believe him."

"That's just what he needs right now," Ohija thought aloud, "people who believe in him. Now you know what I wanna ask girl. So how was it?" Ohija listened to what was said next as if her life depended on it.

Shemone didn't answer right away. "It was . . . I never . . . felt like . . ."

"Wha—at," Ohija said. Her eyebrows rose to the top of her forehead. "Was he that on point? You mean, he left a sistah speechless?"

"Yes," Shemone said as she lowered her voice. "Girl, he told me to stop thinking so fucking much."

"No way!" Ohija screamed. Just then a customer came through the door and began browsing through the clothes.

Ohija sat, still stunned. She wanted Shemone to finish telling her what had happened with Darnell.

"Take care of your customer, Ohija!"

Ohija pulled herself away from Shemone, to the customer. "May I help you?" she asked.

"I'm just looking for now, thanks," the tall, thin woman answered.

Ohija came back over to Shemone and whispered, "Are you serious?"

"Yes, very!" Shemone replied, beaming.

"Does this come in a size eight?" the woman interrupted.

"Uh—let me go in the back and check that for you," Ohija told her. She made a face at Shemone as she went past her, to the back.

"That's a pretty outfit," Shemone told the customer.

"I think so, too," the woman answered.

Ohija came out with a size eight. "The dressing room is in the back," she said as she handed over the outfit. "Give me a holler if you need any help."

"Thank you," the customer said, walking to the back.

"He told you to stop thinking so fucking much?"

"Yes, how many times are you gonna ask me that?" Shemone chuckled. "It wasn't, like, in a bad way, it was, like, in a sexy way. And, Ohija, he looks so fine now. You've got to see him."

"Well, it wasn't like Darnell was ever ugly."

"That is true," Shemone agreed in a giddy teenage tone. "He just looks altogether better. It's hard to really describe him in words," she told her friend. "Right about now, the only thing that I can describe in words is that I don't regret sleeping with him. I'm happy, and I'll just have to wait and see where we go with things."

"Sounds like the best unplanned plan I ever heard, girl," Ohija answered with a grin.

"Maybe we can set something up to go out somewhere together," Shemone suggested.

"You mean, like a couples' thing?" Ohija said, smirking.

Shemone returned the smirk, rearranging the sentence so that it sounded better to the ear. It was also one that flowed easier from her mouth. "Maybe a friendly couples' thing."

"Whatever you say. Friends don't do what you and Darnell did together," Ohija playfully teased.

"Miss, could I get some help back here?" the customer called from the back.

It was Shemone's convenient cue to leave. "Ohija, I'm gone. I'll call you later. I'm meeting up with Darnell for a movie later, and I'm telling him what you said, too," Shemone said, blushing her way out the door.

"You do that," Ohija answered as she scooted to the back of the store with a friendly wave, saying, "I'll tell him so myself when I see him." She added, "And keep me posted."

Shemone got behind the wheel of her shiny SUV and started toward the freeway, heading to White Plains, New York, where her mother had moved to after she graduated high school. Obligation was calling. It had been a while since she'd actually seen her mother, Ruth, and she never had gotten around to returning her phone call. Time simply didn't permit her to see her mother as much as she might have wanted to. Well, no, that wasn't completely true. She supposed she could always make the time, but Shemone wasn't sure she wanted to. Her mother wasn't the easiest person to be around. There was always a strained tension between them. It seemed like the more Shemone did, the more her mother went out of her way to prove that it wasn't enough.

She pulled into the driveway of the French-blue-and-white-painted house and beeped her horn twice. Ben, Ruth's handyman acquaintance, had been out front sweeping the sidewalk. Ben, or Mr. Ben, as Shemone often called him, had to be under some kind of bewitching love spell as far as her mother was concerned, Shemone thought. It was the only way to explain his outright dedication to Ruth. One paid roofing job two years ago had turned into nothing but free use of his extra time and contracting services ever since. Unfortunately, the feeling didn't appear to be mutual on her mother's part. The only attention Ruth ever gave him was when she was bossing him around to complete a task. Just like she was doing now. Ruth had abruptly taken the broom away from Ben and begun to sweep herself. "This is how it should be done," she told him. Ben stood off to the side like it wasn't a problem. Shemone thought to herself again that the man was probably too kind for his own good.

Shemone rolled down the tan-tinted window on the passenger side and yelled out, "Hey there, Mr. Ben. Mom, do you need me to help you with that?"

Mr. Ben gave Shemone a friendly wave hello, while her mother waved her off, continuing to sweep. Ruth finally walked over to her daughter's SUV, leaving Ben to finish what was left of the job.

"Mom, Mr. Ben was sweeping okay," she tried to tell her mother.

"I know, but he wasn't doing it right. You'd never get any dirt up with the way he was holding that broom. I had to show him the proper way. If you're going to volunteer to help someone do something, you need to do it right," Ruth explained.

At the age of fifty, her mother, Ruth Waters, didn't look a day over thirty. A salt-and-pepper blunt cut and a narrow waistline couldn't deny it. When they did go out together, which was seldom, people often identified them as being sisters and not a mother-daughter pair. "Mom, you could stand to be a little friendlier."

"Shemone, please," Ruth interrupted. "I'm the mother, remember?"

Shemone stepped out and around the SUV, slamming the door. It wasn't worth arguing the point, she thought to herself. It always had to be her mother's way.

Ruth was still inspecting Ben's technique as he swept near the curb.

Shemone purposefully stood in front of Ruth's view, then gave her mother a hug. A very quick, strained hug, the kind they'd given each other for years.

"Let's go inside," Ruth told her.

"Can't, I need to get back to my home office. I've got a story to work on that just can't wait."

Ruth sighed softly as they stood in front of the house. She asked herself why her daughter had even bothered to drive out to see her in the first place. What they were having amounted to a telephone conversation. "So what else have you been up to lately?" Ruth decided to ask.

"Pretty much the same stuff, Mom, you know, writing, related things," Shemone replied. She didn't care to go deeper into conversation. She summed things up in a sentence: "I'm just working hard, just working hard, Mom."

"I guess so. You don't get over here much anymore. You must be giving some worthy man all of your time," her mother joked, hoping that really was the case.

"Why does it always have to be about a man, Mom? Can't I be busy working, too?" This was why she had to go. Her mother never had anything good to say. There she was, undermining her and what she was doing for a living. And to think she'd wanted to bring up the topic of actually being happy, the prospect of being back in the relationship loop.

"I don't wanna argue with you, Shemone. I merely meant to suggest that it might be time for you to get out and mingle a little bit more. You never know who you might meet. A doctor, a lawyer, or even one of those little writer friends of yours," Ruth said. Her daughter wasn't getting any younger, and still had yet to meet proper husband material. All Ruth knew was that the world was cruel, and going it alone for the rest of her life, like she was, was not what Shemone deserved.

Shemone frowned. "Mom, I love you, and please don't take this the wrong way, but how would you know what I do, and who I'm meeting?"

Ruth answered in an exasperated tone of voice, "You just said that all you've been doing is working, didn't you? Other than that, I really wouldn't know." She continued, "A mother always wants the best for her child, Shemone." Part of Ruth wanted to reach out for her daughter and take her in her arms like when she was little. It was the only time that Ruth remembered Shemone still needing her to make decisions for her. The truth was, Shemone was an adult now. An adult who was determined to make unnecessary mistakes all on her own. "Why don't we just have a nice mother-daughter visit today? Won't you come inside for a piece of cheesecake? It's fresh from the bakery," Ruth said.

"Mom, you worry too much. Do I look like I need anything?" Shemone forced a smile.

"You look like you need a slice of cheesecake." Ruth laughed.

Shemone gave in and laughed back. "Maybe I do."

They walked toward the house together, but Shemone made sure to add, "I can't stay long."

Ruth looked over at her daughter and answered, "That's fine." She was used to Shemone saying she couldn't stay long. She never could.

9

Raise the Roof

Darnell felt like a new man. He thought to himself that making love with Shemone had been one of the best things that had ever happened to him. It was more than just getting himself some, even though he'd been locked down for so long without making love to a woman. It was getting her that he was glad about. Shemone had let her guard down and given him a shot in her life. It was what he'd always wanted, and Darnell couldn't get enough of spending time with her. Two nights before, they'd held hands and kissed throughout an entire two-and-a-half-hour movie. It didn't even matter that they'd both left the theater not remembering what the story line was about.

After the movie and getting a bite to eat, they'd strolled back to her place, made love, and talked about life up until the wee hours of the early morning. In a way, it almost didn't seem real. Shemone Waters had finally made things official. It was more than just a year of phone calls and friendship. The only thing now was his next move. Yeah, he'd been real set about telling Shemone to stop asking What now? after they'd first slept together, but he knew what she meant. Darnell also knew how she meant it, and deep down, he wanted to know the same. One thing was for sure, he couldn't go back to the way things used to be because even where he lived had changed.

On Friday afternoon, Darnell rode the elevator up to the tenth floor in the Stratford housing projects where he lived. He almost hadn't recognized his own street when he'd first returned. The complex had a new children's playground, colored benches, and landscaping, all thanks to the housing renewal improvements going on in Harlem. His surroundings were different, and so were many of the people. A lot of his close friends were either dead or locked down somewhere, part of another sad statistic. No one—and Darnell had looked—who used to hustle on the streets with him was out there anymore, with the exception of Pop. Only Pop wasn't out there dealing drugs anymore. He was doing the nine to five thing with transit these days, and seemed to be happy doing it. Darnell had yet to figure out exactly what he wanted to do with himself. The odds were that it wouldn't be easy. There was no real money in a nine to five. Real money was what they used to bring in on a daily basis. Probably five to six times what Pop was coming home with from transit. Yeah, and as much as everything had changed, it was comforting to know that some things did stay the same.

His family had had the same three-bedroom apartment at Stratford since he was in elementary school. His mom, brother, sister, and her baby still lived there, and, since his release, so did he. Darnell walked along the hallways looking at the new paint job. His tag name, D-Boogies, had been scribbled all along the elevator and walls years ago. It was a way of marking his territory back in the days when he and his drug-selling crew had ruled Stratford. Now there were signs all over that identified the New York City Housing Authority as being the ones in charge. "No loitering. No spitting. No gambling." "No old friends" the signs might as well have said. But he had his Shemone, and Ohija, and Pop, too.

Darnell made his way inside the beige-painted boxed-in apartment. His mother, Louise, was in the kitchen stirring a steamy pot of something. He looked at her brown face. It was intense. Louise was always intense when it came to her cooking. One could easily tell that she had been a beauty back in her day, although now her face was showing signs of wear. Maybe it was because of all that she'd done in being such a dedicated mother. She'd worked hard her whole life taking care of them. Darnell thought he had inherited many of his facial features from his mother. Her skin was smooth and even, and her eyes deep set and dark, like bottled Karo syrup. These days it didn't seem to matter to her how she looked. Louise wore a multicolored scarf around her head, and underneath, pieces of a black, bushy wig stuck out. The wig was probably as old as she was, and it matched the age of her clothes. Her floral print housedress looked like something that someone would wear outside on a porch somewhere in the backwoods of the Deep South.

Darnell knew that it wasn't easy for his mother raising three kids in the projects with no steady father figure. All three of them had different daddies. Now that they were mostly grown and still in the house made it all the more harder.

Louise added butter beans to the boiling smoked turkey on the stove. She was cooking, but she was also thinking about her kids. Well, she thought again, they weren't all exactly kids anymore. Monica was the oldest, thirty-one, with a new baby and no job. The spitting image of her daddy, cream-colored, with a face and body that would bring any natural-born man to his knees. Sad thing was that Monica knew it. Monica made a career out of her relationships, always out to get something from a man. Monica dressed only in top designer clothing, carried designer handbags, and wore a new hairstyle almost every week. Louise was a Bible-toting, praying mother. She prayed daily that her daughter would do something more with her life, not only for herself, but for her young son, Julius, who was only six months old. It just wasn't a healthy thing for a grown woman to not know the feeling of being responsible, and of having her own independence. Especially if a woman was trapped in the situation Louise had been in with Monica's father. Sadly, Louise had had to flee from him because of the physical abuse that she'd endured.

James was the youngest, and he looked like his daddy, too, only of a darker shade. Such a handsome little thing. At fourteen, he stood almost six feet tall. There was one thing that no one could deny: Louise had herself some pretty kids. James had the most personality of the three, and from what Louise saw, the most promise, a freshman in high school and a star basketball player. James made his mother proud. He got decent grades, and kept his nose clean. Louise had gotten James involved in a Big Brother program not too long after his brother had gotten sent off to prison. She wanted James to know that there was more out there, and that he didn't have to be another product of a bad environment. James's father wouldn't have been so bad to have around if he hadn't been such a compulsive procrastinator. The next day was always the day he would be looking for a job. Louise got tired of supporting a man who didn't have anything besides loving to offer. James was going to be more than any woman's lover. From the way he was going, he'd be making it big in the sports world, and have a solid degree to back it up with.

Then there was her Darnell. The middle child who took on the responsibility of being the oldest. There had been many a time that Darnell had paid the rent or kept the phone going after having gotten a final disconnection notice. He was hardly ever home before he got locked up, but when he was, he made time for his family. He was a solid provider. Louise knew that all that money and the cars weren't from a legitimate source. She prayed for her son to find his way out of that fast-money maze. Unfortunately, like in Monopoly, it had led him directly to jail. She so feared the worst now that he was home again. There was no telling what he would be up to. It was all that she knew of him doing, illegal activities. She still loved him, and she had loved his daddy, too, before he'd died tragically of an early heart attack. His father, Lewis, had been the best man she'd ever had.

"Darnell Williams, don't you slam my door!" Ruth told her son.

It smelled like home. The aroma of spicy greens filled the house. Darnell smiled and gave Louise a loving kiss on the cheek. "How's my favorite mama doing? Why don't you get dressed up and let your son take you out for a nice dinner for a change?" He lifted up the lid from one of the pots. "Come on, Mama, put these pots away just this once," he said.

Louise slapped his hand away. "Boy, I don't want to go out and eat nobody else's food. You know that I don't eat everybody's cooking like you do," Louise scolded. "And you'd better stay from out my pots with them dirty hands! I know I taught you better than that."

Darnell had known his mother would refuse. He remembered the time he'd bought her a new living room set. The one they had was plaid and worn beyond even looking like furniture. His mother, unbelievably, had sent the new one back to the store. She'd told him that there was nothing wrong with the set they had. That's just the kind of woman she was. That same couch was still there, with a cover over it. But it was clean. "Sorry, Mama, I'm just hungry," Darnell replied. "What time is dinner gonna be ready?" he asked.

The front door slammed again. Young James came through the door bouncing a basketball.

"You kids have lost your natural mind!" Louise pointed a stern finger at her youngest son and said, "James, don't make me bounce that ball upside your head!"

James gave his mother one of his handsome, boyish smiles, then acknowledged the presence of his big brother "What's up, D.?" James said. "Dinner ready, Ma?"

"No, dinner is not ready. Go take yourself a shower and then maybe you can talk about eating!" she answered, nodding her head.

James poked out his mouth. Louise took a piece of meat from out of one of the pots, and carefully blew it cool. She stuffed it into James's mouth. He was spoiled and she knew it.

James chewed the flavorful meat with a grin, and, without another word, went off to the bathroom to shower.

"None for me, Mama?" Darnell asked.

Louise did the same for him.

"Mmm, that's good. Mama, you know, you should open up a soul food restaurant one day," Darnell told her.

"Yeah, I should," Louise answered back quickly. She heard it from everyone all the time. From the people at James's school functions to the committees at church. Her baked macaroni and fried chicken were always on the top of the request list.

"How much longer until dinner, Ma?" Darnell asked.

"Goodness, you children act like you've never eaten before. Give it another hour." Louise turned on the faucet to make some pink lemonade Kool-Aid and added, "You know that I don't rush my cooking for nobody."

"I know, Ma. I'm going to go back out for a little bit, then," Darnell replied. "I'll catch you later." Darnell gave his mother another peck on the cheek and was out the door.

"That boy," Louise said as she sucked her teeth. Yes, she sure did love her kids all right. She thought, Now where was that Monica at with my grandchild?

Darnell took a walk over to the next building, where Pop lived. It was after six in the evening, so he should have been in from work by now. He rang his bell.

"Who?" the intercom answered, echoing static.

"Yo, Pop, it's Darnell, come down, man," he said.

"Be right down," Pop answered. Pop came down five minutes later. He had changed from his work clothes into blue sweats and sneakers. The two gave each other a hello pound and a hug.

"You not driving?" Pop asked Darnell.

"No, my car's parked. I'm just waiting for my mother to finish cooking," he said.

"So what's the deal?" Darnell asked Pop. He wanted to tell him how right he was about everything. He and Shemone had only slept together twice, but he could already feel progress in the air when it came to the potential of their being a couple.

"Just trying to stay sane," Pop answered. "My girl was upstairs flipping out on me."

"Oh, word?" Darnell replied. He sat down on the outside steps of the building, and held on to his good news to hear his friend out.

"Word," Pop confirmed, sitting, too. "She's talking about me asking for a raise at my job." Pop took out a piece of chewing gum. He offered Darnell a stick.

"No thanks," Darnell replied.

Pop popped the stick of gum into his mouth and continued, "I'm saying, I've been at my job for a few years and everything. But let me be the one to decide. I know when it's time for me to ask for a raise. It doesn't take her to tell me."

"Wha—at, it's like she's calling the shots like that?" Darnell asked. He was hearing a completely opposite side of the relationship thing all of a sudden. His friend continued.

"Women always trying to dictate shit. I stopped hustling, I do the nine to five, I don't fuck around on her. I take care of my son . . . still ain't enough," Pop complained.

"Yeah, how is the little man doing?" Darnell asked.

"Oh, he's keeping himself busy. He's got a smart mouth just like his daddy." Pop chuckled. "That's why I'm trying to nip that right now. You know what I'm saying?"

Darnell laughed, too. "True, true, yeah, I feel you on that women thing," he said, trying to be sympathetic. "It's got you singing a different tune today, huh?"

"Tune about what?" Pop asked as he tinkered with his watch.

"You know, at the bar, you were like, one-on-one relationships are so great. That white T-shirt stuff you told me about," he said.

"Nah, I mean it's still all good," Pop answered, rubbing his stomach. "Every relationship is gonna have some problems now and then, regardless."

"You know I'm no expert on that, Pop. I've always been more the stick-and-move type," Darnell answered, thinking to himself that he'd never been in a real relationship before, and quite honestly, wasn't sure how to keep one.

Pop burst out laughing. "Yeah, yeah."

The two slapped hands. Pop said, "We've all been there, the casual-sex thing." After their laughter died down, he told Darnell, "But for real, there's more to life than that, you'll see."

"You need your own damn talk show," Darnell joked.

"I know, right," Pop agreed. "So what happened with you and Shemone? Everything turn out all right after you left Shark's?"

"Yeah, did it." Darnell's cheeks hurt from smiling so hard. "She's special, man. I feel on top of the world when I'm around her. I'm, like, trying to map out my future now, and she's definitely a big part of it."

"Wha—at?" Pop replied in amazement. He thought to himself, Damn, I'm good. His words of wisdom had helped Darnell to hook up with the woman of his dreams. "I'm happy for you, man," Pop told him. He took another wrapper off a piece of gum.

"More gum? Is it that good, or do you just have problems?" Darnell joked, then added, "Let me find out I gotta take you to a meeting at gum chewers anonymous!"

Pop laughed again. "Man, I just like chewing gum. I do it when I'm stressed." He placed the stick in his mouth. "I can fuck up some gum!" he said.

"So what are you gonna do about your situation?" Darnell asked him.

"What else?" Pop sucked his teeth. "Ask for a raise."

The two laughed again, then Pop's expression became serious. "Oh, boy, here comes one that they need to put under the jail," Pop told Darnell. He was referring to an old friend of theirs named Red.

Red, in a silver Lexus, drove up to the building where Darnell and Pop had been talking.

So I've been wrong, Darnell thought. Some of his old friends were still around. He just hadn't looked hard enough. But they'd found him. Red had been in the drug game back in the day, and Darnell had a familiar feeling that he still was.

"What's going on, baby?" Red asked in a glad-to-see-you tone of voice.

Same Red, Darnell thought to himself, light tan with freckles. That's where he'd gotten his nickname. His seat in the car was reclined way back, like he was almost lying down and driving. He and Pop came over closer. Darnell gave Red a hello pound on the hands, but Pop didn't. "You're living the life," Darnell told Red. "The Lexus." Darnell checked out Red's ride from where he was.

Red held his hand over the steering wheel so that the two could see both the diamond ring and the bulky gold bracelet on his wrist. "Thanks, paid for it with all cash," he said.

"All cash?" Darnell replied in an impressed tone.

Red grinned a proud, wide grin. "You just getting home?" he asked him.

"Yeah, man, like three weeks ago."

Pop stepped back away from the car. "Darnell, man, let me go do what I gotta do," Pop suddenly told him.

"All right, then, I'll catch up with you later," he answered. Darnell slapped Pop five on the hands and went back to the car to speak to Red. He noticed that Pop hadn't said good-bye to Red. He thought that it seemed out of character for Pop. He usually got along with everybody. "Red, you and my man got beef?" Darnell asked him.

"Nah, it's nothing like that. We just got an understanding, that's all. He stays out of my way, I stay out of his," Red replied.

Darnell only nodded. He'd ask Pop about all the controversy later.

"Yo, get in, let's ride," Red told him.

Darnell obliged, and went around to the passenger side. He thought to himself that his mother probably hadn't finished cooking anyway. Though the inside of the car was rose-scented, Darnell knew that there was nothing sweet about Red. He'd taken down many a man, and gotten away with it.

"So I'm surprised to see you out and about," Darnell looked over and said to him as they rode. "You got locked up around the same time as me, didn't you?" he asked.

"Yeah, man, but I beat that sentence. I got someone else to do the time. I'm not trying to be locked up behind no bars." Red drove around the block. "It's too much money out here to be made. You know what I mean?" Red said. He turned and looked at Darnell.

"Yeah, wish I could have beat my sentence," Darnell replied, thinking out loud. Darnell wondered if his life would have been any different. Maybe he and Shemone would have gotten together a long time ago.

"How much time did you do?" Red asked him.

"Three years, man," Darnell replied.

"Damn." Red slipped silence in between them. "So what are you trying to get into now?" he asked him.

Darnell thought about it. "I'm feeling out different things, man. Just feeling things out," he replied. He really wasn't certain. His passion was fixing things, but he didn't know where to start looking to get a real job doing it.

"Let me introduce you to some cool peoples of mine," Red said as he drove up the avenue.

Darnell thought that being introduced to some cool people of Red's, that was not the best thing. But with him being back in the neighborhood, it did help to know faces, just in case anything went down. It damn sure didn't mean that he was going back to selling drugs again, he told himself.

A group of guys was converged in front of the grocery store around the way.

Red and Darnell got out of the car.

"This is the infamous D-Boogies," Red told them all.

Darnell slapped hands with the group of men. He could tell that an introduction coming from Red went a long way, as each extended him a welcome hello pound. They all looked hard, as if they'd lived a hard life. Although he was just standing there with a group of guys in front of the neighborhood store, there was a lot that was busy. Illegal drug transactions were being made for sure behind the scenes. No, some things hadn't changed at all, Darnell thought to himself. He wasn't going to let Red all up in his business, but like he'd said before, there was nothing to stop him from feeling things out and deciding what to do now that he was home.

* * *

"Hello?" Shemone whispered in a sleepy voice. Rap music blared in the background of the caller.

"Shemone, it's Darnell. Can I come over?" his voice yelled over the sounds of the song.

Shemone checked the time and sat up in bed. "Darnell, it's two-thirty in the morning. Are you crazy?"

"I didn't mean to wake you. I just wanted to see you, baby-girl," Darnell answered. He and Shemone had been taking turns calling each other, back and forth, on the phone for the past few days. With all of the time they'd been spending with each other, they'd both agreed that they needed to come up for air to get some things done. Actually, he thought, it had been more his idea. He wanted to show Shemone that he was taking some initiative when it came to the matter of his future. Darnell had been busy getting all of his paperwork in order so that he could find a job, and a reluctant Shemone had obliged, staying busy with her own writing assignments.

Shemone thought to herself while she had him on the phone that sure, she'd wanted to see him, too, but not at this hour. And since she and Darnell never had a problem with communicating, she was gonna communicate. Shemone angrily watched as her digital clock jumped up another minute. Soon she'd have to get up and get to her work. "Not at two thirty-one A.M. in the morning, you don't," Shemone told him. She hung up the phone, rolled over, and went back to sleep. And for the very first time she thought, I hope I didn't make a mistake getting myself involved with this one.

10

Urban Chivalry

It was the very next day. No, really, it was more like the same day, only the sun was up, shining this time. Shemone was just about to return to her apartment from emptying some garbage in the trash compactor when she heard the elevator chime. When she looked back to see who it was, Darnell was getting off. With conviction, Shemone stood there, at the entrance of her front door. She hoped that Darnell had cleaned up his act, too, by throwing out the late-night calls that she considered to be garbage as well. Namely, because she wasn't having it. "What are you doing here?" she asked him. He was looking all sad and apologetic-like, holding a fragrant bunch of mixed flowers that consisted of bright-hued tulips and a combination of red and yellow roses.

"Here," he said as he reached out to her. "I got you these."

Shemone took in the sight of the beautiful way the bouquet was arranged. "Flowers aren't the answer to everything, Darnell," Shemone replied in an unimpressed tone of voice. She turned her head away.

Darnell was left holding the bouquet. "I never said that they were, but it is something." He paused, thinking about what else he could do to make the situation right again. "I'm sorry, okay? It's just—I'm used to keeping late-night hours on the outside." Darnell smirked, and went on to explain. "It's a street thing. But the thing is, I wasn't even in the streets. I was at home. Just realizing that everybody is not on my schedule is something I need to get used to. I know that you got your own agenda baby-girl," he told her.

Shemone thought to herself that yes, Darnell had made mention of his late-night drug runs in the stories he'd told her. He'd explained that the nighttime was the best time to move around. Legally, it was harder to identify a person who couldn't be clearly seen. But this wasn't a drug run, and she wasn't a drug-enforcement officer. Darnell was going to have to let go of his streety ways.

"You gonna wait for my hands to fall off or what?" Darnell asked in his best Billy Dee Williams tone of voice.

Shemone caught on, remembering the line from *Mahogany* very well. It was one of her all-time favorite movies. "Your name is Darnell Williams, not Billy Dee Williams," she said. "But I will take them," she said, finally giving in and taking the flowers from his hand.

"Good—finally. Are you going to let me in, or am I just stopping by as the flower-delivery man?" he jokingly asked.

Shemone smiled in his direction for the first time. "You might as well come in, but I'm working on a story, so excuse me if I'm not that entertaining," she said, letting Darnell through the door.

"Doesn't matter," he told her. "I don't need to be entertained," a happy and now-forgiven Darnell replied. "You might have something around here that needs my fixing skills," he beamed.

"No, I don't think so," she replied. Everything in her place worked just fine because she was used to staying on top of things before they could ever go wrong or break down. But there was that new DVD player still in the box that she hadn't gotten anyone to hook up yet. She knew Darnell had some gadget- and electrical-mending talents, but she hadn't yet tried him out for herself. "I just might have something," she told him in an optimistic tone. She opened a closet and showed Darnell the box with the DVD player in it.

"Is this all?" he boasted. "You want me to hook this DVD up to the TV for you?" Darnell chuckled. "Baby-girl, it'll be my pleasure."

Shemone smiled, grabbed her gigantic mug of coffee from the counter, then walked toward the bedroom to get back to work, leaving Darnell to his.

"Ain't you forgetting something?" he asked. He was trying to get a quick kiss in.

Shemone turned around and asked playfully, "Oh, coffee? It's in the kitchen, by the refrigerator, go on and help yourself."

"I wasn't talking about coffee," Darnell said as he rushed up on Shemone, chasing her into the bedroom. Shemone fell onto the bed laughing, with Darnell on top of her.

"Get off of me, I told you I had work to do, now quit!" She chuckled loudly.

"You know the morning brings out the sexiness in you," he said, giving Shemone a kiss on the lips.

She returned the kiss because she had missed him, then spoke because there was no way in the world that he could have not heard her, as close as they were physically to each other, body to body on the bed. "It's not going to be the way you want it to be all the time, Mr. Darnell," she told him. "I have rules and yes, an agenda. The first rule is, don't call or show up at my door past twelve A.M. The second rule is that you can't just come by and disrupt my workday whenever you feel like it."

"Okay, I can understand that," Darnell answered. "It's your house, your rules. I gotta obey, right?" Darnell added, "If we're gonna be together."

"That's right," Shemone said. "Rules and togetherness both work for me," she told him.

Darnell gave her one last peck before lifting himself from being on top of her. He was about to get to hooking up that DVD player of hers. It wasn't even five minutes after he'd started that he heard Shemone scream. Darnell rushed into the bedroom. "Shemone, you all right? Why'd you scream?"

"I was typing on my PC, then it just suddenly switched off," she answered in a hyper tone of voice. Shemone hit the power switch on her computer, but nothing happened. "No!" she shrieked loudly. "I know that this computer did not just go out on me! All of my work, it's gone!" she said, panicking.

"It just went out, like that?" Darnell asked her. He immediately went to check on the power line. "Are you sure it's plugged in? Is everything connected?" he asked, double-checking. Everything was connected. Darnell tinkered around in the back of the computer.

It made Shemone nervous. The kind of nervous that if she'd smoked, she would have finished a full pack of cigarettes. It was one thing to be gadget-knowledgeable, but another to be a computer technician, she thought to herself. She knew that he'd taken an intro electrical class in jail, but what it covered she didn't know.

Darnell pulled power cords out, then plugged them back in again.

"Do you know what you're doing back there? Please don't make things any worse," Shemone told him in a worried voice. She stood up to see exactly what he was doing. The suspense was killing her.

"I think I discovered what the problem is," Darnell informed her. "Do you have a spare one of these?" He held up one of the cords he'd taken out. "This one seems like it has a short in it. You must have mistakenly stepped on the cord."

Shemone took the cord from him. "I think I do." She went around to the front of her desk. "Somewhere in the bottom of this drawer." There were about a million cords inside, of all colors, lengths, and widths. She'd put every electronic accessory in it for every item she'd ever owned, and now couldn't figure out which was which.

Darnell came over and pulled out just the one she needed. It was like second instinct with him. "Here it is," he said, showing her. He replaced the old with the new, hit the power switch, and presto, Shemone's work was back up on the screen again.

She heaved a mega-huge sigh of relief. "Darnell, thank you so much," she told him in an earnest tone. "That was amazing, what you did."

"All I did was change a cord," Darnell replied modestly. "It wasn't nothing."

"Maybe not to you, but to me it was. This computer is my livelihood. I've become dependent on it. And even though I'm supposed to have a backup of everything I write, I don't always make one," she explained.

"Well, anytime, baby-girl," Darnell told her. "I'm gonna get back to the DVD. I'm just about done there, too," he added.

Shemone smiled widely at him, and then got back to work. She was feeling really pleasant about the fact that her man had stepped up to the plate to help his lady out.

11

Fairy Godmother

Hello."

"Raymond? Hey, how are you? It's Shemone," she said into the phone Friday evening. Ohija's husband had answered.

"I'm fine, thanks. I was just on my way out. You looking for Ohija?"

"Well, who else would she be looking for?" Ohija joked loudly in the background, then said, "Not you!"

"Mind your business, please!" Raymond joked, "How do you know that Shemone and I don't have something going on?"

" 'Cause then I'd have to open a can of whoop-ass on you both." Ohija laughed. "Y'all don't want none of this!"

Shemone and Raymond cracked up with laughter.

"Hold on, Shemone," Raymond told her. "She's right here."

"Thanks, and take it easy," Shemone said.

"You, too," Raymond replied.

"Hey, Shemone, what's new? I don't hear from you, I don't see you. You too busy being an in-the-house freak or what?" Ohija playfully asked. She hadn't seen Shemone, and she still hadn't seen Darnell. But it didn't take a genius to figure out the mystery.

Shemone just giggled.

"I'm right, ain't I?" Ohija said to her.

"I didn't call you for all that, so don't start," Shemone playfully warned her friend. "Did I catch you at a bad time?"

"No—not at all. I was just looking through my cabinet for some crackers," Ohija answered.

"Crackers?"

"Like morning, noon, and night nausea crackers."

"Ohija—you're pregnant!" Shemone shrieked happily.

"Yeah, girl, unbelievably eight weeks' pregnant. I didn't even know I was because I still had my monthly, girl."

Shemone screamed into the phone. "You're kidding! Congrats, to you and Raymond!"

"Of course, we'll want you to be their godmother," Ohija casually replied.

"Did you say 'their'?"

"Yes, I'm having twins, girl!"

Shemone screamed again. "What took you so long to tell me?"

"Well, I was trying to call you after we first found out. Your phone just rang off the hook."

Shemone thought back, trying to think of what she had been doing. Probably something with Darnell. She grinned, glad that Ohija couldn't see her face through the phone. "You should have kept calling me!" she said.

"I did! Check your machine, Shemone. You've probably got some new stories from your editors to write that you don't even know about!" Ohija joked.

"Oh, girl, I'm ecstatic!" Shemone told her, going to get her date book. "When's your due date?"

"They're telling me sometime in June."

"I'm going to spoil those twins," Shemone told her matter-of-factly. They were going to be the closest practice she'd be getting to having her own children for a while.

"I'm leaving now, honey," Raymond told Ohija from the background.

"Okay, don't work too hard," Ohija answered.

"Raymond off to work again?" Shemone asked.

"Yeah, girl. He's doing double overtime now that the twins are on the way. We're saving up for a house. This little cubby of a Queens apartment's not gonna do us a bit of nothing after the babies get here."

"Your apartment is so nice, though," Shemone told her.

"Nice, but small."

"Sublet it out if you can."

"We just might," Ohijah replied. "That brain of yours is always working."

Shemone told her in an excited tone of voice, "Speaking of working on something, I had no idea that you and Raymond had been trying to have kids."

"We weren't, really. But it was, like, if it happens, it happens. We're stable, married, and not getting any younger." Ohija chuckled. "And boy, did it happen."

"Twins!" Shemone couldn't help but exclaim. It almost felt as though she was missing out on something in her life. Shemone made a brief comparison in her head with herself and Ohija. She was stable, but not as a couple. She wasn't married, but intended to be in the next few years. She wasn't getting any younger. Okay. That was common ground. "So whose side do twins run on?" she asked.

"Raymond's, there are, like, three sets of them on his mother's side," Ohija told her.

"And you mean to tell me you knew that and still married him?" Shemone joked.

Ohija burst out laughing. "Yeah, I guess you could say that I was asking for trouble."

"So it's too early to tell the sexes, right?" Shemone asked. She was full of questions. She'd never been a godmother before, let alone one to a set of twins.

"Girl, we're not trying to find that out. Just as long as we have two healthy babies is all we care about."

"I hear you, that's what's important," Shemone replied. "Well, I can't follow up your news, but that does bring me to the reason for my call—"

"Don't tell me, you're pregnant, too!" Ohija said loudly, trying to make a guess.

Shemone attempted to get her announcement together. "No! I am not pregnant," she confirmed. "I just wanted to invite you and Ray to a dinner party that I'm having next Friday."

"Shemone's pregnant?" Ray asked, repeating what he'd overheard just as he was stepping out the door.

"See what you started?" Shemone playfully replied, giggling.

"No, Ray, Shemone's not pregnant," Ohija informed him. "She just wanted to invite us to her dinner party."

Ray relayed a message through his wife. "Tell her that we'll be there!"

Ohija spoke once again into the phone. "Girl, Ray says what I say, that we wouldn't dare miss being at your dinner party."

"Great, so I'll see you guys when you visit, and take care of my godbabies!"

"I will," Ohija said as she hung up the phone. "Oh, and let Darnell know that I'm looking forward to seeing him," she added. She wanted Shemone to convey the message, just in case he didn't know. She had yet to see him since he'd been released from jail. In all likelihood, Ohija thought to herself, she'd have to wait until that dinner party

"Will do," Shemone replied, not making anything of her friend's extra comment. Shemone's spirits were in high gear. So high that she'd even decided to invite her mother to the dinner party that she planned on giving. Shemone was going to step out on a limb, just this once, with her mother. Ruth would get a chance to get familiar with the new man in her life, which was something she'd been pushing for all along, wasn't it? For her to be more sociable? She couldn't dial the number quickly enough from being so excited. She thought to herself that this new relationship stuff had her going on a natural high. "Hello, Mom?" Shemone said into the phone.

"Shemone, is everything okay, dear?" Ruth asked. She heard something different in her daughter's voice, but couldn't quite zone in on what it was.

"Oh, yes, everything's fine, Mom. I just wanted to call you and invite you over to a little dinner party that I'm having next Friday."

Ruth was startled. Shemone seldom invited her over unless it was to help with charity work or some duty around her apartment. The last time she had been by her place, Ruth had stayed and waited for the cable people to come and install a new converter box. Shemone had had an outside meeting that day, and wasn't able to be in two places at once. "Friday, let's see that's—"

"The twenty-fourth. Mom? Can you make it?"

"I suppose. Who else is on the guest list?" Ruth asked.

Shemone began to give her a list of names, "Ohija—"

"Ohija?"

"Beatrice, Mom, remember? She changed her name, I told you—" Shemone sighed.

"No, I don't remember you telling me anything about that, but okay, who else?" her mother asked, sounding unexcited.

"Ohija, her husband, Raymond, you, me, and Darnell."

"Darnell?" her mother asked in a puzzled tone of voice.

"Darnell, who I went to Monroe High School with." Shemone wanted to tell her then that he was the man she was slowly but surely falling head over heels for.

Ruth paused. "Isn't that the boy who went to jail?"

"He did his time, Mom. And he's not a boy, he's a grown man now," Shemone told her, on the defensive.

"So you invited an ex-con to your dinner party?" Ruth asked her.

"Mom, he's always been a friend to me." First a friend, now her boyfriend, Shemone thought to herself.

"I don't know, Shemone," Ruth said in a stern voice. "I'm thinking that it might not be the brightest idea for me to attend." She thought to herself that this Darnell person from her daughter's childhood was back on the scene again. It didn't appear to be the best thing.

Shemone wasn't about to give up. She was convinced that her mother would like Darnell once she saw him again and gave him a chance, just as she had. Shemone couldn't come up with a reason for why she wouldn't. Darnell was personable, handsome, and jobless, but Ruth didn't have to know about that last part just yet, she figured. Introducing Darnell as the man she was involved with would have to be a gradual process, and by then he would most likely have found a job. Besides, there would never be a right time, she thought to herself. "Please come, I'd really like you to," Shemone asked, whining slightly.

Ruth was hesitant, but did give in. She supposed that it couldn't hurt to meet Darnell. It would probably prove that she'd been right about him being all wrong for her daughter anyway, Ruth thought. Shemone hadn't once mentioned that she and this Darnell fellow were an item, but she didn't have to, she knew that they were. "Okay, I'll try and make it," she told her. "I've got to run. I've got a facial appointment that I can't miss," she said.

"Terrific, and good-bye, Mom," Shemone said, hanging up. She was getting her way, and was content about it. Her mother would be attending. Accepting Darnell was a whole different matter.

12

HIGH HOPES

Shemone leafed through *Sister Soul Magazine* until she got to the page where her monthly column was. Without fail, she smiled, as she always did. She admired her name, and her own words in print. Once again, it made her feel accomplished. She thought to herself that it would only be a matter of time before she was truly recognized for all of her hard work and effort.

"Shemone, can you come in here for a second?" Darnell yelled from the shower early Saturday morning.

"Just a second," she answered in a low tone of voice. She thought that the shower was as good a place as any for him to be as of recently. He was spending more time at her place and had even taken her by to visit his mom, Miss Louise. Shemone didn't think that Miss Louise would recognize her, but she had. She told Shemone that she still had the same pretty face, just in an adult body. Shemone got the chance to see how close Darnell and his mother were. It was amazing to her. She'd seen how the two interacted. They laughed at things together in regard to his own family and Darnell had that same protective manner that he had with her. During their visit, he'd gotten all worked up about where his sister and brother were. As it turned out, his sister had gone to the hair salon and had taken her son along, and his brother was at basketball practice. Shemone couldn't help but be a little envious, wishing that she had the same thing going on in regard to her relationship with her own mother, Ruth.

"Shemone," Darnell called out again, "I said, can you come in here for a second?"

Shemone put the magazine down, got up from the sofa, and replied, "Hold on, I'll be right there." She walked inside the misty-filled bathroom but didn't see any signs of Darnell's silhouette inside the shower stall. She pulled the curtain back.

"Hey, you looking for me?" a naked Darnell asked from behind the door. He delicately reached for her waist, then pulled her body toward his.

His body was wet and inviting, and the way he gyrated gave Shemone no choice but to help in removing clothes that were all her own.

Super, mad, crazy, sexy love was made, specifically, in the middle of the bathroom, leaned up against the edge of the sink. And right after, they hopped into the shower where a strong, thugged-out Darnell took gentle hand actions, washing Shemone's hair. She thought to herself at that moment, If only his boys could see him now.

Back in the bedroom, on the bed, Shemone returned the favor by applying coconut-scented lotion on Darnell's bare skin. She saw a scar on his lower chest that she hadn't noticed before. "What happened here?" she asked him. Using her finger, she delicately outlined the mark.

"Long story," Darnell replied, staring up at the ceiling.

"Tell me," Shemone urged him.

"I got shot," he answered plainly.

"Really?" Shemone gasped, "Oh my God, how?"

His voice wavered. "Me and this kid had a confrontation. Somebody wasn't going to be walking away—"

"You mean you—" Shemone began to say.

Darnell knew what she was thinking. "No, I didn't kill him," he told her. "But he'll never walk again. He's paralyzed from the waist down."

Shemone didn't say anything else. The mere thought that Darnell could have been so violent disturbed her.

Darnell sat up and kissed her sweetly on the cheek. He wanted her to know that she was always safe with him. "That was a long time ago, Shemone. It was a different time back then," he said.

"I know, Darnell, but it still happened. You just can't erase the fact that it did."

"Yeah, well, I can't erase a lot of things," he replied in a regretful tone of voice.

"What are you talking about?" Shemone asked him. She twisted the cap back on the lotion.

"There's something that I need to tell you, right now, while I've got the chance to," he said.

Shemone immediately sat up in the bed at full attention. "What? Is something wrong? Is someone after you?" she asked. Worry was all in her voice.

"Let me finish," Darnell told her.

Shemone leaned back against the iron bed headboard and listened.

"I know that you think about stuff when it comes to me. You probably thinking that because I don't have a job or nothing going on—"

"Darnell—" Shemone interrupted,

"No, let me say this," he continued. His face was serious-looking. "I want you to know that I don't mind doing for you, and that I'm not trying to live off of no woman." He went on, "You know I have a few material things—my car, some clothes, and a few other things. But the truth is, before I got locked up, I was able to hold on to some cash. Something in the neighborhood of thirty thousand dollars. I've had it hidden in my mom's house, underneath the floorboards, the whole time."

Shemone covered her mouth with her hand, stunned. At least now she knew where that big wad of bills came from that first time, when he'd come over and they'd ordered pizza. It also explained why Darnell's pockets had never been empty. He wasn't spending lavishly, but it did still require money to do the things that he did. She thought, Thirty thousand dollars. It wasn't a fortune, but it was something. Darnell had read her mind and he spoke again, saying. "I know it's not a lot, and that it's not a cool thing how I got it, but I want to turn things around. I want to put it to some good use," he told her.

"What exactly do you mean when you say 'turn things around'?" Shemone asked him. She was interested in hearing what he wanted. She wanted to know what his hopes and dreams were.

"Baby-girl, I mean turn me around, as in getting myself a new start. That's my word. I'm gonna get me a real job, doing what I'm best at, electrical work." Darnell beamed as he sat up in the bed and continued, "That's nothing but me right there," he told her.

Shemone wanted to believe in him, and what he was saying, particularly because of what he was starting to mean to her. She showed her support by giving him a hug.

Darnell hugged her back and smiled positively. "You know, you wear a brother out, don't you?" he said, referring to their lovemaking. "My mind is so at ease now that I told you everything." He devised a plan. "How about we grab a nap, and when we wake up, I fix you a late breakfast?" he offered.

"You've got yourself a deal," Shemone answered, thinking that there was nothing more to be said. She could neither say, nor do, anything to change Darnell's dark past. Besides, she'd gathered that Darnell wanted more from life, and that was a solid beginning. Shemone continued, "Everything minus the nap part." She got up out of the bed. "I've got a story to finish, and I want to jump the gun before Monday morning."

"Okay, baby-girl," Darnell replied. He'd mumbled something before drifting off to sleep. Something about her needing to step to one of her editors about getting a raise, because she deserved one. The rest of what he'd said was difficult to make out only because Darnell was too busy sawing down trees, snoring hard in a deep sleep.

Glancing over her shoulder as she sat at her desk, Shemone made a silent promise to herself to really work on the promotion raise/thing, thanks to what he'd said. She thought that yes, Darnell wanted to be an electrician. She wondered if a little bit of her strong career drive had rubbed off on him. She smiled, then got to typing.

HELPING TO JUMPSTART YOUR MATE'S CAREER

by Shemone Waters

The millennium Prince Charming you've been looking for just might be heading straight for you, but be alert. Sometimes the man doesn't come to you on a white horse. Sometimes he just might be coming on the bus, or the train . . .

"Darnell, wake up," Shemone said.

"What time is it?" he asked in a whisper.

"It's one-thirty," she answered. Shemone stood by him, next to the bed.

"One-thirty? Man." Darnell yawned, rubbing his eyes. "I promised you breakfast, right?"

"It's more like lunch now," she replied.

Darnell looked up at Shemone and smiled.

She giggled, as if she'd just saved the day. "Good thing I didn't hold you to it. I threw together a salad," she said.

"A salad?" Darnell paused. "And what else?"

She told him what her menu was. "It's a tricolored bow-tie pasta salad, and there's some garlic bread to go with it."

"Shemone, I can't get full off of no salad, baby. I gotta eat-eat," he said.

She provided him with what she believed was a sensible solution. "Then order out if that doesn't fill your appetite," she told him.

Darnell got up out of the bed, and thought to himself that his baby-girl had gone out of her way to fix him a meal when he was supposed to do it. Therefore, he was gonna like every bite, even if it literally killed him. Shemone's cooking record was iffy.

Shemone smiled. "You plan on eating naked?" she asked him as he sat on the edge of the bed.

"We both should," he replied. Darnell hadn't thought of it himself, but the idea alone made him eager. "Take your clothes off."

"Darnell, no!" Shemone answered in a playful tone of voice.

"Why not? You're such a goody-goody!" he teased.

"I am not!" Shemone said, sticking up for herself. She thought about it. In the dining room? Never done that before. Heck, it was a room, too. She grinned, and in a bold move slipped her dress over her head and led the way, putting a sexy walk on. She knew that Darnell was watching her behind. Next, she took out some candles and lit them. She set the pasta salad and bread out, and then opened a bottle of white wine.

"Do your thing, girl," Darnell told her as he sat down at the table. Shemone brought out one fork, and fed Darnell from her chair.

"Yeah," Darnell said, grinning. The single diamond in his ear sparkled under the candlelight. "I like this. It's freaky, but classy."

Shemone and Darnell took turns feeding each other until the wooden bowl of food was empty.

"That was delicious, Ma," Darnell told her. He had never eaten a three-colored pasta salad, with wine. He'd never known it even existed. Surprisingly, he thought to himself, it was quite filling, too.

"Ma? Darnell Williams, I am not your mother," Shemone told him.

"It's just love, Shemone." Darnell moved from the chair to the floor, onto his knees. "Calling you Ma is, like, a nickname. It means that you take special care of me."

"Oh, I see," Shemone answered with a playful smirk. "You've been taking care of me, too—Pa."

Darnell burst out in laughter. Only his baby-girl could rearrange slang lingo like she did.

Shemone laughed, too, just because being around Darnell made it naturally contagious.

13

SHACKING UP

Well, the wheels were certainly in motion. Shemone hadn't formally given it a name yet, but she believed the term was still the same: "shacking up." Three weeks ago it had only been a thought, but now she found herself actually doing it. Without a doubt, she and Darnell were shacking up, and it was only because she'd allowed it. She'd allowed it because it felt like second nature having him by her side, and snuggly in her bed. It had also been a plus that Darnell had been serious when he'd told her that he wasn't trying to live off her. He was shelling out $500 a month toward the bills, since the day they'd dined on pasta, by candlelight. She planned on telling Ohija, and was doing her best to prepare her mother as well by inviting her to the upcoming dinner party. But at the top of her list was Darnell. She and he hadn't officially had the move-in discussion yet, as backward as it sounded. He had a filled dresser drawer, and a few outfits taking up space in her closet. Shemone made what she considered to be one very necessary call, to Darnell. She decided to have a conversation with him before she . . . decided to add his name to the lease. "Hey, boo," Shemone said cheerily.

"Who is this?" Darnell asked from his cell phone.

"Excuse you? This is Shemone. Who else would be calling you Boo?" she asked him. So much for heartfelt street jargon, she thought. Ruth had raised her to speak proper English at all times, and here she was calling some man boo.

Darnell seemed pleasantly amused. "You know you threw me, right? I'm not used to hearing you talking street slang," he said.

"I know, it's my way of keeping you on your toes," Shemone replied.

"That's my girl," he told her. "What are you up to? You working on that story of yours? Or a better question is, you call that editor-lady boss of yours yet?" Darnell added, "It's about time you stepped up to the plate and laid your qualifications on the line."

Shemone responded in a laid-back tone of voice, "I know. I will, Darnell. It's the timing. I want it to be right. And anyway, I've been busy doing research on another article." Shemone changed the subject. "I'd like us to have a talk when you get in," she said. She twirled herself around in her office chair.

Darnell didn't let the work subject go. "What you need to do is get street on those people. Just let them know where you stand." He added, "Like you do with me all the time."

Shemone chuckled, but she knew that Darnell had a point. Her overly professional by-the-book methods wasn't bringing in much in the way of results. It was like being patted on the head like a dog whenever she submitted an article on time, or mostly in advance, as she often did.

"All right then," Darnell told her. "So we'll talk later. Let me let you get back to your work."

"You trying to get rid of me?"

"Never," Darnell replied.

"Think you can bring something home for dinner?" Shemone asked him.

"What do you want?" he asked.

"Some food from that terrific Spanish-American place on Broadway," Shemone replied. She'd had a taste for Spanish food for a while, and this restaurant was the best. It was always packed full with diners.

"It's a done deal," Darnell told her.

"What time?"

"Let's say around one A.M., to be on the safe side," he said.

"Darnell, remember our house rules."

"But I'm giving you advance notice, though," he reasoned. Sirens could be heard going off in the distance. "And I have a surprise for you," he told her.

"Do you?" a curious Shemone replied. She wondered what the surprise was, but wondered more if those sounds in the background were ambulance sirens, or police sirens. "Darnell, where are you?" she asked.

"I'm around my way, stop worrying. I'm a big boy, I can take care of myself. I'll see you later, okay?" he reassured her.

"Okay." Shemone reluctantly added, "Just be safe." She knew that Darnell was no stranger to the streets. He had been raised on them all his life.

"I will," he answered. "I'll see you when I get home, and we can have that talk."

Darnell folded his cell phone closed and thought to himself that what he needed was some time to let loose. Some time to just kick it with some of the boys from the neighborhood. This searching for a job stuff was no joke. Especially when no one was trying to give him a shot. Already, he was willing to settle for less than what he'd really wanted. Darnell had applied to a sporting-goods store, a clothing shop, and, in his darkest hour, a popular fast-food chain restaurant and still had come up with nothing. He wasn't about to let on to Shemone that he wasn't having any luck. It was as if she'd grown to depend on him, and it felt too good to have the woman he loved behind him the way she was. Admittedly, being just her male best friend wasn't enough anymore, not when Darnell knew what it was like to be her lover, too. He had the best of both worlds now.

Shemone hung up her telephone. He was gonna see her when "he got home." It was home to him by now. Unable to deny it, she couldn't wait for her Darnell to get home.

14

Home Visitor

"Well, look what the cat dragged in."

"Shut up, Monica," Darnell playfully told his sister after he'd strolled through the door late that Saturday evening. "Where's my nephew at?"

"He's asleep in the room where he's supposed to be," she answered. Monica rolled her eyes at her brother. "What wind blew you over here?"

"The mind-my-business wind. Why don't you try getting lost in it?" Darnell joked. He and Monica rarely saw each other, but the two bickered every chance they could get. It had been like that ever since they'd been young. "Where's Mama?" he asked.

"Sleeping, boy! Will you stop asking me questions? Do I look like the six o'clock news? Can't you see that I'm busy doing something?" Monica quickly replied. She was taking the single boxed braids out of her hair. "Don't everybody keep crazy hours like you!"

"I'd rather keep crazy hours than be crazy!" Darnell jokingly snapped back.

"See, you starting." She waved the wide-tooth comb at him. "You and your old big-head self. I said your hours are crazy, not you." His sister continued, "And, really, I'm a night owl myself. My peoples move around at this time, so it's nothing new to me," she let him know.

"Your peoples, huh? What kind of peoples have you got, girl?" he asked her.

"Don't worry about that. I've got them, and that's all you need to know, little brother," she said.

Darnell was bigger than Monica, and stronger than she would ever be, but yet she insisted on calling him "little brother." He hated that. He also hated the countless number of times that he remembered his friends coming on to his sister or asking him to hook them up. He could fight them off then, but now that she was older and all grown up, you couldn't tell her anything. Since he'd gotten out, she'd gotten worse. He was surprised that she was even home on a Saturday night. Darnell thought that he was more like a big brother to his little sister. He didn't care what a calendar said, or even what Monica said, for that matter. But then, Monica probably knew that already, Darnell thought.

Darnell made a beeline for the fridge. There were plenty of leftovers sitting inside, sealed with aluminum foil. He chose to wrap up some smothered turkey wings, cabbage, and rice to take home for Shemone and himself. It was late, and he was too drained to stop at the Spanish restaurant. Darnell had had the best time laughing and joking around with Pop and some of his boys. Before he'd known it, the hours had rapidly gone by. Being out had helped him to relieve just a little of the stress that he was under from trying to find a job. Anyway, he didn't think Shemone would be that disappointed, not after seeing the surprise that he'd gotten for her. It would more than make up for not having the food she'd wanted him to bring.

Monica held her head down low as she loosened a braid. "So, I hear you're seeing Ms. Shemone from your old high school, and that you two have cozied up somewhere together."

"There you go again, all in my business," Darnell replied. He found a plastic supermarket shopping bag and carefully put the food in it.

"Don't go getting all high post on us now, little brother," Monica remarked.

Darnell ignored her comment. "Tell the family I love them, and tell Ma thanks," he said as he went out the door. He slam-locked it, knowing that his sister was not going to get up to lock the door after him. Her hair was way more important than that.

Darnell rang the doorbell at 1:05 A.M., Sunday morning. After searching through all of his pockets, he discovered that he'd left his house keys at his mother's by mistake. After not getting any answer, he rang the bell once more.

"Are you for real, no keys?" Shemone asked, rubbing her eyes. She'd fallen asleep on the couch trying to wait up for him.

"Sorry, left my keys by mistake, baby-girl," he said.

If she hadn't been so hungry for that Spanish food, she'd have killed him right then and there.

"I brought the food . . . my mama made it," Darnell told her with a smile.

"You mean to tell me that you never even made it to the restaurant?" Shemone asked in a disappointed tone of voice. She left the door wide open and walked inside the house for Darnell to follow.

"There's no restaurant in the world that can out-cook my mama's cooking," he said, trying to make the best of the situation.

Shemone questioned whether Darnell had just said what she thought he'd said. She thought that he was trying to excuse what had happened by pacifying her with some food his mother had made. "That's not the point," Shemone answered sternly. It was the whole principal of the situation that bothered her. "The point is that you didn't follow through with what you said you were going to do, and on top of that, you knew that I wanted us to talk." Her anger was further fueled as she was giving him the rundown on each his faults. "I feel like you're taking what I say to you too lightly. I could have had someone deliver the damn food," Shemone made sure to say. She marched into the bedroom.

Darnell entered the bedroom right behind her. He knew he had a point to make, too. "You think about that. This is not about the luxury of having someone to bring something in for you, it's about us eating together," he told her. "And here I am, with food, when I said I would be," he added.

Shemone sighed, he was right. This living-together stuff called for compromise, and Darnell had owned up to his part of the bargain. He'd come in when he said he would, and brought them both food to eat. "I apologize," Shemone said, walking up to him.

Darnell playfully bopped around her in a full circle, looked her up and down, then answered, "Okay, apology accepted." He wanted to say more, though. He wanted to tell her what he'd really been out doing, laughing and joking around, but not a damn thing illegal. He just needed one night of relaxation before getting back to pounding that pavement again. Darnell reached into his pocket and pulled out a rectangular, maroon velvet box. He'd been at the jewelers to pick it up the first time she'd called him earlier in the day. It wasn't expensive, but when he saw it in the window, he knew he had to get it for her.

"What's this?" Shemone asked him. "My surprise?" She looked at the wide grin on Darnell's face, and then down at the pretty maroon box that she held in her hand. She thought, What woman doesn't like surprise gifts? She opened the box. Inside was a silver bracelet with a pendant heart charm. "Darnell, it's beautiful, I love it," Shemone told him, giving him a big hug. She thought about his spending. Darnell had his stash, but hadn't told her anything about finding a job yet. It was far from the stability of a Keith Jenkins move. But then, Darnell was no Keith Jenkins. He was just the opposite. On the upside, he was sexy, hard, and unpredictable, yet he had an innocence to him that made him lovingly vulnerable.

"It's just a little something I wanted to get for you," he said. "It didn't cost me much. I'm holding on to the rest of my money for the things we really need until I find me a job," he told her.

Shemone thought to herself, she couldn't have asked for more.

"Now what was it that you wanted to talk to me about?" Darnell asked. He smirked, aware that Shemone had appreciated her present. He remembered that she was the kind of woman who liked nice things. And as her man, he had to maintain.

Shemone felt no apprehension about her words. "Yes, I did want to talk to you about something," she said. "I just wanted to tell you that it's all right for you to move in, if that's what you were waiting to hear."

"Thanks," he told her in a really flattered tone of voice. He thought to himself that, hopefully, he had a place in her heart, too. Darnell knew that he'd done the right thing by not letting on about his job situation. Something was bound to come through soon. "I love you, Shemone Waters."

Shemone took a deep breath and returned the sentiment. She'd felt it, but never voiced it to him before. "I never thought I'd be saying this, certainly not so soon anyway, but I guess this kind of thing can just creep up on a person. Even a planner like me." She smiled and told him, "I love you, too, Darnell Williams."

Darnell put the charm bracelet on her wrist and gave her a long kiss on the lips. He worked his tongue. She worked hers. Every movement held meaning. The two came along with the sun and ate his mama's dinner for breakfast.

15

Friends to the End

Ohija was busy meditating on Sunday evening when she heard a knock at the door. Meditating was crucial business for her. The interruption would have been ignored any other time, but something told her to see who it was. "Who is it?" she asked.

"It's Darnell," the voice answered. "I came to pick up the money you owe me," he joked.

Ohija chuckled, blew out her candle, and got up from where she was. She opened the door to her Final Four friend.

Darnell had his arms wide open to greet her. "Hey, Ohija," he said.

"Hey, you," Ohija replied in an excited tone of voice. She hugged him so hard, she thought she would break him in two. She was so happy that she didn't have to wait until the dinner party to see him, like she'd thought she would. Darnell Williams was right on her doorstep. "Look at you!"

Darnell joked that he tried looking at himself.

"You're still a fool!" Ohija chuckled again. "You went and bulked up on me," she said to her handsome friend. Ohija felt one of his muscular arms. "You would have given Terrance a run for his money now, that's for sure," she said.

Darnell blushed. "Cut it out now, Ohija," he told her. "You know that I was always the slim, sexy one, and that Terrance was the muscular, athletic one."

"I'm telling you, you two would have had the same build now," she said. "Come on in here and make yourself at home." Ohija led him inside.

Darnell did just that. "I hope I didn't disturb you. I wanted to come by and surprise you," he said.

"And what a surprise this is," Ohija answered. "It's a good one."

Darnell looked around. There was a picture of Ray hanging on the wall. "Ohija, is that your husband?" he asked her.

Ohija got up from her chair. "It sure is, that's the love of my life, Ray. He's working overtime today, so you'll probably meet him another time." She went into the kitchen, and came out with refreshments. It was all natural trail mix, and cold, sweetened pear nectar.

Darnell glanced down at the tray she put on the table. He asked, "Is it time to feed the horses or something?"

Ohija gave him a playful tap on the shoulder, and laughed.

"Ohija, I heard about you being into this natural stuff. I still love you, though," he told her.

"And I still love you," she answered with a smile as she took a seat. She took the opportunity to tell Darnell everything that had been on her mind lately in regard to him. "I was thinking about the last time we ran into each other, you know. I know that I was kind of distant."

"Ohija, please," Darnell told her. "I forgave you for that a long time ago. I understand why you did what you did."

She took up a handful of trail mix, then spoke. "I just wasn't used to seeing you caught up in that lifestyle. I knew that you were heavily into selling those drugs," she said. "You had a lot of money, I'm sure, but to me, no matter what you had on, you looked bad."

"Yeah," he replied. He wasn't about to try and deny it.

"You wanted to know if I needed anything, and I brushed you right off," she told him.

"Yeah."

"I didn't know what to say. Part of me wanted to ask you if you knew what you'd gotten yourself into. I didn't want to have to think about possibly losing you to the streets."

Darnell nodded; he really did understand where she was coming from. "That day did bother me, Ohija, for a long time. I'm just glad that we get to forget it, and do it over again. You're still my friend, right?" he asked her.

"You just try and get rid of me now," she told him with a smile. "I made myself scarce while you were locked up, for all the same reasons, but I'm here to stay now, no matter what, this time," she assured him.

Darnell grinned, then scooped up some trail mix and chewed. "Not bad horse feed," he said.

Ohija laughed. "So, tell me about this romance you and Shemone have going." She then let him in on a little secret she had held on to for years. "You know, I always knew that you two would get together one day."

"Get outta here," Darnell replied. "How? Shemone wouldn't give me the time of day back in Monroe High."

"That's because you were too busy chasing behind every other female in the school," she replied.

"No!"

"Yes!" Ohija confirmed aloud. "Women want to stand out from one another," she explained. "My Ray still sweeps me off of my feet."

"What does he do?" Darnell asked her. He thought that it wouldn't hurt to take a few lessons from the people he heard were the pros. He took notice. His friend Ohija beamed when she spoke about her husband.

Ohija smiled. "Ray does . . . things that he knows I like. He does original things, like reading me a sexy poem in the middle of a hectic work week. He's hardly the Romeo-looking type. I always say that he's my average guy, who does above-average things."

Darnell thought, Impressive. He couldn't wait to meet Mr. Smooth himself.

"Don't try to dodge my question by asking me all about my Ray. How's the romance going with you and Shemone?" she asked him for the second time.

"It's going real good," Darnell told her. He had a smile all of his own. "I'm in love, that's for sure. I never felt nothing like it."

"Yeah? That sounds very promising," Ohija said, grinning. She told herself that she would stick to her friend-confidentiality clause. It meant that no one friend could know what the other had said to her.

"Ohija," Darnell said, "I know that you and Shemone talk to each other about everything." He added, "I also know that you know we live together now." He thought that those two weren't getting over on him.

Ohija's brown eyes bulged from their sockets. She thought to herself, No Miss Waters did not tell me that. She told Darnell the same thing. Only this time, aloud. "No, Miss Waters did not tell me that."

"Oh-kay," Darnell replied; he'd just realized that he'd let the cat out of the bag. He had been sure that Ohija knew.

"You mean you two have shacked up?" she asked again, just to be sure.

"Yep," Darnell told her, "we've gone and shacked up. It's like we've been on a honeymoon every day," he confessed.

"Mmmm . . . You don't say," Ohija replied. "I'm so happy for you two." She added, "Even though I am just finding out."

"Oh, and speaking of just finding out, congrats on the babies," he told her.

Ohija thought to herself that he had her there, they were even.

Darnell and Ohija both chuckled the afternoon away. It felt nice to be sharing news with each other again. It was as if they'd taken up right from where they'd left off.

16

Along the Lines

Shemone looked into the bathroom mirror at 9:30 A.M. Monday morning. She thought that there was something bittersweet about being the woman who felt close to having it all, both the budding relationship and the busy career. She stepped into the shower stall, and allowed the cool water to fully awaken her for the day's work ahead. Darnell had already left the house. There were big changes taking place in her life, and she hoped that it was all for the best. Change was acceptance. She was involved and no longer lived alone. Change was also the shared cleaning duties, if only Darnell could remember to put the toilet seat back down behind himself. Right about then, the only change that wasn't to her liking was the date of the dinner party. It had been postponed. The twins were giving Ohija a time, it being her first pregnancy. Ohija even had to hire her sister to fill in for her at the clothing boutique, which was regularly bringing in a steady flow of customers. Just then the phone rang.

"Hello, Shemone, it's Jane, from *Simply You Magazine,*" she said.

Terrific, Shemone thought to herself. One of her freelance writing–gig connections. She hadn't spoken to her in a while, a long while. "Jane, how've you been? It must be deadline time." She laughed nervously. "That's the only time that you call."

"You've got me there," her editor answered.

Shemone noticed that Jane wasn't laughing.

"So how's it going?" Jane asked.

"My article, right?" Shemone stalled. "I was just in the process of finishing it up," she told her.

Her editor made a noise as she sifted through papers. "Shemone, you had over sixty days to complete the piece," she told her.

Well, Jane was right. Not completing an article with a sixty-day deadline? Impossible for her, she thought to herself. Shemone got out her date book, and flipped pages that took her back two months. It seemed that she'd written in the assignment, but had failed to do her usual week-before-the-piece-is-due follow-up. There was no excuse for not completing the assignment, but she wasn't about to throw in the towel by not at least trying. "Jane, I apologize, but I've just been so busy juggling other projects," she told her. "I really am about to finish this one up," she said. Shemone knew what the truth was. She'd been too busy juggling the benefits of being in a new relationship.

"I see," Jane answered. Her tone of voice was very different from the one that Shemone knew as cordial. "Perhaps you have too much on your plate . . . I could pass the project along to one of our backup writers," she began to suggest.

"No," Shemone answered abruptly, "that won't be necessary. You'll have it, Jane. First thing in the morning, guaranteed."

"Shemone, you know how this works. It's not personal, this is a business."

"Yes, I know," Shemone answered. "Thank you for calling, and I'm so sorry for the inconvenience, Jane." Shemone placed the phone down gently on its receiver. She thought of the big picture of how she was living her life. This kind of thing had never happened to her before—falling for someone like Darnell, letting him move in so fast, and being on the verge of missing her first writing deadline ever. She rationalized that it was no one's fault but her own. Her regimen was slipping because she'd been too busy playing kissey face with the ex-con live-in. Hot damn. This was one for the books, she said to herself. She couldn't wait until Darnell got in to let him know that she was buckling down, and that he'd notice the difference in her. It was happening at a time when a strong woman such as herself only wanted to get recognition and upward mobility in her writing career.

Shemone thought about it some more. Oh, she'd let him know, all right. She'd tell him that structure had always worked for her before, and suggest that he use some of it for himself to get the job wheels turning. And no, Jane from *Simply You Magazine* would not be calling her again if she didn't get her act together and get that story out. Hers and Darnell's new living situation was becoming way too comfortable. Any sane person could figure it out, and as a writer, she should have known. It spelled trouble.

Later that afternoon, Darnell came in. He walked into the bedroom, where she was at her computer, and gave Shemone a sweet peck on the head. "Hey," he said to her.

Shemone didn't return his greeting. She was too occupied in trying to remember the sequence of all that she wanted to tell him.

"Everything okay? You getting quiet on me today, baby-girl?" Darnell asked.

Why should she hold her troubles in, all to herself, this time? The order of it all wasn't important. Shemone got right to the point. "It's just that I almost missed one of my story deadlines today. That's got me a little upset. But I'll get over it. I just don't intend missing another one." Shemone didn't go into further detail with him. In that instant, she'd come to the conclusion that her actions would speak louder than any words she could ever use. That's just how she intended to convey how serious she was about sticking to her work habits. Just as she thought he would, Darnell freely shook off what she'd said, as if it wasn't a problem. Not his, or hers.

"Shemone, if it's a money thing, it's not even worth getting worked up about," Darnell replied. "That's why I'm here, to help. You don't have to do it all by yourself anymore," he told her.

"Is that right?" Shemone swiveled around in her chair. "You care to tell me why not?" she asked him. This was one she had to hear.

"'Cause you just don't, that's all," he said bluntly. Darnell went over to the dresser drawer and looked for something to put on. He didn't like the idea that Shemone was feeling stressed about work. They sure didn't both need to be, he thought to himself. His job search still wasn't going well, but he had a new plan.

Shemone evaluated her boyfriend's statement. Darnell could be such a dreamer at times. Well, she was being a realist, and in the real world, outside the prison system and with limited capital, life was filled with problems.

"Baby-girl, I'm going to need you to help me out with something just this once," Darnell told her.

Oh boy, here we go, Shemone thought. It was the probable moment she'd dreaded from the start of day one. She didn't feel the need to keep a running cash balance on something that was his, but maybe she should have. Was his money all gone? Would she have to carry all the bills? First it would happen one time, and then it would be all the time. There was absolutely no way this relationship could work if this was how things were going to be.

She looked over at Darnell, and prepared herself. He had just dug out his boxers from in between his butt cheeks. Shemone frowned, wishing she could have missed what she'd just seen, and more so, what he would probably say next.

"You think you can help me to put together one of those . . . resumé papers?" Darnell casually asked her.

Shemone was completely dazed. "You mean, as in for a regular job?" she asked in disbelief.

"That is what it's for, ain't it?" Darnell asked with a laugh. So what if he couldn't be an electrician right off the bat. Whatever he did would be an honest day's work. Besides, he thought to himself, he couldn't live off his stash forever.

"I am so proud of you, sweetie," Shemone told him. She could hardly control what to say next from being so excited for him. It was as if she was speaking another language, she was speaking so fast. "So what kind of job are you going to look for? I know just the place for you to go. My mother has this friend who works at the board of ed, and I'm sure that I can get her to—"

"Shemone," Darnell interrupted her flatly, "I don't need you to get me a job." Darnell sighed and shook his head as he stood at the closet. He began to noisily drag plastic hangers from one side of the rack to the other until he found what he was looking for. "I bet you do know just where I can go," he suddenly said sarcastically. The mood of the conversation had taken a turn for the worse. Not only was Darnell offended that Shemone was trying to take over in his job search, but it was also as if she was saying that he couldn't handle the responsibility of being a man. He walked over to the side of the bed, and stepped into his jeans. Then he assured his girlfriend with a little attitude of his own. He told her, "I got this."

"But, Darnell, a little help from me can take you much further. It'll be easier. You most likely won't even have to—"

"Will you let it go already?" Darnell yelled, interrupting her. "I said that I don't need your, or your mother's, help!" He thought about it. Maybe he could have been a little more grateful, but he just wasn't the handout type. Asking for help with the resumé was enough, or at least it should have been.

Shemone stayed quiet for a moment as she settled back down into her chair to stare blankly at her computer monitor. "I really do just want to help you, you know."

"Whatever, Shemone," Darnell replied in a short tone of voice. "For the second time, I'm saying that I can handle getting my own job, but thanks," he told her.

Shemone was beginning to resent the vibe that he was giving her. "You really are being pretentious, Darnell."

He slipped his sweater over his head, and thought hard to himself. This woman just wouldn't let it go. She just has to prove that she's got more to bring to the table than I do, even though I'm busting my ass trying to do the right thing by her. Her and all that overeducated bullshit, he thought. "That's right," he told her, "use fancy words so that you can feel big, Shemone, Darnell can't understand. You trying to make me feel like I'm stupid or something?" he asked her.

Shemone snapped, "Darnell, I won't tiptoe around words just to make a point to you."

"Exactly, so speak in plain English then," Darnell huffed back. He continued, as he rose from sitting on the bed where he'd been putting on a fresh pair of socks, "You know, I might not know a lot of big words like you, Miss Writer, but there's plenty that I do know that you know nothing about."

"Such as?" Shemone asked. The whole conversation was getting more ridiculous to her by the minute, she thought. All she'd done was offer to help the man get a job.

"Such as, what nerve does the dentist use to numb your mouth when you get a needle?"

"Now how would I know something like that?" Shemone asked him.

"Exactly, baby-girl!" Darnell told her. "It's the trigeminal nerve, Shemone, the trigeminal nerve." He wanted her to know how it felt to not know about something for a change. Everything was not as clear-cut to him as it was to her. Like the reason she was holding on to a vase full of dead flowers, he thought as he glanced at the nightstand nearby. "And what is this dead-flower thing about?" he asked her.

Shemone took her time and answered, "It's a dried floral arrangement, Darnell."

"Don't you think they're about ready for the garbage?" he asked her.

"You want me to throw them out?" Shemone asked, her temper flaring up now. Darnell and his shortness and sarcasm had finally gotten to her. "Then I will." She went over to the flowers, took them out of the vase, and dumped them inside the wastepaper basket. "You satisfied?"

"Yeah, I am," Darnell answered as he walked out of the room.

"Wonderful. Those are the very first flowers that you ever gave me, you big jerk! I was saving them!" Shemone yelled. She grabbed her car keys and left the apartment, slamming the door behind her. She wondered how the whole argument had begun, and where it was going.

17

Life's Work

I gotta get me a job," Darnell told his friend days later, once they'd stepped through the door and into the living room. It was Pop's first time visiting the apartment.

"Man, you weren't lying. This place is laid!" Pop said, taking in what seemed to be a showplace palace around him.

"I don't know what to do. I still need to get me a resumé," Darnell told him in a frustrated tone of voice. He slid his keys down on the coffee table, and continued, "And even when I get that, I'm not sure who's gonna want to hire me after they find out I got a criminal record." With no job experience and a record, who was gonna hire his ass? he thought to himself. Darnell needed something to happen, and soon. But one thing was for sure, it was gonna take more than one dumb argument with Shemone for him to give up on himself. They'd barely resumed talking to each other, and she hadn't brought up the resumé subject once. Neither had he, but he planned to because he still needed one.

"Does that fireplace work?" Pop asked him. Black-and-white photos of Shemone and her family in big, ornate silver frames adorned the length of its mantel.

"Pop, yo, are you listening, man? I said, I've got to get me a job. I already told Shemone about my stash, and I feel like it's time for me to step up to what I gotta do."

"I'm sorry, D., yeah, I feel you," Pop answered, giving Darnell his full attention this time. "Welcome to my world, man, welcome to my world," he told him. Pop took a moment before speaking. "I'm saying, I can always see if there are any openings at my spot."

"Thanks," Darnell replied. "I'll keep that in mind. There's just so much to think about. I know that my relationship with Shemone is still real new, but I wish that she'd trust in me a little more. Sometimes I think she thinks that I'm still out there hustling."

Looking as smooth as a hustler himself, Pop chuckled. "It's just time for you to fill in the gaps, man. Shemone needs to see that you're working, or making the effort to, at least," he told him. Pop wore a long-sleeved black T-shirt and baggy black jeans. The hems were cuffed to show the black Timberland boots on his feet. A single platinum herringbone chain hung around his neck; he had a watch to match.

"She knows," Darnell told him. "She just doesn't know about all the whens and wheres."

"Why is that?" Pop grinned at him and asked. He'd known Darnell for years, and drug selling or not, he knew that his friend was one who liked to handle his own responsibilities.

"Because she'll try to take over, that's why," Darnell answered. "Shemone loves to be in control of things. It was a big thing for her to even accept me in her life as her man and not just her friend," he added.

"But she did," Pop told him.

"And I will find a job on my own, too. Everything can't be on Shemone's terms, Pop. I'm already willing to make changes that will benefit us both down the line," Darnell replied. "She has to make some changes, too, now that we're a couple."

"That's the key word, man," Pop told him. "You and Shemone are a couple now. So just keep working at it. Things will be all right." Pop added, "Just watch the company you keep, that's all."

"You know what, Pop? You're wise way past your years, man," Darnell joked.

"I know, that's why you keep me around as your friend," Pop joked back. "But what I said, it's true. You hang around Red and them cats on the avenue sometimes. You and I both know that you're not out there dealing drugs, but they definitely are. Nobody wants you to get caught up in that mess." Pop took a sip from the glass of soda that Darnell had brought him. "See, a man like me, I keep distant from all that. You know what I'm saying? Because I've got a family to take care of now. It ain't about that no more."

"I know you're right, Pop," Darnell said. "Relationships, my first and last real one with Shemone and her high-post ass," he joked. He went on to compare the differences between the two of them.

"I like beer.

"She likes wine.

"I like action movies.

"She likes that drama crap.

"I like jeans and sneakers; well, she likes Dolce and Gabbana and Gucci.

"I'll just put it like that. She walks around here in Prada slippers and shit, man."

Pop laughed a throaty laugh. "Man, that's all good. That's probably what got you two together from jump street. Don't give up on her, Darnell." Pop looked around the spacious apartment. "From the looks of things, you definitely got a solid thing going on here."

"Yeah, you know, I might just humor her, and run for office one day soon."

Pop chuckled. "D. for mayor, baby, all the way."

"What mayor? I'm thinking about D. for president!" Darnell told him, thinking big.

Pop chuckled again, even harder, then spoke. "Yo, I heard that the hospital is hiring maintenance people."

"Okay, that's another lead for me. Thanks," Darnell replied. Pop was just trying to help. Now that he thought about it, Shemone had just been trying to help, too, in her own stuck-up-pushy kind of way.

"Anytime, D. Now you gonna finish giving me the tour, or what?" Pop asked him.

Darnell chuckled. "Yeah, man, I'll finish giving you the tour."

Keys jingled in the front door.

"She's back," Darnell told Pop.

"Should I leave?" Pop asked. They were standing inside the kitchen.

"No, man, stick around. I want you to meet her," Darnell told him.

Shemone came in with a handful of department store shopping bags.

"Somebody go shopping?" Darnell asked after he'd entered the living room.

"What does it look like?" Shemone said sarcastically, dropping the bags down on the sofa and kicking off her shoes. She felt that she was only giving Darnell what he'd given her for no reason—attitude.

"All of that wasn't even called for," Darnell snapped back. It made him want to hold off on communicating with her if she was going to be nasty. When he'd been locked up in jail, he'd looked forward to speaking with her all the time. Now that they were in each other's faces every day made it different. Not bad, just different. As in a you-have-to-watch-the-way-you-say-things different.

A neutral Pop stepped out into the living room. "How you doing?" he asked Shemone.

Shemone turned around, slightly embarrassed. "Why didn't you tell me we had company, Darnell?" She began pushing what seemed like ten bags from the couch.

"Because you were too busy giving me attitude, that's why," Darnell answered in a truthful tone of voice.

Pop broke up the tension in the room by extending his hand to Shemone. "It's nice to meet you, I'm Pop."

"Pop, I'm Shemone," she replied. She shook his hand firmly. "I apologize for my behavior."

"No problem," Pop told her with a smile. "My girl and I argue, too."

Shemone smiled it off. "Darnell has told me a lot about you."

"All good, I hope," Pop said.

"Yes, all good," Shemone answered.

"And I hear that you're a writer," Pop said.

"Yes, I am."

"So how do you like it?" Pop asked. He took a seat on the armchair next to her.

Darnell took a seat, too, and just listened.

"It's great. It has its days. But I love it overall," she told him.

"Yeah? That's cool. I need you to write my life story for me," Pop joked.

"Man, what life story?" Darnell said as he joined the conversation. "You ain't got no life story to tell!"

The three laughed aloud.

Shemone thought to herself that it was the first time she and Darnell had laughed together in days, and she missed it. She had still been trying to figure out what she'd done that was so wrong. He'd been the one who'd raised his voice, caught an attitude, and insulted her dried flowers.

"Now, my life," Darnell told them, "my life would make some kind of story. It would be a sure best-seller."

"Wha—at?" Pop joked. "So they'd want to put you in your own movies and shit?"

"No doubt," Darnell joked back.

"Yes, well," Shemone made sure to interject, "it's a shame that I only write magazine articles, isn't it?" An edge of sarcasm was in her voice.

"Maybe you should try something different. Maybe kick it up a notch or something," Darnell told her. He was referring to Shemone and her promotion situation. If Pop hadn't been there, he would have reminded her about it again. Yeah, she was all ready to jump on him and his career plans, but wasn't following through on her own. Shemone had said weeks ago that she was going to approach her editor and still hadn't, he thought to himself.

"Maybe you should do something different, too," Shemone said to him. She was swift with her reply.

Darnell and Shemone exchanged deadly glances.

"So, what's the worst part about being a writer?" Pop asked, deciding to interrupt before things got out of hand.

"I think that the worst part is the pressure of having to come up with work that's fresh and new, especially once you've developed your own style." Shemone sighed. "People can expect so much from you."

"Mmph," Pop mumbled, "that's something."

"Pop, would you like to have something to eat or drink?" Shemone asked.

"Oh, no, but thanks, we already ate. I'm about to get on home."

"You've got to come by for a visit again. Maybe you can bring your girlfriend the next time. Did Darnell tell you that we were having a dinner party soon?" she asked.

Darnell looked at Shemone, then at Pop.

"Nah, I didn't get a chance to yet," Darnell said. He was thinking that Shemone had beat him to the punch of telling his own friend about the dinner party. She was taking control of things again.

"He's rude. Anyway, I'd like for you guys to come. It's next Saturday at seven," Shemone told him, continuing to play hostess.

"Can I get back to you on that?" Pop asked. "Let me just run it past my girl to be sure that she's not doing nothing else."

"Sure," Shemone answered. "Just let me know." She took the shopping bags and didn't look back once at Darnell as she disappeared into the back, inside the bedroom.

"I'm sorry, man," Darnell told Pop as he got up to leave.

"Don't worry about it. I'm gonna just think that you really forgot to mention it to me, that's all. It couldn't have been that you were ashamed to invite me or nothing like that, I know." Pop added, "Because we go way back." He knew in his heart that Darnell would never do such a thing to him.

"Right, right," Darnell replied, giving him a quick hug and a pound on the hand. "You need me to drop you off at your house?" he asked.

"No, I can jump on the train. It'll probably be quicker," Pop said as he went out the door. "All right then, later."

"Later," Darnell replied as he shut the door. No, he wasn't like that. He would never not invite one of his best friends over to Shemone's fancy dinner party. Never that, and not him. Not unless he truly didn't get the chance to.

18

Pregnant Pause

Ohija sat in the wide, winged armchair on Friday evening, her feet soaking in a basin of warm water. She felt a natural love for the two babies that she knew were growing inside her. Her heartfelt maternal feelings were just starting to kick in, but the whole pregnancy experience, now that was another thing altogether. In a matter of months, her life had been reduced to sudden late-night combination cravings for licorice and potato chips, ice cream and tofu. At the same time, she was nauseous, and vomiting, and her feet were swelling up by the minute. She flicked the television set on to her newly favorite 8 P.M. vegetarian cooking show. Ohija watched as the chef tossed together brown seasoning and green leafy ingredients inside a huge mixing bowl. A wave of nausea came upon her, about to spiral, then suddenly ceased in its motion. A false alarm. Ohija shoved a cracker in her mouth, then heaved a sigh of relief. In all likelihood, she wouldn't be doing this baby thing again, she thought to herself. A woman like her only did this once.

Raymond walked into the living room all spruced up in a black polo sweater and neatly ironed khaki-colored cargo pants. It had been a while since Ohija had seen her Ray dressed up. It was usually the sanitation uniform, home, a shower, then strictly comfort wear for him in the house. Her mind wandered for the first time in years, taking her back to a time when she and Raymond were first courting, and Raymond was dating other women. And out of the blue, the thought came. Other women. Who was to say that somebody couldn't be after her husband? Ray was an attractive man. He wasn't very tall, at only five-seven, and no, he didn't have a complete full head of hair, but he had some right down and around in the back. Ohija chuckled to herself as she looked over at him. She glanced at the roundness of his stomach. Some days she was fooled into believing that he was the one having the babies. Raymond didn't exactly follow her healthy eating habits and nutritious-food regimen.

The best part was that at least he was hers. Ohija had been serious when she'd told Shemone that she was glad she had married Ray. He was an ideal husband, and she considered herself to be a very lucky woman. Cheating. Of course she was being silly. Ohija quickly dismissed the thought, attributing her reaction to her physical and mental state. Ray would never cheat on her. It was nothing but those new hormones coursing through her body. She gave her husband a wide smile.

"How are my babies doing?" Ray asked her.

"Your babies are doing just fine," she said as she held her stained denim maternity shirt up. Ohija had just finished snacking on a pack of butterscotch pudding cups an hour before. A few spoonfuls hadn't quite made it into her mouth. She wiped at the smudges with a nearby paper towel.

Raymond noticed and smiled. "You're still my sexy baby!"

"Stop!" Ohija playfully told her husband. She checked Ray out. "You look handsome."

"Thanks, honey. I'm off to the poolroom to shoot a few rounds with Tim. Can I get you anything before I leave?"

The telephone rang before Ohija could reply. Raymond answered it, walking off into the next room.

It was a good thing that she was secure in herself and her husband's actions. Ohija knew that trust was an important factor in any relationship. Anyway, Ray deserved a night alone to hang out with the boys. They rarely spent much time apart, and when the babies came, they probably wouldn't get too many more opportunities to go out with friends.

Raymond reentered the living room. "So I'm gonna go now, big mama. You're sure that you don't need anything, right?" he asked.

"No, I'm fine, go on out with your friends," she said.

"You have my pager number?"

"Yes," she answered. Her husband always gave her everything she needed and more.

Raymond gave his wife a kiss on the lips, and put his leather jacket on. He went out the door.

Ohija squinched her nose up; her sense of smell was phenomenal, and the strong aroma of Raymond's after-shave cologne didn't help. Pregnancy. Wow. Like she said, a woman like her only did this once.

"Shemone, it's me," Ohija said over the phone an hour after Raymond had left.

"Oh, hey, girl," Shemone replied. Her tone of voice was short.

"Did I catch you at a bad time?" Ohija asked.

Darnell interrupted as he stood in the bedroom doorway. "I'm going out."

"So then go," Shemone snapped, staring at him from her desk.

Darnell walked out of the house, nodding his head. He promised to put an end to their misunderstanding just as soon as he got back in.

Shemone began talking once she heard his keys locking the door. "Yes, I'm here, girl," she said, resuming her conversation with Ohija. "Darnell was just going out, that's all."

Ohija chuckled. "Girl, you wouldn't believe how silly I am." She chuckled even harder, then couldn't stop.

"In what way?" Shemone asked. "Will you stop laughing and tell me, already?" Shemone asked her in an overeager tone of voice.

Ohija chuckled again, but finally did get the words out. "I actually had a thought that Raymond might be cheating on me."

"Now, that is funny," Shemone replied with a laugh. "Everybody knows that man worships the ground you walk on."

"I know it," Ohija said. She rubbed her tummy. "I told you that it was silly, didn't I?"

"Very. What in the world would make you think something like that? It might just be your hormones, you know," Shemone replied, not giving Ohija a chance to answer. "I'm sure that they must be out of sorts by now."

"That's just what I thought," Ohija agreed, adding, "I won't let my crazy hormones get out of control and make me jealous. You know how together I am, girl."

Shemone giggled and confirmed, "Yes, Ohija, you are the most together person that I know."

"Better ask somebody," Ohija replied in a sistah-girl tone of voice.

"So how's your kunta meditation going?" Shemone asked. "Are you still able to do it with you being pregnant and all?"

"It's kundalini meditation, and, yes, I can still do it. I go faithfully to a six o'clock P.M. mommy meditation class three times a week now."

"So it's helping to relax you?"

"Oh yesss, girl," Ohija replied with a burst of enthusiasm.

Shemone smiled. Her friend could be so dramatic.

"But it's how the meditation helps to relax me that makes it such an invigorating experience. It helps me with my breathing techniques, which I'll definitely need once I get inside of that labor room." Ohija demonstrated, panting in deep, quick breaths of groups of three.

"You know, that is so interesting," Shemone told her just as Ohija was about to start off on her second set.

"I know that you're patronizing me, but I won't hold it against you," Ohija joked. "Besides, your day will come, and you know what that automatically makes me, don't you?"

"No, what?" Shemone asked.

"The expert!"

Ohija and Shemone giggled into the phone with each other.

"I like hearing you laugh," Ohija said. "You didn't sound like you were in such a great mood earlier. You wanna tell me who, or what, was behind it?"

"Who else? Darnell. What, is that I offered him some help to get a job." Shemone added, "A legitimate job. We're kind of on the outs. We haven't been doing much communicating lately."

"So I heard," Ohija said, referring to the good-bye that Shemone had given him a few minutes before. "You mean to say that you think he's still in the streets hustling?" Ohija asked.

"No, but the potential for him to does exist," Shemone told her friend. "I do know that much. I think that he's just anxious for any kind of work to come through, at this point."

"Potential to happen doesn't mean that it will," Ohija told her. "You must be over there doing some mean private detective work."

"Not really. Let's just say that it's a fear of mine. It's beginning to stress me a bit," Shemone told her.

"Mmph, don't let anything stress you like that, girl. Meditate on it. It's not worth risking your mental health," her friend warned. "What's important is that you trust in him. Trust is everything in a relationship. That's how I was easily able to rule out the cheating theory with Ray," she said.

Shemone thought to herself about the trust concept. She and Darnell hadn't touched the topic. It was more of an implied thing with them. She trusted him when he said that he wasn't dealing drugs again, but knowing that still wasn't giving her peace of mind.

"Are you sure that Darnell is the focus of your trust issues, girl?" Ohija went on ahead and asked.

The picture in question came clear as Shemone realized what her friend was trying to get at. "No, he's not the focus of my trust issues," Shemone replied. She leaned her head back as far as it could go in the chair. "It's not at all about me not trusting Darnell. I think it's more about me trusting myself, the decisions that I've made, and will continue to make."

"Deep!" Ohija replied enthusiastically.

"I need to trust myself, and be comfortable with it," Shemone said assertively.

"That's right, and how long has it been that you and Darnell have stopped speaking to each other?" Ohija asked her in a this-all-is-crazy-to-me tone of voice.

"It's been a few days," Shemone confessed. "The thing is, I've been racking my brain trying to figure out what was so wrong with offering him help in the first place."

"In a word, it sounds like pride," Ohija told her.

"Probably," Shemone answered. "Darnell is a proud man, but he needs to get over that. He doesn't have anything to be ashamed of around me."

Ohija quietly exhaled. She knew that Shemone would figure out the solution on her own, just as she eventually had done with her own trust situation with Ray. She encouraged her by saying just that. "Don't worry too much about it. The solution will come to you, probably when you least expect it."

Shemone took her friend's advice and carried on with the conversation. She switched subjects. "So what's going on with the clothing shop?"

"It's going, business is better than ever. My sister is helping with managing it now, you know," Ohija told her. "I figured I needed to get someone in there that I could rely on. There's just no telling how long I'll be out."

"Just be grateful that the boutique is doing well."

"That's true. Ray and I are going to need all the money we can get," she said.

"Are you scared about being a new mother?" Shemone asked. She thought the input from her friend would be useful for her latest article.

"No, not really scared. I'm eager, and I'm curious. Two babies are bound to be an experience." Plastic paper rattled in the background on Ohija's end of the phone. It sounded like Ohija was digging into a bag of something.

"Right, but you'll have plenty of help between me, your own family, and your in-laws," Shemone told her.

"That's true, until the newness of it all wears off."

"Ohija, please," Shemone replied. "I can't speak for everyone else. But I'll be there for you for as long as you need me to be. I'm not about to go anywhere."

"Thanks, I know you will. Listen, is your dinner party still on?"

"It had better be. I've been putting it off long enough," Shemone said.

"Sorry about that. I know it's my fault with the pregnancy situation," Ohija told her.

"Don't apologize, girl—you have to take care of yourself and those twins. You guys come first. Now that you're doing a little better, you can come on and enjoy yourself."

"That's right, girl," Ohija said. "So who's invited?"

"There's you and Ray, myself and Darnell, of course, Darnell's friend Pop, his girlfriend, and my mother."

"Your mother?" Ohija asked her in a surprised tone of voice.

"Yes, my mother."

"Shemone, I'm proud of you. You don't include her in your life nearly enough."

"Whatever. I'm there as much as I can be for her. She knows that."

Ohija didn't debate the topic. She knew that conversations about Shemone's mother were a touchy subject. "How's work with you? You churning those articles out?"

"I'm still on track," Shemone answered, truly glad that she was. "I'm working on a story about motherhood now. I'm finishing it up tonight."

"Okay, then I won't hold you up any further," Ohija said. "I'm so thirsty I could drink a gallon of water. Eating all those crackers do it to me every time."

"I knew you were chomping down on something," Shemone said. "I suppose I should get to cracking again myself. Talk to you later?"

"Sure thing, Ms. Writer," Ohija replied.

Shemone laughed, "Okay then, girl." Shemone popped some popcorn in the microwave and got to typing.

SHE CALLED ME MAMA

by Shemone Waters

She called me Mama, I thought to myself. For most first-time mothers, the word "Mama" first uttered, gurgled, whispered, or awkwardly pronounced comes in as melodic music to the ears. Eyes widen, and the world opens up as you then realize that you're truly someone's mother and that you're connected.

Wow. She stopped typing to think. Ohija was going to be someone's mama. Shemone wondered if she ever would be. A two-parent household was her ideal. Shit, right now the employment of two people in her household was an ideal. She just wasn't the somebody's-baby's-mama-on-a-talk-show kind. On second thought, Shemone didn't wonder. She wasn't ready to have kids, and she wasn't ready to be married either. Not that anyone had asked.

19

As We Lay

Shemone?" Darnell called.

Shemone stirred in the bed, still half asleep. Were the lights on? she asked herself. She opened her eyes fully and turned around to find Darnell wide awake, next to her in the bed.

Darnell called out her name again, this time in a more serious tone of voice, "Shemone."

"Darnell, what time is it?" she asked, yawning widely.

"It's late, a little after one A.M."

"Can't it wait until morning?" Shemone asked, attempting to rub the sleep from her eyes.

"It is morning. I have something important to tell you. Are you listening?" he asked.

"Yes, I'm listening," Shemone replied groggily.

Darnell turned to face Shemone on the bed. "Darnell, speak up, what is it?" Shemone asked, wanting to go back to sleep.

"Baby-girl, I will get a job, you know. It's not like I'm no loser or nothing," he said. Darnell ran his hand over his head. He'd been deep in thought about it ever since his head had first touched the pillow.

Shemone didn't utter a word. The expression on her face said it all. She smiled, and rose to give Darnell a kiss on the lips, secure with the fact that she was backing up the man in her life. "Okay, Darnell, I'm just glad that you're getting a job. I'm still proud of you, and I finished that resumé you wanted."

Darnell smiled, too. He hadn't even had to remind her about his resumé. His baby-girl had been in his corner all along. "Thanks, Shemone," he answered, cutting the light off. "It means a lot to me to have you behind me," he said.

Shemone glanced back at the lamp on his bedside table. "My favorite lamp. I thought it was broken." Darnell had fixed it for her, and she was just noticing it.

"Yep, it was broken, until I fixed it," Darnell replied.

Minutes later they'd both fallen back off to sleep. That is until Darnell mistakenly kicked her with his foot. His long legs had spread over to her side of the bed. No, Shemone thought to herself before dozing back off again, nothing was perfect, but life with Darnell was close to it.

* * *

Raymond crept slowly and quietly into the bed early Sunday morning so as not to awaken Ohija. It was nearly 1:30 A.M.

"Good night, Ray, you have a good time?" Ohija asked him.

"Hey, honey, we sure did. I was trying not to wake you," Raymond said. He got into the bed and underneath the covers.

"Don't worry about it. I was already up," Ohija replied. "I couldn't sleep. Body aches. These babies have got me on a schedule of their own."

"You need a back rub?" Raymond asked as he yawned.

"No, you don't have to," Ohija said. "It's late, and I know that you're tired."

Without a second thought, Raymond reached over to the nightstand and switched on the lamp, getting out the tube of massage cream. Then he lifted Ohija's long maternity gown up over her head and helped her to get comfortable, positioning her on her side. He squeezed a bit of the cream onto his palm, lightly rubbing both of his hands together and massaging it onto his wife's back and shoulders.

"Oh, that feels like heaven," Ohija said as Raymond worked magic with his fingertips. She looked over at the clock, which read 1:55 A.M. "Mmmm," she said aloud with pleasure. There was sure nothing like a late-night rubdown.

Raymond continued massaging, rubbing in all of the cream on his hands. His hands drifted, down to her lower back and then over the length of the soft cushion of her buttocks.

It had been a few weeks since she had given the hubby some loving, she thought as his hands made their way around to cup her breasts. They were usually tender, but tonight it felt damn good to her. She moved her body so that she felt Raymond in back of her.

Raymond held her from around the waist, kissing her along the back of her neck. "Have I told you how much you mean to me, and how happy I am that you're having my babies?" Ray asked his wife.

"About as much as I tell you how happy I am to be your wife and the mother of your children," Ohija replied.

"Are you in the mood?" Ray asked.

"You bet I am," Ohija answered.

Ray delicately and skillfully entered her from behind. His motions were loving and gentle. He worked at it as if he was still giving her that massage. Only this one was full body.

Yeah, the hubby sure did his job, rocking her to sleep that night.

20

All in a Daze Work

It was Monday morning. Darnell stepped off the shiny golden elevator with his new resumé that Shemone had made up for him in his hand. He walked over to the door with the gold-embossed lettering that read "ABC Refinishers," and was buzzed in. To his surprise, the room was nowhere near empty. Eight people sat in the fancy red-carpeted room of the main office.

A Caucasian woman and an Asian woman were working behind the front desk. Darnell walked over, nervously loosening his tie. Shemone had made the knot too snug. As a matter of fact, the whole suit thing was making him feel uncomfortable, as in elementary-class-pictures-taking uncomfortable. The gray two-piece that Shemone had surprised him with as a gift was nice, if you were into suits. Not being into suits was him, and simple actions like walking weren't even the same. His strides were more upright, and less relaxed. Anyway, wasn't a person supposed to be at their best when they were comfortable?

The other problem was, this was a refinishing job. It wasn't his passion, like doing electrical work was, but he'd acquired some other skills at Pennington, too, namely, refinishing. Compared to the fast-food restaurant venture, it was a big step up money wise, Darnell thought to himself. This was, after all, what he wanted, a shot. *The* shot. He was determined to give it his best shot. Newfound confidence guided him to the front reception desk. "Uh, good morning," Darnell told the petite Caucasian woman. "I'm Darnell Williams. I'm here for the refinishing job," he said.

"Do you have an appointment?" the woman asked, looking over slate-blue round glasses.

"Uh, yes, ten o'clock," he answered.

The woman looked up at the clock. It was exactly 10 A.M. on the nose.

She picked up some papers and a writing board. "Take this, fill it out front and back, then bring it back to me when you're done."

Darnell reached over the plastic partition. "Thanks."

The woman didn't return his eye contact.

Just as he was about to look for a seat, to his relief, a brother got up. Darnell sat and glanced over the application. It was the longest form he'd ever seen. All of this for a refinishing job? he thought. It had to have everything to do with the $1,000 a week salary the job was paying. Darnell began to fill in the blanks. The top part was the easiest, because it was just general information. Sure. Name: Darnell Williams. Address: 224 Manhattan Avenue, and yes he was a male citizen. Prior experience: refinished library and office furniture for big facility. Darnell scratched out the word "big," and replaced it with the word "large." This application stuff wasn't turning out to be that hard. A half hour later brought Darnell back to the front desk. The Asian woman took his paperwork and told him to have a seat until his name was called.

Darnell took advantage of the time. He took a walk over to the water fountain and had a drink. A little got on his shirt. What the hell, Darnell thought, it was only water, it would dry. He sat back down and eyed the rest of the applicants, all of whom were men. There was the one other African-American, one Hispanic, and the rest were all Caucasian. They were like carbon copies of him, otherwise, dressed the same, with the same job-getting intentions. Darnell wanted to make himself stand out. Still in his thoughts, he heard his name being called ten minutes later.

"Darnell Williams."

Darnell accompanied the Asian woman into the interviewer's office.

"Have a seat, Mr. Williams, Mr. Trent will be right with you," she told him.

Darnell sank down instantly into the plush velvetness of the spacious antique chair. He sat up straight once the tall, thin man with the expertly trimmed goatee entered the room.

"Mr. Williams?"

"Yes, sir," Darnell said. He got up to give him a firm handshake.

"No, please sit," the interviewer told him. He walked around the long mahogany desk.

Darnell remained seated.

"So, let's go over your application," Mr. Trent said as he examined Darnell's papers. "I see here that you did library and office furniture refinishing?"

"Yes," Darnell answered. He didn't know what to do with his

hands. What would Shemone want him to do? He folded them in his lap. Smart choice.

"What facility were you employed with? Perhaps I'm familiar with it," he asked.

Darnell hesitated at first, then decided to just come out with it. "It's a correctional facility, Mr. Trent."

Mr. Trent looked up from Darnell's application and over at him. "I see," he answered. In a believable tone of voice he added, "Well, it's the kind of work you do that counts. Mr. . . ."

"Williams," Darnell said, smiling nervously.

"Yes, Mr. Williams. We'll review your application and be in touch."

"That's it?"

"That's it," Mr. Trent said in an airy tone of voice.

Darnell got up and gave Mr. Trent another firm handshake.

Darnell couldn't believe it. He actually had a chance of getting this job. He knew he could do it. He just knew that he could. Darnell high-stepped out of the office with a big grin. Oh, yeah, he was feeling damn comfortable now, especially because he was going home to change out of these clothes.

"Baby-girl, I did it!" Darnell yelled. He came in like a bandit, picking Shemone up off the floor and spinning her around.

"You got the job?"

"Pretty much!" Darnell replied cheerily. "Baby-girl, it was almost too easy!" he told her. He put Shemone back down.

"Cut it out, seriously?" Shemone asked excitedly.

"Baby-girl, I told you!" Darnell said. He began loosening his tie and removing his jacket. "I told you that I could do it on my own!"

Well, so he had, she thought to herself. Shemone was clad in workout gear, a shiny black DKNY sports bra and matching spandex pants. In the background, an aerobics workout videotape played in the VCR. "I'm so proud of you," she told him.

"How proud?" Darnell asked her over the sound of the television set. He was looking as if he had a different kind of workout in mind for her.

"We'll make a special toast to you at the dinner party, over the weekend, to celebrate," Shemone told him.

"Yeah, we should do something," Darnell agreed. He lifted her up off the floor, playfully spinning her into the air once again for the start of what else but an early celebration.

21

TABLE MATTERS

Shemone put the final touches on the medium-size dining room table Saturday evening. Everything looked festive. The olive-green candles, the floral centerpiece made of sunflowers and lemons, the olive-and-terracotta-colored plates, and the cream chair slipcovers that she'd expertly matched to complement the tablecloth and runners. Taking a step back to admire her work, she heaved a sigh of satisfaction. With a glance at her wristwatch, she calculated that she had forty-five minutes until her guests would begin to arrive. "Darnell," Shemone called out.

"What?" Darnell answered from the bedroom.

"You almost ready? Don't forget to take that earring out," she said. She could already imagine the way that her mother would gape at it, automtically labeling him a thug, which he wasn't.

Darnell came into the dining room area fidgeting with his shirt. "Nope, the earring stays. It's a part of me. Your mother will just have to take me or leave me," he told her. "I already agreed not to mention that we're living together." He continued, "I also agreed not to answer the phone if it rings, because it might be her and she's not supposed to know about us yet." He made a *tsssk* sound with his teeth. "You're lucky I love you so much, but don't ask me to do anything else because I won't, I'm doin' enough."

Darnell thought to himself. He was being a trooper, he didn't agree with Shemone and the reasons why she had resorted to her cover-up methods. He'd known all about the problems she and her mother had. It just wasn't understandable to him how she and Ruth could remain so mentally distant from each other.

Shemone laid on a hopeful smile. She was appreciative, and as far as she was concerned the situation was temporary. She dropped the earring subject, and moved on to another. "Darnell, please, I asked you to dress yourself in everything but your shirt." She complained, "Linen wrinkles so easily."

"It's gonna wrinkle anyway," Darnell replied. "My jeans and a regular shirt, that's what I should be wearing," Darnell huffed. "You act like we're about to meet the president or something. The lady can't be that bad, Shemone, she is your mother," he said.

"I just want everything to run smoothly," Shemone said as she one-handedly helped Darnell strip from his black linen shirt down to his T-shirt. She made use of the other hand, running it along the tablecloth, making sure that it lay flat. "Now, all that's left to do is to get myself together." She hurriedly scurried off into the other room.

Darnell took in the sight of the dining room. He knew his babygirl was something else, but she'd really outdone herself tonight. "Fancy-ass," he said aloud. He reached for one of the candles on the table, wondering if it smelled as pretty as it looked.

"Darnell, don't touch anything in there please."

"Damn, I'm not," Darnell joked. "You just do what you gotta do, and let me handle me, Ms. Eyes-in-the-Back-of-Your-Head Person."

Shemone was way too busy with herself to respond. Darnell went into the living room to look through one of his sports magazines to kill some time before Shemone killed him.

Forty minutes later, Shemone emerged, making her grand entrance. "So, how do I look?"

Darnell's eyes nearly bugged out of their sockets. "Eatable."

Shemone blushed. She wore a two-piece camel-colored ultra-suede outfit, which meant that it had the look of suede but was of a thinner fabric. The design consisted of a tube top and a mid-length matching skirt with a scalloped edge. On her feet, she wore strappy shoes. Her makeup was flawless, with just the right amount of sparkle on her eyelids and glossy shimmer on her lips.

"I could eat you up!" Darnell said as he got up to go toward her.

"Darnell, stop it!" she said in a playful tone of voice. "You're gonna get me all mussed up!"

"C'mon, baby-girl, let's have a quickie."

"No!"

"Yes!" he urged.

The intercom sounded.

"See," Shemone said as she hurried to get Darnell's shirt and help him into it. She picked up the receiver. "Who is it?" she asked.

It was Ohija and Raymond, on their way up.

"Greetings, greetings," Ohija said. She entered through the front door with the scent of jasmine and her husband, Raymond, following not too far behind.

"Hello, everybody," Raymond said at the same time that he helped his wife remove her coat.

"Ohija, Raymond, thank you for coming. Let me have those coats," Shemone replied. She gathered everything from Ray.

Ohija took in the overall feeling from the room and immediately spotted Darnell. She yelled loudly, "Hey there, Darnell Williams."

Darnell grinned as he hurriedly made his way toward her, stopping to bend and do a few *GQ* model poses. He gave her a big hug and flashed her a smile.

"You'll never change." Ohija chuckled.

They took a second, then let go of each other.

Ohija looked even prettier than the last time he'd seen her. His friend's face glowed like tan velvet. He thought to himself that she was wearing her pregnancy well. "You're looking good, girl," he told her.

"Please, I'm beginning to look like a big old beached whale," Ohija answered.

Darnell laughed and gave her stomach a little rub. "Don't talk about the babies like that. You know they can hear you, right?" he said. Seeing Ohija pregnant was so mind-blowing for him. There were actually little people inside her. It proved that the world would still have been spinning, locked up or not.

Ohija grinned, then rubbed her protruding tummy.

Ohija the mother, he thought again to himself. Ohija always had been the mature one of the group. "So, when are the twins coming? Shemone told me, but I forgot," Darnell asked her.

"They're saying around the middle of June, and I can't wait," she answered.

"I know what you mean," Darnell replied.

"You do? You don't have kids, do you?" Ohija asked. Shemone hadn't mentioned that he had any, but with new relationships one never could tell, she thought.

"No." Darnell chuckled. "I mean, I can imagine how much you'll have to carry around, that's all."

"Thanks, Darnell." Ohija felt like playing around with him. "So when are you and Shemone gonna have you some babies?" she asked.

"Why you starting up trouble?" Darnell joked. "You know that we're still real new with the couple thing," he answered, grinning.

"Mm-hmm," Ohija quickly replied. It was a sensible answer. Shemone and Darnell were definitely building a relationship based on a friendship.

"Who knows what the future will hold?" Darnell said in a hopeful tone of voice. "So you hoping for boys, girls, what?"

"Just healthy babies is all I want. But between you and me, at least one boy who resembles Terrance would be nice," she told him.

Darnell paused to reminisce and reflect. "Yeah, I miss him, too. That would be something if the babies looked like Terrance. You two were cousins." He added, "It might happen."

"So how are you doing otherwise?" Ohija asked, changing the subject. She wanted to get to know all over again who Darnell was. The man who was standing before her was not just her Final Four buddy, or the drug-toting streetster she'd last seen. He appeared to be changed somehow, in a better way.

"I'm good," Darnell answered, and just then his face brightened back up from having been talking about Terrance. "I might have me a new job lined up as a refinisher."

"Really? I didn't know you refinished. Shemone never mentioned it to me," Ohija said. A sense of relief overcame her as she learned more about the Darnell who was on the path of the straight and narrow.

"Yeah, well, I was kind of keeping the job situation under wraps. The refinishing thing is another trade I picked up while I was locked up."

"Another?" Ohija asked him. Shemone had told her about his electrical skills, but she wanted to hear it from him.

"Yeah. What I really love is electrical work. Wiring, you know," he told her. "That's my first love, next to Shemone."

Ohija was her usual optimistic self. "Of course, and I think that it's great that you made use of your resources while you were away. Definitely, pursue your passions, man."

"Yeah," Darnell answered. "I figured I had to do something." He hesitated momentarily. "I mean, refinishing work isn't my favorite thing to do, but the numbers look right. You know what I mean?" he said.

Ohija nodded emphatically. "Oh, I do know exactly what you mean," she replied. "I've been there many times before myself. You need money to pay the bills. You can still set short-term goals with the electrical work until you get where you want to be. In the meantime, I think that it's a gift to be able to use your hands to make furniture look so beautiful, and congratulations!"

"Thanks," Darnell replied modestly. There was an absence of enthusiasm in his reply.

"So when do you start?" Ohija asked.

"I don't really know," Darnell answered as he took up a celery stick and dipped it into the smooth bleu cheese dressing. "Should be any day now, I guess."

"Okay," Ohija replied, hoping that he found out sooner rather than later that the job was a sure thing.

"How's the clothing-store business going?" Darnell asked. He made a loud crunch as he bit into a stalk of celery.

A modest Ohija replied, "It's doing okay."

"You don't wanna brag, go ahead and brag, girl. I know you're doing well for yourself," he told her in a loud tone of voice.

Ohija chuckled. "Let's just say that it's still doing all right. I miss working, though. The doctor has me on bed rest. I told you that my sister is managing things for me while I'm out, right?"

"Right," Darnell replied. "You know how I feel about family, family is number one."

"Yes, truly, family and friends," she agreed. "Life with Shemone still treating you good?" Ohija asked. She took a small plate and began to cram it with appetizers. Just watching Darnell eat his celery had made her hungry.

"Life is sweet, as always," Darnell told Ohija. "You know she's an African princess, but her heart's in the right place."

Ohija laughed again. "Yes, I know. She has a heart of gold. Have you seen Ruth?"

"Her moms?" he asked. "Oh, no, not yet. Not since we were teenagers," he answered.

Ohija made a face.

"I know that face means something, but I'm gonna leave it alone," Darnell responded in a joking tone of voice. So far, meeting Shemone's mother seemed as if it would be like meeting the president.

22

The Main Course

Shemone came over and abruptly made an announcement to Darnell and Ohija. "My mother's on her way up, busy yourselves."

Ohija patted Darnell on the back. "Darnell, come on and meet my husband," she told him. She led him toward her Ray.

Raymond had made his way over to the mini-bar setup, and was trying to decide what to drink for the evening.

Ohija lit up. "Darnell, this is my husband, Raymond. Raymond, this is Shemone's other half and my very good friend from Monroe High School who I always talk about, Darnell."

"It's real nice to meet you, man," Darnell told him.

"It's nice to finally meet you, too," Raymond replied as he shook his hand. Darnell thought about what Pop had told him. V-necked sweater, white T-shirt underneath, and checked garbadine pants. Yep, in a relationship.

Ohija walked off toward the couch to sit down, leaving the two men behind to talk.

That's when Shemone's mother, Ruth, came through the door. Her expensive perfume entered before she did.

Ohija felt a sudden urge to throw up. She made a mad dash to the bathroom.

"Hello, Mom, thanks for coming," Shemone said at the door.

Shemone's mother gave her an air kiss. "How are you, darling? Is something burning?" Ruth asked.

"No," Shemone answered. "I cut the oven off and took the Cornish hens out a long time ago." The restaurant she'd ordered them from had explicitly assured her that reheating everything was all she needed to do.

"Cornish hens?" Shemone's mother sighed. "I was hoping you'd have some of those wonderful stuffed turkey breasts that you get catered in." Ruth removed her jacket and gave it to her daughter.

Shemone wouldn't allow herself to get caught up in her mother's negativity. She just wanted her to see Darnell again, the man who was bringing her mostly joy these days. "Mom, I'm going to call Darnell over. It's been such a long time since you've seen him," Shemone said. She summoned Darnell over with a wave from the other side of the room.

"Good luck, man," Raymond told him. Even he had known his wife long enough to know about Ruth.

Darnell chuckled. "Yeah, thanks. I have a feeling I'm gonna need it." Darnell kind of bopped his regular walk over to Shemone and her mother. He decided that he was going to be himself, and no more.

"Mom, this is Darnell. Darnell, this is my mother, Ruth," Shemone said.

"How do you do?" Ruth said. She extended an expertly manicured hand to him.

Darnell gave her a handshake. "It's nice to see you again, Ms. Waters," he told her in a well-mannered tone of voice.

Shemone stood there almost expecting something to go wrong. It was like watching the ball travel to and fro in a tennis match. Hopefully, she thought, it would be more about the sport and less about the competition.

"Are you and my daughter involved?" Ruth cut to the chase and asked him.

Damn, she was forward, Darnell thought to himself. He'd never thought she'd ask if they were dating, and one thing he was not was a liar, not to his mother or anybody else. So he answered, "Yes, we are."

"I see," she answered back. "Shemone, go and get your mother a Bloody Mary."

Shemone's stomach did a bungee jump, straight down to the floor, but she couldn't get angry with Darnell because she hadn't told him to outright lie if Ruth asked if they were dating. He was just being honest. For her, it had always been okay to tell Ruth what she called little white lies, because it avoided arguments and conflict. Lies like, she had to get right back to her home office, or, no, she wasn't dating anyone at the time. "I'll be right back with your drink, Mom," she told her. Shemone was also going to get one for herself to deal with the aftermath because Ruth knew now that she and Darnell were involved. Oh well. Darnell and his earnest demeanor seemed to be the way to go, with everything, she thought to herself. Shemone tossed her mother a you-behave-yourself look before going off to the bar.

Light jazz played in the background, but there was nothing light about the conversation.

"So, how long have you been seeing my daughter? Darnell, is it?" Ruth folded her arms over her chest, and then hit him with another statement, even before he could answer her first question. "I had no idea she was even dating," she told him. Ruth had recognized him on sight. This was that same slim, scrappy boy she'd seen from the window. The one who'd liked to follow her daughter home from high school.

Darnell went along with her, and answered both of her questions. "Yes, it's Darnell, and not for that long." He thought about it for a minute. He'd been talking to Shemone over the phone much longer than he'd actually been seeing her. "I'd say it's been a few months."

Ruth stared at the lone diamond that sparkled in his ear.

"Are you a rapper?" she asked in a disgusted tone of voice.

"Do I look like one?"

Ruth snickered.

Just then Shemone arrived back with the drink for her mother, one for Darnell, and, of course, a double for herself. "Here we are," she said as she handed the drinks over.

"Shemone, I'm gonna go and put a call in to Pop to see if he left," Darnell said. He'd had all he could take of the nonfriendly chatter. He thought to himself that being protective of your child was one thing, but Ruth Waters was another case altogether. It made him more than thankful to have the mother he had.

"Okay, Darnell," Shemone replied. The expression on his face conveyed that he couldn't wait to get away. Shemone turned and asked her mother, "What did you say to him?"

Ruth replied innocently, "I just asked him what line of work he was in, that's all."

Shemone could feel the blood rising to her head. "I know, I planned to—it's just that we don't talk like that—" Shemone whispered, trying to explain to her mother. Shemone leaned on trusting her own judgment again. "And so what if he's not working right now? It's not the biggest deal in the world, Mom," Shemone told her. "He makes me very happy." She didn't feel the need to explain the extras about Darnell's savings and what he contributed, or the fact that he'd taken the reins and was actively pursuing full-fledged employment.

"Actually, I didn't know that Darnell was unemployed, but thank you for telling me. I'm certainly learning a great deal this evening," Ruth said suddenly, feeling the need to saunter away from her daughter. The contents of her Bloody Mary helped to float her over to the couch, where Ohija, who had since returned from the bathroom, had been cozily sitting. Ruth couldn't put her finger on it, but there was something she didn't like about the girl, and never had. "Beatrice, dear, how have you been?" Ruth asked with a wicked smile. Of course she was aware of the name change, but she was acting as though she wasn't. "From the look of things, you must have been pretty busy—you're huge!" Ruth overexaggerated. She casually took a sip from her glass.

"Ms. Waters, always a pleasure to see you," Ohija replied with a pained smile. She couldn't stand Shemone's mother. When they were in high school and she'd come to visit, Ruth had always watched her. It was as if she thought she was going to steal something from her house. Ruth had just never thought that Ohija was decent enough to be Shemone's friend. It was a fortunate thing that Shemone thought differently.

"How's your little shop, Shadows, doing?" Ruth asked her.

"It's called Shades, Ms. Williams, and it's doing quite well, thanks," Ohija replied.

"Yes, I remember the one time that I went in there. The clothes are really . . . cute."

Ohija knew that "cute" wasn't meant to be a compliment, but she acknowledged it anyway. "Thank you," she replied. She was not going to let this woman ruin her evening, not while she was in the company of good food and good friends.

The doorbell rang. Pop had finally arrived, with his date. Darnell met him at the door and slapped him a hello five on the hand.

Ruth turned around to see what all the extra banter was about. She turned back around after discovering that it was just her daughter's new secret boyfriend and his common street friends.

Shemone had gone over and joined them. "Pop, so glad you could make it. We were starting to get worried about you."

"Oh, nah," Pop replied. "It was wifey over here. She was busy getting herself on point, you know how that is."

"I sure do." Shemone gave Pop's date a warm smile and introduced herself. "Hi, I'm Shemone."

"I'm Monique, thanks for inviting us." Monique's eyes aimed straight down at Shemone's feet. "Your shoes are hot!" Then Monique took a look around the apartment. "And this place is gorgeous!"

"Thanks, and I like your outfit, too," Shemone replied, complimenting Pop's date. Monique was pretty. She stood a petite five-four and had a medium-copper complexion and tiny, neat, long black-colored braids down her back. She was stylishly dressed in zebra print pants, a black turtleneck, and black leather boots.

Shemone and Darnell made the rounds and introductions as they allowed people to circulate and mingle before sitting down to dinner.

Shemone's mother sat solo on the sofa, satisfied with the company of her drink. Ohija chatted it up with Pop's girlfriend, Monique, while Darnell, Pop, and Raymond male-bonded in a corner of the living room. In a few minutes, Shemone would call everyone to eat.

"Shemone, everything looks on point," Pop said. He took a seat at the table beside Monique.

"It really does," Ohija agreed. "You should start a part-time business as a party planner or something."

Ruth chose to join the conversation. "Oh, didn't you know? My daughter already has a job. She's a wri-ter," her mother said slowly, emphasizing the syllables. She placed a dinner napkin on her lap.

It was a tense moment. Everyone just looked off somewhere else, as if Ruth hadn't said anything.

Darnell was fed up with Shemone's mother and her rude remarks to everyone, including himself. He was trying to get along with her, but he had to defend his girl on this one. He thought that Ruth should have been a little more supportive. "Yeah, she has a job, and she's a pro at it, too," Darnell answered.

"I should think so," Ruth replied as she fingered her ear and clip-on earring. "I mean, she'd have to be a pro at it if she wants to be able to carry you both the way she must plan to."

Raymond's eyes darted briefly from right to left, not knowing quite where to focus. He sat in the hot seat, between Darnell and Ruth, longing to make himself disappear from all of the friction in the room. Ray disliked confrontation, and didn't like pretending that he was at ease when he wasn't.

Ohija looked across the table at Ray sympathetically. She pouted her lips to softly blow him a comfort kiss, and he accepted it.

"Now wait just one minute, Mother," Shemone said. "You're out of line."

"I'm out of line? You're taking up for this man over your own mother?" Ruth noisily backed her chair up from the table. "That's fine. I'll be leaving now."

"Mom, wait," Shemone pleaded, feeling guilty. The evening was a personal disaster for her. Everything had gone just the opposite of the way she'd planned. And she still had to let Ruth know that she and Darnell were living together.

"Yo, let her go," Darnell urged. He wanted Shemone to work through things with her mother, but it didn't seem like the right time or place. Enough damage was done, and there was still an apartment full of people to attend to.

Pop put his hand over his mouth. He chuckled quietly to himself, thinking that Shemone's uptight mom had set herself up for everything that had gone down this evening.

"I'll call you," Shemone told her mother before she walked out the door. It was meaningless to try and persuade her to stay. No one else seemed to mind that her mother had left. The rest of the dinner party was peaceful and quite enjoyable. At least for everyone but Ruth.

23

DRIVE-BY

Shemone girl, you sure know how to throw a dinner party," her friend said as they drove in Shemone's SUV down the highway, toward the mall, the next day.

"I don't want to discuss it, Ohija," Shemone replied. She kept her eyes on the road ahead.

After driving in silence for maybe two minutes, Ohija started up again. "Have you spoken to your mother at all?"

Shemone didn't reply.

"You know, she's still your mother. I'd give anything to have mine closer to me." Ohija continued, "I'm just glad that she's coming up here to stay for a while after I have the babies."

Shemone still offered no comment.

"Shemone, you need to talk about this. Say something. It's not good for you to be so quiet." Ohija dug in her oversize leather handbag. She took out a bunch of pamphlets. "Let's see, reading one of these should help."

Shemone looked away from the road for a second. Curiosity had gotten the better of her. What was Ohija looking for now? she asked herself.

Ohija found the pamphlet she was looking for. "One of these tells you about St. John's wort," Ohija continued. "It's supposed to help destress you and bring your mood level up to a positive place."

"Ohija, I'm not interested in any of your miracle pills today. I'll be fine." Shemone put a DMX rap CD into the SUV's CD player.

Ohija took the case and examined the inside. "Well, I see Darnell is having a big influence on you."

"Not you, too," Shemone said, thinking about her mother's last words before storming off. "And what's so wrong with listening to rap and letting Darnell have an influence on me? There's a particular song that I'm looking for. DMX gets down to it. It's what I'm feeling now, put to music." Shemone listened to rap quite a bit these days. Before, it wasn't that she'd never liked it, but that she'd never really listened to it. Both Darnell and rap music offered her a new dynamic of street tough. And these days she could use a little toughness on the outside.

Ohija looked out the passenger window at the passing scenery. "I never said that there was anything wrong with Darnell or listening to rap music. I listen to a little every now and then myself." She looked back over to Shemone and added, "No need to be hostile, girl."

"I apologize. I didn't mean to snap, and there's no hostility." Shemone sighed. "I just don't know what to do. My mother is important to me, but Darnell is important to me, too." The music soothed her, it enabled her to open up. "My mother and I don't have a lovey-dovey relationship. Okay, fine, but can't she and Darnell at least be sociable for my sake?"

"Shemone, I think that Darnell did put the effort out there," Ohija replied. "You and I both know that your mother isn't exactly the easiest person to get along with."

"I know, I know," Shemone quickly replied. "My mother needs to meet him halfway." She signaled, then turned off at the next exit. "Maybe he can learn to tolerate her."

"You mean, just like you do?" Ohija asked.

Shemone didn't answer right away. It was as if she was waiting until just the right moment to respond. "Yes, just like I do," she finally admitted aloud.

Ohija arranged her pamphlets back in a neat stack. "Well, I guess you won't be needing these," she said as she stuffed the brochures back into her bag.

"No hard feelings?" Shemone asked with a smile.

"Never, girl," Ohija answered. "You know I'd never try to force any of my stuff on you. I love you for the person you are and you know that."

Shemone's eyes began to fill with tears. Cut it out, Shemone. You're stronger than this. Don't break down, the all-knowing voice in her head told her. But by then it was too late. "I can't believe I'm doing this in the car, right here and right now," Shemone sniffled. "I'm used to taking charge of my emotions."

"It's okay to release, Shemone. You can't always be in control," Ohija told her. "You need a minute to pull over? It's okay to be yourself around me."

"No." Shemone took out a tissue and blew hard. "I'm fine now. I just needed to release, like you said. I'm slippin', I'm fallin'," Shemone sang out loudly, along with the CD.

Ohija was silent as they drove the rest of the way to the mall. She spoke only after her friend found a spot to park the SUV. "Shemone, the best advice that I can give you as a friend is to work it out. Your mother is always going to be your mother, and Darnell seems to be a big part of your life now. So work it out. That's all you can do, is try."

"I've been trying," Shemone told Ohija. "I called my mother three times the same night of the dinner party. She won't take any of my calls. I don't know why I'm torturing myself like this." She took a minute to grab her friend's hand and give her a positive nod. "I know that this might sound a little crazy, but I was just wondering—"

"If we could stop by your mom's house since we're so close by?" Ohija finished for her.

Shemone laughed. "How did you know I was gonna ask you that?"

"It's called divine intuition, girl, and believe me, I have it."

Shemone hadn't put the security club on the steering wheel yet. "I'd like to stop by there first, before we start shopping, if that's all right with you," she said.

"Heck yeah, it is. I don't need you dragging around behind me in the mall, looking all depressed, bringing me down," Ohija joked. "It's probably better that you go and see her as soon as possible."

"That's what I was thinking, too. She was really upset when she left my house last night," Shemone said as she started up the ignition. "And Darnell and I are going to have a talk about her tonight, too."

"That's the woman I know," Ohija replied with pride.

They arrived at her mother's doorstep in record time. The trip was a short distance. Her mother lived only a few minutes from the mall they were going to.

"Are you coming?" Shemone asked her friend just as she was about to open the SUV's door.

"No, you go on ahead and handle your business. I'm fine here," Ohija said. She took her pamphlets out of her bag again. "I'll just be right here, reading."

"Are you sure? You're welcome to come."

"Yes, I'm sure, now go. My presence will probably only sidetrack things anyway."

"Now, Ohija, you know my mother likes you as well as she can like anybody."

Ohija giggled. "You said a mouthful there!"

Shemone laughed, too. "Okay, then I'm going in." Shemone got out of the SUV, smoothing her white cotton shirt before walking down the concrete path that lead to Ruth's door. For some reason, her heart was beating really fast. She knocked on the door lightly at first, and got no response. She knocked again, this time much harder, wondering where her mother could be. "Mom, are you in there? It's me, Shemone," she said aloud, hoping that the sound of her voice would make her mother open the door if she was inside. Shemone gave the door a hard knock, one last time, before walking off, and headed back toward the SUV.

"Not there, huh?" Ohija asked her once she'd stepped back inside.

"No, not there," Shemone said in a sad tone of voice.

"Don't let it get the best of you, now," Ohija told her. "The point is that you tried to reach out to her. You can't help it if she's not home. Remember what I told you about control."

"Right, I do," Shemone replied. "I'll just try calling her later on tonight from home. Now let's go spend some money on those babies!"

"That's the spirit," Ohija told her as they sped off toward the mall.

Ruth slowly opened the curtains, only wide enough for her to see the SUV before it took off outside the house. No, she wasn't home, and that was her final decision. It was no telling when she'd be home for her daughter. Not after it appeared that she'd chosen him over her.

Shemone came through the door later that afternoon.

"How's my favorite girl doing?" Darnell asked. His nose was stuck in the middle of a book.

"Not too great," Shemone said as she flopped down on the couch. She and Ohija had shopped until they'd almost dropped, finding the cutest toys and infants' clothes for the twins. Right after, they'd grabbed a bite at Ohija's favorite deli-restaurant. But Shemone still wasn't feeling good about the day. It had more to do with her mother not being home. "What are you reading?"

Darnell finally looked up. "*Of Mice and Men,* by John Steinbeck," he said.

Shemone was taken aback; she recognized the worn cover. Darnell had gotten it from her book collection.

"This Lennie character is something else," Darnell continued, like he was making a comparison of some kind. "He's slow, but he still has it together, you know?"

"Yes, you're right about that," Shemone agreed, even more pleased. Her man was soaking up all kinds of knowledge.

He stopped reading and asked, "So how's Ohija doing?"

"She's fine," Shemone answered. "Do you know that she actually thought for half a second that Ray might have been cheating on her?" she told him.

"So that's what's bothering you? Shemone, I'm not even sure that half a second counts as cheating. Ray might be good, but he can't be that good!" Darnell said with a laugh.

"That's not what I mean," Shemone told him. "He wasn't cheating. It was like a passing thought of hers, as in a human characteristic. Ohija's way too secure for that kind of pettiness," she said. Shemone got out her clear nail polish from a nearby basket filled with manicure supplies. She added, "She doesn't even go there."

"I see," Darnell replied. "You still haven't answered my question, though. What's not so great with you? You decide to go there with me or something?"

"I don't know," Shemone replied in a wistful tone of voice. "It just got me to thinking about, you know, the direction that our relationship is going in." Shemone paused, then asked, "Darnell, do you think that you could ever cheat on me?" She didn't want to think the worst, but she did want to know. Maybe her mother was right, and had a solid reason to be angry with her. Darnell was straight out of jail, he didn't have a real job yet, and already she'd let him into her world, fast and furious. Who was to say that they were even compatible with each other? she thought to herself.

"Baby-girl, you're already a handful. Believe me, I wouldn't have the time or energy to cheat on you!"

Shemone playfully hit Darnell against the head.

"Seriously, though," he admitted, "I'm very happy."

"But I don't mean when you're happy, I mean when you're not. You know all those reasons that they say a man strays. The arguing, nothing in common, or if I became unattractive to you."

"Shemone, I could never say never, but you've been there for me, and I'll always love you for that. You were all I had after I found out that Terrance was gone and when I was locked up, and even now that I'm out."

"You can still love me and not be in a relationship with me," Shemone said.

Darnell burst out jokingly, "No, I'm not gonna cheat on you. I love you too much, okay?"

Shemone smiled. All she needed was a little more of that reassurance he was so good at giving her. She'd never really had that before. She thought back to that first time when Darnell had called her from jail and told her that he loved her. Shemone passionately kissed Darnell as if there was no other. The center of his pants rose to the occasion.

"I want you so much," he told her.

"I want you, too, but not tonight. I have some important research to do for a story. And before you ask me, yes, I am about to speak to my boss about getting that promotion, you'll see," she said.

Darnell looked at Shemone with fiery eyes. "Okay, and I'm gonna behave myself today and understand," he said, giving her one last peck. "I think I'm gonna head uptown to play some ball."

"Darnell?"

"Yeah?"

"Be careful."

"Oh, I am, baby-girl, always. You don't have to worry about me getting caught up out there," he said. "Did anybody call me earlier today?" Darnell asked her.

Shemone was almost positive of who he meant in particular. He was asking about them nearly every single day. "ABC Refinishers? No, not today," she replied.

"I was talking about your mother, but okay," he told her. "And ABC Refinishers still hasn't called? Damn, it's been long enough. I'm starting to wonder if they'll ever call me."

"Darnell, be patient," she told him before he went out the door. "It's all about office politics, they'll call." Shemone tried to relax back on the couch. She sure hoped they would.

24

FAMILY TIES

Ohija, can we talk?" Ray asked his wife on Wednesday evening as he walked into the brightly lit kitchen.

"Of course, I'm all ears." Ohija stirred a wooden spoon into the stew of turkey cutlets, mushrooms, green peppers, and cut-up chunks of fresh garlic.

"You know that I've always been straight with you about things," Raymond said, leaning against the counter to face his wife.

"Yes."

"And you know that I love you very much."

"Yes," Ohija answered. She brought the spoon up and blew on the hot brown sauce. "Here, taste this for me."

Raymond sipped at the sauce. "It's delicious."

Ohija smiled. "I'm sorry to interrupt, honey, now go ahead. You were saying we're straight with each other, and we love each other," she repeated out loud.

Ray began, "Well, the other night . . . The night that I went out to shoot pool was the night that the doctor called me and said that I should come in for further testing. Ohija, I might be really sick."

"'Further testing'?" Ohija asked as she continued to stir the pot. "And sick like what, Ray?"

"I think you need to know." Raymond paused. "You deserve to know. I went to the doctor to get myself checked—"

"Raymond, please stop stalling and just tell me!" Ohija pleaded, still stirring.

"Cancer, Ohija," Raymond blurted out. "I might have cancer."

Ohija dropped the spoon on the floor. "What?"

"I went to the hospital last week to start the testing because I discovered blood in my urine about a month ago."

"Why didn't you tell me?" Ohija asked as tears began to stream down her face. She consoled her husband with everything she had, holding him tightly in her arms, and listening closely with her ears.

Raymond continued, "I guess that I didn't want to believe it myself. It took me a while to get to that hospital. Tim was the one who convinced me to go. He told me to tell you then, but I didn't want you to be worried. I didn't want to get you worked up if the results came back negative."

"Raymond, baby, you know that I'm strong. You could have come to me whether you knew for certain or not," she said to him.

A single streak of a tear rapidly made its way from one of Ray's eyes. "I guess it wasn't about you. I was scared. I just panicked. I know better—we always communicate with each other about everything. This was the first time that I didn't."

"We're in this together," Ohija said as they rocked each other and wept. "So then you still don't know anything for sure yet?"

"No," he answered. "I only went once, for, like, a general exam. I haven't been back since."

"Ray, we're going to make an appointment for you to go back to that hospital and really get tested, the way you should be. No more playing around."

"Okay, honey, okay," he agreed.

"But what makes you think that it's cancer, Ray?" Ohija guided her husband over to the table to sit down. She picked the spoon up from the linoleum-tiled floor, and cleaned up the spot of sauce.

"The doctor says that I've got the symptoms—blood in my urine, and problems urinating. My dad had prostate cancer, you know." Raymond stared off into the room. "It happened so fast. One minute he was up and around and the next he was gone. That's just how cancer is. It just creeps up on you, and before you know it—"

Ohija fell silent. "I thought you said your dad died from a heart attack."

"No, it was cancer, just before we started dating. They tried radiation therapy on him, and it worked for a while, until . . ." Raymond's eyes refilled with tears. "It just stopped working altogether. He lost so much weight, his face . . . was so thin and sunken in. I hardly recognized him after he was gone, lying in that big silver metal casket."

Ohija took her husband's hands in hers. "You never talk about your dad, Ray."

"I know, it's painful for me. We were real close. Ohija, I want to be a good father to my kids, like he was to me. I need to be here for them."

"Everything will be all right, Ray," Ohija reassured him.

"How do you know that everything will be all right, Ohija? I'm thinking about the outcome of all this," Ray said. "I don't want you to do it alone. I don't want you to have to raise two children and run a household all on your own."

"I don't want to have to raise the kids without you either, Ray, but you said part of it right, honey. If I have to, then I will. Believe you me, these kids will know you like I know you. They'll know that their father was special."

"Ohija, you've always been such a positive woman. I don't know how you do it." Ray held the weight of his head up, resting his elbow on the table. "It's one of the reasons I'm so attracted to you. You have no idea how much you're helping me, just by staying positive now."

Ohija kissed her husband softly on the lips. "Things are different now. Scientists have developed all kinds of new treatments. I'm sure something will come through."

"Right, technology, I know, and this is a new age," Raymond said without much emotion. "But hey, who says I even have cancer? I still haven't been fully diagnosed."

"Ray, let's just be realistic about this. We need to take things one step at a time."

Ray smiled. "Okay, baby, just one day at a time then."

25

TOMORROWS

Darnell lay across the bed on Thursday evening munching on a Ritz cracker from an open pack. "Dang," he said. He attempted to sweep away the loose crumbs from the sheets.

"Darnell, please watch getting those crumbs in the bed. I hate it when you get food everywhere," Shemone told him.

"Yes, Mommy," Darnell joked.

"Very funny," Shemone replied as she read through the pages of her monthly issue of *Black Enterprise* magazine. It was always productive for her to read about other African-Americans doing well in their careers, she thought to herself. The inspirational entrepreneurial stories always motivated her. It was exactly what she needed as an added push now. Darnell had already encouraged her. All she had to do was find the nerve to approach her editor about that raise/promotion situation.

"I just can't believe that Dawg might have cancer," Darnell said.

"His name is Raymond, Darnell, not Dawg."

"Do you always have to correct me like I'm some child? It's just an expression." Darnell stuck the roll of crackers back in its box. "Any way you put it, it's cancer, and that's still real critical," he said.

"I apologize," Shemone replied, still engrossed in the article she was reading.

"Apology accepted."

"I know," Shemone suddenly continued, "I can't believe it either." Getting the news from Ray and Ohija late last night had devastated them both.

"He might die, right?" Darnell asked her.

Shemone shuddered to think so, turning the page. Her best friend's husband could really die. "I suppose so," Shemone answered in a sad tone of voice. Life was so unpredictable. Shemone thought about her mother and the dinner party fiasco. Her mother probably thought she'd taken sides with who, in her eyes, was the enemy, the enemy being Darnell. Ruth had always been big on appearances, or maybe from her point of view, not being betrayed. She and her mother weren't close, but like she'd told Ohija, they had certainly always been lovingly tolerant of each other.

"You think I should try and make up with my mother?" Shemone suddenly turned to Darnell and asked.

Darnell picked up the TV listing guide and looked through it. "There's nothing on worth watching tonight," he told her.

"Darnell—I'm talking to you."

"Oh, I heard you, about your moms. I'm saying that you're already trying to make up with her. You went over there, right?" The only thing running through his mind then was the fact that Ruth had insulted and stereotyped him. He thought, But Ruth isn't my mother, she's Shemone's, and so yeah, she should try to work things out with her, because if it was my mother, I would. He put the TV listing down and said, "Yes, I think that you should try and make up with your mother."

"But I did," Shemone answered, realizing that she really had already put her best foot forward in trying to reach out to Ruth.

"That's all you can do, baby-girl, is try," Darnell replied. "Speaking of trying, I think I'm gonna try and give ABC Refinishers a call in the morning and find out what's going on."

Shemone hesitated, then said, "That's probably a good idea." Maybe her next move wasn't, but she was going to put it out there anyway. "Maybe you should start looking into other avenues," she told him. It had occurred to her that Darnell should move on.

"Look into other avenues? Why would I wanna do that? I got the job, baby-girl. I was there when the man said it, remember?"

Shemone looked up over her magazine at Darnell. "Did he actually tell you that you had the job? I mean, did you hear him say the actual words 'You've got the job'?"

Darnell thought back. The man had said that he'd give him a call. That had to be the same thing. Why would someone call to tell a person that they didn't have the job?

"I'll find out in the morning," Darnell huffed, "that's for sure. They better not make me have to go down there, that's all I know."

"Darnell, you can't bully anyone into giving you a job."

"Did I say that I was gonna bully anybody?"

"Well, then why would you go down there?" Shemone sighed. "You know what? This is turning into an argument, and I don't feel like arguing."

"I don't feel like arguing either." Darnell turned over in the bed. "Damn."

"Damn what?" Shemone asked him.

"I'm still hungry."

"You're always hungry. Darnell, it's, like, eleven-thirty at night. Why don't you go to sleep?" Shemone flipped another page, and added, "Or have some more crackers."

"I don't want any more crackers. I'm no parrot. 'Darnell wanna cracker, Darnell wanna cracker,'" he joked. "I'd be full if you'd cook something once in a while," he told her. "A man can't live just on take-out food all the time."

"You know that I don't cook like that, Darnell. What do I always tell you? You want home cooking, go visit your mama."

Suddenly, things weren't a joking matter anymore. "My mistake, you act like one sometimes," he told her.

"That's because you're acting like a child," Shemone said. "I'm telling you that I don't want to argue and yet you're still pushing for an argument. You're pushing for an argument because it's sinking in that you might not have that job you want."

"You know everything, so I'm not gonna answer." Darnell forced his eyes shut and thought, If this job thing doesn't come through, I just might have to look in to other avenues.

The next day Shemone printed out and signed the last of the new story queries that she had written to be sent out to the newest magazine-release editors. She hoped that her submissions would continue to bring in even more work. She'd planned on keeping the respect she deserved in the publishing industry. She thought that it was important for her not to lose focus. She was a professional woman with wants. And hopefully, Darnell would be getting his act together soon, and they'd make it to that next level, together. She thought that it wasn't as if he didn't want to work. Darnell still helped with the bills, and as of late, had agreed to put half of what he had in an interest-bearing savings account, and half in a CD account, where his money could grow.

Her businessman, Shemone thought to herself. Darnell had left the apartment early that morning, dressed in slacks and a dress shirt. She hoped that he would keep to his word by not starting anything with the people at ABC Refinishers. As a surprise for all of his efforts, Shemone had gone food shopping the day before. She planned on fixing her man a real down-home southern dinner. Fried chicken, macaroni salad, and biscuits. Shemone got up from her workstation to get to the cooking. Darnell would be in soon.

"Ouch!" Shemone yelled as a drop of the hot frying grease popped onto her arm. "I knew there was a reason why I don't cook," she said aloud to herself. The dark brown pieces of chicken sizzled in the hot oil as she continued to turn them over onto the other side. They were a little dark, more like closer to Cajun.

"Is that my baby-girl in there cooking for her man?" Darnell asked as he walked inside the kitchen. Shemone hadn't heard him come in.

"Yes, it's baby-girl in here cooking for her man," Shemone replied. She coughed at the same time. The smoke from the burning chicken set off the high shrill of the smoke alarm. "I don't know what made me think I could do this," she said, fanning at the alarm with a dish towel.

"Shemone, cut the gas down," Darnell suggested. "The fire is up too high. You don't need to cook the food so fast." He remembered patiently waiting in the kitchen while his mama had prepared meals when he was younger. Seeing her make her soul-food creations had always been magical to him.

"You know what, this wasn't the smartest idea I've ever had," Shemone told him. A pot of elbow macaroni puffed out slow bubbles on the back burner of the stove.

"Shemone, baby? How long has that macaroni been boiling on the stove?" he asked her.

"How should I know?" Shemone answered. "I was too busy trying to get the chicken together. I had to clean it, and season it, didn't I?"

Darnell cut both burners off and reached over to give his girl a hug as she sobbed in his arms. She'd failed performing this task, big time.

"It's all right, I wanted to surprise you and take you to dinner at Negril's anyway, to celebrate," he told her.

"Celebrate?" Shemone asked as she looked up at her boyfriend. "Celebrate what? Darnell, you got the job!"

"Not at ABC Refinishers."

"You went down there?"

"No, I called today from outside, on my cell phone. They just told me that the position had been filled. But it's okay, I still came through with something. It ain't much, but after I left ABC Refinishers, I just started walking the streets in that area. I was asking everybody were they hiring. All I knew was that I wasn't coming home without a job. Everybody was turning me down until I got to this one place. They needed somebody real bad because a guy had just up and quit on them the day before. It's a packing company. It doesn't pay a lot, but, baby-girl, it's a job!" Darnell said with a big grin.

Shemone grinned back. It was a start, and that was all that counted. Her man had gotten himself a legitimate job. She looked over at the mess she'd created in the kitchen. "Let's get out of here and get some real food. I'm starved," she said.

26

Stormy Weather

"Mom, open up this door! It's your daughter," Shemone yelled. She rang the front doorbell over and over on Saturday afternoon. "I won't go away. I can see your shadow moving around through the window," she said. Shemone leaned her head on the big colonial-style cherry-wood door. "Don't make me use the spare key under the potted plant, because I will," she told her. She thought about it. Enough was enough. It had been going on too long since she'd last seen or heard from her mother.

"Just hold on," Ruth yelled out to her from inside. "I should call the authorities on you." She unlocked the door and Shemone stepped inside.

Her mother's house looked like something out of *Metro Homes*. It was done up in rich burgundy plaids, emerald greens, and rust. The entire house was carpeted in a plush wine, and ornate floral-inspired runners were spread throughout. It was a bit busy for Shemone's taste, but it worked completely for her mother. Ruth walked into the den and switched on the Tiffany-inspired lamp that Shemone had bought her as a Christmas gift two years before.

"So what can I do for you, dear?" Ruth asked as though nothing had been going on.

"Mom, you know what you can do for me. I've been calling you, I've been leaving messages, I've been coming by—"

"Yes, I suppose, more than you ever have," her mother quickly replied.

"What's that supposed to mean?" Shemone asked. She took a seat in the large green upholstered chair.

"It means that you don't usually come by, unless you have a reason to."

Shemone became defensive. "Mom, that's just not true. You know how busy I get."

"Not too busy. You've got time for that new secret man of yours," her mother said. She disappeared into the kitchen and returned with a tray and two cups of hot tea.

"How can I make things okay between us, Mom?" Shemone asked her. Word of Ray's sickness had truly brought out her compassionate side. "You know, Ohija's husband may have cancer."

Ruth barely flinched.

"How can you sit there and be so insensitive?" Shemone asked.

"The world is insensitive, Shemone. I thought I taught you better than that." Ruth took a sip from the steaming cup. "I've always raised you to go for the best. How do you think it is that you've made it to where you are today? I'll tell you how, it's because I worked hard to give you all the good things you needed and deserved, that's how."

"What does having good things have to do with insensitivity?" Shemone asked, not interested in her cup of tea.

"It has everything to do with it. You go in, get what you need to get, and then get out. It's the only way to the top. If I had only followed my instincts then . . ." Ruth's voice began to waver. "To have danced with the Dance Theatre of Harlem—"

"Mom, I know," Shemone said as she got up from the chair. "I know that you could have been a professional dancer for the Dance Theatre of Harlem. I know that it was at the same time that you met Daddy, and then got pregnant with me." Shemone spoke as she gazed up at the photograph of her mother in the heavy brushed gold frame on the wall.

Ruth was a younger woman then, with jet-black hair pulled tightly into a neat bun. She stood erect, on her toes, with a slim waist, and long legs, dressed in a navy leotard with white tights. Undoubtedly, against the backdrop of a curtained stage, she'd been blessed with the perfect dancer's body.

Shemone continued on, and her voice changed to match Ruth's. "The dance troop was on the verge of going on a multicity national tour and you couldn't go along with them. Your dreams were all diminished, because of little old me. Your wealthy parents disowned you and eventually so did Daddy, who was never to be seen again. Then you found out later on that the only love of your life had died only years later of a heart attack.

"You say that it made you a stronger person. It forced you to grow up, and be responsible even if you had to struggle for a while. You were the single parent without parents, and without a husband. Learning a trade was all that you could do. So naturally, you became the best head administrative assistant that the Channel 64 network ever had. You dedicated yourself, did your years there, and then retired early with benefits. You built a nest egg, bought this house, and in the process, gave me the best life had to offer.

"Guess that makes me the lucky one," Shemone told her. "I get to prove that I haven't deserted you."

"Shemone, you don't have a thing to prove to me, only to yourself," Ruth interrupted.

"Right," Shemone answered cynically, remembering her true purpose for visiting her mother. "All I want to know is, what's so bad about Darnell? He's paid his debt to society, Mom. Are you going to continue to make him pay, too?"

"What, are you his attorney now?" Ruth asked. She took another sip from her teacup.

"No, I'm not his attorney, but I am his girlfriend." Shemone added, "We live together, and I'm in love with him."

"You're in love with him? Shemone, have you lost your mind? That man can't offer you anything. Does he even work?"

"Yes," Shemone said with pride. "He's got a job."

"Really?" Ruth took a cigarette from its pack, lit it, and inhaled. "Where?"

"Darnell works for a packing company, Mom."

Ruth laughed aloud. "You can't be serious! His paycheck probably won't even be enough to cover your phone bill!"

"Maybe not, but that's our problem, Mom, don't you think?"

"No, I think it's your problem, and when you realize why, then you'll agree that I'm right." Ruth took another drag from her cigarette, then squished it out firmly in the ashtray. She thought about what a huge mistake her daughter was making by taking this man in.

"If you just gave him a chance—"

"I don't need to. You have to sleep with him, I don't," Ruth replied. "Time will prove the obvious. That man was used to not having, Shemone. You've gone and given him everything, and now you think he's going to be happy with a menial packing job?"

"Yes, I do," she replied.

"Then you're stupid."

"I'm stupid?" Shemone said. "You know what? You're right. I was stupid, stupid to try and come over here and talk some sense into you. You'll never change, Mom." Shemone took up her purse and jacket and walked out the door without looking back. She hated to have to choose. But if she had to make a choice, Darnell would be the one.

* * *

Darnell stepped inside the bedroom. Shemone was sitting at her computer working on a story. "Hey, my workingman, how was your first day?" she asked him Monday evening.

"Work was work, I guess," he answered, removing his baseball cap from his head.

"Mmph, that doesn't sound very enterprising," she said back as she scrolled through one of her work documents. She stopped, then looked up at Darnell so that he'd know that she was interested in what he had to say next.

"It's a job, Shemone, that's what I wanted to get, right?" Darnell replied. He began to take off his work clothes.

Even dirty, the man looked inviting. Shemone was tempted to jump on him and make his day a whole lot better.

Darnell was back to the details of how his day had been. There wasn't much detail to discuss. "I pack the boxes and seal them up for shipping, pack the boxes, seal them up for shipping. I do it all day until six P.M. when my shift is over," he told her, walking out of the room to go into the bathroom. "I'm going to take me a shower."

Somebody was Mr. Negative, she thought to herself. Shemone kept at her story, thinking that the best thing she could do for him would be to stay out of his way until his mood passed.

Darnell came back in the bedroom with a white towel wrapped around his waist. "That shower made me feel like a new person. It was just what I needed," he said.

"Is that so?" Shemone asked him. She came up behind him and began massaging his shoulders. She'd chosen to disregard what she'd originally said she was going to do, leave him alone. Just the sight of him half naked was turning her on, and besides, he'd even said himself that he felt like a new person. Shemone couldn't resist the temptation of kissing Darnell on the side of his neck, so she did.

"Shemone?"

"Yes . . . ," she asked him in a sexy voice, just about ready to make a move out of her clothes.

"Not tonight."

"I understand, you're tired," she said, bringing the mouth play to an immediate halt. Darnell had never refused her advances before. But then, there was a first time for everything.

27

Decisions, Decisions

I tell you, I never thought this cancer thing would hit so close to home," Ohija told Shemone. It was almost one week later, in the living room of Ohija's house on Sunday evening.

Shemone leaned Ohija's recliner back to its farthest position.

"Ray is trying to be strong, but I know that he's scared. I know him better than anyone else," Ohija said.

"And you? How are you holding up?" Shemone asked her friend. Ohija didn't need to answer. Shemone could see for herself that Ohija's face was washed over with worry.

"I'm holding up," Ohija replied. "I can't tell you that I'm not shaken, because I am. But I have to be strong for Ray and the babies now. The little ones sense things, even from the womb," Ohija added, rubbing her stomach.

"So you guys went and had the tests done?" Shemone asked.

"Yeah, yesterday. It took all day."

"What kinds of things did the doctor do?"

"Oh, girl, there was all kinds of testing," Ohija replied. She ate from a Baggie filled with cut-up apples and oranges. "The PSA exam, lab tests, imaging, and then there was Ray's favorite." She smirked.

"What's that?"

"The digital rectal exam."

"Eww, you're kidding. You mean Ray liked it?"

"No, girl. He didn't even want to take it. He insisted that he have a female physician or he wouldn't go through with it."

"Wha—at?" Shemone exclaimed.

"Yes, because you know with that rectal exam, a gloved finger goes up his you-know-what."

"His ass?"

Ohija laughed, hard. "I know it's not funny but, Shemone, if I don't laugh about something, I'll start crying. I refuse to take this thing lying down."

Shemone got up from the recliner and joined her friend on the couch. She rubbed her back and gave her a hug. "Remember what you told me? It's okay to not always be in control." Shemone put her arm around her friend's shoulder. "Is there anything that I can do? You need me to drive you anywhere or run any errands for you?"

"No, I'm fine, really. I've still got my meditation practices and everything." Ohija added with a faint smile, "It helps."

"Okay, so you're making all of your GYN appointments, then?" Shemone asked.

"Yeah, I am. These kids will need to have at least one healthy parent."

"So what happens if Ray's tests come back positive?" Shemone asked.

Ohija couldn't hold it in any longer. She just started crying. "I'm so glad that Raymond's not home to see me like this. He thinks so much of me."

"I know, I know," Shemone told her. "He still will, and it's okay to be yourself around me, too. That's what I'm here for."

Ohija sighed, sniffled, and continued. "If the tests come back suspicious, then the doctor will probably recommend that Ray get what's called a transrectal ultrasound. If that comes back positive, then it's just a series of more tests."

"And what's the transrectal ultrasound?" Shemone asked. "As if the digital rectal exam wasn't enough."

"The transrectal is when they use sound waves from a small probe. It creates an image of his prostate on the screen. It can detect any tumor that's too small to be picked up by the digital rectal exam."

"Oh, Ohija," Shemone said. She was really at a loss for words for her friend.

"That's the hardest part, not knowing. All the tests make it even scarier. I just wish that Ray could have been from a different family."

"Oh, so then it's hereditary?"

"Yes, it can be." Ohija went on to explain, "And African-American males are more likely to develop the disease than anyone else. Diet and age could also have a lot to do with it."

"I see you've been doing your homework," Shemone said.

"Shemone, I just want to find out all that I can about the disease that's trying to take hold of my husband," Ohija told her. "I'm sorry, I'm so caught up in me. What's going on with you?"

"We don't have to talk about me. My problems are nothing compared to yours."

"Gee, thanks," Ohija replied.

"I'm sorry," Shemone apologized. "I didn't mean it like that, girl."

"I know you didn't. Now go ahead, tell me about what's new with you. How's Darnell doing?"

"Darnell is alive and well."

"Uh-oh, that doesn't sound too promising. Did he start his new job?"

"Yes, but he didn't get the refinishing gig. He works downtown, as a packer," Shemone told her.

"A packer, huh?" Ohija said, trying to sound cheerful. Darnell had sounded so excited at the dinner party about getting the refinishing job. She knew he was disappointed.

"Right, I know it's not exactly the best position he could have, but it's an honest day's work," Shemone replied.

"True," Ohija agreed.

"But it's like when he comes in every day, his whole mood is thrown off."

"What do you mean, 'thrown off'?" Ohija asked as she resumed eating from the bag of fruit. She offered Shemone some.

"Thanks." Shemone took out a piece of sliced Granny Smith. "I mean he seems to be angry about something. He doesn't want to do anything but jump in the shower and go to bed. And on the weekends he's uptown sitting by his mother's house in his old neighborhood. We aren't really even doing things together," she told Ohija.

"Yes, it certainly does sound like there's been some changes."

Shemone sighed aloud. "I don't really know what to do. He's not even in the mood to make love."

"Girl, you gotta put it on him. Buy yourself some new lingerie, some sweet-smelling oils, light some candles . . . He'll be in the mood all right!"

"Would you believe me if I told you that I've been there and done that, and the rooster is still not cocka-doodling?"

Ohija burst out with laughter. "Then it's got to be that job."

"I know it is, but I won't tell him to quit. Then he'll think it's okay to go from job to job. Darnell will never learn stability," Shemone said.

"You're right about that. I don't know what to tell you, girl. Just keep believing in him, and be there, the same as I'm doing with Ray."

Just then, Ray came through the front door. "Hey, family, how's everybody doing?" he asked.

"Perfect, now that you're here, baby," Ohija answered.

Raymond came over and gave his wife a kiss on the cheek.

"Oh, spare me!" Shemone said jokingly. "You guys are making me sick with all that sweet talk."

"Don't be jealous," Raymond said. "If you fatten up that man of yours, you can have a love belly, too!"

Everyone laughed aloud. It was refreshing to forget about worries, if only for a while.

"How is Darnell doing?" Ray asked Shemone.

"He's okay—thanks."

Ohija spoke. "Shemone, I was thinking, maybe Ray could lend some insight into that little dilemma we were talking about."

Shemone thought to herself that it wasn't a bad idea. It would be constructive to get the male perspective. "Ray, I think you just might be the one to help me with this, since you're a man and all."

"You know that I charge by the hour, right?" Ray kidded, his hand extended out for a cash payment.

Ohija nudged him gently. "Ray, this is serious. Listen to what Shemone has to say."

"Okay, okay, I'm all ears," Ray replied as he took a seat on the couch, next to his wife.

Shemone began to tell her story. "Well, Darnell started this new job. He was supposed to get a position as a refinisher—"

"Yeah, he was telling me about that at your dinner party," Ray told Shemone.

"Will you let the woman finish?" Ohija said as she looked at her husband. "Here, stuff this into your mouth until she's done." Ohija handed Ray a chunk of apple.

Shemone continued, "So, right, well, he didn't get that position. He wound up having to take a job as a packer. He's been coming home every day in a messed-up mood, and all he wants to do is shower, eat, and go right to bed."

"And he hasn't had any interest in sex either," Ohija announced.

"Now look who won't let the woman finish!" Ray turned to tell his wife.

"I just didn't want her to leave that part out," Ohija answered quickly.

"She's right," Shemone confirmed. "He has no interest in much of anything lately. It hasn't been very long, but I'm already concerned about it."

"Well, how long has he been working at his new job?"

"Just a little over a week, actually," Shemone told Ray.

"And how long has it been that you two haven't slept together?"

"I'd say the same, a little over a week."

"Oh, Shemone." Ray chuckled. "Maybe the man just needs a break. Men don't have to have it every day you know. He's probably just stressed out. It's possible that he just has a lot on his mind." Ray thought to himself that he would know. He had lots to worry about.

"That's what I was thinking, too," Shemone replied.

"Listen," Ray told her, "all you need to do is be there for him. Tell him that you'll be there to support his decision if he wants to work somewhere else. Let him know that you love him, that's important. Don't forget, this is all new to Darnell. It's going to take some time for him to adjust to working a normal nine to five."

"Thanks, Ray," Shemone said as she got up to get her coat. "I'm gonna go home right now and tell him that."

"You go do that, girl," Ohija told her. She struggled to get on her feet.

Raymond stood and helped his wife up.

"Now I want you guys to call me if you need anything," Shemone told them before she walked out the door.

"How about starting an account to fund our children's college education?" Ray joked.

"Ray, will you stop playing around?" Ohija said to her husband, giving him a gentle nudge.

"I'm not playing. Do you know how much it costs to put a kid through college these days?" Ray chuckled.

"Good night, Shemone," Ohija told her, trying not to laugh.

"Good night, you two, I love you guys," Shemone said on her way down the stairs. She admired the love that Ray and Ohija shared. Even in what seemed to be the worst of times, they were still able to give her relationship advice. They would be the ones. She couldn't have found a better source.

"We love you, too," they both answered at the same time.

Shemone got into her SUV and slipped Faith Evans into her CD player. She turned the volume down and used her cell phone to call home and see if Darnell had gotten in. Hmph, Shemone thought to herself, nothing but the answering machine. She decided to go and pick up some dinner. She stopped by a Chinese restaurant, and got an order of shrimp egg foo yung and an order of beef and broccoli, thinking that they wouldn't have to hunt in the refrigerator for old leftovers tonight.

Shemone strolled through the door of her apartment with fresh flowers and the good-smelling bags of food. She dropped the mail on the table. Darnell still wasn't home, and there weren't any messages on the answering machine, inside the bedroom, from him. Most likely, he was at his mother's, she thought. She couldn't imagine that Darnell would be out too late since he had to get up and prepare for work the next morning. Shemone went to take a shower and slipped into her newest purchase from Frederick's of Hollywood, an all-black number complete with stockings and garter belt. Then she set the table up with candles and wine. Next, the petals of the pink roses, which she scattered about, from the living room to the bedroom and finally onto the bed. As a final touch, she slipped her Faith Evans CD from the car into the home CD player. Darnell was in for a surprise tonight, one he wouldn't be able to turn down.

Four hours later made her think very differently. "Where in the hell is this man? This is crazy," Shemone said to herself loudly. The candles were burning down, the food would have to be reheated, and Faith was growing tired of singing. Shemone decided to call him on his cell phone.

"The tel-subscriber you have called is unavailable. Please try your call again later," the recording said to her.

It was 11:30 P.M. according to her clock, and she was starting to get worried. Suppose Darnell had been in an accident? Or maybe he had gotten himself into some kind of trouble. She followed her first instinct, and went into her phone book to get his mother's number, thinking he might be there.

"Hello, is this Miss Louise?" Shemone asked.

"Yes? Who is this?" Darnell's mother asked in a sleepy tone of voice.

"I know it's late, and I'm sorry to disturb you. It's Shemone, Darnell's girlfriend."

Miss Louise's voice cracked. "Oh, yeah, sugar, how are you? Is there something wrong?"

"I was just calling to see if you'd seen or heard from Darnell. He's usually home by now," Shemone explained.

"Well, baby, he was here. I don't know where that boy is now. He could be anywhere," she told her. "But don't you worry yourself none. I'm sure he's all right," she said.

Shemone thought that his mother spoke as if what she was saying was the gospel. "Thank you, Miss Louise, and sorry to wake you," she replied.

"No problem. Don't you be no stranger now, you hear?"

"Yes," Shemone answered, "we'll have to get together again soon. Good night." Shemone went into the dining area and blew out the candles. Then she put the food back in its containers and placed it inside the refrigerator. She supposed he was all right. There was no use in worrying about a grown man.

Shemone's alarm clock sounded off loudly the following morning. She reached over to her night table and cut it off, both eyes still closed. "Darnell, it's time to get up for work," she murmured, patting his side of the bed. After opening her eyes, she saw for herself that Darnell really wasn't there, sleeping next to her. Shemone instantly hopped out of bed and put on her robe. She walked into the bathroom, then checked the living room and kitchen just to be certain she wasn't losing it.

"Well, I'll be damned, Darnell hasn't been home all night," she said. Just then the telephone rang. "That's probably him calling with some excuse right now," Shemone said as she went to pick up the receiver. "Hello," she said with attitude.

"Hello, Shemone, this is Jane."

"Oh, hi, Jane, glad you called. The story is on its way to you. Can you give me fifteen to warm up the fax?" Her voice went up, shielding the disappointment that it hadn't been Darnell.

"Sure, no problem. Call you later?"

"Okay, then. Good-bye, Jane." Shemone hung up the phone and went into her home office to turn on the fax and send the story out as she had promised. She was a woman of her word. Too bad all people weren't. True to their word, that is. Darnell hadn't come in all night, and it had her playing the guessing game. Was he back to his old ways just that quickly? Out there, in the streets somewhere? Avoiding her, avoiding work. Avoiding hearing her mouth shooting off at him for staying out. Shemone thought that sooner or later he'd have to confront her. For now, one thing didn't have anything to do with the other. She had her own work to do, enough to keep her busy for weeks.

"Shemone, this is Darnell. It's around nine A.M. I just wanted to let you know that I'm okay. I just needed a minute to get myself together. I need to sort through some things on my own," Darnell said into the phone. "I'm gonna be at my mom's for a few days." *Beeeeeep,* the answering machine sounded. The red light blinked brightly while Shemone was in the shower.

28

Bye and Bye

Ray, come on now, they're calling us," Ohija said Tuesday afternoon, taking hold of her husband's arm.

"I'm on my way," Raymond breezily answered as he lagged behind his wife.

Ray's oncologist, Dr. Berg, had phoned and asked them both to come in and discuss the test results.

"Follow me," the nurse told them. She led them down the orange-painted hallway and into the examining room. "You can change into a robe, and Dr. Berg will be right with you," she said before she left.

"I can't stand hospitals," Raymond told Ohija.

"I know, baby," she answered, helping Raymond out of his clothing and into the blue hospital robe.

"I don't know why he couldn't just give us the results over the phone. The results are still going to be the same," Ray said.

"I'm sure he has his reasons, Ray," Ohija replied.

"Dumb reasons," Raymond muttered. "Doesn't he know that I have a family to support? If I keep taking days off work, I'll never be able to."

Ohija didn't say anything. She was going to let her husband say whatever he needed to in order to feel better. He was just nervous, and although she wasn't showing it outwardly, she was, too.

"Good morning, Ray, good morning, Ohija," Dr. Berg said as he entered the office. At fiftysomething, Dr. Berg stood at what looked to be six feet tall. He was monochromatic from head to toe. From his neatly groomed salt-and-pepper hair and beard, to his white medical coat and pants, down to his feet, on which he wore beat-up gray sneakers.

"Good morning." Ohija was the only one to reply.

"Looks like those babies are popping," he said to her.

"Yes, Doctor, it's already getting to be quite a load to tote around," she replied.

"And, Ray, how are you today?" he asked, realizing that his patient hadn't spoken to him yet.

"Terrific," Ray answered in a sarcastic tone of voice. "Just terrific. Let's not waste time. Just give it to me straight, Doc. Am I gonna live or not?"

"Well, why don't I examine you first, and see how the vitals are doing?" Dr. Berg said with a cheerful smile. He listened to Ray's heartbeat. "Breathe in, Ray."

Ray breathed in.

"Now breathe out."

Ray breathed out.

"Sounds strong," the doctor told him.

Ohija looked on closely, hoping for the best.

Dr. Berg took Ray's blood pressure. "Well, everything appears to be fine with your vitals."

"That's good to hear," Ohija replied.

Dr. Berg went to his desk and jotted down some notes. "Have a seat, please," he told them. "As you know, I called you in to discuss the results of your DRE, or digital rectal exam," Dr. Berg told them both. "Unfortunately, the results came back as inconclusive, and the results from your PSA, or prostate specific antigen, blood tests came back as suspicious. So what we want is to run further tests on you today, Raymond."

"Is that the transrectal ultrasound?" Ohija asked Dr. Berg.

"Right. I see someone's been doing her reading. Now as far as we can tell, Ray has not tested positive for prostate cancer." Dr. Berg paused. "But we'd like to be sure."

"That leaves us right where we started out, then," Raymond said in an exasperated tone of voice.

"Not really. Until your tests come back positive, we just won't know. And that could be a good sign."

"So what if I do have cancer? Then what?" Raymond sat with his head slightly hung down. Ohija took hold of his hand.

"There are several treatments, but it depends on a number of factors. The stage of your cancer, if you do have it, and, of course, the risks and benefits."

"What types of treatments are there, Dr. Berg?" Ohija asked.

Dr. Berg crossed his legs and spoke as he looked up from Ray's medical chart. "There's surgery, which we refer to as the radical prostatectomy. That's when we remove the prostate and some of the surrounding tissue. Then there's radiation therapy, which you might already be more familiar with, where we use radiation to kill the cancer cells." Dr. Berg continued, "And last, there's hormone therapy, where we give the patient hormones, and administer drugs that cause the cancer cells to shrink."

Ray sighed. "Thank you, Doctor, I believe we've heard enough. Let's just see how the tests come back so I can know what to do, and move on with my life."

"But, Ray—we need to know all we can about this disease."

Raymond looked over at his wife sternly.

Ohija kept quiet.

"Well, then, why don't we start the testing?" Dr. Berg said as he got up from his chair.

"Yes, let's start the testing." Raymond squeezed Ohija's hand. It was his way of letting her know that he hadn't meant to be short with her. "How long will it take to get the results back?"

"Not long," Dr. Berg answered. "The test itself will be a bit uncomfortable at first, but it is generally painless, and we should be done in about twenty minutes."

"Let's do this," Raymond said.

"Can I stay with him, Doctor?" Ohija asked.

"I don't see why not," Dr. Berg told her.

Ohija forced a brave smile.

* * *

"Hey, Ohija, it's Shemone."

"Hey, girl," Ohija answered into the telephone later that same evening.

"I've been trying to call you all day," Shemone told her friend as she tapped at her computer.

"I'm sorry, girl. Today was Ray's doctor's appointment. We were there all day even though it was only supposed to take a few minutes. They needed to retest Ray on some other things," Ohija said.

"Okay, then," Shemone answered. "So, Ray's done with the tests?"

"Yeah," Ohija replied, "at least for today he is."

"So, how did everything go?" Shemone asked her.

"So far—okay," Ohija said. "The first tests came back as being inconclusive."

"Well, you know what they say, no news is good news."

"Mm-hmm," Ohija agreed. "We're hoping for the best. Ray's acting like he's dead already. Talking about wills and stuff."

"Well, Ohija, it is important to have those matters in order." Shemone added, "Whether he's sick or not."

"Yes, that is true."

"So where's Ray at now?"

"In the bedroom, lying down in bed watching the game. We get the results back in three days, over the telephone."

"That's quick," Shemone answered.

"I hear you tapping over there, keeping yourself busy. You're working on a story, aren't you?"

"You know I am."

"Mmph," Ohija mumbled. "Any news about Darnell? It's been a couple of days. I'm starting to get worried. He's my friend, too."

"Believe me, I realize that it's been two days," Shemone told her. A total of forty-eight hours and fifty-five minutes to be exact, she thought to herself. She wasn't about to let on about what Darnell's odd disappearance was doing to her. Ohija had enough to worry about as it was. "Oh, I didn't talk to you, you weren't home. That's why I left you a message," Shemone told her. "He called."

"He did?" Ohija exclaimed. "Why didn't you say something sooner?"

"Because you were talking about Ray, and because he called and left me a message saying that he was all right. He said that he needed to sort through some things on his own." Shemone continued, speaking in an airy tone of voice, "So, I'm going on with my schedule. Frankly, it's allowed me to accomplish plenty of work." Shemone resumed her typing. "You know how self-sufficient I am, girl," she told her.

"Mm-hmm," Ohija replied in a cynical tone of voice.

"I mean, don't get me wrong or anything, I do care about Darnell. I'm glad to know that he is okay and safe at his mother's."

"Well, I suppose so," Ohija replied. "You do miss him, though, don't you?" Ohija asked her.

Shemone ceased typing. Her work suddenly didn't seem as appealing as the thought of seeing Darnell home again. "Of course I miss him. What kind of question is that?" she asked Ohija. She thought to herself that she had never been good at concealing things from her friend. And then Shemone just burst out with everything all at once, everything she missed about Darnell. "I miss him leaving his stupid million pairs of jeans, shirts, and underwear all over. I miss him scavenging through the fridge at all hours of the day and night, and I miss being with him and laughing at all the dumb jokes he makes," she admitted aloud.

"Then what are you waiting for?" Ohija asked. "Go and get your man and work it out, girl!"

"Get my man? I couldn't!" Shemone said. After thinking about it, she said, "You know, I should. I should go over there to his old neighborhood and get him!"

"That's my girl," Ohija told her in a supportive tone of voice. "You need me to come along with you?"

"No, I'll be fine," Shemone replied. "Your place is with Ray right now. I can do this alone."

"Okay, but you had better keep me posted."

"I will," Shemone said, "and thanks, girl. I appreciate having you in my life."

"Me, too," Ohija replied.

Shemone drove to Darnell's old neighborhood that same night. She rarely made it over to that part of town, not since Darnell had brought her there, and before that, not since she was a teenager. Most of her friends had moved on and out into different areas of the world. Shemone thought to herself as she glanced through the driver's-side window that her block was so much cleaner. The area had improved, but it wasn't quite there yet. Garbage still littered the streets, and folks loitered outside around the apartment buildings. But there were improvements. A lot of construction projects were going on. Shemone made a mental note to look into purchasing a brownstone as an investment property for herself some day. It wouldn't be long before the entire neighborhood would do a one-eighty.

Some of the people still had a ways to go, though. People stared at her as she drove through their streets in her SUV. She paid them no attention, focusing only on the reason for her journey uptown. Thankfully, the sign for the Stratford housing complex where Darnell's mother lived came into view. Shemone parked as close to the building as she could, then, after putting the anti-theft club on the steering wheel and activating the car alarm, set off.

A group of young black men was fast approaching.

"Hey, miss, looking for me?" one of the guys asked. He tried to stare her down.

"You got a lucky man, baby," another one said.

"That SUV is it. I'm gonna have mines next year, no doubt," another one said.

"Keep dreaming, kid," the first guy told him.

Shemone knew better than to reply as she walked in front of them. She kept going toward her destination, thinking that maybe it hadn't been such a clever idea for her to come out alone. She held on tightly to her pocketbook, and reprimanded herself for not leaving her wallet at home. The night wind stung her face and her shoes made a sound as she walked across the concrete pavement. *Clickety-click. Clickety-click. Clickety-click.* Her mother had once told her that you could tell expensive shoes by the sound they made. Damn. She walked like money, even if her shoes had been purchased as a hot deal through a sample sale, she thought to herself. Shemone walked into the building and pulled on the gated entrance door. It was open. She rang the bell once she was inside the vestibule, but got no answer. Shemone was just about to leave when a woman exiting the elevator approached her.

"You looking for somebody?" the woman asked.

Shemone thought her face looked familiar. Oddly familiar. It was the woman from Shark's bar, Hope. Shemone cordially replied, "Yes, as a matter of fact, I am looking for Darnell." She tried to make it appear as though she wasn't looking too hard for him.

"Is that right? So you came slumming to look for your man, huh?" Hope asked in a heavy sistah-girl tone of voice. "What's wrong, can't keep him at home?" she added with a sly grin.

"Have you seen him or not?" Shemone asked. She wasn't the least bit afraid of this woman, or what she had to say.

"No, and if I had, I wouldn't tell you," Hope replied, cutting her eyes, and swaying her head back and forth.

"Then we don't have anything else to talk about," Shemone said right back, walking away from the building. She briefly glanced over her shoulder to see if Hope was anywhere on her heels, but she wasn't. Hope was still back at the building, running her mouth a mile a minute to some other woman. Shemone thought to herself that the conversation had to be about her and her trip uptown. It didn't matter either way. She walked the desolate block, back in the direction of her car. A bald, dark-skinned heavyset man was making his way toward her. Shemone's heart sped up as she debated whether or not to go in the opposite direction. His footsteps quickened. He pushed his hands deep in his pockets and gazed directly at her. It was Pop.

"Shemone?"

"Pop?" she asked, relieved to find that it was someone she knew.

"What are you doing out here at this time of night by yourself?" Pop asked her.

"I'm trying to find out if Darnell is at his mother's," Shemone told him. "He hasn't been home in days."

"Damn," Pop replied in a shocked tone of voice. "I haven't spoken to him in about a week. I know that he started that new job. I just thought a brotha' was tired from working. I know how things can get." Pop rubbed his two hands together. "Damn, it's chilly! How did you get up here, a cab?"

"No, I drove," she answered.

"Your SUV?" Pop asked. He had ridden in the cleanly kept car several times before with Darnell. It would be a prime target for car thieves in the neighborhood who didn't recognize the vehicle as being familiar.

Shemone nodded yes.

Pop chuckled. "Yo, Shemone, you better get back to your car. I can put feelers out on D. for you to follow up. You should have just called me instead of coming out here trying to be some kind of female superhero."

"I know," Shemone answered. "I was just worried. It's not like him."

"So you checked over his mom's house already?" Pop asked.

"Yes, I just came from his building. I rang the bell, but I didn't get any answer," she replied.

"Oh, okay," Pop told her. He thought to himself that Darnell was probably staying with Miss Louise, but just hadn't been in the house when Shemone buzzed. "That's not like D. to be disappearing on you like that," he said, knowing how much his friend really cared about Shemone. She was all he ever talked about.

"This way, my car is over this way," Shemone said, starting off in the direction of where she was parked. During the short trek, she asked herself how Pop would know what wasn't like Darnell when it came to her.

The same group of young guys she'd encountered stood next to her SUV. It was unclear whether they were trying to do anything to it or not.

"See what I mean? Perfect timing," Pop told her, referring to whether or not the group had been plotting. He knew them all, but wouldn't trust any of them once his back was turned.

"Pop, that's you?" one of the guys asked.

He slapped him five. "Nah, this is D.'s girl," he told them. "But we peoples."

Shemone made sense of what they'd said. She had been around Darnell long enough to pick up the latest street lingo. They wanted to know if she was Pop's girlfriend. Pop said no, but that they were close friends.

"Yeah, that D.'s a lucky man," the same guy who'd spoken to her before told Pop.

Shemone got into her car, and the group of guys walked off down the street.

"Shemone, go straight home," Pop told her as he stood outside the driver's-side window. "Enough of this *Murder She Wrote* shit," he joked.

Shemone laughed. "Okay, I promise, I'm going home."

Pop told her, "Good. I'll let you know when I hear something."

"Thank you, Pop," Shemone said, and with that she pulled off. She could see Pop nodding his head. He probably thought she was out of her mind. Shemone set off down the street thinking that maybe she was.

29

Bread Pudding

Shemone was glad to be back home, safe inside the confines of her own apartment building, Tuesday night. As she rode the elevator on its way up, she wanted to break down. This wasn't supposed to be happening, she thought. Not when she hadn't done anything wrong. Not when she'd taken a chance on loving like this, and not when she'd trusted so hard in her own judgment. She opened the door to her apartment and went in and said in an exasperated tone of voice, "Darnell, where are you?" She wasn't expecting him to be there, or to actually answer her.

"I'm in the bedroom," he said.

Shemone could hardly believe her ears. She followed the voice that led her to the bedroom.

Darnell was inside, sitting down on the foot of the bed, bent down and holding his face in his hands.

"What is this all about?" she asked him.

Darnell looked up at her. "I'm sorry, baby-girl. I've been going through something. I wasn't sure how you were gonna handle it," he answered.

"Darnell, get over here and give me a hug," she told him. She was happy to see him, and didn't care what he was doing in that instant.

Darnell came over and held her tightly. "I'm so sorry, baby-girl."

"But what happened?" Shemone stood back from him and asked. "Now I can kill you," she said. "I just left your old neighborhood."

"You did? You and who?" he asked her.

"Me, myself, and I," Shemone answered boldly. "No one else was there."

"Baby-girl! You didn't." Darnell sighed. He couldn't imagine her going through his neighborhood all by herself in the dead of night. "The doorbells are broken," he told her. "The management people have been promising to fix them for weeks," he said.

"You had me worried," Shemone said. "You went and did a disappearing act on me. Darnell, this is my life, not a Terry McMillan story," she told him. And that Miss Hope never said a word about the bells being broken, Shemone thought to herself, betting that Hope had known all along.

Darnell looked directly at her. "That's why I came back, to face up to things," he said. "Shemone, I quit my job at the packing company. It was like, when I left for work that morning, I knew that I wasn't going back there again. It was like, it just wasn't me."

"I know, Darnell, I called them the day after to see if you went in. They told me that you didn't work there anymore," she said.

Just then the phone rang. Shemone hadn't planned to get it, but she decided to answer it anyway.

"Hello?"

"Hey, Shemone, it's Ohija."

Shemone expelled air. "Girl, he's home safe," she said.

Ohija heaved a sigh of relief. "You found him?"

"Not exactly, he kind of found his way back, on his own," she said, smiling.

"For real? Mmph," Ohija remarked, "I was about to go after you. I should have gone with you to look for him in the first place. I care about what happens to that man, too. Just let him know that for me."

"I was okay," Shemone explained. "I ran into Pop. Everything worked out. And Darnell knows that you care about what happens to him, too," she added.

Darnell nodded his head in the background. "I sure do, that's love right back at her," he replied.

Ohija chuckled knowingly. "Well, I'll let you get back to him then. That's good enough for me. Knock him up side the head once for me, too," she told her.

Shemone smiled. "Thanks, girl, I will. I'll talk to you tomorrow. 'Bye."

Darnell spoke after she had hung up the phone. "So you saying you knew that I quit?"

"Yes," Shemone said. She sat down on the bed. "But why did you go to your mom's house?"

Darnell sat next to her. "Because I knew I could, without a problem. And without having to explain why. It's just the way it's always been between us. She's my mother," he said.

Shemone tried to be understanding. "You could have just told me that you wanted to leave the job." She stood up. "I'm not sure what to say. You're not the only one who can be a good listener, you know."

Darnell found something to say. He wasn't ready for things to be over between them if that's where she was heading. "I am trying, baby-girl, that's why I went and got my job back today. I told my boss that I was out on a family emergency. Lucky for me, he went for it. My boss decided to give me another shot. He said that he didn't want to lose me because I'm a hard worker."

"Yes, well, I suppose I can't give up on you. Not as long as you're not giving up on yourself, I won't," Shemone told him.

"I hope you never do," Darnell replied. He wanted to take the opportunity to open up and talk, since she was willing to listen. "It's not easy being with a headstrong woman like you. It's like," Darnell continued, "you don't really need me. You have no idea how much I wanted to tell you about me hating my job, from that first day. I thought to myself, where does that leave you when my stash runs out?" Answering his own question, he replied. "On your own again, that's where. You'd been paying your own bills and everything before I ever came along, and now it's like I'm trying to find my place as your man."

"A relationship is more than paying bills, Darnell," Shemone told him.

"Your mother doesn't feel that way. She hates me," he said.

"My mother hates herself," Shemone replied.

"Whoa," Darnell responded in a shocked tone of voice. He wasn't expecting Shemone to say that her own mother hated herself. He thought, That's some real lie-down-on-a-couch-and-talk-to-a professional shit.

"We're both going through adjustments with this relationship," Shemone told him. "But I am learning that you have to make the most out of what life gives you, and then work on making it what you want it to be. Darnell, nothing happens overnight. It took me a while to get to where I am today," Shemone said. "I'm glad that you went and got your job back."

"Yeah, and that's why I'm holding on to that packing job even though I still don't like it. I'm going to make it work for me just like you said, until I can get something better. I think better is on its way soon," he told her, smiling, going into more detail. "See, my younger brother, James, won a contest at school. He got a computer. It's real cool. It's, like, a candy-apple red, and it's got speakers and this same CD thing that you have." Darnell got up and showed her on her PC. He sat at the desk in front of it.

"Really?" Shemone replied with interest.

"You know how you always trying to get me to go on your computer and mess around on it?"

"Yes," Shemone answered.

"Well, James taught me how to use it. And while he was in school, I was on it all the time." Darnell grinned proudly. "Baby-girl, you wouldn't believe, I even know how to use the Internet now."

"You're kidding!" Shemone shrieked. She couldn't believe it.

"That's how I found out about the program," he told her.

"Darnell, no! You found a program on your own?"

"Yes, I did. I was"—he excitedly tapped on the computer monitor, trying to jog his memory—"what do you call it, riding the Net?"

"You mean that you were surfing the Net?" she asked.

"Yeah, right, surfing the Net." Darnell caught his breath. "I'm sorry, baby. I'm just so amped right now."

"It's okay, take your time and tell me. I'm not going anywhere," she assured him.

Darnell anxiously continued, "Yeah, so, I was surfing the Net and I came across someplace where they offer ex-cons a way back into society. They ask what you want to do in, like, your career and stuff."

"Go ahead," Shemone told him, wanting to hear more.

"Well, they, like, lead you through the steps to make it happen, so I hurried up and went to sign up." Darnell grinned. "I'm registered and everything. It's right around here, a few blocks away. The best part is that they're offering a course that teaches you everything you need to know to be an electrician. I already got me a counselor, Mr. Lane," he said. "He told me I can go part-time and still work. And that I'd get money for going, 'cause it's a government-based program. And—they help you with job placement!"

"Darnell, that's wonderful!" Shemone said. She threw both arms around his neck and gave him a big hug.

He let go of her embrace only to take her hands in his. "I must seem all mixed up, job wise, to you. Starting out wanting to do music when I was younger, then the refinishing gig, which would have been okay if I had gotten the job." Darnell's voice took on a strong tone as he continued. "But I really do want to be an electrician. I'm sure about this."

"Then do it!" Shemone said, encouraging him. "You can do whatever you put your mind to. It's not like you don't already know how to fix things. I've seen that for myself." She thought about the computer and the clock, the DVD, the lamp. Eventually there had been the toaster, and the broken kitchen outlet.

"Baby-girl, there's so much I want, and so much I want to tell you. I'm looking forward to my future," he told her.

"And I wanna hear everything you have to say about your future, Darnell." She pushed her body into his, taking the initiative to stick her tongue in his ear. His overwhelming decisiveness was a major aphrodisiac.

"Oooh, baby-girl, don't do that," Darnell warned. "You know how that gets me all open." He slowly lifted himself up from the chair, in a way that would not interrupt Shemone and her moves on him.

"Get open, baby, I want you to get open," Shemone urged, pursuing him even more as she stuck her tongue down deeper into his ear.

Darnell stepped out of his pants and underwear. His T-shirt stayed on. He'd warned Shemone to stop. It made him savagelike in the way that he pulled off Shemone's top, sucking wildly back and forth on her breasts. Grabbing her fingers, he placed them erotically in his mouth while removing her pants and underwear. Shemone screamed out in high notes of pleasure. She'd missed his touch, but not for long. Darnell lifted her from the floor, entering her while she was up in the air. Shemone breathed in deep, short gasps as Darnell pumped up and down, up and down. She wrapped her legs around him, clawing feverishly at his back. Each held on tightly to the other, as if life itself depended on it. It was a physical agreement that said they never wanted to be separated unnecessarily from each other again. Darnell made a deep, throaty moan, pumping even faster until he exploded, bringing them both down onto the bed, and into the realm of bliss.

"I love you," Darnell told her as he lay under her. "I mean it, baby-girl. I love you, and I'm glad to be back home."

"I love you, too," Shemone replied in a satisfied tone of voice. Their lovemaking had been wild and sporadic, yet truly emotional.

"So how's Ray making out?" Darnell asked as he turned over on the bed onto his stomach. His naked body was wrapped up in the sheets.

"Ray is doing okay, he's still getting tests," Shemone answered as she moved in closer to him. She lay across his back. She noticed the set of lengthy scratches she'd made during the heat of their lovemaking. A sistah had been into some serious loving. It must not have bothered Darnell, because he'd never said anything about feeling them at all.

"It must be pretty hard on Ohija right now, with her being pregnant and everything," he told Shemone.

"Yeah, it is, but you know Ohija. She's strong."

"She sure is," Darnell replied. "Shemone?"

"Yes, Darnell?"

"Do you think Ray's gonna make it?" he asked. "I'm saying he's not that old. It can't be his time to go yet."

Shemone stayed quiet for a bit. She thought about Ray, and she thought about why she loved this man next to her so much. The man who undeniably had a soft side for the people he really cared about. She answered Darnell's question about whether she thought Ray was going to make it as best she could, only she couldn't. All she could say was, "I only wish I knew."

Darnell sighed. "I feel like I want to do something to help."

"Like what?" Shemone asked.

"I don't know, just something. I think I'm gonna call Ray and ask him if he wants to go hang out with me." Darnell figured Ray could use some guy time. Something that would make him forget about being sick for a while.

"That might be nice," Shemone told him.

"I just hope that he pulls through this thing okay," Darnell said.

"So do I, Darnell, so do I," Shemone answered.

Darnell had turned around to hold her. He was snuggling, yet he was holding on to her so close. He thought to himself that there was no way he could ever imagine having to give up someone after you'd discovered that they were your soul mate.

30

Male Bonding

Pass the barbecue!" Darnell told Pop on Saturday as the three men sat at the table of the Barbecue Shack, or the Shack, as it was otherwise called. The restaurant sold some of the best hickory-smoked barbecued food that one could buy. It wasn't a big place. Its decor was quite predictable. There was paneling on the walls, picnic-style red-and-white-checkered tablecloths, rounded tables, and simple wooden chairs.

"All right, calm down, D., a brother's acting like he don't eat!" Pop joked.

"That's because I don't!" Darnell replied. He helped himself to the tender-cut pieces of barbecued ribs from the platter and continued, "It's not like it's a secret. Everybody here knows that I'm in love with Ms. Take-out herself."

Laughter went around the table.

"Ray, man, I'm just glad that you were able to come," Darnell told him while taking a big bite of rib. Ray's whole experience was making Darnell think about what a changed man he was becoming. In the old days, when he'd been running the streets, he would never have cared about someone like he was doing now. His enemies could have firmly attested to that. "Yeah, it took us a while, but we finally made it out." He had been trying to get together for over a week since he'd talked to Shemone about doing something special for Ray. What made him push even more was that Shemone had found out that Ray's tests had come back positive for what the doctors called an irregularity with his digital rectal exam.

"Yeah, it's good for the fellas to get out sometimes and vent, too," Pop added. He speared a forkful of thick-cut french-fried potatoes. "All that *Waiting to Exhale* shit! All you gotta do is just breathe through your nose!"

Ray couldn't help but laugh.

"Speaking of movies, how did you like the movie we saw tonight?" Darnell turned to Ray and asked, trying to get him to open up.

"Oh, I enjoyed it very much. That Chris Tucker is one funny guy." Ray chuckled as if he was remembering a comical part from the film. "This is real cool, the movie and dinner thing. I can't remember the last time I had ribs." He added, "Ohija isn't really big on red meat. I like it because it really sticks to your bones, especially after putting in a hard day's work."

"True, true," Darnell and Pop agreed, nodding their heads in unison.

"So, how is work?" Darnell asked. "Things haven't gotten to be too much, have they? I mean, are you still able to maintain yourself physically and everything?"

"Work is okay, and yeah, I'm still out slinging those garbage bags. It's just sometimes that I get pains in my lower back, or in my upper thighs," Ray told them.

"So your job doesn't know yet?" Darnell asked.

Ray had to take time out to think before he could reply. "You know, I've been working for sanitation for seven years, and it's like I still don't know what to say." He mocked the way he would tell his boss: "'Oh, listen, by the way, I might have prostate cancer.' It just doesn't sound right. Plus, I'm still getting tested. The final step is for me to have a biopsy, which is a small tissue sample."

"Word?" Pop asked as he looked, surprised, over at Ray. Darnell had mentioned that Ray was sick, but he hadn't said with what. He'd never known anyone with prostate cancer before, and wasn't one for disguising his feelings. "Then you'll know if you have it for sure?"

"Yeah," Ray told them.

Darnell interrupted, feeling the urge to explain. "Ray, I hope you're not mad that I brought up the how-you-feeling topic, especially around Pop. I just wanted us all to hang out together." He added, "And it's not like Pop's a stranger, he's one of my best friends."

"It's okay," Ray assured him. "I don't mind that he knows. I think it helps me to come to grips with what's happening. It could happen to any man."

The table was silent as both Pop and Darnell thought about it happening to them.

Ray took a bite of the still-warm corn bread. "It's real important to have people in your corner."

"But you don't have to worry about that, Ray, you've got Ohija. Man, I've known her for years. That's a strong woman behind you. She's like family to me. She helped to get me out of a lot of jams back when we were in high school." Darnell took a sip from his oversize glass of root beer.

"Oh, that I know," Ray agreed. "But who wants their woman to take on all that responsibility?"

"Right, right," Pop replied.

"You got a point there," Darnell agreed. Of course he could relate, but in a different way. He had school and his packing job, but dollars and cents wise, he still wanted to be able to bring in more money. Shemone had said that money wasn't everything in the relationship, but she didn't know what it was like to be a man. One who wanted to provide more, and be the breadwinner. Darnell continued, "I had a conversation with Pop about that. I know damn well that I'm not pulling in money like I want to." He skillfully finished the meat on his rib, then began chewing on the gristle part of the bone. Barbecue sauce was getting all over the oversize bib he had on. "Shit, I can barely afford to keep up with my half of Shemone's monthly living expenses. That makes me feel like less sometimes. It's a lot to live up to."

"But, D., you're striving," Pop interjected. "You out there doing your thing. You're in a program and you have a job." Pop nudged Ray on the arm. "A lot of people don't have that."

Ray nodded. "Pop is right, Darnell. Now, I know I'm a little bit older than you guys, but there's a lot we can all relate to in just being a man."

Darnell knew that the guys were right. He'd tried to leave Shemone before, when he'd felt himself coming up short, ego wise, but love just wouldn't let him. Honestly, he thought, if it wasn't for her, he wouldn't be able to say that he had a career to focus on now. Darnell had to repeat it to himself again, it sounded so good. Him, with a career as an electrician. And with Shemone by his side, he'd make her his wife-to-be. The thought of it was definitely crossing his mind.

Just then the waitress came over. A shapely sistah with a short black Caesar hairdo. Her apron hugged her in all the right places, wide hips and thick thighs blessed her with a walk to go with it. "Can I get you handsome boys another round of ribs?" she asked.

"As long as you're here to serve them up, you can," Pop replied with a flirty smile.

"Okay, one more round of ribs coming up." The waitress returned the smile tenfold, for the hefty tip that she was expecting to get. She walked away, and the three men's eyes closely followed as she went to the back to get their order.

"See, that's what I'm talking about," Ray said. "We all like to look."

"Right, just as long as we don't touch," Darnell added.

"I'm saying ain't no crime or nothing like that," Pop chimed in.

Ray asked, "So, Pop, what about you? We're all putting our cards out on the table, what's your gripe with life?"

Pop took a minute and thought. "I don't know. I guess, you know, just trying to better myself, and wanting more out of life. You know, the usual things. I'd like to get married and make it official one day. Maybe have another kid and a big house somewhere." Pop munched on a rib. "It just ain't happening yet."

"Okay, right," Ray said. "I mean, that's good though. It's good that you set goals for yourself. You-all seem to be pretty mature."

"Thanks, man," Darnell said as he gave Ray a friendly slap on the back. "I appreciate you saying that."

The waitress returned with the next round of ribs.

"Here you go," she said as she laid the huge platter down on the table with one hand.

"Thank you," Darnell told her as he dove in.

"The pleasure is all mine," she answered, showing her teeth.

"Am I the only one eating here?" Darnell asked. He finally looked up from his plate and noticed that both Pop and Ray were staring at him.

"Darnell, read my lips: The food is gone," Pop told him with a laugh.

"You might be needing this," Ray said. He passed Darnell a fresh napkin.

"It's all good," Darnell replied as he laughed along with them. "When I eat, I enjoy my food." Then Darnell thought for a minute. "Pop, call the waitress over here."

"D., for what? Don't tell me you trying to hit on that," Pop said to him.

Ray gave Darnell a look, too. "Yeah, Darnell, you got a keeper at home, man. We all are lucky."

"What are you talking about? I'm trying to get me another order of ribs to take home!" he told them.

Pop, Darnell, and Ray all doubled over with laughter.

"So, dinner and the movie went well?" Shemone asked. She sat up in bed with her glasses on, looking through her date book.

"It sure did. Ray is real cool people," Darnell said. He pulled his sweater off. "I told him that we'd go with him to the doctor's office to find out the test results from his biopsy."

"That was really sweet of you, Darnell." Shemone blew him a wet one from across the room.

"The thing is, that Ray doesn't want anybody to come along. He said that Ohija and him would just let us know when they knew something." Darnell stepped out of his jeans. "I can respect that, they probably need a moment to themselves."

"Probably," Shemone replied. She looked back down, not really able to concentrate on her book. She was thinking about her mother, Ruth, and how short life was to be arguing. There had to be a way that she could have both her mother and her man, and not have to choose.

Darnell got into the bed in just his underwear and T-shirt. "Good night, baby-girl."

"Good night," Shemone told Darnell. No more needed to be said for that night. She knew what she had to do next.

31

WHATEVER WILL BE WILL BE

Baby, we can do this," Ohija told Ray as, days later, she took hold of his hand, following the pale yellow line that led to Dr. Berg's office.

"I'm not afraid," Ray assured his wife. He tightened his fingers around hers.

Dr. Berg sat at his desk looking down and scribbling notes.

"Dr. Berg?" Ohija said. "The floor nurse told us that you would be in here. We've come for Raymond's test results."

Raymond stayed quiet. He calmly pulled up a chair and sat down.

Ohija sat next to him.

"Yes, of course." Dr. Berg looked up. "I'm not going to beat around the bush here." Dr. Berg glanced over at Ray, then down at the papers on his desk before speaking. "Ray's tests came back positive for prostate cancer."

"Oh no!" Ohija said aloud. "Are you sure? Can we retest?" she asked in a shaken tone of voice.

Raymond hung his head low. He hadn't made eye contact with his wife since the doctor had announced the news. Ray thought to himself. What had he done to deserve this? He worked hard, and had never missed a day until recently. He took care of his family, working years on a job that most people wouldn't want, and this is what he got in return?

"Yes, we're sure. We generally run the tests a few times just to make certain." Dr. Berg scribbled in his notes again. "Ray, are you going to be okay?" he asked.

Ray didn't answer.

"Raymond, the doctor's speaking to you, baby, say something." Ohija's eyes welled up with tears, and her face saddened. She reached out for her husband's hand again.

"Yeah, I'm okay," Ray said. He nodded his head slowly in disbelief. "So now what, Doctor?"

"Well, the next step, now that we have a positive diagnosis, is to proceed with a treatment," Dr. Berg explained. "But before we can do that, we need to determine whether or not the cancer has spread."

"So, more tests?" Ray asked. "I don't know how much more of this I can take, Doctor, I've got a family to support."

"Yes, you remember that, honey," Ohija replied, folding her hands on her lap. "You can't get better if you don't get treatment."

"Just one more test," Dr. Berg promised him. "You've been the ideal patient."

Ohija heard Ray mumble something to himself about not having any other choice.

"The test is called an MRI," the doctor told them.

"I think I know what that is," Ray said in a less-than-enthusiastic tone of voice. "I lie down and go through a big machine, right?"

"Exactly," Dr. Berg confirmed. "Then we can go on and treat you, Ray."

"Then that's what we'll do," Ohija said.

Ray shifted uncomfortably in his chair. There was something else he wanted to ask. "Dr. Berg, I've heard that if I have to get my prostate removed . . . I won't be able to—"

"Perform sexually?" Dr. Berg said, completing Ray's sentence. "There have been a number of improvements and advancements in surgical techniques that now allow most patients to maintain normal sexual function."

"Whew!" Raymond sighed in relief.

Ohija tossed her head back and laughed aloud. "Now that's the man I know!" she said.

Even Dr. Berg had to chuckle. "Okay then, we can order the tests to be done ASAP."

"We'll be right here," Ohija told him. "Won't we, Ray?"

Ray could think of a thousand and one places he'd rather be. But Dr. Berg was right there, watching his every move. Ohija was also right there, watching his every move. So much was riding on this. They both were patiently waiting for him to respond. He did the only thing he could in a situation such as his. "Yeah." Ray sighed again, and then answered, "We'll be right here, Doc."

32

Maternal Instincts

Ruth repositioned the string of white pearls that hung loosely around her neck. She stood in front of the wall-length mirror of her Laura Ashley–inspired yellow-and-mauve floral bedroom Wednesday morning. From the outside, she looked perfectly, well, perfect. The two-piece designer plaid skirt and jacket suit complemented her two-tone hair, which was pulled back tightly in a traditional chignon style. In her world, she settled for nothing less than the best. Ruth used her hands to tug up on her face, considering for the first time if she'd ever get a face-lift. Sure, everyone always told her how young she looked, but what she actually saw in the mirror was an altogether different thing.

Her maintenance regimen of manicures, pedicures, and exercise was an absolute must. Ruth longed to recapture the youth and vitality that she'd once had, before she'd had Shemone. It was a time when nothing had sagged, and a time when she actually felt excited about who she was. Now it just wasn't the same. Part of her felt unmotivated. There was a void, and an inner emptiness that remained unfulfilled. The face in the mirror wasn't hers anymore. Just then, she heard someone knocking at the door. It was a welcome distraction.

"Just one moment," Ruth called out from the bedroom. It was probably the car service she'd phoned to take her to the nail salon. Ruth didn't rush. She slipped her coat on, then picked up her purse. When she opened the door, it wasn't who she thought it was. "Shemone," she said in a surprised tone of voice. After that last argument, Shemone was the last person Ruth thought she'd be seeing.

"Hello, Mom," Shemone replied. She stepped inside, just close enough to give her mother a hug.

Ruth stood stiffly, while her daughter held on to her, and said, "Shemone, what are you doing here? You didn't call or anything. It's not like you to just stop by." The hug her daughter gave her struck her as being a little different. Ruth thought that it was probably her daughter's conscience. But to her, Shemone had made her decision already when she'd chosen to have that man, who would only bring her down, in her life.

"No, Mom, I'm not in the habit of just stopping by," Shemone told her. She made her way past her mother, and through the door. "But maybe I should be."

"Shemone, I was just about to go out—" Ruth began to say. "The car service should be here any second now." She added, "In fact, to be honest, this really isn't a good time for me."

"Oh?" Shemone said. "Where are you headed?"

"To the nail salon, I've got an eleven o'clock appointment," Ruth replied.

Shemone looked down at her nails. She could use a coat of polish, she thought to herself. "Great, then I'll just tag along."

"Shemone, you know how particular Kim's Nail Salon is," Ruth told her, trying to discourage her. "They work by appointment only."

"But I'm with you," Shemone replied, getting up from the chair. "You've certainly been going there long enough for them to accommodate your own daughter. I don't think it'll be a problem."

Just then, a silver-gray sedan pulled up directly in front of Ruth's house.

"Oh, good, our ride's here," Shemone told her mother as she peered out the window. "Hope you have everything." She looked straight ahead, and made her way out, toward the car.

Ruth did the only thing she could do. She locked her front door, frowned, and followed Shemore.

Kim's Nail Salon wasn't crowded. Shemone could tell from just walking through the front door. It was empty except for the five employees she'd effortlessly counted on sight. Her mother had exaggerated. Clearly. Shemone turned to look at her mother's facial expression. She wanted to see if guilt was written on it; instead, it was like seeing a blank canvas. Ruth had already seated herself in one of the chairs, seemingly engrossed in her nails and the nail technician.

"Nails done?" an Asian woman asked Shemone.

"Yes, I'll just need to get a new coat of polish, please." Shemone picked out a metallic platinum color. She purposefully sat in the seat next to her mother. "Mom, what do you think of this color?" She held the bottle up for Ruth to see.

"It's—really modern-looking," Ruth replied as she quickly glanced over at her daughter and the bottle of nail polish.

"Thanks," Shemone answered, deciding to take her mother's response as a positive one.

As the nail woman redid her nail wraps, Ruth thought that this child was forcing herself on her. What nerve. The apple sure didn't fall far from the tree. When a Waters woman set her mind to doing something, she did it.

"So how is Beatrice's husband doing?" Ruth asked without looking up from her nails.

Shemone's body felt a jolt. Well, I'll be. I got her, she thought to herself. It wasn't important that she had gotten Ohija's name wrong. "Raymond is holding up, under the circumstances. The tests came back positive for cancer. They're running more now to see if it's spreading." Shemone tried to make eye contact yet again and added, "I'll tell him that you asked about him."

Ruth swallowed hard. "You do that."

Shemone smiled from her chair. "Look, Mom, I've been thinking a great deal lately, just about life in general."

Ruth listened.

"I've come to the conclusion that life is too short to argue, and I don't want us to not get along."

"Dear, no one said that we weren't getting along," Ruth answered in a soft tone of voice.

Shemone gathered that she was on the right track. At least she was "dear" again. "Mom, there's been more of a strain on our relationship, now more than ever, and I think we both know why," Shemone told her. "Or should I say who?"

"I don't think this is the time, or place, for this conversation." Ruth stuck out her pinkie finger. "Make sure to get the cuticles on this one," she instructed the manicurist.

"You're doing a great job," Shemone told her own nail tech. It was interesting to see how so the same, but yet so different, she and her mother were. "It's never going to be the right time or the right place, Mom," she said.

"For heaven's sake, we're in a nail salon, Shemone!" Ruth's voice went up, attracting the attention of the nail workers who knew little English.

Shemone called her mother by her first name, in the hope that she would take her more seriously. "Ruth, I'm making the effort to reach out to you," she said, not caring who heard. "Why don't you just admit it? Darnell is the reason why you're being so distant toward me."

"Hmph, I'm the one being distant?" Ruth asked in a nonchalant tone of voice. "I don't think so." Her daughter had been the one who was always too busy. Her daughter had been the one to take up for that man despite her opinion.

"Yes, you are being distant," Shemone told her. "I took time off from my work to come and see you because you wouldn't take my calls or return any of my messages."

"Please hold still," the nail tech told Shemone as she steadied her hand. It was trembling.

"You know what? Fine," Shemone huffed. She rose from her chair, and pulled a crisp twenty from her front pocket. Her nails were still wet, but she didn't care if they got smudged.

"No finish?" the nail tech asked as she sat looking at Shemone, puzzled.

"Yes, I am finished," Shemone said as she laid the bill down on the table. "Thank you. My mother wants to see what distance is, so I'm going to do her a favor and show her." And with that, she walked out the door.

Ruth sat anchored in her chair. She looked at the door for a long time, continuing to get her nails done.

"Same color, Miss Ruth?" her nail tech asked her, already knowing what her response would be. She'd been a faithful customer for three years, since the salon had first opened.

"Yes," she said with a stone face, "I'll have the same color that I always have."

33

Same-O, Same-O

"Ohija, girl, I could have screamed!" Shemone told her friend over the telephone the next day. "It took everything I had to calm myself down," Shemone said after playing out the episode she'd had in the nail salon with her mother.

"So has she tried to call you?" Ohija asked. She opened the huge denim bag that sat next to her chair. She'd started to learn how to knit, and was well on her way to making each of the twins a blanket.

"I don't see it happening," Shemone replied. "You know how stubborn my mother can be."

Ohija left that one alone. Her mother could be stubborn, and so could Shemone. She let her friend vent.

"I mean, you should have seen me when I went over there. I made that woman spend time with me," she said, referring to her mother. Shemone sipped hard from the straw of her fruit drink and continued, "And just when I thought I had her—everything went wrong, all because I mentioned Darnell." Shemone sipped again. She made a slurping sound.

"Girl, what are you over there doing?" Ohija couldn't help but ask. All of that slurping was throwing her knitting off.

Shemone apologized. "I'm sorry, I'm drinking juice. I think the straw has a hole in it or something. Nothing's coming out."

"Well, get a new one," Ohija replied. She pulled loose the two rows that she had just done. "You're making me mess up my knitting rhythm," Ohija added. "Fix the straw, and fix the relationship with your mother."

"Ohija, have you heard a word of what I've been saying to you? Hellooo—I've been trying to reach out to her. What else am I supposed to do?" Shemone asked with an edge to her voice. "I know you like the world to be, like, picture perfect, and everybody all together and stuff, but it doesn't always work that way."

"Shemone, I'm living through that now. But just because things don't go the way you want, when you want, doesn't mean that it's time to throw in the towel." Ohija gave her the edgy voice right back, which was a rare occurrence. She hardly ever used anger to express her feelings to someone. "Just imagine if I were to do that. Then where would Ray be right now?"

Shemone sighed. "You're right. I apologize again, and again. I'm not gonna give up on my mother."

"Good," Ohija told her. "But do you really think she dislikes Darnell that much? You keep telling me that he's the problem between you two."

Shemone tossed the handicapped straw on the table, and replied, "I don't know what else to go on."

"Hmm . . ." Ohija thought aloud. "It doesn't seem to me that your relationship was so great with your mother even before you and Darnell became an item."

Shemone's call waiting beeped in.

"Can you hold on?" Shemone asked Ohija.

"No, you go on and take the call, I've got to get my clothes ready for my prenatal exam tomorrow anyway," Ohija said. "But think about what I told you."

"I will," Shemone replied. "Thanks, girl," she said before she clicked over to see who was on the other line. "Hello? Hello?" There was no answer on the other end. She hung up the phone, looked at it, then picked it up again, this time dialing *69 to find out who was calling her but not saying anything.

"The number you are trying to call cannot be reached by this method. If you know the number, please dial it directly," the automated male voice told her.

Hell. If she'd known the number she wouldn't have dialed *69, she thought, gently placing the headset back on its cradle. Playing phone games had not been on her to-do list. It was a waste of her time. Shemone sat at her desk and turned her computer on, to review and edit an article before sending it out. She went through it word for word.

HAIR TODAY, GONE TOMORROW

by Shemone Waters

Looking for a change in all the wrong places? Well, then look no further, because there's evidence in the fact that what looks good can feel good in sporting your new 'do. From deep shades of black to bright shades of blonde, you can make a statement that you won't soon forget. So be strong, and muster the nerve to make a trip to a professional stylist. Go ahead, have them take it all off before you have a chance to change your mind. There's no fuss and no muss when it's done the right way. Getting out of your house in the mornings for work can be as easy as applying a good pomade and walking on out the door.

Don't believe it? Then just ask some of the many celebrity artists who have taken a walk on the wild side. Actress extraordinaire Jada Pinkett-Smith, Ruff Ryders rap artist Eve, and *Essence* beauty editor herself, Mikki Taylor, are only some of the few. Most of these cuts do require a weekly visit to the salon for a quick trim, but the upside is that this technique can take less than ten minutes to do. Here are a few things to keep in mind before taking the big plunge:

Make Sure That Your Hair Is in Healthy Condition

Make sure that your hair is in its healthiest state for your most optimum look. This is the rule of thumb for any hairstyle.

Have It Done by a Pro

Don't try to save a few dollars by saving yourself a visit to the salon and cutting your own hair. The results could be something you'll live

to regret. The stylist also knows about shaping, and can help you with finding a particular style based on the contour of your head, i.e., a part on the side.

Maintain Your New Look

Maintenance, maintenance, maintenance! Maintenance is key when deciding to get this new cut, or else, why even bother?

Having kept these helpful tips in mind ensures that you will be at your best 100 percent of the time. So here's to the new you!

Shemone proofed for spelling and grammatical errors. Everything checked out fine. She ran her hands along her own textured short do.

"Boo!" Darnell said as he sneaked up on her from behind.

"Darnell Williams!" Shemone said as she held on to her chest. "You scared me!" she said.

"I know, I wanted to sneak up on you and make sure that you weren't tripping out on me!" Darnell joked as he hugged her tightly around her shoulders.

"Please," Shemone said. "I'm the one who somebody doesn't want to talk to." She wasn't about to make the call an issue. She only wanted to let him know about it. "Someone called here today and hung up on me."

"Oh, yeah?" Darnell replied, thinking that it could have been anybody, anybody who might have just dialed the wrong phone number.

"Yeah," Shemone mocked. "Sure it wasn't one of your women?" she asked, just joking around with him.

"Shemone, don't you even go there. You know you're all the woman I need!" Darnell began to sing and shout, "I come home to my baby every day!"

She had to laugh. "You are such a clown."

"But you love this clown, don't you?"

Shemone grinned. "I don't know why, but I do," she admitted. She knew that it wasn't any other women calling the house for him.

Most likely, it was just a wrong number, she thought to herself; it happens. "You're home early today," she said to him.

"I know, teach let us off early for good behavior," Darnell answered as he looked through his work bag. He was taking out electrical supplies. "I got my tester, switches, outlets, and some wires," he announced proudly. "Everything seems to be in there."

"Those are all of your tools already? You're kidding me," Shemone said.

"Nope, I earned them. The more you learn, the more you get," Darnell told her. "My instructor, Mr. West, told me that I'm one of the best students he has in the class. He said that they shouldn't have one bit of trouble placing me for a job, baby-girl."

"Do tell," Shemone said in a wowed tone of voice.

"So that's why I'm home," Darnell continued. "To get my gold star from you for good behavior."

Shemone smiled and thought to herself that well, she had finished her work for the day. She began to remove her clothes. She made Darnell see a lot of stars that day. Lots of shooting stars.

* * *

"Ray, I'm pleased that you came along with me for my prenatal exam," Ohija said to her husband the following day as they drove home from the doctor's office.

"Honey, they're my kids, too," Ray told her. He was still clothed in his green sanitation worker's uniform. "Sorry I had to come and meet you dressed like this," he said. "It was the only way I could make it on time for your twelve o'clock appointment."

"I'm just happy you were able to be there." Ohija asked him, "So back out to the hospital on Monday for your test results, huh?"

"Yep," Ray answered. He continued to drive. "Back out to the hospital again."

"We're going to make it through this, you know," Ohija reassured him.

"Oh, I know we are," Ray said. He sounded more confident than he ever had.

Ohija was relieved about the change. "Ray, where are we going? This isn't the way home," she told him.

He turned, and then made a left on the following corner. "I know," Ray answered calmly. "We're going to my lawyer's office."

"Since when do you have a lawyer?" Ohija asked.

"Since I found out that I might be dying," Ray answered outright.

Ohija didn't respond, but got out her book of daily affirmations. She felt like she needed to read something positive.

I have learned throughout my life that what really matters is not whether we have problems, but how we go through whatever we are facing.

—ROSA PARKS

Mmph, Ohija thought to herself. That one was right on the mark for today. Her husband was just protecting his family's interests. Ray was doing what he felt he needed to do as a man, and she would be there for him, right there by his side.

"Mr. Edwards, this is my wife, Ohija. Ohija, this is our new attorney, Fred Edwards," Ray said as he introduced the two.

"Pleasure to meet you," he told her. "Please, have a seat."

Ohija and Ray sat down in the burgundy leather chairs that were placed just in front of the huge fancy desk of their lawyer. He swiveled a few times in his own chair, which was twice the size of theirs, before he began speaking.

"Okay, so we're here to go over matters of the last will and testament of Raymond Jones," the attorney told them both.

Ohija felt nauseous, like when she'd first found out that she was pregnant. She leaned for support on the thought of the affirmation that she had just read. Sitting up strong and erect, she convinced herself that she could get through this. Ray seemed to be doing fine, sitting there like a man who was simply handling his business.

"That's correct," Ray said, speaking in a clear and decisive tone of voice. "We're here to go over my will."

The attorney broke it down for them. As Raymond's wife, Ohija would be the sole beneficiary of all of his assets. This included the car, his life insurance, and his job pension. Monies were also to be set aside for the twins' college fund. Ray signed on the dotted line.

"Thank you so much," Ray told Mr. Edwards, giving him a firm handshake as they brought their meeting to a close.

"Yes, thank you," Ohija said, too.

"That's what I'm here for, and good luck to you both," their lawyer replied.

It had been a long day, but Raymond and Ohija were on their way home. "Ray, I'm glad that we went and took care of things today," Ohija told her husband.

"I am too, honey." Ray smiled widely. He felt the best that he'd felt in a long time, despite the circumstances.

34

The High Life

Darnell woke up and got out of the bed early Saturday morning. He'd decided that he was going to go and get a haircut, and maybe shoot a few hoops with his boys over in Stratford. He looked around the room for Shemone. "Baby-girl," he called out. He didn't get any answer, so he yelled out again, thinking that she might have been in the shower, or busy somewhere in the kitchen. "Baby-girl!" There was still no answer. Darnell dragged himself into the kitchen. There was a handwritten note attached by a magnet to the fridge.

Darnell, went out shopping to
the Price Club Warehouse for
food. Will see you later.
P.S. Saved you a croissant for breakfast.
Love,
Shemone

"Croissant?" Darnell pouted as he opened the refrigerator. It was empty except for a few old cartons of take-out. "Dang!" Darnell said loudly. "I should have listened when my mama was trying to tell me to learn how to cook for myself." Turkey bacon and grits would have hit the spot right about then, he thought to himself. He looked in the bread box. There was the one last croissant that Shemone had promised would be there. He took it out and devoured it in two bites, not bothering to heat it. He washed it down with the last of the orange juice, which was in the refrigerator.

After breakfast, Darnell cut the stereo on, and switched on the CD player, listening to the sounds of Coltrane as he did his jazz thing. Yeah, turned out that jazz was all right. Shemone had hipped him to the music that sounded so soothing. He went to the closet, looking for something to lay out and wear before he showered. Darnell chose his dark denim jeans, a white T-shirt, and an Enyce sweater to go over it. After bathing and dressing, he slipped into his sneakers and put on a Yankee's baseball cap until he could get his hair cut.

Shemone had taken his car, so he took the SUV. He walked over to the Montero and got in. Its exterior shined, like that of a newborn baby's bottom. Shemone always made sure of that. He revved up the engine and slipped in another jazz CD. Darnell hummed along knowing that he was indeed a fortunate man. He was in love with a beautiful, accomplished woman, lived in a beautiful, spacious apartment with all the luxuries a person could ever want, was in a solid educational program working toward doing something that he actually had an interest in, and still held down a salaried job. Life just couldn't get any better, he thought to himself.

The neighborhood barbershop wasn't far from his old Stratford apartment building. The familiar swirling red, white, and blue candy-cane-striped pole in front of it had just come into sight. Joe, his barber, was inside, at his chair. The place looked busy, which wasn't uncommon on an early Saturday morning. Every chair was occupied. One guy was getting a bald head, another a shave, and another a shape up.

Darnell strolled through the door and a bell chimed.

"Well, look who's here," Joe announced.

Darnell walked over to him.

"Mr. Moneybags is slumming today," Joe joked. "I can afford to take my lady out for lobster tonight." Joe was of a dark complexion, with a medium Afro and long, thick sideburns that grew down each side of his face. To look at him, you would never have thought that he was a barber. There was just no reason why he couldn't cut his own hair, except that he liked the way it looked.

"Oh, you got jokes?" Darnell answered with a grin. "Okay, Issac from the *Love Boat*."

Everyone in the shop burst out with laughter, even the customers had been amused.

"Okay, okay, you got me, young buck," Joe told him. "You know that I'm always glad to see you. You're my number one customer."

"Joe, any customer who pays you and gives you a tip is your number one customer," Darnell replied. He took a seat at a chair against the wall.

Joe chuckled. "Right is right, young buck. Give me a few minutes and I'll be right with you," his barber said, continuing to cut his customer's hair.

"I'll be right here waiting," Darnell answered. He picked up an abandoned newspaper from the floor and began to read.

The bells chimed again. Three guys came in making a lot of noise, deep in dialogue, discussing the highlights of the last Knicks/Bulls basketball game.

Darnell had the newspaper in front of his face, so all he could do was hear them. He didn't look up until he heard one person call another person by name.

"Red, man, I'm telling you the Knicks are never gonna make it to the finals," one of the guys had said.

"Red?" Darnell asked. He put the newspaper down and got up. It was a small world. They both got their hair cut in the same place.

"Yo, what's up, Darnell?" Red said as he gave Darnell a hello five and a hug. "I haven't been seeing you around here much. Where've you been at?" he asked.

Darnell replied after they'd all taken a seat. "I've been kind of staying on the low, man, my plate is real full right now," he told him.

"Oh, yeah?" Red answered. He crouched over in the chair, and his hand palmed his chin. "D., don't tell me you been holding out on me. I know you gonna hook a brother up with some of that action. What, you working out of state now?" he asked. His questions shot out like cannon balls, one after the other.

It became apparent to Darnell that Red thought he was back to his old lifestyle, dealing drugs again. Darnell lowered his voice, then spoke. "Oh, nah, man, it's nothing like that. I'm strictly on the up and up now," he told Red. "I'm not trying to go back to Pennington—"

"Yeah, well," Red said, cutting him short. "What's life if you can't take some chances, right?"

"Hey, young buck, there's a traffic officer outside eyeing your car. You might want to hightail it on out there," Joe warned.

Darnell leaped up from the chair and rushed outside, leaving Red and his boys to gape at him reasoning with the woman traffic officer. He'd made it out just in the nick of time, and avoided getting the ticket.

After returning to the shop, he sat down. A bad feeling in the pit of his stomach told him that trouble was brewing. Darnell willed himself to think differently. He wasn't looking for trouble, all he wanted was a haircut. "You almost done, Joe?" he asked.

"Just about," Joe replied. "Just got to add my finishing touches, and I'll be ready for you."

Darnell said, getting back to the conversation he'd been having with Red, "Sorry, man, I had to run out and handle my business, you know?"

"I understand how it is," Red replied, looking out of the front window of the shop. "That your ride parked out front?"

"Yeah—well, it's mine, and my girl's. I just saved us from getting a ticket," he said.

"It's sweet," Red replied. There was a look of something different in his eyes, and something about the way he spoke had changed. "So what's your plate so full with, D., you were saying?"

"Oh, man, just school, work, and my lady. You know I've got to give her time," Darnell said with a grin.

"Right," Red replied. "You gotta give your lady time. That's only right. I know mine have got to have theirs," he boasted. "So, I hear you moved."

Darnell thought to himself that Red wasn't about to get any specific information from him. He was smarter than that. "Yeah, but not too far away," he told him.

"Not about to give up the home address, huh?" Red asked in a sly tone of voice. Red's friends laughed to themselves. They were slapping each other five. "You even sound different."

Darnell let the comment go. He was also about to let the conversation go with Red before it went any further.

"Yeah, just make sure that you don't forget where you come from," Red told him. "Remember to keep it real. Just keep it real," he said, pounding a fist into his own heart as a sign of solidarity.

"I always do," Darnell answered. He thought to himself that he was making new changes in his life, for the better. To him, that was keeping it real.

Red spoke again. "I mean, just don't go getting all ritzy on me, D., we got history and shit."

Joe flapped a new red smock out at Darnell. "Okay, young buck, you're up," he told him.

Darnell couldn't have been happier for the excuse to get up and away from his ex-drug-running buddy. "Yeah, well, I'll see you around, Red. You heard the man, I'm up next."

Red nodded and squinted his eyes. Darnell could feel his eyes on him, from the time he sat down in the barber's chair up to the time he drove off toward the basketball court to shoot some hoops.

"Teddy, over here," Darnell said, urging his teammate to pass him the basketball. He took hold of it, then slam-dunked it into the round metal hoop. "In your face!" Darnell shouted out to the other team. He was working up a steady sweat, playing hard on the court, when his cell phone went off in his jacket, which was nearby.

Spectators who were watching from the sidelines heard it as it sounded off. "Darnell, man, I think your phone is ringing."

Darnell left the game and rushed over to the fence to answer it.

"Yo, hurry up on back, man," his team members told him.

"I need to take a time-out," he replied. "Give me a minute." Darnell got his phone out, pressed the button labeled Talk, and spoke. "Hello?"

"Hey, Darnell," the caller said. It was Shemone.

"Hey, baby-girl. How did the shopping go?" he asked her.

The team members on the court made kissing sounds in the background, which he ignored.

"It went well. I bought plenty of food," she told him.

Darnell could hear Shemone removing items from out of the boxes as they were being shifted into the constantly opening and closing cabinets.

"Now all we need is someone to cook it," Shemone joked.

Darnell laughed. "Exactly."

"So what time are you coming home? I have something special planned for you," she said.

"Oh, yeah?" Darnell replied with a smile. He could feel himself getting worked up, just from the sound of her voice. "You going to tell me what?"

"It's a surprise. You'll have to come home to find out," Shemone teased.

"I'll be home in ten minutes," Darnell told her.

"Okay," Shemone answered, knowing she'd be getting her way.

Darnell clicked his cell phone off and went to grab a towel out of his gym bag. His boys noticed that he was getting ready to leave.

"Uh-oh, somebody's got to be home before the street lights come on," one of the guys yelled out to him.

"That's right, hater," Darnell said with a big grin. "You just jealous because you ain't got no home to go to," he joked.

"Jealous? Please, it's not about me being jealous." He walked toward Darnell to make his point. "It's about you being whipped!"

All the guys on the court roared with laughter.

Darnell stuffed his towel into his bag and went on his way. "Whatever, then," he said. "I'll be that." He pressed a button to turn the car alarm off, and hopped inside the vehicle, going back to the apartment, he thought, 'cause, just like the Jeffersons, he was movin' on up.

35

Model Man

Darnell reached home in record time that afternoon, eager about his surprise, like a kid on Christmas morning. He wondered if Shemone had ordered new lingerie. Fredricks of Hollywood was his favorite. They'd leafed through the catalog together before, and it wasn't difficult to envision Shemone in the sexy black leather number that he'd pointed out. He couldn't wait to get upstairs.

Darnell whistled a catchy tune all the way up to the apartment door. "Honey, I'm home," he said loudly, locking the door behind him.

"Hold on, I'll be right there," Shemone answered from what sounded like the bedroom.

Darnell peeked in the hall to see if she was in the bathroom. She wasn't, so he dashed inside for a quick cleanup. He came out of the bathroom minutes later all refreshed, only to find Shemone in the living room, fully dressed, sitting leisurely on the sofa doing a crossword puzzle.

"So?"

"So what?" Shemone asked with a sly smile.

"Where's my surprise at, woman?" Darnell kidded.

"Calm down, let me finish this last word," Shemone teased. She tapped the pencil on the book as she thought, playing along.

"Shemone," Darnell said impatiently. He stood over her waiting.

"Okay, okay." Shemone laughed. "I'll go and get your surprise." She got up from the couch, and disappeared into the bedroom.

Darnell fiddled with his fingers, waiting in anticipation. It still wasn't too late for the lingerie.

Shemone came out of the room with a huge plain white box. It had a red bow tied around it. "This is for you," she told him, placing it on the floor in front of him.

The box was light. Darnell only smiled. He didn't waste any time unwrapping his gift, tearing off the bow and opening the big box. He pushed the tissue paper aside. There was a note that said, "Your gift is in the bedroom." Yeah, buddy, Darnell thought to himself. Maybe Shemone had ordered the whip, too. He dashed into the bedroom with Shemone on his heels. On the bed lay a garment bag with some European name printed on it. He unzipped the bag and removed a black three-piece tuxedo, complete with cummerbund and bow tie.

"A tux. Whoa," Darnell told her. "I don't know what to say." He gave Shemone a hug.

"And that's not all," Shemone announced, unable to contain her excitement. "I'm also supposed to let you know that we will be attending the MWIW banquet in three weeks. They're giving me an award!" Shemone added, spinning around the room. "Darnell, you just don't know how rewarding it feels to finally be recognized for my hard work," she said.

"MWIW?" Darnell asked.

"Minority Women in Writing Awards, and we're going!" Shemone yelled out, still in a happy tone of voice.

Darnell stood there stunned and smiling, smiling and stunned. He eyed his fancy new tux. Now he had a suit and a tuxedo to add to his wardrobe, all thanks to the generosity of his baby-girl girlfriend. "This is something," Darnell said. "I'm proud of you, and I am glad that you're getting an award and everything, but," he told her, "I don't remember you asking me if I wanted to go. It seems like you just decided for me."

Shemone waited for him to finish speaking. She knew there was more to come.

Darnell sat on the end of the bed and looked at his new tux again. "You must have laid out some big cash for all of this," he said.

"It's not about the money, I just want you to be there." Shemone added, "By my side."

Darnell rose from the bed. "Look, baby-girl, I appreciate the tux and you wanting me to be there with you and all, don't get me wrong."

"So then, what are you saying? Don't you want to come?" Shemone asked him. She held the tux up to admire it. It was a fabulous tux. And she'd gotten a great deal on it from this store that was going out of business, 70 percent off. When she saw it, she knew. Every man should have a selection of formal wear in his closet, for special occasions.

"We should have had this conversation before you bought the tux, that's what I'm saying," Darnell replied back shortly.

"Is that what this is all about? A tux?" Shemone shook her head. "I can't believe this, but I understand now." She continued, "You're upset because I bought you the tux, which, by the way, was on sale," she said, throwing in a laugh.

"You're damn right, I am upset. The count is up to two now. One for the interview at ABC Refinishers, and now one for your dinner thing," Darnell told her. "I'm your man, not your child. You need to discuss things like this with me instead of being such a control freak all the time. It's not always about you telling me what I need in my life, Shemone."

Shemone tilted her head way to the side and folded her arms over her chest. "A control freak? Are you sure that's what you want to say?" she asked Darnell. She was giving him a chance to take it back.

"Hell yeah, I'm sure," he said. "Shemone, you manipulated this whole situation to go the way you wanted it to. You figured you'd buy me a tux and make it a surprise so that I'd have to go to your fancy dinner."

"First of all, it's more than a dinner, Darnell," Shemone snapped. "It's an awards banquet. And yes, I do want you to be there. Is that so terrible?" Shemone went over to the window and looked off into the distance. She was on fire. "Maybe I should have surprised you with a denim outfit."

"Oh, so now you're making fun of the type of clothes that I wear?" Darnell asked her. "Because I remember a time when street clothes were a turn-on for you. I believe that I've even seen you wearing some of my stuff sometimes."

Shemone turned from the window and explained, "No, Darnell. That's not it. I'm just trying to point out to you that I don't think that you would have been this upset if I'd gotten you something that you really wanted. I love you in anything that you do or don't wear. I just think that, sometimes, change is for the best."

Darnell didn't say anything. He was looking at her, and she was looking at him. Then he spoke. "You think you think you think. What did I tell you about thinking so fuckin' much? It can't always be about you, and what you think."

Shemone continued, "Then I won't say 'I think.' I'll go out on a limb and say that I know." She spoke boldly. "I know that part of you is afraid to go to that banquet with me."

Darnell immediately became offended. "What? I'm not afraid of nothing, baby-girl, not anything," he told her. She'd struck an obvious chord with his masculinity. "I can hold my own, I maintain."

"Then prove me wrong," Shemone dared him.

Darnell thought about it for a moment. "Your friends are stuck up. I don't even know if I want to be around those kinds of people."

"You haven't even met any of my coworker friends, Darnell. We usually conduct business over the phone." Shemone added, "And it's not about them anyway, it's about me. It's my night."

Darnell sat back down on the bed like a man that loved his woman. He wanted to prove that he was up to the challenge. "Okay, so I'll go," he said.

"You're for real, right? You're not gonna cancel on me at the last minute?"

"Nope," he replied, smiling. "But hear me when I say this: We are in a relationship together. No more making decisions for me, okay?"

Shemone hopped onto Darnell's lap and kissed him long and gently on the lips. "Oh, yes, and thank you, baby, for understanding. This means a lot to me."

"You're welcome, baby-girl," he replied. While she was kissing him, he was kissing her back even harder, but not as hard as he was still eyeing that tuxedo.

"Unbelievable," Pop told Darnell on the telephone the next day. "Darnell Williams is about to get his mack on at some fancy-schmancy awards dinner. Unbelievable," he said again. Darnell had just given him the rundown on the whole story.

"I just can't believe that I told her I would go," he said.

"You'll be okay," Pop said. "Hold on a minute, man. What—do you want something to drink? Wait, I'll get it." He added, "Juice, no soda. This boy know he loves himself some soda," Pop told Darnell. "Okay, D., I'm on again. What was I saying?"

"Oh, you're watching the little shorty today?" Darnell asked, referring to Pop's son.

"Yeah, man, my girl went someplace up in Yonkers with her sister. The thing that gets me is that he knows better. This boy is always trying to test me and see how far he can go."

"Sound familiar?" Darnell asked with a laugh.

Pop laughed back. "Too familiar. But for real, D., what was I saying before that?"

"You were saying that I'm gonna be all right, and I was saying that I don't think so," Darnell replied.

Pop sucked his teeth. "Darnell, just walk in there with your head up high, that's all. Just be you. You were good enough for Shemone, so you're damned sure good enough for her saddity friends."

"Good enough might not be good enough. Shemone's going all out herself. This is really a big thing for her," Darnell answered. "She went out to go and find a dress today."

"For real? The dinner is still, like, almost three weeks away, isn't it? Malik, I said don't mess with that!" Pop told his son. "Well, you have to go now. What else could you do?"

"Fake her out, like I'm too sick to go."

"Nah, don't do that, Darnell, you probably won't feel right about it the next day. And suppose she feels like she needs to miss the whole dinner, stay at home and take care of you? My girl was right when she said that sometimes the stuff that you do comes back to haunt you."

"I know you're right," Darnell answered with a pang of guilt. "Shemone would never forgive me for that one."

"You better believe it," Pop answered. "Man, just relax. You're living a different lifestyle now. You gotta learn how to blend in."

Darnell laughed. "Yo, you say some funny shit."

"I do?"

"Yeah, funny but true."

"What can I say," Pop told him in a playful tone of voice. "It's a gift."

"So, how's work going? Did you ever ask your boss for that raise?" Darnell asked him.

"Malik, put that clock back on the table," he suddenly told his son. "All the toys you got in here and you want to play with stuff that you shouldn't be messing with. I'm sorry, Darnell," Pop continued into the phone. "No, they trying to say that I need to put in some more time. They say that I haven't been with them long enough."

"Get out of here," Darnell replied. "Ain't that something. You probably work harder than most of the employees that they've had working for them for years."

"You ain't lying," Pop told him. "But it's all good. I told my girl that if she wanted to see more money coming into the house, then she'd better get her ass a second job."

Darnell burst out in laughter. "Stop it, Pop! No you didn't."

"For real, I bet that shut her up. We're in the 2000s now. Women can bring that money in just like we can."

"That's definitely true," Darnell agreed. "Shemone makes sure to hold down her own and then some."

"Don't even go there," Pop told his friend. He knew that Darnell had a hang-up about Shemone bringing in more money than he did.

Darnell didn't say anything.

"Hello—"

"Oh, you talking to me? I thought that you were talking to Malik again," Darnell said.

"Yeah, I'm talking to you." Pop paused and thought. "Come to think of it, he has been kind of quiet. Could you hold on for a minute while I go and check on him?" he asked.

"Yeah, go ahead, man," Darnell replied. This dinner thing would probably be the first of many that he'd have to subject himself to. Someplace he didn't belong. Blend in, his ass. Darnell waited on the telephone, wondering what Shemone was doing. He thought to himself that she was probably buying up the whole damn store.

36

Comfort Zone

I didn't feel like I belonged there. I felt so closed in," Raymond told Ohija in the kitchen on Wednesday evening. It had been the first time he'd spoken about his MRI experience since he'd found out he had to take it on Monday. "And that elevator music they played for me inside didn't make it any better," he said.

"Ray, I'm sure the doctors did everything they could to make you feel comfortable," she replied.

Ray popped open the tab on a can of cold beer. "Well, I wasn't. I'm comfortable in my own house, that's where I'm comfortable at," he told her. He walked out of the kitchen and into the living room.

Ohija went on with what she was doing. She opened the jar of spaghetti sauce and then dropped thin noodles into a pot of boiling water. Then she cut up the ingredients for an easy salad of lettuce, tomatoes, and cucumbers. Dinner would be done in a matter of minutes. At least some things were still easy. Dealing with Ray on a day-to-day basis since he'd gotten ill certainly wasn't. He was so moody. At one point he'd be up and joking around with her, and the next he'd be serious or angry. Ohija knew that Ray was under a great deal of pressure. She was glad that they knew what was wrong with him. All they had to do now was try and cure him. "Ray, dinner's ready, go wash up while I set things out on the table," she told him from the kitchen.

"Okay, honey," he answered from the other room.

Ohija knew that Ray shouldn't be drinking, but one beer wasn't gonna kill him. That night, it had actually helped to mellow him out.

Ray came downstairs and sat at the table. "Mmmm, food looks tasty. I worked up a real appetite laying down in that machine for an hour today."

"Mm-hmm," Ohija replied, thinking that saying too much might cause him to get worked up. She thought to herself that sometimes the less said the better.

Ray sprinkled Parmesan cheese on his spaghetti. "It really wasn't that bad, Ohija." He continued, "I just wanted to say thank you for being there and putting up with me."

Ohija smiled at her husband and then twirled spaghetti around her fork. She lifted it up to her husband's mouth and put it in. "You're very welcome."

Ray chewed and then spoke. "I don't want my wife and babies to be all stressed out." Then he did the same for his wife, feeding her a piece of leafy lettuce.

"Oh, we're not going to be stressed," Ohija replied with a giggle.

"Baby, I'm serious. I want you to know that I like the fact that you take the time to talk to me about the, uh," Ray stammered, "the cancer and everything."

"Anytime, Ray, you know that." Ohija took a sip of juice from her glass.

Ray felt like talking some more. "You know, I was reading the brochure that Dr. Berg gave us. It was pretty interesting to read about the MRI and then actually go through it."

"Was it?" Ohija asked. She listened closely.

"Yeah, that MRI thing is nothing but one big old magnet and radio waves, you know."

"Really?" Ohija replied in a surprised tone of voice. She wasn't going to let on that she had already read the same brochure several times herself. She was thankful that he was finally opening up.

"Yes, its like hydrogen bombs in the body that react to the magnets. The computer analyzes the results and makes pictures of the inside of my body."

"That is so fascinating," Ohija told him. "Mmph, technology."

"Yes and mmph, my wife." Ray smiled. "I know that you've already read the brochure, and if I know you, it's probably been more than once."

Ohija gave Ray a wink, not confirming if she had or not. She wanted to continue to encourage his openness when it came to talking about his illness. "We find out something from the doctor, as soon as he gets the results from the radiologist," Ohija said.

"I just hope that it hasn't spread," Ray told her.

"Me, too," Ohija replied. She finished the last bit of food on her plate to keep her energy up. She was going to need it. The day still wasn't over for her. She had to look over both the revenues and expenses month-end report from the boutique. Her sister was doing an excellent job, but Ohija still had to do a lot of the paperwork from home. Having a brain, and an accounting computer program, helped.

"Dinner was delicious, baby." Ray got up from the dinner table. "I think I'm gonna go and take myself a little lie down," he said.

"That sounds like an idea," Ohija replied. "I'm gonna put these dishes into the dishwasher and then start on my work from the shop."

"Baby, you do too much sometimes. I know the obstetrician said you can do a little more, but don't overexert yourself."

"I'll be fine," then she ordered, "now get," slapping him gently on the rear end.

Ohija sat at her computer twenty minutes later, ready to look over the reports from her boutique.

Raymond walked into the den. "Come on," he told her.

"Ray, what?" Ohija asked. "I can't, I have work to do."

Ray helped to pull his wife up on her feet. "Come on." He led her into the bathroom. The old-fashioned clawfoot tub was filled high with foamy bubbles, and her book of daily meditations was right beside it. Her favorite vanilla-scented candles burned brightly as the only source of light. Ray had even taken the time to set out her best pajamas, robe, and slippers.

"Ray, you shouldn't have," Ohija turned to tell him.

"You deserve it and more, now enjoy," he said, kissing her on the lips. Ray disappeared past her, to the other side of the door.

"There are so many things I should be doing," Ohija said aloud to herself, looking around the bathroom. Her husband had gone to so much trouble. It truly would be a shame to waste his unselfish deed. "Oh, the heck with it," she finally said, removing her clothes. Tomorrow was another day. She sank down into the silkiness of the water and reveled in the comfort that it gave her. Closing her eyes, she began to meditate on all of the positive things that were going on in her life. The upcoming birth of their twins. Entrepreneurship and a lucrative business. A roof over her head, and a loving husband who, even in his illness, could take time out to think of her and prepare a bubble bath.

37

Gone Solo

Darnell couldn't concentrate. He was trying to review the notes for his electricians' class exam the next day. It was important for him to do well. He'd managed to get high grades on both the written and hands-on exams so far, and he wanted to keep it up. Between work and school, he didn't have time for much else. Darnell flicked on the television set, and put his book down to try and unwind for a bit. A basketball game. For the man who couldn't focus on his studies, it was an easy diversion. He'd review for class later, the Lakers were about to take on the Spurs. Darnell thought about Terrance, as he always did whenever he watched a game. Terrance would have been so proud of him because he was going to school.

Yeah. After he'd finished his internship, Darnell would be making some nice money, he thought. He'd really be able to help Shemone out the way he'd wanted to. As it stood, Darnell was contributing his entire check from the packing company, and using his stipend money for himself. Compared to what he was giving from his stash before, it barely made a dent in staying on top of the monthly bills. Constantly, he was haunted by something he'd once told her: If it's a money thing, it's not even worth getting worked up about it. But he still did, even though Shemone agreed to stick by him through his schooling, and as long as he was bringing in some money from his job.

While a commercial was on, Darnell went into the kitchen and stockpiled snacks. His all-time favorite was pretzels covered in milk chocolate; Shemone had introduced him to it. Darnell filled up a bowlful, and got half of a leftover deli sandwich and a raspberry wine cooler from out of the fridge. Shemone walked through the front door with a small shopping bag at halftime.

"Don't tell me you're still out there shopping," Darnell said.

Shemone came over to him and gave him a kiss on the lips. "Hello to you, too," she answered with a smile. "No, I'm not still out shopping. As of today, I'm all done. I just needed to get some accessories to complete my outfit, that's all."

Shemone handed a bag to Darnell and hung up her coat. "Look inside, there's something in there for you."

Darnell sighed. "Shemone—what did I—"

"I know, I know," she said, not allowing him to finish. "You don't want me buying anything for you. Okay, so then you can just owe me," she said. Shemone sat down on the couch next to him. "How's that?" Her reasoning seemed logical enough to her. If Darnell didn't want her buying things for him, she wouldn't.

Darnell set the bag down on the coffee table unopened. He listened to Mary J. Blige croon a soulful song on the TV.

Shemone couldn't help herself. "All right, then, I'll open it for you," she said, wanting to get his reaction. Inside the box was a set of sparkling silver-toned cuff links. "You like?" she asked him.

"No, I do not like. Listen, Shemone, we gotta talk."

"I can take them back if you don't want them. I still have the receipt," she told him.

Darnell got up from the couch. "Then, yeah, take them back. I don't like how you continue to just"—Darnell spun words around in his head until he had just the right ones—"disregard my feelings in this relationship."

"Darnell, I—"

Darnell didn't let her finish. "I'm talking. You're doing it again. You're disregarding me, and how I feel," Darnell said in an angry tone of voice. "We've already been through this. You went out and bought me a tux without asking me. You decided that I was going to a banquet without asking me. You're bringing accessory shit in for me that I didn't ask for, and now you gonna have the nerve to tell me that I can owe you for it?"

Shemone sat on the couch totally stunned, her head turned to him as he continued.

Darnell thought about his decision before he spoke. He saw it as being the only way to get through to her. "Shemone, I'm not going with you to the banquet," he decided aloud. He'd really planned on making it, but changed his mind right after she'd handed that bag with the cuff links to him. He needed to take a stand, and Shemone needed to understand where he was coming from. He'd agreed to all of her rules, but he had some rules of his own, too.

"What?" Shemone said as she stood up. "Darnell, you can't be serious. The banquet is only days away. You promised me that you wouldn't cancel," she huffed. "You know this is so—typical," she spat back. She had no problems finding words for him.

"And what is that supposed to mean?" Darnell asked.

"I mean it's typical for you to go and cancel now. You knew you didn't want to go, why did you even agree to go in the first place?"

Darnell thought to himself about the reasons why he had agreed to go: to make her happy, because he loved her, because she'd already gotten him a tux, and to prove that he could go to one of those high-saddity affairs of hers. Instead, he answered completely differently. "I'm starting to wonder the same thing myself. As a matter of fact, I'm starting to wonder about a lot of things. Shemone, I won't let you control me," he told her.

"'Control'?" Shemone sighed heavily and nodded. "Control you how?"

"With money and your education, that's how," Darnell yelled.

"You just can't get past the fact that I make more money than you, can you? It's not always about money, Darnell, how many times do I have to tell you that?" Shemone pointed at him sternly. "This is about you, and your own hang-ups."

"Right, it's always a hang-up when I'm not doing what you want me to do," he replied.

"So what do you want from me, Darnell? You want me to tell you that it is all about the money? You want me to tell you that there can't be any romance without the finance?" she asked him.

"Shemone, I just want you to be more aware of how I feel about things before you do them." Darnell leaned against the couch as he spoke. "It's about respect. You own everything in this apartment. If I left today, I could fit all my thing in two duffel bags. A man does have his pride."

"Yes, and?" Shemone said, resting a hand on her hip. "So you're saying that you want me to move, start over with you, and throw out all of my personal belongings that I've worked so hard and long for?"

"You're a real piece of work. Do you know that?" Darnell said as he walked off into the bedroom.

"So what are you gonna do now? Run home to Mama again?" Shemone yelled out as she paced the floor. She added, "Go ahead and see if I care."

Darnell yelled back, "No, I'm not gonna run back to my mama's. I'm gonna finish watching the game, if you don't mind. Then I'm gonna finish studying for my electricians' test," he answered, slamming the bedroom door.

Shemone went into the bathroom and slammed the door right back at him. He wasn't the only one in the world who could make loud noises. It was immature of her, but yet satisfying. She turned both jets of the bathroom faucet on full blast, and sat down on the edge of the bathtub for a long, soulful cry. Her emotions were way out of control. She was angry, she was sad, and it hardly seemed fair. She'd opened her home and heart up to this man, and all he wanted to do was punish her for being mildly successful, but why? She was certainly nowhere near rich. Her mother didn't want anything to do with her, and Darnell was close to distancing himself from her at a time when she really needed him. It seemed the only one she could depend on was herself. Shemone splashed water on her face, then buried it deep inside a towel. Yes, the only person she could depend on now was herself. An idea for an article suddenly came to her. She marched out of the bathroom and into the bedroom, where Darnell was. As far as she was concerned, he wasn't even there in the room with her. Shemone sat at her computer, turning it on, typing fast and furious at the keys on her keyboard.

GIRLFRIEND STRIKE

by Shemone Waters

In a monogamous relationship but feeling like you just can't win when it comes to making the one you love be at the right place at the right time? Has he stopped uttering the right things, like he used to when you first met? Well, maybe it's time for a girlfriend strike! No need to raise the signs or shout out loud because he'll instantly get the point once he sees the action behind your words. Less dramatic than a breakup, a girlfriend strike allows you to have the short-term space you need while you both get a chance to sort out your thoughts. It's not nearly as devastating as an all-out breakup, and you get a chance to truly cater to yourself. There's more of it's about "you" than of "him," and less of what you're making for dinner and where's the remote.

But there are a few rules that you need to follow:

- **You must not call him. Not on the job or even in the house unless it's an absolute emergency. If he calls you, then remember to keep it brief. He needs to feel what life would be like without you in it, just so that he appreciates you more.**
- **You have to look your best. Make sure you visit the salon for complete hair and body treatments. It's important to feel confident about yourself. Know that if push comes to shove, you can get somebody else. If you have to.**

- **Go out with your girlfriends, take a class, do something different; don't just sit at home waiting for the phone to ring. Make the most of your time because the strike won't last very long.**
- **Don't see other men. Give your partner that respect. At least while you're still in a relationship with him. This lets him know that you can be loyal, but that you can still mean what you say.**

The average girlfriend strike should last a week or two, tops. Watch the results. Just like any strike, demands should be met. Air your grievances and concerns with your mate face-to-face. Try to meet each other halfway and come to a compromise. And if the girlfriend strike lasts longer than that, and you find that he is enjoying the space you put between you two a little too much, then maybe it's time to consider getting out of the relationship. If you are enjoying the space, then perhaps you should consider the same thing. Being alone isn't always the worst thing. At least you'll find out that you enjoy doing things for yourself and that there's less to complain about. Because if you don't love yourself, no one else will. But when you do, you'd be amazed by who might come your way. So look out, world!

Shemone smiled with satisfaction after saving her new article. One of the best things about being a writer was that she could put some of her feelings on paper and was able to get paid for it. She rose from her chair and walked out of the bedroom fine with the fact that she'd be going to the awards banquet solo. There was no way she was going to miss it, Darnell or no Darnell.

Ray and Ohija were determined to weather the storm together.

"The MRI results are in," Dr. Berg told them. They sat waiting inside his office on Friday afternoon. "You'll be relieved to know that the cancer is in its local stage, meaning, it hasn't spread. It's pretty much confined to your prostate."

Ohija and Ray both heaved a heavy sigh.

"Dr. Berg, that's wonderful news," Ohija replied. She leaned over and hugged Ray.

"Of course we want to move along with a treatment as soon as possible," Dr. Berg told them.

Ray smiled slightly, a first for being in the doctor's office. "So then, I'm gonna be okay, Doc?"

Dr. Berg smiled back. "We don't want to give you any false hopes, but I feel confident in saying that with proper treatment, things looks bright for you."

Ohija felt her stomach. "So what type of treatment are you going to give my Ray?" she asked. The babies within her felt like fluttering butterflies. Ohija took it as a sign. They were responding to the news about their father.

"We're looking at surgery. Its medical term is a 'radical prostatectomy,'" Dr. Berg began to explain.

"Is it painful?" Ray asked. His eyes were wide with curiosity, and from what Ohija could see, even a little fearful-looking.

"No, the surgery itself isn't. You have the choice of choosing between two types of anesthesia."

"Wow, two?" Ray exclaimed. "Sounds like pain to me."

"Ray, let him finish," Ohija told her husband.

Dr. Berg went on. "For a confined tumor such as yours, a radical prostatectomy is the best alternative. The surgery is intended to effectively cure your cancer by removing all of the cancerous tissue from your prostate."

Ohija and Ray hung onto Dr. Berg's every word while he continued.

"The two types of anesthesia are general and epidural. With general, the patient is completely unconscious. With an epidural, a spinal block is administered to numb your lower body."

Ohija was concerned. "What are the risks, Doctor?"

Dr. Berg hesitated, and forced out a response. "As with any surgery, there are risks."

Raymond told him, "Just spit it out, Doc, tell us."

"There is a risk of urinary incontinence and impotence," Dr. Berg replied.

"There goes my manhood," Raymond said aloud. "I knew there would be some price to pay," he added, bolting up from his chair.

"Ray, please sit down," Ohija pleaded. "Let's just hear him out."

"Ohija, what more is there to say?" Ray replied.

"Ray, Ohija," Dr. Berg said, "there have been numerous advances in medicine. One of them being nerve-sparing surgery, which can help reduce the chances of impotence and other side effects."

"Okay, so what's urinary incon—" Ray asked. He was having difficulty pronouncing the word.

"Urinary incontinence, Ray," Dr. Berg told him. He took his time and carefully explained. "That means that you might have difficulties controlling your urination from time to time."

"Diapers, Doc?" Ray asked in an overwhelmed tone of voice. All of this information was really getting to be too much for one day. He suddenly felt light-headed.

Ohija got up from her chair. "Ray, baby, come on and sit down for me," she said.

Ray sat down. He'd do anything for his wife, even before himself. He was relieved to sit; his head stopped reeling for a moment.

"Ray, like I told you before, there's a chance that you'll come out of this okay. I haven't diagnosed you with either impotence or urinary incontinence. You're still considered to be relatively young to have prostate cancer. That actually works in your favor," Dr. Berg said in a positive tone of voice. "Why don't we just hope for the best?"

Ray sighed and nodded slightly as he tried to put up a front for his wife. He wasn't ready to die. He wasn't ready to be impotent, and he wasn't ready to be wearing diapers right along with his babies.

38

Seeing Is Believing

"How about some hot tea?" Shemone asked Ohija as they sat in the living room of Shemone's apartment the next afternoon. "I bought some of that herbal peppermint kind that you especially like."

Ohija smiled. "That's sweet; you considered me and my natural teas while you were out food shopping," Ohija said.

"I sure did," Shemone told her in an upbeat tone of voice. Ohija hadn't said what the doctor had told her and Ray, but she had a feeling that it wasn't anything she'd want to hear.

"No tea, thanks," Ohija replied. "These babies are tired of me and my teas by now, I'm sure."

Shemone giggled. "Yeah, I bet they are. So are you doing okay? You and the twins are all right?"

"Oh yes, better than ever," Ohija said. "The doctor said that I could even go in a few days a week at the boutique if I wanted. I just can't do too much." Ohija continued, "You know, no lifting or stuff like that."

"Oh, of course not," Shemone said. "Just let me know if you need me, I'll be glad to help out."

"You already are, just being there for me." Ohija fidgeted with the silver bangle on her arm. "Well, it looks like Ray does have prostate cancer—"

"No!" Shemone shrieked, about to cry. Her tears were quickly replaced with a look of empathy for her best friend. Breaking down was not going to help the situation, or Ohija, who was together and perfectly fine with what she was about to finish telling Shemone.

"Don't cry, at least now we know that Ray has prostate cancer. Luckily it's confined, meaning it hasn't spread. They want to perform a radical prostatectomy. The name actually sounds much worse than the procedure itself. They'll remove all the cancerous tissue from the area." Ohija kept speaking, and her tone of voice stayed the same, not a sign of "losing it" to be found. "There's a chance that Ray could come out impotent or with urinary problems. That's not to say that it will happen for sure." Ohija rubbed her stomach and smiled. "We're gonna make it through this, Shemone."

"Poor Ray, but I know you'll be okay, and I'll be there for you guys every step of the way," Shemone replied. "How is Ray taking things?"

"Oh, you know Ray, he's my warrior. He's real moody now, but I understand. I'm just trying to give him the space he needs to take this in and be positive for his surgery." Ohija added, "He's still got a lot to live for, and if I know my Ray, he'll realize that, too."

"Yes, of course he will," was all that Shemone could say. Ohija was always inspiring and uplifting, but Shemone knew that if the shoe was on the other foot, she'd probably go nuts. Shemone decided to change the subject of the conversation. "You know that I'm going to the awards banquet solo."

"Get out, Darnell's not going with you?" Ohija asked in a surprised tone of voice.

"No, Mr. Darnell feels that I'm trying to control him." Shemone made it sound as if it were the most bizarre thing in the world to hear about herself.

"You aren't, are you?" Ohija asked. She knew that her friend did have some issues with control.

"Ohija! I don't believe you asked me that! Of course I'm not trying to control him. Darnell Williams has always been his own person."

"So then what would make him say something like that?" Ohija asked. She munched on some chocolate chip cookies that Shemone had put out.

"Like I know!" Shemone answered quickly. "The man is delusional." Shemone paused. "Just because I bought him an inexpensive tux, and some cuff links—"

"Wait," Ohija asked. "You bought him a tux?"

"Yes—is there something wrong with that?" she asked.

"It all depends," Ohija answered.

"On?" Shemone asked inquisitively.

"On how and why you gave it to him. I hope you asked him if he wanted to go to the banquet with you first." Ohija looked across at Shemone for an answer. "Shemone, you didn't!"

"I most certainly did, and still don't see anything wrong with it."

"Shemone, you know Darnell is a proud man," Ohija said. "Most men are."

"I told him he could pay me back for the cuff links—"

Ohija burst out with laughter, unable to respond right away. "See, you're gonna have to work on that," Ohija finally managed to say. "I'm not saying stroke his ego, but be respectful about the way you treat him. Darnell is not your son, he's your man, girl. You have to know where to draw the line. The point is to have your man thinking he's in charge, while you make the decisions. Think about it," she said, getting up from the sofa.

"Where are you going?" Shemone asked her, wanting to know more.

"Home to the hubby. He went to work today, and I'm ordering dinner in for my workingman. Last week he ran me a bubble bath, and took care of me. Hint, hint, two-way street." Ohija winked at her friend.

Shemone got up to help a very pregnant-looking Ohija on with her coat.

"I'll call you!" Ohija said on her way to the elevator.

Shemone waved and closed the door. She hadn't told Ohija about the girlfriend strike she was on. She thought about what Ohija had said about men being proud and all. But what was stopping Darnell from being the man he wanted to be? Not her. She was encouraging, supportive, and sexy. Hmph. As far as she was concerned, the girlfriend strike was still on.

"Darnell, you've got, like, all the channels a brother could ever want. You got the illegal cable hookup or what?" Pop asked a week later as they sat in front of the wide-screen living room TV set.

"Naah," Darnell answered. "Shemone and I both pay for it."

Pop chuckled, not from what his friend had just said, but from the way that he had said it. "You back on that old trip again? When are you gonna let that bullshit in your life go?" he asked him.

"When Shemone lets it go, that's when. When she stops buying me monkey suits and throwing things up in my face," Darnell said in an angry tone of voice. "That's when."

"Darnell, man, for real, I don't even think it's that serious."

"Oh, it's serious all right," he told Pop. "Sistah-girl has been walking around here for a week saying next to nothing to me, like she lives here by herself. But it's cool. She probably thinks I'm gonna up and leave because of how she's acting, but I'm not planning to. That's irresponsible, and it's exactly what she thinks I'm going to do."

Pop used the remote control to flip to the numerous TV stations. "You're losing me. What is going on with you two?" he asked Darnell.

"For starters, I'm not going with her to that awards dinner," he told Pop.

"Ohhh," Pop replied. He suddenly understood everything. "That would do it."

"It's not just that," Darnell went on to explain, "it's her trying to rule me all the time. She makes decisions for me. I hate that she does that," he said.

Pop stopped on a college basketball game. "Did you talk to her about it? You know it's important to talk to your woman about these things."

"Yeah, I have, Pop. It's gotten to the point that I'm tired of repeating myself."

"So then why don't you just go ahead and break out?" Pop asked, knowing that leaving wasn't what Darnell wanted to do.

"You mean leave? I told you already, that's what she thinks I'm gonna do because I've done it before. I ran home to my mother's the first time. But I'm a bigger man than that," Darnell told his friend in frustration. "I'm only dealing with this because I—" He paused.

"Because you love her?" Pop said, helping Darnell to finish his sentence.

Darnell sat in the chair with his hand under his chin. "Yeah, 'cause I love her, man. I love every stuck-up, creative, smart, sexy thing about her. The only problem is, I don't know how long I can deal. If she doesn't realize this and get it together soon, then I'll have no choice but to walk away."

"Darnell, you can't mean that," Pop told him.

"Yeah, I can say it and mean it. Love is love, but I won't be nobody's fool for too long. I'm making the changes in my life, and if she doesn't see that, or if it's not quick enough for her, then we don't belong together in the first place."

Pop didn't respond verbally, but he nodded. Right was right this time and Darnell was entitled to feel what he felt.

Later that evening, Shemone sat at her computer keyboard toying around with an outline for a new story. She kept coming up blank, so she decided to call it a day. Truth be told, she'd saved almost a dozen new story ideas already. Her girlfriend strike had given her more than enough opportunity to focus on her work. Just as her own article advised, she'd gotten a new retouching of color on her hair, been to the nail salon, and gone out on a mini shopping spree for clothes and discounted designer shoes. The nail-salon trip made her think of her mother, Ruth. She hadn't phoned or gone by her house since they'd been to the salon together. Pre-girlfriend strike, Darnell had told her to keep trying. He'd said that it seemed as if her mother might be hurting from stuff that had happened in her past. Shemone sighed. No, she still wasn't giving up on Ruth. She was just giving her a little space to think, which was what Darnell was a master at doing at the present moment. As long as he didn't say anything to her, she was fine. Then he did.

"Shemone, you want me to order in some dinner?" Darnell asked as he loaded his books back into his bag. It was his way of making an attempt at smoothing things over between them. Pity, though, it seemed Shemone wasn't quite ready to throw up the white flag.

"No thank you. I'm just going to make myself a tuna sandwich," she replied flatly.

"Oh, so it's like that? Fend for yourself around here for everything, huh?" Darnell asked, angrily walking out of the room. He regretted reaching out to her for a truce.

Just then the telephone rang. Darnell was closer to the phone, but he let Shemone pick it up since she was doing everything for herself these days. He went into the kitchen and opened the kitchen cabinet. He took out two packages of flavored noodles from the cupboard. He didn't want any tuna. Suddenly he heard the sounds of Shemone's loud laughter coming from inside the bedroom. It wasn't a regular kind of laughter that she shared between words with Ohija or any of her other female friends. Apparently, Shemone was finding someone or something quite amusing. Darnell left the kitchen and inched quietly toward the bedroom to see what was so damn funny. He soon found out.

"Oh, Keith, you are hilarious," Shemone said into the phone.

Darnell was sure that Keith wasn't one of her female friends. He thought to himself, So it's a male, so what? He was okay with a male calling, just as long as Shemone was on the other end letting him know that if it wasn't business related, that made it personal. And she already had a man. Darnell waited as he heard Shemone laugh again.

"No, I haven't been to Shark's in a while," he heard her say. He held his breath. The Brooks Brothers brother, he remembered. She'd better be getting her ass ready to make that tuna sandwich.

"Really? You got a promotion at your job, head accountant? Impressive," Shemone told her caller. "We've just got to go out and celebrate that."

Celebrate? Darnell thought. Was she crazy? He couldn't hear what the response was on the other end but it must have been interesting because Shemone's voice lowered. Then he heard, "Okay then, I'll be in touch," a giggle, then a flirtatious, " 'Byeee."

Darnell walked into the bedroom.

Shemone hung up the phone and looked up at him and smiled, then got up and went into the kitchen to make her sandwich.

Darnell wondered. So she was having tuna tonight, but what about tomorrow or the next day? He wasn't about to confront Shemone on her intentions. Not when she knew exactly what she was doing. Darnell wasn't about to be made a fool of by anyone, not in his own house, or not in her own house, or whatever. Period. He'd known the game all too well himself.

39

FEELING THE FIRE

Ray, it's okay, it really is, baby," Ohija said late Tuesday evening, in their bedroom.

"No, I can do this," he replied as he tried again.

Ohija nibbled at his neck and ran her fingers down his back as she attempted to help get her husband excited.

Ray abruptly rolled off her and got up from the bed. "Sweet mercy!"

"Honey, it's okay, I told you that," Ohija said as she sat up and slipped into her robe. She'd rarely ever heard her husband swear.

"It's not okay," Ray answered. "This type of thing never happens to me. I can't even pleasure my wife. I don't understand this."

Ohija walked over to him and rubbed his back. "It's probably just stress, you've got a lot on your mind. I read that something like this could happen, even though you haven't had the surgery yet."

Ray continued to harp on the negative, and not pay attention to anything that his wife was trying to tell him. "I'm not gonna be of any use to you now. I just didn't think that it would happen so soon."

Ohija interrupted, "Raymond, you're talking crazy. Listen, in a week and a half you'll have had your surgery and a month and a half later you'll be a new father. Don't let this thing control you, you control it," Ohija ordered. "Now, I'm here to support you, but if you're gonna keep feeling sorry for yourself, then, Raymond Jones, go somewhere and find yourself a room or something to sulk in." Ohija's voice was adamant. "I mean it, Ray, I won't let you take this family down!"

Raymond plopped down on the bed like a little boy. He was still naked and looked so susceptible to being hurt.

Ohija wrapped her arms around him, rocking him as he cried.

"I'm sorry, baby. I don't want to leave the house. I want to be here with you and the twins. I'm gonna be strong," Raymond vowed.

"You don't have to leave, Ray," Ohija said. "But you do have to make some effort. There's more to us than sex. That's not what makes you a man."

"You're right," Ray replied. Ohija kissed his salty tears. And just then, something wonderful began to happen. "Ohija, look," Ray said.

"I know, baby, I told you it would happen," she said, smiling down at the hardness between his legs. "It's on now."

When Ohija awoke, hours later, she got up and walked into the living room, to find her husband engrossed in a huge red medical book on prostate cancer. "Getting some reading in?"

"Yeah, baby, come here for a minute," Ray said, holding up the book, urging her over to sit on his lap.

Ohija sat.

"This is some really interesting stuff in here. That nerve-sparing procedure that Dr. Berg was telling us about, I can get it done." He read from the page. "'It leaves intact one, or both, of the neurovascular bundles that pass close to the prostate capsule. The bundles maintain an erection.'" He closed the book and kept talking. "The best news is that if I still have good erections before the surgery, and all goes well, the results can be excellent. Just reading about these new procedures gives me hope, baby."

"I'm so glad to hear that, Ray," Ohija told her husband. She only hoped that he didn't get too carried away with new tech cures and technology. "Ray, remember what Dr. Berg said, now, we just need to see what happens."

"I know, I will. I'm just anxious to have this surgery so that we can go on with the rest of our lives, that's all."

"Every day that God wakes us up is going on with our lives, Ray," she told him.

"You got me," he agreed. "Speaking of lives going on, how are Shemone and Darnell doing?" Ray asked.

"They're okay, both of them are going through some kind of couple thing." Ohija got up from Ray's lap to go into the kitchen. "Love will get them through."

"It usually does," Ray replied as he reopened the book to continue to read.

Ohija yelled out from the kitchen, "Ray, you want to split this hero sandwich with me?"

"No, baby, you go on and eat it. I'll just heat up the leftovers from the other day when I get hungry," he said.

"You sure?" Ohija asked.

"Yes, go ahead and eat it." Ray was so wrapped up in the medical book that he wasn't thinking about food. As he read on, he found some more new information. The chances of impotency and incontinence were very likely if there was a history of the disease in your family and if you were of African-American descent. Ray slammed the book closed. He thought, Will it always be like this? One minute on top of the world, and at the bottom the next? Ray got up from the chair and went into the bedroom to lie down. He could hear Ohija calling his name in the next room. He closed his eyes, making believe he was asleep. Ray didn't want his wife to know that his mood had changed just that quickly and that he actually just wanted to lie down and die at that very moment. It felt as if he was running into brick walls, again and again.

"Ray?" Ohija said as she walked into the darkened room. "Ray, are you sleeping?"

Ray stayed still on the bed.

"I guess so," Ohija said. She left the room chomping down on her hero sandwich.

He told himself, Ohija thinks all is well, but she guessed very wrong.

40

ON THE DOWN LOW

"I can't believe you're here, boo, in my bed."

"Believe it," Darnell answered early Friday afternoon, on his day off. He ran his hand up and down the smooth thickness of Hope's thighs, and didn't say anything. He only kept on with what he was doing, kissing her shoulders, and steadily working the fabric of her tank top farther and farther up. In an odd way, being with Hope was making him feel superior, in a way that he hadn't felt with Shemone. With Hope, he didn't have to try to live up to her, or to any kind of high standards. Overhearing the conversation with Brooks Brothers had been the best thing that could have happened, he thought to himself. It let Darnell know that whatever he did, or tried to do, would never be good enough for Shemone.

"Does your uppity girlfriend know that you're here with me?" Hope asked him in a breathless tone of voice. She was grinning, and soaking up all of the attention that Darnell had to give.

Darnell whispered in her ear, in a low voice, "I don't want to talk about her right now." Instead, he undid her bra.

"I knew that you wouldn't," she boasted, as Darnell squeezed her breasts. "A fine, smart man like you needs to feel like a man should, and I know just how," Hope said. "I knew that you'd be coming to see me sooner or later." Hope couldn't have been happier. Ms. Uptight Lady didn't have it going on like that after all. Her man was coming to her, and she was gonna welcome him with open arms, giving him her very, very best.

Darnell huffed and panted, not wasting any time, going right for what he'd come for, first emotionally, and now physically. As he pumped inside Hope, he blocked out all images of Shemone and himself, and substituted thoughts of Shemone and Brooks Brothers instead, and what they would probably soon be doing, any day now, because that was the kind of man she'd wanted all along. He pumped harder. Hope enthusiastically participated, underwear that was at her ankles and a tank top that was pulled up above her chest. There was no time for romance. Darnell lifted Hope up from the bed and went at her on the dresser in her room.

"Give it to me, Darnell, yes, ooohhh . . .you are the best!" Hope loudly yelled, urging him on with nothing to stop him but a condom between them. Darnell yelled out and came, his eyes squeezed tightly shut. When he opened them, Hope was smiling, wide and hard. Darnell released her, immediately pulling up his jeans. There wasn't the usual kiss and cuddle after having made love like he did with Shemone. This was a fuck.

Hope hopped down from the dresser and flung herself on the bed as Darnell buckled his belt. "Whew! That was something! It was so hot I could go for another round!" she told him in an excited tone of voice. That's when she noticed that Darnell was about to leave, and not about to join her on the bed for a rest and then another go at it. "Where are you going?" she asked.

"I've gotta bounce," Darnell answered, opening the door to her bedroom. "I'll see you around," he told her. He went out through the front door of her mother's apartment thinking that it was a good thing she wasn't home. It made for an easier exit.

"Call me later, boo," Hope told him, the sheets pulled in between her legs. Because if he didn't, she was going to call him.

Darnell headed straight home after leaving Hope's that afternoon. He needed to hurry and shower before going to his electricians' class. Shemone wasn't there when he got in. Of course his mind told him that she was probably with Brooks Brothers. Somehow, it made him feel okay about what he had done just an hour before. After showering and changing his clothes, about ready to go back out, Shemone walked in, in sweats, as if she'd just come in from jogging.

"Hello," Shemone said in a casual tone of voice. She felt like acknowledging him that day, for some reason, but still kept walking past him, toward the bathroom.

"Hello," Darnell replied in the same tone of voice. Oh, today she was speaking, Darnell thought to himself as he went out the door, on his way to class. Still, he didn't feel a bit of guilt.

Shemone showered and put on a pair of boxers and an oversize T-shirt. She hadn't gone jogging in Central Park in a long time, and the run had done her wonders. She was able to stay fit while working off some steam. The steam was from the girlfriend strike, which was still going on. While out on her run in the open air, she'd had a chance to really think about things. The girlfriend strike really wasn't working. Now it seemed more petty to her than anything else. Darnell didn't seem to be all that troubled by it. Mr. Cool Guy. She wasn't even sure if Darnell had been troubled by the Keith Jenkins phone call, and the way things had gone down. Imagine, she thought, the entire time that

Darnell's been living with me, Keith hasn't called, but now that he has, I took the ball and ran with it. Flirting with him on the phone, with the promise of going out to dinner with him on a day that would never come. And forget the fact that she hadn't found it necessary to let on that she and Darnell were living together.

Shemone knew that dating Keith was out of the question, and the next time he called, she'd let him down softly, telling him exactly that. If anything, the whole experience just let her know what a strong person Darnell was for not giving in to her and her silly games. Throughout the entire time, he'd worked hard, stayed busy and focused, Shemone thought, just like she did. It occurred to her that she was affecting Darnell in the best kind of way. He was really trying hard to do right by her. He'd called her a control freak, but was he right? Shemone thought about everything. Going to that banquet in her honor without him hadn't been easy, but she'd done it. Part of her couldn't help but wonder whether, if Darnell had been by her side, she'd have done things differently. She really could have asked him if he wanted to go, and gotten his input on what he wanted to wear. Ohija had told her and so had Darnell; she just hoped it wasn't too late to realize on her own that she needed to give up some of her controlling ways.

Shemone was watching a movie in bed and eating some popcorn when Darnell came in from class. It seemed as if he was going in slow motion, because it had taken him so long to get inside the bedroom. She heard the kitchen cabinets open and close, the refrigerator door open and close, and the microwave go off. She heard him in the bathroom, flushing the toilet, and she even heard him kicking his sneakers off in the living room. Darnell finally entered the bedroom, dressed only in his boxers and a T-shirt.

"Good evening," Darnell said as he sat on the edge of the bed.

Suddenly, he was just *so* engrossed in the movie that played on the television, she thought to herself. "Good evening," Shemone answered. "Darnell, I need to talk to you if you have a moment," she asked. She thought that in trying to resolve some of her controlling ways asking him to have a conversation would be a better choice than telling him.

"Sure, baby-girl, shoot," Darnell casually answered. He turned the covers back on the bed, and then laid down next to her.

"Well, I want to apologize to you. It took me a while, but I realize how I was wrong. I actually even understand why you didn't come with me to the banquet," she said. "I was trying to teach you a lesson, and in the end, you wound up teaching me one," she confessed.

"I taught you a lesson?" Darnell asked. He turned on his side and smiled. "What?"

Shemone turned on her side, too, and faced him. "I learned that you are your own man, and that I don't need to try and control you." She added, "I don't need to buy you things without your permission, even if they are on sale."

Darnell chuckled. "Under those conditions, I accept," he answered right away. He thought to himself that Shemone's vocabulary had managed to work its way into his speech, too. He sat up and grabbed Shemone playfully by her hips, squeezing her as if she was his long-lost teddy bear. He'd forgiven her. But not without asking how things had turned out with her little outing. "So how was your date with Brooks Brothers?"

"Date with who?" Shemone asked. She was aware of who he was talking about. "Oh, you mean Keith Jenkins? Darnell, please, you didn't actually think that I was going out with Keith Jenkins, did you?"

"But I overheard you on the phone," Darnell said. What had he done? he thought. He couldn't even begin to try and make sense of the mess he'd made.

"That will teach you to listen in on my phone conversations," Shemone joked. She told him, "It was just talk," and gave him a kiss on the lips.

And suddenly, it was back to the street lingo again. "Yo, Shemone, you shouldn't play like that. I didn't think that shit was funny at all," Darnell said in a serious tone of voice, stifling her lips with his. Oh, what had he done? he asked himself again. That talk had sunk him to the point of no return. Thanks to listening to that conversation, he'd thought that he wasn't enough of a man for Shemone. "But what about his promotion?" Darnell asked.

"Oh, he got one, but it didn't end up with us celebrating. Keith doesn't have enough money to pay me to go out with him. Don't you know that I could have had Keith in my life if I'd wanted him? You are the one I want, Darnell Williams," Shemone said, kissing him again, fully on the lips.

He kissed her back, but was still stupefied.

Shemone smiled. "And I promise not to play any more games, control or otherwise, if you promise not to eavesdrop. All I want to do is learn to love you better." Shemone's eyes lit up. "I'd like to one day get to where Ohija and Ray are."

Darnell sighed. He wasn't about to tell her what had happened. He knew that if he did, it would really be over between them. And like his friends Ohija and Ray right now, all he could do was stay positive. "We're gonna make it happen, that's a promise from me, too," Darnell told her as the two moved closer to each other for some fabulous makeup loving. All he wanted to do was forget about the past and move on to the future, something more permanent, like in a Mr. and Mrs.

Darnell woke up from making love, ironically, with Hope on his mind. But his thoughts weren't pleasant. What had happened with her was just plain sex, nothing like what he and Shemone shared. More important, it would never happen again. Shemone could never find out about the big mistake he'd made. He was just grateful that he'd used protection. Yeah, he was sure things would work out fine once he told Hope that it was a one-time thing, and that he was sorry if he'd hurt her.

Just then the telephone rang. It woke Shemone from out of her sleep. "Hello," she said in a just-got-her-some voice. "Oh, hi, Pop, how've you been? I'm well, thanks, hold on, yeah, your boy's right here, next to me," she told him. Shemone handed Darnell the telephone.

"Hey, Pop, what going on?" Darnell asked cheerily.

"Darnell, tell me it ain't so," Pop said. His tone of voice told Darnell that something was very wrong.

"What?" Darnell asked, trying to sound as if he had control of the conversation. Shemone cuddled up right next to him, smiling, her eyes closed.

Darnell switched the handset over to his other ear.

"Hope is around here telling everybody in the neighborhood that you two are together, and that you got rid of your girlfriend." Pop added, "It's just that serious."

"Oh, okay," was all that Darnell could say without displaying too much emotion. "All right, I'm going to be over that way, then. It's not like it can get to where I am," Darnell tried to say in code. He questioned whether or not Shemone could hear his heart as it pounded loudly in his chest. "All right, so I'll ring you when I get uptown," Darnell said to Pop.

"Yeah, you do that. I sometimes think that girl's elevator doesn't go all the way to the top floor, D. You better do something."

"I hear you," Darnell replied, knowing just what Pop was getting at. "All right, 'bye." Darnell gave Shemone a peck on the forehead and sat up in bed. "Baby-girl, I've got to run over to my old neighborhood for a minute."

"Right now? Do you have to?" Shemone asked, trying to persuade him out of it by kissing him along his chest.

The thought of staying home was tempting, but he had to handle his business. This thing with Hope had to be resolved right now, before things got out of hand. "Yes, I've got to go and do this."

Shemone made herself not go there for the last and final time as she watched him get out of bed. No, it's not anything drug related that he's going uptown for. It's something else, it's anything else, and I am not in control of it, she said to herself. My man is in school and working, and he doesn't have time for that nonsense. Now those thoughts sent her, easily, right back to sleep. It was about trust.

Darnell dressed quickly, before heading uptown. He took the shortcut, the fastest route possible.

Meanwhile, back at the apartment, the phone was ringing again. "Hello," Shemone said groggily into the receiver. "Hello?" she said once more. There was no answer. She hung up the phone. Somebody was trying to get the best of her, and she didn't like it one bit. Shemone didn't make a big deal of it, opting to dial Ohija instead. She wanted to wish them the best for the next day, which was Ray's surgery date.

"Ohija? Hey, it's Shemone," she said.

"Hey, girl—how's it going?" Ohija asked into the phone.

"I'm well. Darnell and I just wanted to wish you and Ray the best for tomorrow with the surgery."

"Thanks," Ohija told her in a high tone of voice. "So, it's Darnell and you again, huh? Sounds like you two are a definite item."

"We're trying," Shemone answered happily. "You know how relationships are, you have to be constantly working at them. I was the bigger person. I apologized first."

"Get out!" Ohija replied in an astonished tone of voice.

"That's right. I'm gonna try and make changes when it comes to Darnell, especially since he's doing so much to change for me," she said.

"Shemone, that is wonderful. I know you two will make it."

"Well, I'm going to let you go and get yourself ready for tomorrow. Call me when you get back in to let me know how things went," Shemone told her.

"You know I will," Ohija replied, then hung up the phone.

Shemone hung up on her end, too, thinking that Darnell needed to get way more credit then she'd given him, and from here on out, he was going to get it.

41

Consent Slips

Hope, there's somebody here to see you," an older, roller-clad woman yelled out after opening the apartment door that same day. Darnell assumed it was Hope's mother. They looked alike and were both loud. It felt strange to him needing permission to step inside. He had just been in this woman's house yesterday, with free rein, buck naked, in the act with her freaky daughter.

"Who is it, Ma?" Hope yelled back from the room in the rear.

Her mother had attitude. "What did you say your name was?"

"Darnell, ma'am," he answered, keeping his tone of voice mannerly.

"It's a Darnell, and come on." Her mother added, "I don't have all day to be standing here with my front door wide open."

Hope was at the door in Guinness-book time, welcoming Darnell and pulling him inside. She pushed her lips onto his. "Hey, baby," she said, greeting him warmly. She noticed her mother standing in the kitchen watching them on the square stick-on mirrors that hung in the hallway of their apartment. She told her, "Mama, this is my new man, Darnell."

Darnell looked embarrassed, knowing full well that he'd never claimed Hope as his girlfriend or anything else, but he did nod. A minute would be all he needed once he'd had the chance to say what he really wanted to say.

Hope's mother's attention was diverted elsewhere, on to a videotape of what looked like soaps. His presence there didn't seem to faze her much. Hope probably had lots of boyfriends, Darnell thought to himself. She led Darnell straight to her bedroom, wearing a short denim dress with a sparkle design, and she had bits of sparkle on her eyelids. Compared to the class act he had at home, Hope wasn't even in the running.

An over-twenty-one Hope closed the bedroom door behind them. "Baby, I missed you so much." She took Darnell's hands and placed them on her behind.

Darnell snatched his hands back, as well as the rest of his common sense.

Hope leaned her body against his as he stood by the wall, in her room.

She was literally making things very hard for him, but Darnell was determined to let her know what was up. "Hope, that thing that happened the last time I was here—" Darnell began to say.

"Yes, wasn't it off the hook?" Hope asked. "It felt so right to me, kind of like we were meant to be together. You want to go and do it up on the roof?"

Darnell wasted no time with his reply. This was the minute he needed. "No, Hope, and we're not meant to be together, that's why I'm here. It can't happen again." Darnell reworded his statement. "It won't happen again. I made a mistake. You and me are not a couple, and I have a girlfriend. I need for you to stop telling people that we're together."

"What?" Hope asked as if she had misheard him. She stood upright, bringing her body away from his instantly.

"I'm sorry, Hope, you're sweet and all, but it just can't work. I've got a girl," Darnell continued in an attempt to spare her feelings. "If things were different, who knows what could have happened?"

Hope placed both hands on her hips, and tilted her body to one side. "You weren't trying to say that yesterday." She nibbled on the end of her fingernail for a few seconds, then spoke again. "Oh, so now all of a sudden you remember that you got a girlfriend?"

"Hope, I always did. I can't explain it—" Darnell began to say.

"I know you can't explain this motherfucker, but I can. You used me. Now you walking up in my house with this? Oh, no," she said, riled up. "I can't believe this." She sat on the edge of her bed shaking one leg. "So it's your uppity girl, right?" she asked.

Darnell didn't want to say yes or no. He was just there to let her know what the real deal was, that he couldn't be with her.

"Answer me!" Hope threatened. "That's the least you can do," she told him. Since she was getting nothing out of him, Hope chose to take another route. She thought to herself that she'd have to be smart about what she was going to do next. "I mean, if you're in a relationship and everything like that, I can respect it," Hope told him, lying. "Just tell me that you and I don't have a chance of being together, that's all."

Darnell sighed. Hadn't he told her that? He cooperated anyway. "Yes, Hope, I'm still with the same person, and no, you and I don't have a chance together." He removed his baseball cap, then rubbed his hand over his head. "My girl and I were just going through something. It was one of those things, and you sort of got caught up in the middle. I didn't mean to hurt you."

"Okay then, Darnell," Hope replied.

"Okay then? So then we're cool?" he asked. By looking at the calm expression on her face, one would have thought so.

Hope paused, then nodded. She stopped shaking her leg. "Yeah, we're cool." She added, "You know how we do." She stood up, walked over to him, and gave him a hug. A friendly one and nothing more.

Darnell reciprocated, more at ease because everything had turned out without the heavy drama.

"Let me walk you to the door," Hope told him.

"Thanks," Darnell replied. Hope's mother was snoring loudly, having fallen asleep in front of the television set, or he would have said good-bye. "So I'll see you around then."

"Bet," Hope said. "I'll see you."

Darnell wasn't gone thirty seconds before Hope was back in her room and on the telephone dialing away. "Hey, Lashawn, it's Hope."

"Whassup, girl?"

"Listen, your cousin still working at the telephone company, right?" she asked.

"Yeah, girl, going on six years now," Lashawn answered.

"Perfect, I'm gonna need her to do me a favor," Hope said with a devilish grin. Somebody was about to be in for a big surprise.

42

Under the Knife

Well, today's the big day," Dr. Berg announced on Saturday morning. Ohija accompanied the nurse, who was wheeling Ray from the lobby toward one of the prep rooms inside the hospital.

Ray looked over at his wife, frowning. "Is this wheelchair really necessary? I mean, I can still walk," he said.

Ohija readjusted her bag over her shoulder. It was filled with things to help get her through the experience of waiting while Ray was in surgery for his radical prostatectomy. Inside were books, munchies, her personal journal, and Ray's cell phone, just in case she needed to call Shemone. "Ray, I'm sure it's just part of hospital procedure," she replied.

The nurse handed Ray a hospital robe to change into once they were inside the prep room.

"I can't stand these hospital gowns. They're so open in the back," Ray complained.

Ohija spoke to him from the other side of the curtain, which the nurse had pulled across. "Honey, I'll bring you some other clothes when I come back to see you," Ohija said, attempting to make Ray feel more at ease. She was feeling quite nervous herself, but knew she shouldn't get too excited, for the sake of the babies.

"All set?" Dr. Berg asked before pulling the curtain back open.

"Yeah, guess so, Doc," Ray replied, fully changed into his blue gown and matching slip-over slippers.

Just then, two orderlies rolled in a bed, which would transport Ray directly into surgery.

"Ohija, we're gonna have to take over now," Dr. Berg told her while rechecking Ray's chart. "Ray's in good hands. We'll take care of him," he said.

Ohija heaved a huge sigh, then took hold of Ray's hand as they helped him onto the gurney. "Okay, Ray, baby, be strong. This whole thing will be over before you know it," Ohija told him. She gave her husband a loving peck on the lips. "We'll see you when you get out."

Ray made himself smile. He'd never been hospitalized a day in his entire life. He was terrified. "Okay, honey, I'll see you when I get out."

Ohija walked out of the hospital room and down the long hall, toward the family waiting area. It was the longest walk she'd ever taken. Just knowing that it might be the last time she'd see her husband was enough to make her go into premature labor. But she planned on staying calm, and waiting. Patiently waiting was the best thing she could do.

Ray drifted in and out of sleep, motionless. Through what could only be described as a blur, he saw masked doctors in green tops. There was a blinding bright light, darkness, and then, finally, once again the light.

"Ray, baby, can you hear me? It's your wife, Ohija."

Ray mumbled aloud, then spoke, "Ohija? Did I make it?" Looking around the room made it clear that he was in recovery. A vibrant red vase filled with colorful flowers sat on the table next to his bed.

Ohija was at his bedside, smiling. "Yes, baby, you made it, and I'm so proud of you."

Ray wriggled his toes, and they moved. He was still alive.

Ohija said, "Dr. Berg said that the surgery went very well. It lasted three hours."

Ray turned his head to one side. "Three hours, huh?"

Ohija was bursting with information. "And I also thought that you'd like to know that the doctor was able to spare both sets of nerve bundles, so recovery of your sexual potency is very possible."

A groggy but relieved Ray replied, "You don't say." He gave his wife a sexy look. "Just you wait until I get out of this getup." Ray was referring to the blue leggings with air bladders that he felt inflating from left to right. They squeezed both his legs.

Ohija noticed him still looking down at himself. "Those are to prevent you from getting an embolism. You know, to keep your circulation going. This is the second time I've been in here to check on you. You were resting. I called everyone and told them that you'd made it through the surgery. I wish you'd let people come visit you."

"No way, Ohija, not with me looking dead, and feeling sick," Ray answered. He touched the tube, which blew cold oxygen through his nostrils. He was also hooked up to an IV.

"Will you just relax and quit it with that crazy talk?" Ohija told him. "You look like my angel."

"I still don't want anybody coming to visit me here," Ray told his wife.

"Okay, Ray, then no visitors," Ohija replied.

A tall, thin nurse entered the room. "Well, look who's finally awake," she said, walking over toward Ray's bed with a form on a clipboard. "Tell me, on a scale of one to ten, what's your pain level? Ten being the most painful." Her voice was soothing.

"A five," Ray lied. Actually, he wasn't feeling any pain at all. It seemed as if he should have been, though. He watched the drainage bag on his abdomen filled with the cherry-red liquid. No, there was no hurt at all.

"Mrs. Jones, can we bring in a bed for you?" the nurse asked.

"No, go on home where you can be comfortable in our own bed," Ray interrupted. "You don't need to be here. I can see you in the morning."

Ohija ignored what her husband had just said. She wasn't about to leave Ray alone in the hospital on his first night. "Yes, please bring in a bed, I'd appreciate that."

The nurse smiled. "I hear you, boss."

Ohija took hold of Ray's hand. He was connected to so many tubes. At least he had made it out of surgery, she thought to herself. That was all that was important.

The past few days had been glorious. Especially after Ohija had broken the news that Ray had made it though his prostatecomy. Shemone and Darnell felt closer than ever, putting more of a value on life and the precious time they spent with each other. The two took turns serving each other assorted meals in bed, went to a play, and even visited an arcade down on Forty-second Street. Everything was as it was meant to be. There was a balance, and a peacefulness, that no other man, woman, or child could touch. Shemone felt inspired enough to put the finishing touches on an article she'd entitled "Break Up to Make Up." She typed the final sentences, feeling like a modern-day Shakespearean playwright.

A lovers' quarrel with your mate isn't always the worst scenario. It's sometimes one of the best ways to release those emotions that you've got bottled up inside. When you let it go, it becomes real that what you have is true, so just let it be, otherwise it was never meant to be.

"Shemone," Darnell yelled from the living room. "Ohija's on the phone for you."

"Tell her I'll be right there," she answered. Shemone saved her document, and then shut down her computer. "Hey, you," she said happily, once she'd picked up the phone. "I miss you guys. How's Ray holding up?"

"Girl, Ray is doing just fine, and we miss you, too." Ohija chuckled and said, "Him and his old mean self. He gives those doctors and nurses a run for their money, that's for sure."

Shemone laughed, too. "I can imagine. So when are we going to be able to come and see him?" she asked.

"You can see Groucho soon enough. He's set to be released in a couple of days. I finally left him at the hospital, to come back home for a spell. I'm going back to see him in a bit."

"That's wonderful," Shemone said. "I'm so glad that he's doing well."

"Darnell sounds well, too," Ohija told her. "We spoke for a little while before you came on the phone. Wouldn't you know it, he's worried about me."

"That's my baby," Shemone replied. She blushed on her end of the line. Darnell's character was something to brag about. His worldly ways and streetwise attitude made him a protector. "Ohija, you two are still, like, best friends. Of course he's concerned about you and how you're getting through this."

Ohija agreed. "Yeah, I'm glad that we're rediscovering our friendship. Time and distance can really separate people." She added, "Darnell was also telling me how happy he is now, girl."

Shemone smiled broadly. She felt warm and fuzzy inside. "I think he's happy we're happy. You know, he's at the top of his electricians' class. His instructor is so impressed that he's trying to line up a paying position for him already, even before he graduates."

"Wha—at!" Ohija exclaimed proudly.

"Yes, and it's top dollar, too."

"See what happens to those who wait?" Ohija replied in a matter-of-fact tone of voice.

Shemone laughed. "Hey, I never said that I wouldn't wait."

"Mm-hmm," Ohija kidded.

"Babies doing great?" Shemone asked her friend.

"Babies doing great, and about ready to make their entrance into the world." Ohija continued, "I'm just hoping everything goes okay all around with Ray. We're not completely out of the danger zone yet, you know?"

"Everything will be okay," Shemone assured her. "Everything's gonna work out just fine."

"You're sounding like me now," Ohija said.

"I know, a real optimist, right? Guess I've been hanging around you for too long."

The two chuckled.

"Girl, I'll give you a call tomorrow, then," Ohija told her.

"Okay, girl, give Ray our best and tell him that we'll see him soon."

"Okay, 'bye."

Shemone hung up the phone. She looked over at her desk. Her paperwork was a growing skyscraper exhibit. Although Darnell had taken his turn in cleaning, she'd asked him to never include her desk. She was the only one who knew where everything was. The wastebasket was within arm's reach, so Shemone began to organize. She discarded any old paperwork or notes that she no longer had any use for, and surprisingly was done within the hour.

Exhausted, she lay down on the bed to relax. The phone rang, and she reached to pick it up: "Hello." There was no answer. Damn, the silent caller was calling again. She had to remember to get that call-blocking feature put on, she was getting tired of this shit. Just as she was about to hang up, a female voice spoke.

"Hello, Shemone Waters?" the voice asked her.

"Yes, this is she," Shemone said in her professional tone of voice, unsure whether the call was personal or business.

"You don't know me, but I know you," the voice said.

"Is that right?" Shemone asked. She sat up in the bed, moving closer to the telephone's base. The voice sounded familiar, but Shemone couldn't put a name or a face to it.

"Yeah, bitch, and I know Darnell, too." The voice made sure to add, "real well."

"Who is this?" Shemone asked, irritated that someone would call her house and speak about Darnell in that way. She was about to call him into the room, but then decided not to. She wanted to get to the bottom of this one herself.

"Oh, don't you recognize my voice?"

"No, I don't, but if you would stop with the games and just tell me who you are, I might," Shemone told her. "You must be a child, because I see you like games."

"You'll know me when I'm ready for you to know me, bitch!" the voice said, slamming the phone down in Shemone's ear.

Shemone sat still on the bed, holding the telephone receiver in her hand. Who would do such a thing? And did Darnell know anything about it? She wasn't going to accuse him and fly off the handle like she usually did. Shemone got up from the bed calmly and headed straight to the living room where Darnell was studying and snacking. She got right to the point: "Darnell, I just got a crazy phone call from some female claiming that she knows you 'real well.'"

Darnell almost choked on the chips he had in his mouth.

"Are you okay?" Shemone asked, patting him on the back.

He had a strong feeling about who was behind this. He couldn't believe that Hope had managed to get his home telephone number. "Yeah, I'm okay, chips just went down the wrong way, that's all," he said, coughing. "Baby-girl, somebody is just playing games," he told her. He grabbed hold of her, and sat her on his lap. "Remember, we're not letting anybody come between what we have. We've got a good thing going."

Shemone rested her head on Darnell's shoulder. "That's just what I was thinking, that somebody is playing around on our phone. But whoever it is, they know you," she told him.

"Baby-girl, do you know how many people I know?" Darnell said, almost convincing himself. "It could be anybody."

"Yes, that is true, but they haven't been calling," Shemone replied, choosing to leave the conversation at that. She wasn't about to let one phone call get to her. She was satisfied with trust, and what Darnell had said.

Darnell felt the need to say more. "It's probably some lonely woman with nothing else to do." And having said that, it wasn't completely all a lie. Hope was a lonely woman with nothing else to do but try and wreck his happy home.

43

Three-day Hospitality

Ray woke up famished the morning of the following day. He craved real food. Something tasty like salmon cakes, home fries, and scrambled eggs. Instead, the nurse brought him brown broth, chunks of celery, Jell-O, and unsweetened tea.

Ohija spoon-fed Ray the broth. It went down, and stayed down. After a few bites of Jell-O, everything wanted to come up. She held the plastic kidney-shaped bowl below Ray's mouth while he gagged. "Ray, do you have to vomit?" she asked him.

Yes, Ray nodded his head up and down. He had to vomit.

Lunch was the same menu, but included a cup of ice cream. This time everything stayed down, and Ray was relieved. He was relieved until that afternoon when the nurse came in and told him that he'd have to attempt to take his first walk down the hall. Ohija still hadn't left his side.

"C'mon, Ray, honey, you can do it," Ohija told him as she and the nurse helped him up on his feet. "I'll be with you every step of the way."

Ray rose from the bed slowly, keeping in mind that there was a slice in his abdomen. The IV cart handle and the nurse helped to serve as something else to lean on, and in no way was he going to try to be heroic. It was about twenty feet to the nurses' station, a turn around, and then back to the room. Ray collapsed weakly, back onto his bed. He felt nauseous again.

The following day was a better one. Ray was feeling stronger. A bunch of his coworkers from the sanitation department had popped in to visit.

"Ohija, I thought I told you that I didn't want anyone coming by here to see me," Ray said no sooner than his guests had walked out of his hospital room.

"You did, but I couldn't stop them from coming. I'm not the only person in the world who cares about your health. Your boss and the people from your job have been very supportive." Ohija continued, "As if it isn't enough that you shooed your own wife out of here last night, and made me tell Shemone and Darnell to wait until you got home and settled."

Ray switched on the television set anchored up in the ceiling, unaffected by his wife's chatter. "I'll say this again: I just don't want everybody coming here seeing me like this."

"Oh, Ray, everybody gets sick sometimes," Ohija told him in a convincing tone of voice. Her husband could be so stubborn.

The nurse wheeled in a silver cart filled with platters.

"Finally, I get some food around here. I hope it's not more of that flavorless broth and Jell-O," Ray complained.

The nurse came over and gently removed the IV from his arm. Then she placed one of the covered platter on Ray's own tray. "No, Mr. Jones, I think that you're in for a pleasant surprise," the nurse said. She smiled. Before she left, she peeked back inside and said, "Oh, and you'll get to shower today."

Raymond lifted the lid off the platter. "Yes, solid food, no more IV, and a shower!" he cheered. Things were looking up, due in part to chicken, rice, and green beans.

"Well, somebody's happy," Ohija said to her husband. It was a relief to see that he was finally elated about something. She didn't quite blame him for being such a grouch. The man had a catheter in his penis, a drainage bag on his abdomen, and a newly bloated waist from surgery.

After he'd hungrily devoured his meal, the nurse came back in and helped him to take a shower. He didn't want to be helped. He was feeling daring, and it was upsetting to him that all the nurse cared about was whether or not he did number two. It just so happened that he had gone earlier in the day. Ray slipped on the new underwear that Ohija had brought him. "Ohija," he called out from inside the bathroom.

"Yes, honey, what is it?" She flipped through the pages of a baby catalog, and was seated comfortably in a chair.

"These shorts you bought me, they don't fit," he said.

"Raymond, they've got to fit. I bought you the same size that I always buy," Ohija replied loudly. He was working on her nerves and, quite frankly, she was glad that she'd be leaving to go home within the hour. She'd get herself some rest and start out fresh, ready see him, the next day.

"Ohija, they don't fit and there's no opening in the front," Ray whined. "Where'd you get this underwear from, the bargain basement?"

"No, I did not. Just change into another gown, Ray, nobody wants to see you and your rusty butt," Ohija joked. "I'll bring you better underwear tomorrow."

Ray came out of the bathroom. "Ha, ha, ha. I bet you love this rusty butt," he told her as he walked back toward his bed.

"Sure do, honey. I love your old rusty butt," Ohija said as she looked up, smiling, from her magazine.

The next day was more than just another day. It was the last day of Ray's hospital stay. "What the hell?" Ray asked himself aloud. He examined the look of his genitals after using the bathroom. Both his penis and scrotum had become grossly discolored and swollen. No books or brochures had mentioned that this would happen, and it had him disturbed. Disturbed enough to rush back into his room and buzz for his doctor. Somebody was going to have to come up with some answers for this one.

"Ray," Dr. Berg carefully explained, after the front desk had paged and located him, "believe me, there's nothing for you to be worried about. I assure you that your condition is normal."

"'Normal'?" Ray asked in an excited tone of voice. Ohija hadn't arrived at the hospital for the day yet, so there was no one to tell him to be calm and listen. "You mean that it's normal for my nuts to look like old shriveled-up rotten raisins?" Ray continued, only because he could. "I swear, I'll sue this entire hospital for malpractice if I have to," he said.

"Ray, I promise you that that won't be necessary. What we did was to remove both of your pelvic lymph nodes; they do repipe themselves eventually." Dr. Berg went on, while he still held Ray's attention, "Meanwhile, your fluids have nowhere to go and have settled in the lowest part of your abdomen."

"And just how long is all of this supposed to take?" Ray asked. His eyebrows were knitted together so closely from frowning that they almost formed the letter *V*.

"It's a slow process. It should shrink gradually over the next few weeks to a month," he said.

Ray sighed heavily.

Ohija walked through the door of his room. "Good afternoon, my love," Ohija told her husband, taking immediate notice of the expression on his face. "What's the matter?"

"My privates are all swollen. It's got me walking bowlegged and everything," Ray quickly said before the doctor could give his medical explanation.

Dr. Berg smiled, thinking that Ray had some way with words.

"Well, isn't that a coincidence," Ohija said, trying to make the best of a sensitive situation. "I've always wanted a bowlegged husband. I think that it's soo-o sexy."

Ray grinned, and did finally sit back and relax on his bed, thinking how good his wife was for him. "Ohija, don't talk like that in front of the doctor," Ray said lightly.

"I think it's just what he ordered," Ohija answered.

Dr. Berg gave her and Ray a wink and slipped out the door to finish his daily rounds. Thanks to Ohija, things seemed to be back under control.

Ohija took some stuff out of a plastic bag. "Look what I got you . . ."

Ray smiled. "Underwear! Just what I needed." He turned them around, both in the front and inside, where the tags were, sizing them up. "These should fit my waistline, and they've got an opening, too. Thanks, honey," Ray said appreciatively. "I'm sorry I was so explosive with you yesterday."

"Apology accepted," Ohija said as she leaned in to give Ray a peck on the lips.

"You wanna see what I look like down there?" Ray asked his wife. "I wasn't exaggerating."

Ohija responded in a serious tone of voice, "Not really. All I want to see is what you look like up here." Ohija pointed to the spot on his head where his brain was. "As long as you've got your God-given senses, you're blessed."

"You're some kind of woman," Ray told her. He looked at his wife's growing belly. Lately, it had been difficult to focus on anything but himself and his medical condition. He realized that Ohija had one, too. "So how are my babies doing?"

"Oh, they're doing fine, just fine. It won't be long now. I'm just grateful that I can still get around to be here for you."

"Me, too, baby," Ray said. "I don't know what I'd do without you."

"I know," Ohija said. "I also brought you some food from home that I cooked."

Ray opened up a package of aluminum foil. Inside were four golden-brown salmon patties. "Jackpot!" Ray said as he instantly began eating the fried cakes. In between bites he spoke. "You know, they're going to be shipping me out of here today. I can't wait to get back home."

Ohija settled herself down into a chair. She'd pulled it next to Ray's bed. "I can't wait for you to be back in your own home, too, Ray."

He continued, "Yeah, the nurse should be coming in to explain some stuff about attending to the catheter and drainage bag."

As if on cue, the nurse entered the room. It was the same tall, slim nurse with the calming voice. In his opinion, she was one of the best things that hospital had going for it. He hated everything else.

"Okay, Ray, I just need to go over a few things with you about your catheter."

"Sure," Ray replied. "I was just telling my wife that you would be in here."

The nurse smiled in a nonthreatening, I'm-just-here-to-help-your-husband kind of way. "There are two urine bags: a large one for bedtime connected to a long tube catheter, and a smaller one for mobility strapped onto your upper leg, to be worn under your trousers."

Ray seemed to beam when he replied, "Nurse, I'd wear that catheter thing on top of my trousers if it means that I get to go home!"

44

Either, or Not Both

Ruth picked up the telephone receiver, then put it back down on Saturday afternoon. She picked it up and put it back down again. She wanted to make the phone call to Shemone, but something wouldn't let her. She'd already phoned a week ago and hung up twice. Was making an apology supposed to be so hard? she asked herself.

Ruth stared at the phone for a few seconds longer, then got up from her chair to go into the kitchen. She took from the freezer two filet mignons that she'd special-ordered from the home-shopping network. To go with it, she'd throw together a Caesar salad, and have a baked potato. Dinner for one, as usual.

It was no picnic feeling lonely. She'd managed to single-handedly isolate herself from the one person in the world who actually cared for her. The telephone sounded off in the other room. It hadn't rung in weeks. Ruth scurried into the living room, hoping that it was her daughter, and her chance to apologize. Ruth would invite her over for dinner, and they'd enjoy a steak meal together, with some white wine. She'd apologize for not speaking to her for so long. It had never been this long.

"Hello," Ruth said in her most pleasant tone of voice.

"Hi, Ruth Waters?" the voice asked.

"Why, yes, this is Ruth Waters," she answered in a concerned voice, hoping that it wasn't the hospital calling to say that something had happened to Shemone.

"This is Verizon—" the female voice began to say.

"Is this an emergency call, or is my service about to be interrupted?" Ruth quickly broke in. She knew it wasn't, and she always made sure to pay her bills on time.

"Why no, ma'am," the voice continued, "this is a courtesy call regarding your long-distance privileges."

"No thank you, please don't phone here again," Ruth said, and with that, she hung up the phone. It wasn't Shemone, just a meaningless telemarketer from the phone company. Ruth got up and went back into the kitchen to prepare her dinner. As she cut up the ingredients for the salad, she thought. A handwritten letter to her daughter could work, but direct would be the better approach. Direct meant having to go and see her. And if *he* was still living there, then that could be a problem.

Ruth was getting angry all over again. She didn't have to like him. He was Shemone's boyfriend, not hers. And if her daughter wanted to put up with some factory-working thug, well, then that was her business. Ruth rolled her eyes up in disgust at the thought. It suddenly occurred to why she had been unable to make amends. She and Shemone had been on the outs before and made up, but this time around was different. It was that boyfriend, and nothing else. Accepting Shemone would mean that she'd have to accept him, and that was something she simply wasn't ready to do. Ruth wasn't sure if she ever would be.

Shemone peddled away madly on her exercise bike, determined to give her body a workout. She had to, since there wasn't the everyday hustle and bustle of having to trek back and forth to a nine to five. It was simple to type away at her computer, then break for a snack, in consecutive rounds. Those pounds added up. Sweat began to drip down the sides her face. She wiped it away with the short white terrycloth towel wrapped around her neck, and watched the digital speedometer increase in its numbers. She thought of things that would motivate her to go even faster, those things in her life that she wanted to escape from or was upset by. Immediately, her mother, Ruth, came to mind. Shemone wanted to escape from all of the turmoil that surrounded their relationship. Darnell was close to his family, and Shemone wanted the same. She just couldn't see her mother being left, miserable, one day dying all alone in that house. Another face-off with Ruth was inevitable. Shemone knew that, somewhere, there was some decency inside her. She thought to herself. The bottom line was that Darnell wasn't going anywhere. He was going to be in her life to stay, but she needed her mother, too.

"Look at my baby in here working it out for her man," Darnell said as he walked into the bedroom.

"Hey, you," Shemone replied. She slowed down, pacing herself on the bike. "And for the record," Shemone stated, "I'm working out for me, not for you, buddy."

"Yeah, yeah," Darnell joked. "Of course I don't expect you to admit to it."

Shemone stopped completely and got off the bike.

"Have I ever told you how it turns me on to see you sweat?" Darnell asked her in a seductive tone of voice.

"Yes, several times, and don't get any ideas because we're supposed to go to Ohija's to welcome Ray home tonight."

Darnell grabbed Shemone from behind. His spirits were high. He'd made another trip uptown, and ordered Hope to stop calling his house or else. Of course she'd broken down crying, but had never denied that it had been her. In her own words, she'd told him that it was her one last attempt to make sure that he really wanted to move on. Darnell was convinced that he had persuaded her this time. He was definitely moving on. Hope vowed never to call the house again. He thought to himself that now he and Shemone could live their lives the way they wanted to. Darnell tickled Shemone under her arms.

"Darnell, quit it!" she said, laughing. "We need to shower and get ready to get out of here for tonight." She laughed again as Darnell kept on with the tickling. "We promised to pick up dinner."

"Okay," Darnell replied, "I'll stop it if you get out of those sweaty clothes and meet me in the shower," he told her.

Shemone looked at him as he stood in front of her now, butt naked. His mouth had asked, and as she looked down, so had his body. She wasn't about to refuse, and anyway, she hadn't quite finished her workout.

It wasn't until almost an hour and a half later that they were ready to go.

Shemone lined her lips with brown liner and added a touch of Bobbi Brown lip gloss. "See how late you've made us?" Shemone told Darnell, who was looking at his rugged reflection in the mirror. He was dressed in a gray sweater, a matching hat, black baggy jeans, and gray Timberland boots. "We're matching tonight," Shemone said, smiling. She was dressed in a gray turtleneck, black knit boot-leg pants, and snakeskin boots.

"Yeah, baby-girl," Darnell admitted. "We do have it going on."

Shemone threw her brush, some perfume, and a makeup compact into a coordinating pocketbook. "Let's go," she told Darnell. The telephone rang. "It never fails," Shemone said, sighing, grabbing her keys from the table.

Darnell was already at the door. "Come on, Shemone," he said impatiently, "just let the machine pick it up. We've got to go."

"Wait a minute," she replied. "It's probably Ohija. Let me just tell her that we're on our way."

Darnell stood at the door tapping his foot, looking at his watch.

"Hello," Shemone said after reaching for the receiver.

"Hey, bitch," the familiar voice said. "I didn't catch you at a bad time, did I?"

"I'm not going to keep telling you this—now stop calling my damn house," Shemone warned, putting bass in her voice to let this woman know that she meant what she said.

Darnell frowned. "Yo, Shemone, who is that?" he yelled from the door.

After hearing the sound of Darnell's voice, the caller hung up.

Darnell walked back inside the house, over to Shemone and the phone. "Who was that?" Darnell asked her again.

"If I knew, we wouldn't be having this problem," Shemone answered, collecting her keys and walking toward the door. "I don't know who it was, but as soon as they heard your voice, they hung up, that's for sure."

Darnell followed her. "So you trying to blame me for something some stranger is doing, something that I have no control over?" Darnell asked her.

Shemone locked the door. "No, I'm not, Darnell," she answered calmly. She threw her handbag over her shoulder. "I'm not blaming you at all." And she wasn't going to blame him, she thought to herself, not as long as she had that caller ID ready to come out of the box and be installed. She'd called the phone company to have the feature added to their services the last time the mystery caller had pulled the same stunt. Score one for the Verizon phone company.

45

Reunions

"I am so sorry we're late, girl," Shemone said as they walked through Ohija's front door. "This one was in the mirror, getting all prettied up," she said, referring to Darnell. Ohija laughed out loud. "Yeah, you know he always has liked the mirror," she joked, giving Darnell a hug.

"Whatever!" Darnell replied. He gave Ohija a kiss on the cheek. "We made it here though, right?"

"Where should we put these bags, and where's Ray at?" Shemone asked.

"On the table," Ohija replied. She took their jackets.

"Ray's on the table?" Darnell joked.

"Darnell!" Ohija gave him a playful nudge. "He's in the bedroom, he'll be right out."

Shemone whispered, "Is he in a good mood?"

"Will you stop whispering about the man?" Darnell said, loud enough for Ray to hear. "Of course he's in a good mood. I'm here now."

Shemone and Ohija chuckled.

"Sure I'm in a good mood," Ray said as he came out into the living room. "Now that the food's here. What's that I smell?"

"Hey, man," Darnell said. He went over and gave Ray a manly hug. "It's Caribbean food: curried chicken, rice and peas, and plantains."

"Sounds tasty, D.," Raymond said as he made his way over to the table.

It was already neatly set for four.

No one said anything about the way Ray walked, his new, bow-legged walk.

"Excuse me if I'm not as hospitable as usual," Ray told them. "I just want to fix myself a plate, and then I'm gonna go back on in the bedroom and lie down."

"Right, right, we understand, Ray," Darnell replied. "We just wanted to come through and support you, you know what I'm saying?"

"I appreciate it, Darnell, I really do," he replied.

"Yes, Ray," Shemone added, "you know that we're always here for you."

"Ray, you need any help taking up your food?" Ohija asked.

"No, I've got it," he answered. His plate was stacked high with a little bit of everything.

Just as he'd said, Ray disappeared into the bedroom, but not without saying, "Thanks for coming, you guys."

"Anytime," both Shemone and Darnell answered in unison.

"You two are like a married couple already," Ray said, causing everyone to laugh aloud. It helped to cut some of the tension that was in the room.

Ohija spoke only after she'd heard the bedroom door close. "I'm sorry, you-all."

"What are you apologizing for?" Shemone asked as they all sat around the table to eat.

"It's just that Ray's been so unpredictable. Before we left the hospital, he was fine, now he's gone and switched up on me again to Mr. Grumpy. I know that your intentions were well meant, but maybe I should have waited a while longer before letting you guys come over for a visit."

"Ohija, please—" Shemone said.

"We're practically family," Darnell added, spooning out a large portion of the aromatic peas and rice from their container.

"I know," Ohija replied. "But you know Ray, he's a proud man."

"Most men are," Shemone said, remembering that Ohija had told her the same thing about Darnell.

Darnell gave her a look. Of course she was talking about him and their last you-buying-me-a-tuxedo dispute.

"Yes, but Ray really doesn't want anyone to see him this way, and they've got him taking painkillers once every four hours."

"Get outta here," Shemone replied. "I can see how that must be hard for him."

"Stop pitying the man, just give him a chance to regroup and get on his feet. That's all he needs," Darnell said.

"I'm trying to," Ohija replied. "But these babies aren't about to be waiting for anybody." She loaded her plate with food.

"Right, right, true, true," Darnell said. "Ohija, just keep doing what you doing," Darnell advised her. "Obviously you're doing something right."

"You two must be doing something right, too. You're both all glowing and everything."

"That's nothing but love," Darnell said as he speared and then devoured two of the sweet plantains on his plate.

Shemone giggled and replied, "Darnell, cut it out."

"Let the man revel in his love for you, girl!" Ohija told her, taking a drink of soda from her glass and rubbing her belly. "You're very fortunate."

"You okay, Ohija?" Shemone asked, concerned about her friend.

Ohija took another drink from her glass, then answered, "Yeah, I'm fine. It's just gas," she replied. "It comes with being pregnant. It won't be for too much longer now."

Shemone thought, Time, right. It was moving along pretty fast. "So have you gotten a chance to do any shopping for the babies yet?"

"Not since the last time you and I went to the mall," Ohija answered in a restless tone of voice. "I haven't had time to do anything, between this pregnancy and Ray."

Shemone dabbed at her mouth with a napkin. "That settles it then, we're going baby shopping." She rose from her chair and got her handbag. "Let's say one week from now, which is . . ." Shemone looked at the dates in her date book. "The twenty-first. We'll shop until you drop."

"I might just drop before then," Ohija joked. "I don't have the same energy that I used to. I don't know what I'd do without my meditation, it helps get me through."

"Oh, you do that nam-rey-yo stuff?" Darnell asked, helping himself to another portion of curried chicken.

Did she do that nam-rey-yo stuff? Shemone thought to herself. Was Ronald Reagan once the president of the United States? "Please don't get her started," Shemone answered. Ohija was the queen of meditation.

"Don't worry about her," Darnell said playfully, ignoring his girlfriend and her comment. "I'm talking to Ohija right now."

Shemone smiled and was silent.

"Oh, absolutely, Darnell," Ohija told him. "I'm very much into meditation. And you don't have to say anything in particular as you do it. It's your choice. Meditation is one of the best things that I could ever have started doing. It really allows you to get to know your spirit, and teaches you that through it, you can grow." Ohija beamed and continued, "Just think about it. When you meditate, you're in silence. You're in a total state of thoughtful awareness."

"That's deep," Darnell replied in a really interested tone of voice. "I might try to get into that. I need to be more focused."

"You're already more focused, sweetie," Shemone said in a supportive way, deciding to rejoin the conversation. "You know exactly what you want, and where you're going." Shemone came over and sat back down at the table.

"But it can't hurt," Ohija said. "It can only make him more centered, Shemone. Darnell, I'm not trying to push you into anything, the choice is up to you, and it doesn't mean that you have to go to classes or anything. Just find a peaceful place in your head, close your eyes, and think positive thoughts. Channel your energy."

Shemone got up and started to clear the finished plates of food from the table. "Ohija's right," she said. "Anything that's gonna make you a better person is worth trying."

"Have you tried it?" Darnell asked as Shemone passed him. He playfully hit her on the behind.

"Darnell, stop it!" Shemone chuckled, then answered, "Not yet, but I've been meaning to."

"Excuses, excuses," Ohija joined in and said with a smirk.

"I will," Shemone said. "I pray, that's a form of meditation right there."

"It sure is, girl," Ohija quickly replied. "I heard that. Prayer is meditation. I pray all the time."

"Go, baby-girl," Darnell said.

"Thanks for clearing the table for me," Ohija told her. She was overstuffed from the meal she'd just had, and couldn't move an inch.

"No problem. I don't mind," Shemone told her.

Darnell got up from the table. "Well, dinner was the best, if you two ladies will excuse me."

"Where are you going?" Shemone asked him.

"I'm going to pop in and see Ray for a quick minute," Darnell replied.

"Do you think that's a good idea?" Shemone asked. "You heard what Ohija told us, Ray just got out of the hospital and everything."

Ohija just looked on.

"Yeah, I heard her, and I still think it's a good idea. It's a better idea than sitting out here having a pity party for him."

Darnell disappeared toward the back and into the bedroom.

Ohija and Shemone let him go.

"That husband of yours!" Ohija said in an upbeat tone of voice.

"He is not my husband." Shemone held out her hand. "There are no rings on these fingers!"

Ohija gave her the eye. She hoped her friend wasn't still waiting for that perfect package in a man.

"No rings, at least not yet," Shemone finished with a broad smile. "Gas gone?"

"Hey, Ray—man, you asleep?" Darnell asked once he'd stepped inside the bedroom. The color television played an old episode of *I Love Lucy.*

"No, I'm awake," Ray answered from underneath the covers. His tray of food sat untouched on the nightstand next to the bed. "Come on in, man."

Darnell walked inside and sat on the end of the bed.

"Tired of being around the women?" Ray asked.

"Yeah—you know how it is," Darnell answered. "Women just love to talk and talk about stuff."

"Got tired of talking about babies and the pathetic husband, huh?"

Darnell laughed aloud. "No, not the babies. You know I love kids." Then he added, "And, man, there's nothing pathetic about you."

This time Ray himself had to laugh. "If you only knew. My privates are all swollen and messed up. I got this catheter and tubes. You just don't know, everything on me hurts."

"Sounds real personal," Darnell joked.

Ray laughed again. "You're funny, you know that?" Ray was able to hurl a pillow toward Darnell's head. "I needed that. I haven't laughed like this in a while. I mean, I've got other friends and everything, but they, like, give me that sympathy crap. I know it's just about them feeling sorry for me. You never do that," he told Darnell.

Darnell joked again, as if he was accepting a Grammy. "I appreciate it, and," he said, pausing, "I love you, man."

The two looked at each other and burst out in laughter.

"So when do you have to go back to the doctor?"

"A week and a half from now," Ray answered. "To get my pathology results. They'll basically just let us know if my surgery was successful or not."

"Okay," Darnell said in a hopeful tone of voice. "That's good to know."

"Right," Ray said. "I am glad to be back at home, though."

"You must be." Darnell looked at the large wedding picture of Ohija and Ray, on their dresser. One day soon, he and Shemone would have a picture just like that.

"Checking out the wedding photo?" Ray asked, switching the subject. The thought occurred to him that he was being just as bad as his wife by talking about his medical condition so much.

"Maybe," was all that Darnell said with a smirk.

"Getting any ideas?"

"Ray, you sure do ask a lot of questions for a sick guy!" Darnell chuckled. Then getting serious, he continued, "For real, I've been thinking about it a lot. I'm about ready to take it to that next level, man."

"Yeah?" Ray answered. "There are a lot of women out there, but to find a really grounded woman is special."

Darnell only nodded. He knew that Ray was right, and that it was his time. He'd be graduating from electrical school soon, hopefully had a new job waiting for him right after, and already had money saved for the ring, from his old reliable stash.

46

Masquerade

Sucker, Hope thought to herself on Tuesday as she ran her customer's items past the scanner in the drugstore where she worked. She could hardly believe that Darnell had fallen for her and her big-time crocodile tears. No wonder his uppity bitch had him wrapped around her finger. But not for long. Hope began to bag her customer's items. She wasn't about to respect his relationship with that woman.

"Have a nice day," Hope told her customer. She pulled out an issue of *Essence* magazine that she had underneath the counter. She opened it to the article called "Girlfriend Strike." Quickly reading the words she made sure. Yeah, it was her story all right. Hope reread the part that said "by Shemone Waters." What made Shemone Waters think that she was better than everybody else? Just because she was a writer? So what if she was still in the projects with her mother and had a job in a pharmacy? Hope thought to herself. Shit, she was on her way to making it to store manager. She knew more than the one they had in charge working in there now. Hope couldn't count the numerous times she'd had to closeout her own register as well as the other cashier's on account of his lack of know-how.

Hope glanced at herself in the store's mirror. Nobody could tell her that she didn't look way better than Shemone Waters. She'd just gotten her hair done in a new flat twist style with burgundy highlights, and it made her look like one of those models in the salon magazines. Her butt and breasts were way bigger, too. Shemone's supposed-to-be-man sure was real happy when he had at them. Hope smiled, thinking that he would be again, because she wasn't about to give up without a fight. It was clear that Darnell didn't know what he wanted, but it was her job to show him. He'd probably wanted to speak to her the last time she'd called. It annoyed Hope that Shemone had picked up every time she'd called. She and Darnell were just meant to be, and Hope was determined to have everything that the uppity bitch had and more.

Darnell had devised the perfect plan, all thanks to what Ohija had told him about Ray and his methods of original thinking. He sat in the living room nervously reading the sports pages of the newspaper while Shemone worked on a story in the bedroom. He looked at the time on the clock on the wall thinking that it was now or never. "Shemone," he called out, "the door buzzed. I think that there's a FedEx delivery for you in the lobby," he told her.

"Can't you get it?" Shemone yelled back.

"No, baby-girl," Darnell lied. "He said only you could sign for it."

"Well, can't he bring it up?" Shemone suggested. She was busy, right in the middle of doing some crucial research on the Internet.

"Shemone, you'd better go. You know how those delivery people are. The FedEx man might just take it back."

She sighed heavily, rushing out of the bedroom. She shot Darnell a look as she took notice of how casual he looked sitting comfortably reading his newspaper. She went out the door.

Darnell sprinted up and into the bedroom. He'd learned enough about computers to find his way around now. He saved, signed Shemone off, and went into the Windows program. Then, on a new blank page he wrote in huge seventy-two-point-size lettering: WILL YOU MARRY ME? Darnell quickly removed the two-carat ring from his jeans pocket and placed it on top of the computer, knowing that she'd be coming back through the door any second.

"Darnell Williams," Shemone yelled out, "I'm gonna kill you."

He met her in the hall, not a second too soon. "Yeah, what happened?" he asked innocently.

"There was no FedEx for me. I went downstairs for nothing," she said.

"For real? They must have gotten your name mixed up with someone else. My bad," Darnell said nonchalantly as he walked back toward the living room.

"Thanks a lot," she said, heading back into the bedroom to finish her work.

Darnell listened closely from the living room until he heard a scream. Fast footsteps followed, as Shemone jumped on his lap.

"Yes, I will marry you," she answered, kissing him on the lips slow and long. She stopped just long enough to admire her ring, which was already on her wedding-ring finger. "Darnell, I love my ring, it's beautiful!" She admired it again, holding it away from her. "And asking me on my computer," she continued. "You are really something else, do you know that?"

Darnell shook his head knowingly. "Yeah, I didn't want to be too corny!"

"Ohija, I've got to call Ohija and tell her," Shemone said as she sprang up from his lap. Shemone used her speed-dial feature, hardly able to get the words out. "Ohija, Darnell just proposed to me, girl!"

"No way!" Ohija said in her happiest tone of voice. "I knew it was gonna happen! I just knew it! Ray, Shemone and Darnell are getting married!" she yelled out loudly to her husband.

Shemone could hear Ray in the background.

"Tell them congratulations, and all the best!"

"Let Ray know that I heard him, and thank you," Shemone replied as she stood, beaming. "Did you know anything about this?" Shemone asked Ohija.

"Yeah, girl, remember when I spoke to Darnell the last time, and I told you that we spoke for a while? Remember when I told you how happy Darnell said he was?" Ohija chuckled loudly into the phone. "Sure he told me that's what he planned on doing. I am one of his closest friends."

"You knew all along!" Shemone burst out.

"It wasn't a definite sure sure. Then when Ray mentioned that Darnell had mentioned something to him—"

"Girl, I'm so happy!" Shemone said, cutting her off. "And you've just got to see the ring, girl. How many carats is it, baby?" she asked Darnell

"Two, but who's counting?" he joked. He knew his woman. She liked nice things. He'd known that from day one, when he'd first started having conversations with her from jail.

"I gotta go, girl," an overexcited Shemone told Ohija. "I just wanted to call you and tell you. I have to spend some time with my husband-to-be," she said.

"Go on!" Ohija replied. "Congratulations again. I wish you both all the happiness in the world."

"Thank you, I'll call you tomorrow, then." Shemone hung up the phone. She held out her hand and smiled. Darnell smiled back. "I think that this calls for a celebration," Shemone said as she slipped out of her clothes. She stood naked in front of Darnell. He stood up, and picked her up off the floor, carrying her into the bedroom. The celebration was on.

Shemone turned over in bed on Tuesday evening. Darnell wasn't there, but a note was.

Baby-girl, went uptown to see Pop to tell him our news in person. Will be back soon. Be prepared for another round.

Love, your future husband, D.

Shemone smiled warmly, and sat up in bed. Her husband, she thought. She and Darnell had sure come a long way, but it had been worth it. She got up, and six-stepped it to the bathroom. She didn't think there was going to be another round. Darnell had put it on her. Shemone turned on the water for a bubble bath. She thought that would help to soothe her, and by the time Darnell got home, she'd be ready again. It hadn't been five minutes that Shemone had been in the tub when the phone rang. Shemone listened to it ring as she sank herself farther down into the tub. She'd forgotten to put the answering machine on. She sucked her teeth, thinking it could be one of her editors. She got up out of the tub and ran to pick it up. Water and suds made a trail behind her.

"Hello."

"Bitch, it's you."

"Yes, it is me," Shemone answered in a bold tone of voice. "I just got out of the bathtub, 555-7159." She examined the caller ID box, which she'd just had installed by her side of the bed. This time, Hope had failed to block out the number she'd called from.

"Oh, it's no secret," the female voice said. "I'm glad you know now. It took your ass long enough."

Shemone wrapped the towel tightly around her body. Her ring

glistened brightly as she looked down at it. "Let me tell you something. If you wanted me to know who you are, you should have just said your name the first time you called," Shemone replied with satisfaction. "Now I'm going to ask you one more time, who is this?"

There was a silence on the line. "You can call me 555-7159, or you can call me Hope, bitch. Either way, I've been sleeping with your man."

"You're a damn liar," Shemone shot back.

"Oh, you think so?"

"You are, and I should have known that you'd be the one to stoop this low after Darnell rejected you for me," Shemone answered in a confident tone of voice. She thought to herself that things with Darnell couldn't have been going any better.

"I don't think that's the way it's going down. You sure you haven't been having any problems lately?" Hope added, "Ms. Girlfriend Strike?"

"Excuse me?" Shemone said in a stunned tone of voice.

"Bitch, you need to stop putting your personal business in your stories. But since you do, I've got some juicy information you might want to put in next month's issue."

"Hope, I'm not going to let you take me there," Shemone spat back.

"Oh, I'm gonna take you there," she said, before dropping the bomb. "Darnell and me made love at my house, in my bed. That's right, bitch, he's been coming to me 'cause you can't handle your business. In fact," she continued, "Darnell's just looking for a way to use your ass all up so he can leave you."

"Don't you ever call here again," Shemone threatened.

"Oohh, I'm so scared," Hope told her with a laugh. "And if I do? What are you gonna do?"

"Let me just put it this way, in plain language that I'm sure you'll understand." Shemone spoke in an even tone of voice: "I know where you live." And with that, she hung up the phone.

Shemone sat on the edge of the bed. Her head was trying to process information as she tried to regroup, and retrack the events in her life from just weeks before. The girlfriend article was real. And it was true that she'd gotten in an argument with Darnell. Could it be? Her Darnell in another woman's bed? And the calls, she thought, the calls had just started. Shemone looked down at her ring. She impulsively snatched it off, and decided to place it on her nightstand until she could hear what his side of the story was. She was going to wait for him, no matter what time he got home. If Hope was telling the truth with what she'd said, Shemone predicted that this would not be the next round, but the last.

47

Ringside

Shemone sat in a dark living room that same night, all the lights turned off inside. It had been hours since Darnell had left to go see Pop. She'd had enough time to make a phone call to Ohija and let her in on what was happening, and polish off almost a whole bottle of Chardonnay all by herself. Right at that moment the room spun around, but her agenda remained crystal clear. She knew exactly what it was that she had to do. Keys rattled in the front door.

Darnell came inside and hung up his coat. He didn't try to turn on the lights, and he didn't see Shemone sitting there as still as an owl on the couch.

"Have fun?" Shemone asked in a loud tone of voice.

"Shemone, you scared the mess out of me!" Darnell said in a startled voice.

"You didn't answer my question." Shemone asked him again, "Did you have a good time?"

"Are you okay?" Darnell asked. He switched on the light, but wanted to switch it right back off once he saw Shemone's facial expression. There was definitely a crazed look in her eyes.

"I'm fine, and Hope's fine, too," Shemone said as she finally stood up. Her legs felt as if they wanted to give out from all the wine she'd drunk, but she remained steady on her feet.

"Hope?" he repeated. "What's she got to do with anything? Is she the one who's been calling here?"

Shemone laughed. "As if you didn't know," she replied. "She had a lot to say about you, and her, in her house, and on her bed—"

"She—" Darnell began to say.

Shemone held her hand up toward his face, defying him to utter another word. "Don't you lie to me, Darnell Williams, don't do it to yourself. I'm only going to ask you this once. Did you, or did you not, have sex with that Hope woman?" she asked him.

Darnell sighed, not knowing what to do. His first impulse was to deny it, but he wasn't sure he could live with himself if he did. He didn't want to start a brand-new marriage based on a lie. He finally decided just to tell her. "Yes, Shemone, I did have sex with Hope."

Shemone had an expression on her face as if she was about to throw up. "Is there anything else that you have to say, anything you need to say for yourself?" she asked him. She didn't want it to be said that she hadn't given him the chance or the opportunity to straighten out this whole nightmare.

Darnell answered, "No, there is nothing for me to say. I did what I did, on my own."

"Okay, then, I want you to leave, and I want you to leave right now," Shemone told him calmly. She continued, "You can get your clothes tomorrow, they'll be waiting for you outside my door."

Darnell looked down at Shemone's empty hand. "Where's your ring at, Shemone?"

"Hope has it," Shemone said in a wicked tone of voice, giving him a hard stare. She was way too upset to be thinking about where his ring was. "Any more questions?"

Darnell turned away, then left to walk into the hallway, his head hung low. It was over, he thought to himself. His life was over, all of his dreams were just over.

Shemone, about to walk back into her bedroom, made sure to add, "And leave my apartment keys on the table."

48

Old Endings, New Beginnings

Raymond and Ohija sat in Dr. Berg's office awaiting Ray's pathology results on Wednesday morning.

Dr. Berg came in. "Hey, folks." He greeted them with a smile, and then took a seat. "Good news—there was no cancer in the lymph nodes we removed. It appears to have been contained entirely within your prostate," Dr. Berg continued, and gave Ray a firm pat on the back. "We'll be looking over your shoulder, so to speak, for the next few years, but I'd say that the odds are excellent for a complete recovery."

"Oh, thank you, Dr. Berg!" Ohija exclaimed as she reached out and gave him a hug. Tears streamed down her face.

Ray sat with a hand covering the top part of his face. He sniffled.

"Ray, did you hear the doctor? You made it through this, honey! We made it through this!" his wife told him.

Ray removed his hand and looked up. His eyes were red from trying to contain his emotions. "Dr. Berg, from the heart," he began to say, feeling all choked up. He stood up and shook his doctor's hand. "Thank you for everything." A single tear fought its way downward.

Ohija smiled.

"You both are welcome," Dr. Berg replied. "This makes my job worth while. "But we still have some unfinished business with you today. We need to get rid of that extra stuff on you. I'm sure it's been weighing you down." He was referring to Ray's catheter, which he'd worn for twenty-four hours a day since he'd left the hospital.

Ray laughed, and said in a happy tone of voice, "Yes, please get rid of it!"

A physician's assistant with a name tag that read "Marla" came in and removed his drainage bag. She also pulled out the tube that fed into it. It came out slowly, a sheet of glistening gray paste rolled up in a long tube.

"Is it painful, honey?" Ohija asked her husband.

"No, nothing's painful now," Ray answered. He grinned as if every day was his birthday, then continued, "It's just a sucking feeling, deep in my abdomen. It kind of feels like I'm getting my intestines pulled out."

Dr. Berg was still in the room, standing by. "Ray, I must say, that does sound painful."

The whole room laughed.

By the time Ray looked down at himself, Nurse Marla had pulled the tube out. There was a sizable hole in his lower abdomen, just to the right of his incision. "Wow, it looks like I've got myself a spear wound," he said.

"It'll heal quickly, Ray," Dr. Berg replied as he scribbled on his chart. "It should only take a few weeks from the inside out."

"I just can't believe that I'm in the clear," Ray said enthusiastically.

"Don't forget now, there's going to be some constant irritation in the area for a while, because the catheter has just been removed." Dr. Berg added, "And incontinence, and impotence, is still a possibility. Incontinence can last for as little as a few months to forever if you happen to be in that small—two to four—percent of men," he told him.

"Doc, I don't think that I'll have to worry about that impotent part at least." Ray hurried and said, "My wife and I are handling things just fine."

"Unfortunately, Ray," Dr. Berg said, "it's still too early to tell. Time will have to be the deciding factor in determining your outcome. You may be impotent for just a short time, and then become able to resume normal sexual activities after a while. In any case, there's always Viagra."

"Viagra, no Viagra, whatever it takes," Ohija said, joining in on the conversation. "We'll just work at it, Ray, honey. I'm sure you won't be needing to take anything with the way you get."

Dr. Berg chuckled. "Optimism is always key," he said. "And if you two need me, don't hesitate to call the office. If something doesn't seem or feel right, just let me know."

"Thanks again, Doctor, and we will," Ohija replied. She and Ray got up, put on their coats, and went out the door. She didn't speak until they had gotten settled inside the car and were on the drive back home. Her mind was weighed down, and Ray's prognosis was not the topic she wanted to speak about. "Did I tell you that Shemone and Darnell's engagement is off?"

"What?" Ray asked. His tone was a startled one as he drove onto the entrance to the highway. "They just told us that they were getting married yesterday, didn't they?"

"Mm-hmm," Ohija replied. She added, "It's such a shame."

Ray stayed quiet for a minute or two. At first, he wasn't about to get involved. If Shemone and Darnell had decided not to walk down the aisle, then that was their business. It didn't mean that they'd never get married. As he switched over to the right lane, curiosity got the better of him, so he asked, "What's such a shame?"

"It's a shame that Darnell was out there messing around on Shemone." Ohija folded her hands on her lap. "I heard the woman called the house and everything." She continued, "I mean, Darnell is my friend and all, but that's just plain deceit right there," she told him.

"So? How does Shemone know that it's true?" Ray momentarily looked away from the road and over at his wife. "That woman could just be saying things to break up their relationship, you know."

"Oh, a woman knows when her man's been cheating, believe me," Ohija said in a confident tone of voice. "It's an instinctual thing. I'm all for positivity and all that, and Darnell is like a brother to me, but wrong is wrong, period. You just don't step out when things are solid for you at home," Ohija told her husband. She rubbed her stomach, calming herself down. The excitement had the babies moving around inside her, and as of late, she was beginning to feel minor back pains, too.

Ray thought to himself that he sure could never say that he didn't know where his wife stood on this one, thanks to his what's-such-a shame question. "I hear what you're saying, honey, but remember, there's always two sides to a story. I just hope that she gave him the chance to defend himself before calling everything off so suddenly," he said.

"Yes, well, maybe she should have, but gut instincts usually don't steer you wrong," Ohija answered. She thought to herself that Shemone hadn't met her at the hospital as she'd said she would, and it bothered her. Who knew what kind of condition her friend was in? Ohija decided to head straight for Shemone's house as soon as Ray dropped himself off back at home. If she hadn't had to find out what his test results were that day, she'd have been right by Shemone's side.

Ray wasn't about to try and take on his wife on the subject of instincts. He knew he'd never win. Instead, he made a mental note to call Darnell and try to find out the truth about what had really gone down. He wasn't about to write him off just because he and Shemone had had a falling out. Ray felt as if he owed him that much. Darnell had been there for him throughout his medical ordeal, and now Darnell needed to have someone in his corner. Ray drove the rest of the way home silently, thinking about his future. Things were finally starting to look up for him again.

49

Charity Case

"You poor dear," Ruth said. She held her daughter close in her arms like she'd actually wanted to, for what was the first time in years, on Wednesday morning. She reached over for the mug a third of the way filled with the slightly warmed-up coffee. Ruth had been trying to sober her daughter up for the last hour, and it was finally working. Shemone was sitting up. Ruth was grateful that her daughter had gotten to her safely, in one piece, and that she had not been taken advantage of by the cabdriver who'd brought her to her house. "Here, try and take another sip," Ruth told her, holding up the cup.

Shemone sniffled, trying to hold back the tears that wouldn't stop coming. She sipped. Everything was like one big blur, especially the part about how she'd wound up on her mother's doorstep. She thought about it as Ruth held her gingerly in her arms. She remembered how quickly her anger had turned to pain. Shemone had broken down completely after Darnell left the apartment. She'd cried herself to sleep that night, but the pain was still there the next morning when she woke up. Her temporary cure stared directly at her from the wine rack. It was that other bottle of Chardonnay plus that hurting pain, like never before, that had done it. The unusual combination of the two led her straight to Ruth's house, where it was as if her mother was there just waiting to comfort her.

After telling Ohija the tragic news, she was supposed to meet her at the hospital that morning, but somehow, she knew that with Ohija wasn't where she wanted to be. Comforting, Shemone thought to herself, was how Ruth was behaving. She could relate for once in her life to what Darnell had been talking about that time when he'd run home to his mother. Of course Darnell and his mom seemed to have a stronger bond, but where she and Ruth were now was a damn good start, even if the circumstances of their reunion weren't exactly ideal. "Darnell just wasn't the one for me," she said, sniffling again.

"Don't you worry now," Ruth replied. She gently patted Shemone on the back. "There are plenty of other fish in the sea. You're attractive, and you're smart," Ruth told her. "You'll find someone else in no time. He won't have to struggle, and he'll be on your level," she added.

That comment, the one right at the very end, was enough to make Shemone stop her wailing. She held her head up, and blew her nose in a tissue. "It's not that he wasn't on my level, Mom, it's that he cheated on me," she replied. Why was she still defending this man? she asked herself.

Ruth just looked at her daughter lovingly, and with compassion. She knew how it felt to be rejected by someone you loved. Shemone's father, and her own parents, had done it to her. This was why, Ruth thought, she had to be there for Shemone.

Shemone continued, "But how could he do that to me? Especially after everything that we've been through?" Shemone asked her mother. "I feel like such a fool," she sobbed. "I should have known once all those phone hang-ups began."

Yes, the hang-ups, Ruth thought. She wasn't about to admit that she had been the one behind some of those calls. To think, Ruth had been telephoning to apologize, but fate had done her one better. She was getting a second chance at being a mother. Good riddance to Darnell, because Shemone was better off without him anyway. Ruth let her daughter know just that. "I know that you might not want to hear this coming from me, but I did try to tell you. Whenever you get involved with a man like that, he's bound to cheat." Ruth added, "Or they'll steal or do just about anything, for that matter. I think you should consider yourself lucky that something like this happened before you made the dreadful mistake of possibly marrying him."

Shemone got up and went over to the window. As she peered out, she thought that maybe her mother was right. It would only have been a matter of time before Darnell and his cheating ways surfaced. She hated to think it, but it rang true: You can take the man out of the ghetto, but you can't take the ghetto out of the man.

Ruth walked over to the window, by her daughter. "Shemone, dear, why don't you take some time for yourself and stay on a few days with me?" she asked. "The rest will do wonders, and you know you always have a room here."

Shemone didn't have a doubt in her mind. The rest and the change would do her good, she thought to herself. She could even bring her laptop over and get some writing in. The best thing was that when Darnell called, pleading and begging her to take him back, she wouldn't be at the apartment. "Okay, Mom," Shemone answered, trying to muster a smile. "I think I'm going to take you up on that invitation. I could use the break."

Ruth smiled broadly. Her intentions weren't at all bad. Wanting to make up for lost time and bond with her own flesh and blood couldn't have been. Right now, Shemone didn't want to have anything to do with Darnell Williams. That was something major they had in common. It was an opportunity that Ruth wasn't about to miss out on.

Darnell and Ray sat at a booth in the Silver Diner restaurant on Sunday afternoon.

"So you're going to be a Dada soon, huh?" Darnell said.

"Yep, soon enough," Ray answered with a proud smile.

"You all ready?" Darnell asked.

"About as ready and excited as I'll ever be," Ray replied. "Man, myself, I'm just glad to be alive and kicking."

"I hear that," Darnell said.

Ray nodded during an awkward moment of silence. He wasn't sure how to approach the topic. He'd invited Darnell out for lunch, his treat, under the pretense that they were celebrating his recovery from prostate cancer. Just by looking at him, Ray could tell that Darnell wasn't doing well. It looked like he hadn't changed his clothes in days, and his face was covered in stubble, giving him the appearance of a much older man. Hell, Ray thought, he was just going to come out with it. He had to say something. "Darnell, I heard about what happened with you and Shemone."

"Yeah?" Darnell replied. The tone of his voice hit an all-time low. "What'd you hear?"

The waitress arrived with their orders. Ray had ordered a steak and fries, and Darnell had ordered a turkey and bacon club with onion rings.

"Thank you," Ray told the waitress. The plates clanked on the table surface as she set them down, then walked away.

Ray continued with their conversation. "I didn't hear much, really," he said, not wanting to say exactly how much his wife had let on. "Just that you two called the marriage thing off."

"Hmph," Darnell replied. "I didn't call anything off. Shemone did that for me."

"I see," Ray said. He poured steak sauce over the top of his steak. Darnell didn't even attempt to touch his own food.

"Aren't you hungry?" Ray asked him.

"I'll get to it," Darnell replied. "Don't think that I don't appreciate you taking me out and everything, Ray—" he said.

"Oh, I understand, you don't have much of an appetite now," Ray answered. He cut off a piece of steak, chewed, swallowed, then finally asked, "Darnell, did you cheat on Shemone?"

Darnell took his time in answering, blowing out a fresh rush of air. "That all depends on how you describe it. It was for all of the wrong reasons. I overheard her talking to this guy Keith, but I was feeling like less of a man way before that. There was nothing to what happened. I'm not in love with that girl, like I am with She—" Darnell started to say her name, but changed his mind. It hurt too much. He continued speaking, until he'd told Ray about everything that had happened between him and Shemone. "Ray, you gotta believe me, it didn't mean anything."

Ray took a drink from his glass of ginger ale. "I believe you, Darnell, but it's not me that you have to convince. Shemone's the one. I mean, have you tried to explain at all?"

Darnell picked up an onion ring, then put it back down. "She asked me if I cheated, I told her the truth, then she asked me to leave. There was nothing I could say then, to make it right. She was up, waiting for me."

"Yeah, it might take her some time," Ray replied. "Did you confront the woman who called the house yet?"

"No, I'm scared that I'll kill her if I see her," Darnell told him. "She knows what she did, all right. That was nothing but spite right there," he said, getting angry just thinking about it.

Ray quickly reminded him, "You know, it did take two. This girl wasn't the only one at fault," he told him.

"Oh—no doubt," Darnell replied. "And that's just what stops me from acting on my feelings about her and her craziness." Darnell continued, "I wouldn't want her now if she was the last woman on this earth."

Ray held his hand up to his temple. He felt for Darnell and what he was going through.

"There's nothing that I want more than Shemone. I can't eat, I can't sleep. I haven't even confessed and told Pop that I really did it. He'll probably just tell me I'm off the charts."

"'Off the charts'?" Ray asked.

"Yeah, it's, like, street lingo. It means 'crazy.' Pop's gonna tell me I did some crazy shit, for sure, sleeping with that girl in the first place. He knows her from around the way."

"So where are you staying?" Ray asked. "You look terrible."

"With my moms again. My mother wants me to see somebody, like in a psychiatric ward or something. She keeps asking me what's wrong," Darnell told Ray. "All I can tell her is that I'm just closed up right now. I told her that I'm going through something. It feels like I've been separated from Shemone forever, even though I know it hasn't been that long," he said.

"It must," Ray replied in an understanding voice. "What you've got to do is keep on trying."

"Ohija hate me, too?" Darnell asked him.

"Hate you? No," Ray told him, "Ohija could never hate anybody. But she doesn't like what you did to her other best friend. You guys are best friends, too, but you know she got Shemone's version of the story first."

"Right," Darnell said, nodding. "And that's not far from the truth." He sighed. "Ray, I'm useless without her. She has a way that just brings out the best in me, you know?"

"Oh, I know," Ray said. "A real woman will do that for you, and vice versa. Just don't give up yet. That's the best I can tell you."

"You've got a steady relationship. What should I do?" Darnell asked Ray in a desperate tone of voice. He wanted advice from him in the worst kind of way. "I don't know how to make it right. I took a few days off from work, and my electrical-school internship is done. I'm just waiting to see if something comes through. I don't know. I just feel like I could go out and get myself locked up again," Darnell told him. "It was safe in jail, in a way. I didn't have to deal with these kinds of problems."

"Get a hold of yourself, man," Ray told him. "You didn't exactly have Shemone when you were behind bars."

Darnell frowned. "You mean, what I had, Ray. Remember, man? I don't have her no more."

Ray couldn't say much, except that he still had him as his friend. "Well, if you need support, just like you told me, I'm here for you."

Darnell slapped Ray five with his hands, across the table. Then he called out to get the waitress's attention. "Over here, can you wrap this up for me? I'm gonna take this to go," Darnell told her.

"You about ready to leave?" Ray asked him.

"Yeah, I guess I'll head back across town," Darnell replied without enthusiasm.

"Well, take care of yourself. I've got the bill this time," Ray told him in a joking tone of voice.

The waitress came back with his food. Darnell held the bag up in gratitude as he got up to leave. "Yeah, thanks, and keep in touch, Ray."

"You, too," Ray answered. He had gotten to the bottom of the story, but wasn't sure if he could help in doing anything about it.

50

BAD CONNECTIONS

Wednesday would make almost two full weeks of being at her mother's house, and Shemone hadn't missed being at her own place at all, she thought to herself. So far, she was surviving, filling her days with work, and her nights with thoughts of purchasing the biggest vibrator she could find in a sex store. Shemone had just finished a new article for *Sister Soul* entitled

LOVIN' GONE WRONG

by Shemone Waters

Liar. Cheat. Love is often overrated before it's gone wrong. If you're reading this article and these signals seem somewhat familiar to you, then it's probably in your best interests to take careful heed. It's often hard to distinguish what is, and what is not, good for you when you're the one in the relationship. Sometimes it takes someone

from the outside to help point things out. So here are a few things for you to be on the lookout for:

- **You don't spend nearly enough time with your friends as you used to. It's okay to divert for a moment while in relationship bliss, but don't get carried away. Those same friends who were there for you before you met this person will probably be there for you after.**
- **Hang-ups on your phone. That's a telltale sign of another interested party, and if they're not asking to speak to you, then I guarantee that it's for your mate. Don't be paranoid, but get to the bottom of it as soon as you can.**
- **Lying. A lie is a lie is a lie, and it's never a healthy thing. If your mate can fabricate the small things, he or she is certain to be able to fabricate the big. That's one to watch for.**

These are just a few things to look out for. You should tailor your own signals by using your own instincts. Make the love you have right! It will last much longer that way!

"Shemone!" Ruth called from the front room. "Ohija's here."

Had she misheard? Shemone asked herself with a smile. Her mother had actually called Ohija by her right name. Wonders never ceased. "Tell her to come back to my room, please!" Shemone yelled back.

"Hey," Ohija said as she waddled through the door. "Did you ask your mother if you could have company?" she asked with a big grin.

"Ha-ha, very funny," Shemone replied with a smirk. "Close the door behind you—and nice scarf."

Ohija closed the door. "Thanks, it's about the only fashionable thing I can wear these days. Of course, it's from the shop. My sister found a new tie-dye vendor."

"It looks hand painted," Shemone replied. "Have a sit down anywhere." Shemone eyed her friend. "Girl, you look like you're about to burst."

Ohija giggled. "Don't I know it. At night, my back aches, and I'm supposed to be on bed rest, but you know, I just had to come and see how my sistah-girlfriend was doing. Even if it meant having to see your always cordial and pleasant mother," Ohija joked.

"Ohija," Shemone said, feeling guilty, "I could easily have come over to see you."

"I know, but I wanted to get out of the house anyway," she replied. "You know, you had me a little bent out of shape when you didn't show up at the hospital. I'm glad that I called your mother's from my place after letting Ray off." In an attempt to make her friend feel better, she added, "It looks like you're doing okay now, though." Ohija took a seat on the edge of the bed.

"I'm coping," Shemone said, answering Ohija's earlier question. "I feel a little bit like I'm in the twilight zone. My mother's been acting so nice to me, approving of almost everything I say and do."

"You're kidding," Ohija said in an astonished tone of voice. "And that's all you ever wanted, right? Her approval."

"Everyone wants their parents' approval, when you think about it. I must say that it is nice that she sees where I'm coming from for a change." Shemone continued, "We're spending a whole lot more time together. We've played cards, gone food shopping, and even watched movies. Ohija, you know that I'm not a drinker, but I was sooo drunk when I got here in that cab. She really did help me to get myself together," she told her.

"Wow, that's nice to hear," Ohija replied. One of her eyebrows was raised higher than the other.

"Well, it's true!" Shemone said, trying to convince her friend that her mother's motives were sincere. "Did you even notice that she called you by your right name?"

Ohija took a look around the room. "Sure did."

"Ohija," Shemone said with a look of optimism on her face.

"Shemone," Ohija playfully mimicked her right back, continuing to look around the room. "I see not much has changed." Amazingly,

Ruth setup the furniture the same as when they were living in Harlem.

"I know," Shemone replied. She switched off the power to her laptop. "I think it's kind of flattering that my mother would go out of her way to keep things the same for me. This room could easily have been a den or a study."

Ohija switched subjects. She didn't want to steer her friend off her optimistic path with Ruth. It went against the rules of everything she stood for. Knocking someone down when they were feeling positive was a no-no, no matter who it involved. "So what kind of article are you working on?" she asked.

"It's an article I'm calling 'Lovin' Gone Wrong.'"

"Mm-hmm," Ohija answered, assessing the title.

"Mm-hmm what?" Shemone asked.

"Sounds kind of angry."

"Oh, I am not angry," Shemone answered assertively.

"Okay, if you say so," Ohija replied. She pushed her arms back on the bed, attempting to balance herself and her large belly on the weight of her elbows. "You know, Ray had lunch with Darnell not too long ago," Ohija said in a la-di-da tone of voice.

"That's special," Shemone simply replied. She got up and began to look for something inside her dresser drawer.

Ohija made it her business to dwell on the topic. She was set to at least try to fix the mess that was going on between Shemone and Darnell, two of her very best friends. Ohija thought to herself, What a mess it is. She and her own Ray had almost gotten into a blowout over the situation because they hadn't communicated the way they should have. Usually, it was something they were in the habit of doing as husband and wife.

This had been one of those rare times when Ohija had formed an opinion about someone without hearing all the facts. Blindsided, it hadn't mattered to her that Ray had tried to tell her that there was another side. It wasn't until after she' gotten a call from Darnell a few nights ago that she'd realized it for herself. Shemone had never said anything about the little telephone game she had played with her male friend Keith. Of course, it didn't warrant Darnell sleeping with another woman, but Ohija could understand how that incident and a number of other "Shemone capers," as she chose to call them, had led him to feel somehow like less of a man. Truthfully, Ohija had determined, they were both in the wrong.

"Listen, girl, I hope that you're not about to start in on Darnell and how he made a mistake. I'm in no mood to hear about his troubles, because I've got my own." Shemone added, "Right now, I'm doing me."

"I heard that," Ohija answered back, taking notice that Shemone was making a mess as she tossed around items inside the drawer.

Shemone abruptly stopped, and turned to face her friend, looking at her but saying nothing.

"Yes?" Ohija asked.

"Nothing," Shemone replied. She'd hoped that Ohija would at least have tried to broach the subject of Darnell a little harder. She still wanted to argue or scream about him and what he'd done to her. Ruth didn't have a problem with not mentioning his name in her house, or even ever again. Shemone still rummaged through the drawer.

"Shemone," Ohija asked, "what are you doing?"

"I'm looking for something," Shemone said, finally slamming the drawer closed. She sat on the bed next to her friend.

"Nervous energy?" Ohija asked.

Shemone nodded.

"Idle time?" Ohija asked.

Shemone nodded again.

"You want to hear about what Darnell told Ray or what?" Ohija asked.

"Only if you call me cuckoo."

"You're cuckoo for not hearing his side of the story." Ohija smiled at her friend. "Cuckoo-cuckoo-cuckoo."

The two chuckled as if they were still teenagers.

"Shemone and Ohija," Ruth called out, tapping on the door.

Ohija shot Shemone a look. It said, Your mother's got perfect timing. I'm sure she's had her ear to the door, listening.

"Come in, Mom," Shemone answered, smiling.

Ruth stuck her head through the door. "You girls want something to eat? I just finished a pot of beef stew."

"No thank you, Miss Waters," Ohija said as she got up. "I really should be getting back home, before the hubby starts to worry." Ohija turned to give Shemone a wink.

"You're leaving so soon? Why, you hardly had enough time for a proper visit," Ruth told her with a fake expression of concern.

"Yes, well, I must," Ohija answered. There was the slightest edge of sarcasm in her voice. She added, "But Shemone was just telling me that she was planning on returning home tomorrow, so we can finish catching up later."

Ruth looked at Shemone in shock. "Is this true, Shemone? Are you sure you're ready to leave?"

Shemone smiled at her mother. Ohija was something. It sure was time for her to go back home and deal with her problems, like a real woman, regardless of what she'd decided on doing. "Yes, Mom," Shemone confirmed. "I was going to let you know today. It just happens that I mentioned it casually to Ohija first."

If looks were deadly, then Ohija and her twins would have been gone in a puff of smoke in just that instant. "Mmph," Ruth replied in a short tone of voice. "Yes, Ohija, thank you for stopping by to visit," she said. Physically, Ruth led her toward the front door, pressing down firmly on the small of Ohija's back.

"Shemone, girl, I'll catch you later, and remember what I told you, now," Ohija managed to say with a chuckle, from the hall. She wasn't about to let Ruth and her usual antics get the best of her.

"Okay, girl, and you take it easy," Shemone replied back. It wasn't hard to tell. *Yes, her mother could be manipulative and nosy when she wanted to be. But she could also be loving and sweet, which was something she hadn't known.*

* * *

Ruth was at Shemone's room's entrance in an instant. "Shemone, you can't be serious, you're leaving me already?" She thought that it had been the best two weeks with her daughter ever, and she wasn't ready to let go.

"Mom, it has been almost two weeks. I don't want to wear out my welcome," she told her.

"Never," Ruth replied. "Frankly, I don't care if it's been ten weeks. I still think that you're not ready," Ruth insisted as she stood in front of her daughter.

"Yes, I am ready, and I will be leaving tomorrow. Thank you for being here for me, Mom," Shemone said as she got up from the bed and gave her mother a hug.

Ruth hugged her daughter back, thinking that it had been good while it had lasted. "If you must leave, then I suppose that I have no choice," Ruth said. She forced herself to let Shemone leave her arms. "I can't very well hold you hostage here."

Shemone laughed. She could almost envision her mother doing something like that.

"But before you leave tomorrow, there is one other thing that I wanted to talk to you about," Ruth told her.

"This sounds serious, should I sit down?" Shemone asked with a smile.

"Yes, and I will, too," Ruth answered. She and Shemone sat on the bed.

Ruth fidgeted with the set of three connected gold chains around her neck before she began. "I wanted to talk to you about the Alvin Ailey thing."

"Mom, you don't have to do this," Shemone said.

"Yes, I do," Ruth replied. "It's a conversation that I've wanted to have with you for some time now," she said. "I'm sorry about the reason for your coming to me, but I can't lie. I am glad that you came here."

"I'm glad, too." Shemone made a bold move, taking her mother's hand into her own. "That you're here for me, when it counted."

Ruth curled her fingers around her daughter's hand in support. She continued, "I just want you to know that I'm proud of you. I think that you are an excellent and talented writer."

"Mom, you're gonna make me cry," Shemone replied in disbelief. She questioned whether or not their conversation was really happening.

"You might as well cry, I know I won't be able to stop myself from doing it," Ruth replied, beginning to sob. "Shemone, I take pride in knowing that you were able to follow your dreams and do something that you're passionate about." She paused. "Because I was never able to."

Great, Shemone thought, frowning. She knew it was coming. Her mother was about to remind her yet again of her dreams of making it as a professional dancer, and the way it had become diminished, all because of her.

"I want you to know that I don't blame you anymore," her mother told her.

Shemone wanted to faint, but not before she heard her mother through.

"I mean, I used to blame you, but I really don't anymore. I realized that you are my dream come true, Shemone, you're everything I ever wanted to be and more."

Tears streamed down Shemone's face. "You really mean it?" she asked. She'd longed to hear those words for such a long time. Her mother understood, and didn't blame her. The burden was lifted. The burden that she had carried with her since she was twelve years old. It was when she'd first found out that her mother could have been a professional dancer, but had settled for being a single mother instead. Shemone had started keeping her thoughts in a journal from that point on. Who knew that writing would take her to where she was today? And to have her mother actually admit that she was a talented writer made all of her efforts worthwhile. It was worth being busy, and worth hiding behind the security of seeing her name printed in major magazines, for this. Now she could emerge, and just be herself, writing for the mere joy of doing what she loved to do the most. Shemone smiled and thought to herself that this was by far one day that she would never forget. And if she had any doubts, her mother made it all clear in her next sentence.

Ruth replied, "Yes, I really do mean it."

"You have any regrets?" Shemone asked her mother.

Ruth paused to think. "I do, but only that I can't go back in time. I never wanted you to feel like it was your fault that I hadn't accomplished something."

Shemone smiled widely. "You have a chance to make the best of it now," she told her.

"What are you talking about? Make the best of what now?" Ruth asked.

"I mean that you could take a class, or even travel. Think about it," Shemone said eagerly, "this is your chance to do anything you ever wanted to do."

Ruth chuckled softly at the thought. "Shemone, dear, thank you, but I think it's a little too late for me."

"No, it isn't, and if you don't start looking into things, then I'll do it for you."

Ruth stared at her daughter for a long time. The moment felt almost surreal. Her busy daughter was taking the time to find out about her, and what she wanted to do. Finally, she thought, someone cared.

•

51

No Place Like Home

Shemone stepped inside the living room of her apartment the next day and looked around. She placed her suitcase on the floor, and her pocketbook down on the couch

The space seemed quieter than usual and it was immaculate. The cleaning lady had been by to clean up, just as Shemone had phoned in and requested. Inspecting each room, Shemone felt satisfied with the work that had been done. She went back into the bedroom. By her nightstand was a note from the cleaning person that said she'd come across a ring behind the nightstand while doing her cleaning and that she'd put it in the drawer. Shemone opened it. There it was, her ring. The ring that Darnell had given her. Its diamond reflected the natural light coming in from the nearby window. As tempting as it was, she didn't pick it up, hold it, or even begin to reminisce for too long. She had refused to go there, after much thought and a lack of sleep, the night before.

Ohija had said that Darnell had his side to tell, but what could it be except something lame that he'd needed time to think up? She'd given him the chance to defend himself the very night she'd found out that he'd cheated. He'd had nothing to say then, and probably nothing worth hearing now, Shemone thought to herself. In any case, she decided to not jump to any conclusions. This was not going to be another break-up-to-make-up scenario. The best thing she could do would be to leave Darnell right where he was, and to move forward with her life.

The answering machine had zero messages. Unusual, but not a

miracle, since she'd been retrieving them from her mother's house during her stay. Just then the phone rang. Shemone answered it, because she wasn't trying to hide from anybody. She wished that Hope woman would have the audacity to call her house again; she was going to let her know that Darnell was all hers now. Shemone grabbed the telephone. "Good afternoon," she said in a professional tone of voice.

"Shemone, don't hang up, it's me."

"Darnell, I don't want you calling here. Do you hear me?" Shemone's voice was firm, the complete opposite of the way she had just answered the phone. "I mean it."

"It's no pressure, I just wanted to make sure that you were okay. I've been trying to call you for a while now, but I didn't get anything but the machine," Darnell told her.

"Yes, well, I've been away." She reiterated, "I'm back now and I don't want you calling here."

"I heard you. You don't want me calling you. I just—" Darnell broke off, then said, "If there's anything I can do."

Shemone cut him off. "Nothing—ever." Then she glanced over at the nightstand. "But since you asked, there is one thing that you can do."

"Anything, baby-girl, you know I'd do anything," he said in a hopeful tone of voice.

"Don't call me that."

Darnell quickly corrected himself. "I mean, Shemone, I'd do anything for you." His words were strong and filled with emotion.

"Please come and get your ring."

"No, that's yours to keep," Darnell told her outright. "That's yours for life, do whatever you want to with it, pawn it or whatever," he said.

"I don't want it, or you," Shemone said coldly, knowing that she was being extra cruel. After what he'd done to her, she felt he deserved it.

Darnell couldn't speak. He was so taken aback by her response. It was as if she was another person. He paused for a long time. "Okay, when do you want me to come and up pick the ring?" Darnell asked. There was no use in trying to talk her out of it.

"As soon as possible. Now, if you can," Shemone replied.

"Okay, Shemone, you got it, I'll be there in a few," Darnell finally gave in and told her.

"Good." Shemone hung up the phone. She picked up the ring as if it was a dead bug, using only her fingertips, and took it into the kitchen. She removed a clear Baggie from on top of her refrigerator, and placed it inside, sealing it tight and leaving it on the counter. "Begone," Shemone said aloud. The telephone rang again. She hoped it wasn't Darnell calling to say that he couldn't make it. The sooner he came, the better. It would all be over with. "Good afternoon," she said.

"Well, hello there, stranger," her mother said. "I'm just calling to check on you."

"That's sweet, Mom," Shemone replied.

"I just wanted to make sure that you got in okay," Ruth said.

"Yes, I'm in fine," Shemone answered. "I was just about to go and run a bubble bath to de-stress." No sooner than she'd said the words, she wished she could take them back. Her mother did not need to hear her name linked with anything close to the word "stress."

"Are you stressed, Shemone?" Ruth asked. "I told you that you left here too soon. You need to get in your car and get right back here, where you belong."

"Mom, I'm fine, really. 'De-stress' is just a manner of speaking, as in relaxing," Shemone explained.

"That man is not over there harassing you, is he?" her mother asked.

"No, Mom, Darnell isn't harassing me at all. But you are," Shemone said jokingly.

Ruth got the joke and laughed. "Okay, I get it, I'll leave you to go and de-stress, or relax, or whatever you want to call it," she replied.

"Okay, Mom, talk to you later." Shemone hung up the phone. She was glad that she and her mother were growing closer, but what she needed now, more than ever, was time. Time, and a little space.

Shemone hadn't told her mother the full truth. She hadn't been about to take a bath, but the idea sounded like a good one, because it really would help to de-stress her. Darnell probably wouldn't be over for a while anyway.

An hour later, the bath salts had felt invigorating, and now so did she. At least on the outside. Shemone redressed in comfortable baggy sweats and a T-shirt. She ordered herself some vegetable lo mein from one of the local Chinese restaurants. That's when, in the middle of her meal, the doorbell rang. "Who is it" Shemone got up and asked into the intercom.

"It's Darnell, Shemone," the voice said.

Shemone had a flashback. It was like the first time he'd come over to see her after jail, only this time, she wasn't about to invite him in. She quickly went into the kitchen and got the Baggie with the ring in it. Then she waited for him at the front door.

Darnell stepped off the elevator, not looking good at all. He looked tired and as if he wasn't taking care of himself, Shemone thought.

"Hey," he told her.

"Hey," she answered, holding the bag out for him to take.

"So this is it then?" he asked her. There was something in his eyes that pleaded for forgiveness.

"This is it," she told him. "I wish you the best, Darnell. Take care of yourself."

Darnell watched her, at the door, for a few seconds longer. He was biting down on his lower lip, waiting for magic words to come that didn't. "Okay, then, you, too," was the best that he could do. Then it suddenly hit him, right before he got to the elevator. He did have one more thing to say to Shemone, his ex-fiancée, his girlfriend for a while, and finally, his Final Four friend. All of the extra reading he'd done had helped to make him into a new millenium Shakespeare. She was still standing at the door, he knew, because he could feel her eyes on him. He turned to her and said, "Oh, and, Shemone, by the way, I am the man I say I am." He paused and then continued, "Are you the woman you say you are?"

Shemone didn't answer, because she wasn't really trying to hear him. She watched him as he bopped to the elevator, what for her would be the very last time.

52

GREAT EXPECTATIONS

Ray, could you come in here for a minute?" Ohija called out to her husband on Sunday evening. She lay in her bed with pillows propped up high under her feet and behind her head.

"Yes, honeybunch," Ray answered as he entered the room. "What can I do for you?" He had just come out of the bathroom. So far, he'd had complete control of his urinary functions.

"Can you help me take off this anklet?" Ohija asked. "Everything is all swollen on me," she complained. "It feels like my circulation is getting cut off."

Ray removed the brown leather band adorned with cowrie shells from around his wife's ankle.

Ohija smiled. "You're going to make a terrific daddy," she told him.

Ray smiled back. He'd had his ordeal in the hospital, and gotten through it. Now he was ready for Ohija to have those twins. Life seemed to be more precious than ever.

"Ray, could you hand me the phone, please?" she asked him.

Ray didn't as much as sigh. It had been like this for the past few weeks. Ray, do this, Ray, do that, Ray, bring this, Ray, bring that. It was refreshing for him to be able to give his wife a helping hand. And although he wasn't 100 percent himself health wise, he felt close to 75 percent. Any way he put it, it was a big improvement. Ray handed his wife the telephone.

"Shemone, Ohija," she said into the phone.

"Hey, girl, how are you?" Shemone asked.

"Tired."

"Really?" Shemone asked.

"Yes, my back's acting up again. At first I just ignored it, but the pain is really starting to get to me now. If it keeps up, I'm going to wind up going to the hospital. It's not that bad at the moment." She sighed. "Other than that, I'm fine," she told her. "What were you doing?"

"Yes, please, Ohija, if the pain keeps up, go straight to the hospital. You don't want to chance anything," Shemone told her. "I'm not doing anything special, just washing a few dishes."

"Utterly fascinating," Ohija replied, joking. Raymond had just walked out of the room. "So how are you doing? We never got a chance to finish having our talk about the other side of the story," she said.

"I'm making it, and I don't feel that it's necessary," Shemone answered.

"For us to talk about Darnell's version of what happened?" Ohija had to ask her. It was as if they weren't on the same page anymore. Suddenly Shemone didn't want to hear what Ohija had to say. She wondered if Darnell and Shemone had spoken and that had changed things. "Has he called you yet?" she asked.

"But of course," Shemone replied. "I told him to come and get his ring."

"Girl, you're something," Ohija told her. "That was fast. I didn't even get a chance to see it before you gave it back to him."

Shemone admitted, "It was nice."

"You sure you were ready to give it back?" Ohija asked.

"I was ready to throw it back at him. I can buy my own," she told her.

Ohija chuckled. "It's not quite the same. You and I both know that."

"Ohija, what would you have done if you were me? I'd really like to know," she asked. "You and Ray are stable, and by now, I know that you can tell if a couple has what it takes, so tell me, what would you have done?"

"I'm not you, and I'm not Darnell," Ohija answered. "But I can tell you that what works for Raymond and me is to listen to each other. You and Darnell miscommunicated, big time, girl."

"So cheating on me is supposed to be written off as miscommunication?" Shemone asked her with a smirk.

"No, it's a result of it. Girl, just ask yourself if it was all worth it," she said. "Ask yourself if you can forgive each other and move on. See if you prefer moving on with or without him, because there is a difference." Ohija called on her husband once more. "Ray, could you bring me a little bit of lemonade with some crushed ice in it?"

Ray stood at the door. "Yes, master," he said, taking a low bow, "coming right up."

Something was trying to register within her the next morning when she woke up. "I am the man I say I am. Are you the woman you say you are?" Those were the last words Darnell had uttered to her. She had to ask herself to be certain. Was he trying to tell her to be the woman that she said she was? Shemone peered at herself in the bedroom mirror. The way she looked on the outside was more than acceptable. But not inside. The inside was different. The inside ran deep. It wasn't as simple as looking at a reflection. The inside entailed feelings, family, and career. Family, for her, was a work in progress. She and Ruth were both attempting to build a foundation. Career wise, she still had hurdles to overcome. Darnell had told her that long ago. Step to that boss lady of yours, was what he'd said. But what had she truly done about it? Shemone sat upright in her chair, picked up the phone, and started dialing. There was no time like the present, she thought to herself. "Yes, good afternoon. Shemone Waters calling for Jackie Simpson, please," she said into the phone.

"Oh, hello, Shemone," the receptionist replied. "You need me to tell her that you're sending in your column?" she asked.

"Actually, no," Shemone answered. "I need to speak to her directly."

The receptionist replied, "Okay, hold the line."

Shemone took a deep breath. Of course, the receptionist was used to her calling and saying that she was sending in her column. She had been, faithfully, for the past two years. Well, it was time for some change. If the staff at *Sister Soul* didn't make it, then she would, she told herself.

"Jackie Simpson speaking," the overly busy voice came on the line and said abruptly.

"Hi, Jackie?"

"Ye-eees," she answered in a bothered tone of voice. "Who is this?"

"This is Shemone Waters."

"Shemone," Jackie said. Her voice took on a softer tone. "Nice to speak with you. I was just about to run into a staff meeting, can I phone you back?" she asked.

Shemone put herself into an aggressive Darnell persona, then spoke. "No, actually this won't take very long." She continued, "I've been working for *Sister Soul* for the past two years now, and I think that my work speaks for itself. I handle all my assignments in a professional way, as well as in a timely fashion. What I'm trying to say is that I'd like to be considered for another position, and advancement of some kind." Shemone went further. She was on a roll. "Jackie, I'd like to take *Sister Soul* by storm by doing more. I feel that I'm truly capable and willing, particularly at this stage of my career."

Jackie responded, "Shemone, we would love nothing more than to promote you, but I'm afraid that the magazine simply isn't prepared to make you that kind of offer as of yet. We've only been in the business for a decade ourselves." She added, "Surely you understand that we consider ourselves to be a new publishing venture."

Shemone rolled her tongue around in her mouth. She'd already done the research on her own. Readership, advertisers, and subscriptions were doing more than adequately enough. *Sister Soul* could certainly afford to up the stakes. "Jackie, I completely understand where you're coming from, however, from my standpoint, I feel like I need change because I'm growing as a writer. I was hoping that it would be with a publication as wonderful as *Sister Soul*, but if not, like I said, I do understand," she told her. The next sentence fought its way out of her mouth. "I'm prepared to resign from my relationship-columnist position."

Jackie, her boss, made it sound as if she was already gone. "Shemone, I'd hate to see you leave, and I do understand that you have to do what you have to do for your own career advancement. I only wish that we could accommodate you. You're one of our best writers," she told her. Shemone was glad that she added, "All I can tell you is that I'll get back to you on this, okay? Let me talk it over with a few of my superiors," she said.

Shemone was about to be sick. She'd just put the best thing she had going for her career wise out there on the line, in the hope of getting something better. This was a huge risk she was taking, and she knew it. The reality was, she could end up jobless. A better question was, So what kind of woman would she be then? She thought, A homeless one.

53

Life in a Nutshell

Who needed a relationship? Not me, Shemone thought to herself. Not a rebound one or otherwise. She was on the brink of discovering the woman she was, and time was still on her side. All she had to do was use it wisely.

It was Tuesday afternoon, and Shemone decided to break up her workday and get out of the house for some air. She was already dressed, sporting a glazed black leather biker jacket, blue jeans, and high-cut pony-skinned boots. She picked up her car keys and her laptop, just in case she felt inspired to write a new article along the way. Shemone hopped into her SUV, and quickly browsed through her CDs. She chose the soothing sounds of Brian McKnight to drive to. Amazingly, the highway was pretty free of cars, so it didn't matter that she had no definite destination in mind. It made her feel free. Her SUV's bass was powerful, and she turned it up as loud as she could without the threat of being served with a summons for the noise.

Shemone cruised along, her window halfway down and the sunroof open. The coolness felt calming, blowing on her face. It satisfied the urge she felt to be out in the open. After driving almost halfway to New Jersey, she turned the car around. When she was nearly home, she took the local streets before she was supposed to get off. A guy in a black Cadillac Escalade watched her as they both stopped at the traffic light. He was a white guy with olive skin. Dark hair, dark eyes, clean cut. He looked Italian; she pegged him as the Mafioso type right off the bat.

He beeped his horn, urging her to pull over to the curb. "You gotta minute, beautiful lady?" he asked. His entire head was all the way out of the window as he spoke.

Definitely Italian, Shemone thought to herself. The accent was a dead giveaway. He needed to work on his pickup lines, but he was still attractive. "Maybe next time," Shemone replied. She smiled politely, and honked her horn back at him. Her man had done her wrong, but she wasn't quite ready to go the Caucasian route yet. It did feel good to know that to other men, though, she was still sexy. Her experience with Darnell had made her feel as if he was the only man on the planet. She double-checked her rearview mirror. Her Italian stallion was right on her. They stopped for another red traffic light.

"You gonna make this difficult for me, huh?" he said with a boyish smile.

Shemone chuckled. It was cute, the way he spoke.

"So what's your name?" he asked her, refusing to give up.

Shemone didn't reply. She grooved in her car with the music that she had since turned down to low.

"I don't have a lotta time here, the traffic light's about to change to green," he told her. "I'm Marcello. Won't you tell me your name? I'll even start you off," he began to say. "Your name is—"

"Shemone," she said, finally relenting and announcing it from her window.

Just then the light changed. Shemone sped right off without looking to see if her new road buddy was following. There was congestion, and a sea of yellow taxicabs ahead. "Damn yellow cabs," she said aloud.

Marcello, no surprise, pulled up right alongside her. "Listen, Shemone, I'm no crazy person. I'm a nice guy. I'd like to take you out for a nice dinner sometime," he told her.

Shemone comfortably rested her elbow outside her car-door window. "You like sistahs, huh?" she asked, daring herself to flirt with him.

"I like beautiful woman," he said.

"Woman, or women?" she asked. "Do you like to date a lot of beautiful women, Marcello?"

"No, only the ones with class, like you. Now I'm not with nobody. It's only me. I get lonely sometimes. I work all the time," Marcello told her. "I gotta nice house, two cars, money, but no one to share it with."

Shemone nodded with a slight grin on her face. The traffic ahead was beginning to move along and this guy was making an impression on her. From thug love to the Italian stallion, she thought to herself. Her cheeks rose and gave way to a full smile.

"Call me," Marcello told her. He handed her a business card, but didn't allow her the chance to respond. This time, he was the one who sped off.

There was something about the move he'd just made. It was cocky, it was confident, and it was undeniably sexy. Shemone glanced at his card at the next light. He was into automobiles. In fact, it looked as though he might have his own dealership. For a brief moment she thought of her mother. Ruth would probably approve of this one. He was right on the level.

When Shemone got back home, there was a message waiting from her mother. She said to call her right back because it was important. "Hey, everything okay?" Shemone asked Ruth over the telephone.

"More than okay," Ruth replied in an upbeat tone of voice. "I got a job today!"

"You got a job today?" Shemone repeated.

"Yes!" Ruth answered excitedly. "I applied to teach a dance class at the local community center in my neighborhood."

"You did!" Shemone exclaimed. "Mom, that's terrific news. How did you hear about the opening?"

"There's a free paper that they give out. It's called the *Home Gazette,* and it comes out bimonthly. I usually never read it, but two days ago I scanned the want ads section. Then I called up, went in for the interview, and landed the job," her mother said, beaming. "I mentioned that I was with Alvin Ailey for a time, and they were so impressed—"

"That they hired you on the spot!" Shemone said, completing her mother's sentence.

"Yes," her mother replied. "Can you believe it? They want me full-time, and I'll be getting a salary and everything!"

"Mom, I'm so happy for you!" Shemone said.

Ruth had stopped smiling, and her face had taken on a different expression. It was a somber one. "Yes, I know that you are, and that's why it makes me feel terrible that I wasn't happy for you and your career sooner. All I ever gave you was a guilt trip. I didn't go on tour as a dancer, and you felt bad about it. Shemone, you were so young. It really wasn't your fault, because you never asked to be born." A lump began to form in Ruth's throat. She'd ached to say those words for such a long time. "I really do apologize for everything, and I realize that all I want is to see you happy now," she told her.

"You know, I don't know how much more of this bonding I can take," Shemone joked with her mother. She could feel her eyes getting wet with tears. All of the damage that had been done in their relationship couldn't be fixed overnight, but she was willing to give Ruth a try.

"Well, get used to it, because we've got a lot more to do. This is just the beginning."

"We should celebrate your new position over the weekend," Shemone suggested.

"I'd like that," Ruth excitedly replied.

"So, then I'll talk to you later?"

"Count on it," Ruth answered before hanging up the phone.

Shemone thought to herself: my mother, the dance instructor. She didn't know which she liked better, the dance-instructor part or the mother part. She thought again, plopping herself down on top of her fluffy bed. The mother part, that was the best. The day just didn't seem real, in a never-say-never kind of way, to her. Marcello also came to mind. His accent, his smile, and then some advice she'd given Darnell on one occasion when they had a falling out. She'd told him that sometimes it was time to do something different. Maybe it was.

54

Pain in the You Know What

Ohija tried to prepare herself on Thursday afternoon for the possibility of the twins arrival into the world. The aches in her back had gotten worse. The pain could only be described as severe, the way she was feeling, and no amount of meditation or herbal medication would make it go away. Ray had phoned the hospital for her ob-gyn, and he'd instructed them to go right into the ER. After checking out her complaints, the doctor found that she was exactly one centimeter dilated. Dr. Wayne had insisted that the hospital administer medicine. They'd given her a shot for preterm contractions, and were keeping her in for a twenty-four-hour observation. So far, nothing spectacular was going on inside her body, which was what everyone wanted. It was way too early to deliver the twins.

Ray had just arrived back in the room with a crossword puzzle book for his wife.

"Did you see Shemone?" Ohija asked him.

"Not yet," Ray replied. "I'm sure she'll be here soon."

"Oh, I know that she'll be here," Ohija said. "I just hope nothing's happened. It's not like her not to call if she's running behind."

"That would be my fault," Ray told her. "I kind of forgot to recharge my cell phone batteries."

Ohija chuckled. "You've got a right to be nervous, hubby. I don't expect you to be on the ball with everything."

Ray heaved a sigh of relief. "Anything exciting happen while I was gone?"

"No, just more of the same," she replied. Ohija sat up in the bed. The fetal monitor pulsed loudly.

"What was that?" Ray asked as he rushed over to his wife's side.

"I think that was my first contraction," Ohija, looking at him wide-eyed, said. She was still able to speak with ease. "Hopefully, it was my last for the day," she added.

"I'm going to get the nurse," Ray said, leaving the room before giving Ohija the chance to call him back.

Ray came back with the obstetrics nurse, who immediately went over and read the paper that fed out of the monitor. "Yes," she confirmed, "it was a contraction all right."

"Is she going to be okay?" Ray asked with a look of concern.

"She'll be fine," the nurse told him. "It takes a while before the shot takes effect. I'll be back," she told them after checking to make sure that everything was in order.

Ray paced back and forth in the room, in front of Ohija's bed. He hoped another contraction didn't hit. He wondered if he should rub her back, feed her crushed ice, or do whatever else it took. "Is there anything I can do?" he asked her.

"Yes, Ray, please sit your ass down," Ohija told him in a joking tone of voice. "You're making me uneasy."

Shemone pushed open the door to Ohija's room. "Well, look at you," she said, attempting to be chipper, as she walked inside.

"You made it, finally." Ohija reached out to give her friend a welcome hello hug. "Ray was just about to drive me stark, raving crazy in here."

"Tell me you're joking. Is he that bad?" Shemone asked.

"Girl, I got one contraction and he freaked on me. Lord only knows what he'll do when I'm really in labor."

Ray sat quietly in a chair in the corner of the room.

Shemone chuckled. "Then I made it here just in time."

"What took you so long?" Ohija asked.

"Bumper-to-bumper traffic," Shemone explained. "You know how it can get."

"Yes, I do, girl," Ohija answered. "I'm just glad that you're here."

"So how are you holding up?" Shemone asked. "You look like you're doing okay."

"Like I said, one single contraction and that was it. Oh, and my back stopped hurting," she told her.

"Was it really bad?"

"Worse. I thought that we might have to come here in an ambulance," Ohija told her friend.

Shemone only nodded, thinking to herself that it seemed as if Ohija shouldn't have to be going through this, especially after everything she'd just gone through with Ray. The turmoil with her mother, breaking it off with Darnell, and even her job situation, none of that stuff seemed as important. In the end, togetherness was all that mattered. Her mother had, surprisingly, come through for her when she'd needed her to. Ohija had come through for Ray when he'd needed her to. Togetherness made it so much easier to get through the rough times.

"Ohija's resting, so how about joining me for a cup of coffee at the vending machine?" Ray asked Shemone. It was hours later the same day. "My treat?"

"How can I refuse?" Shemone replied. She took hold of Ray's arm and they went down the hall.

"You know, I've been meaning to have a chat with you," Ray said. He slipped coins into the coffee machine.

"Really?" Shemone asked. She wasn't totally clueless as to what the topic of discussion would be about.

"It's about Darnell," Ray told her.

"Four sugars, please, Ray," Shemone requested. She took a seat over in the lounge area.

Ray joined her, holding two steaming cups in his hands and a packaged doughnut in his mouth.

She thought, Of course it's about Darnell. "Wow, Ohija sure has you trained," she joked with him. Ray had done well quickly fetching food and drink for them both.

Ray laughed at himself. "Tell me about it," he said. He took a seat next to her and gave her the doughnut and a coffee.

"Thanks," Shemone told him.

"Now I was saying, about Darnell," Ray went on. "We met up for lunch a while ago and I know you might feel like it doesn't concern you anymore, but, Shemone, he looked real bad."

The coffee was too hot to drink. Shemone set her cup down on a nearby table, and began opening up the doughnut package.

Ray continued, "Shemone, he looked bad, and he feels bad about what happened. I just know that girl didn't mean anything to him."

"Ray, no offense, but it's really not your place to say what that girl meant to him," Shemone replied shortly.

"None taken. You're absolutely right," he agreed.

Shemone added the fourth packet of sugar to her coffee. "And anyway, how would you know, Ray?" Shemone asked him. If he was going to be Darnell's personal representative, then he was gonna get some of her flack. "You weren't there, were you? She must have meant enough for him to carry his behind over there into her bed," she said.

"All I'm trying to say is that I think he made a big mistake," Ray told her. "Everybody makes mistakes."

"And everybody pays the consequences for them, too."

"I think he has. Honestly, I'm afraid that he might go back to his old lifestyle again. Ohija told me about how he was before you and him got together. But I'm sure that he knows that he's a better person with you."

Shemone thought aloud, "You would defend him, you're a man. He was probably a cheater before we got together, for all we both know."

Ray took a sip from his coffee. "I've never cheated on Ohija, though."

"And you'd better not," Shemone playfully threatened, "or you'll have me to answer to."

"I'll try and keep that in mind," Ray replied with a smile. "Oh, and there's just one more thing, if you're interested. He told me the reason why he cheated."

Shemone twisted up her face. "Now what logical reason could Darnell possibly have had for stepping out on me?" She added, "*I'm every woman*, Raymond."

Ray chuckled. "Who's not lacking any self-esteem, that's for sure. But I think that Darnell was."

"What are you talking about?" she asked him.

"I'm talking about you and the guy you were supposedly planning a date with on the phone," he said, trying to jog her memory.

It didn't take long for Shemone to remember. Purposefully trying to make Darnell jealous was wrong, but so was the fact that he'd cheated on her. She explained it to Ray. "Hearing something doesn't mean that it's going to be done. Darnell should have known better than that," she told him. Shemone scarfed half a doughnut, then washed it down with the contents of her coffee cup. She stood up to leave. "Tell Ohija I'll call to check on her later."

"Okay," Ray answered, unsure of what Shemone's next move would be. He took a giant bite of the remainder of her uneaten doughnut. He hoped he didn't wind up choking on it, or his words.

55

Blood Hounds

Shemone entered her apartment late that Thursday evening. Inside the bedroom, the answering machine harbored no messages. She flung herself onto her work chair, then turned on the computer. She opened it to the file labeled "Question." The blue screen came up the same, just like the day Darnell had typed it in. The words "Will you marry me?" appeared. Shemone gazed at the monitor for a long time. Darnell was wrong for cheating on her, but what she had done had been wrong in just the same way. Just then the phone rang.

"Hello, this is the receptionist for Tayteck Electronics. Can I speak with a Darnell Williams, please?"

"I'm sorry, he isn't in," Shemone answered, getting out a spare piece of paper and a pen. "Can I take a message?" she asked. Evidently, Darnell still had her down as the contact for his work prospects, she thought to herself.

"Can you please tell him that he passed the second interview, and that we want him to come in for work? His start date is Monday, at nine A.M. sharp."

"Yes, I sure will, I'll be sure that he gets the message," Shemone replied excitedly. "And thank you for calling."

Shemone hung up, smiling. All of his efforts had paid off. Darnell had gotten an electrical job, all on his own, with no help from anyone, including her. He'd be so happy once he found out, she thought. Shemone picked up the telephone, and dialed the number for Darnell's mother's house.

A very unenthusiastic person picked up on the very first ring. "Yeah, hello."

"Hello, this is Shemone. Is Darnell home, please?" she asked in a cordial tone of voice. She was almost certain that it was his sister, Monica, the one who was hardly ever home. It wasn't Miss Louise's voice, and there was only one other female she knew of who lived in the apartment. Darnell had mentioned his sister on occasion. He often referred to her as the "ghetto-fabulous superstar of sorts."

"Is this a creditor?" Monica asked loudly. "'Cause you should know that he don't live here," she said.

Shemone replied, "Uh, no, this isn't a creditor, this is Shemone."

"Oh, this is girlfriend Shemone?" Monica giggled softly and said, "You sound white, girrl. This is his sister, Monica. I thought you was calling for some money or something, don't nobody be calling here sounding like you."

Shemone didn't know what to say to that one. No one had actually ever told her before that she sounded white. First it was Darnell with his shut-ups, and now it was his sister and this. The Williams family had some way with words. Shemone chose to ignore Monica's comment. There was no white or black way to speak. In her book she was simply speaking English. She spoke up, snapping herself back into the reason for why she was phoning in the first place. "So is he there? I have some good news for him."

"No, he ain't here. Ya'll break up or something?" she went ahead and forwardly asked. "'Cause he is truly working my nerves, being all in my business and stuff. You know what I'm saying?" Monica announced to her.

Shemone stammered, at a loss for words for probably the first time in her life. "Uh, it's really important that I find him. Do you have any idea at all where he might be?"

"Well, he's been hanging out with Red and them knuckleheads lately," Monica replied. She sucked her teeth.

"Red? Who is he?" Shemone asked.

"You don't know Red? From Building 122? Short, light-skinned, with freckles? He drives a Lexus. That's right, I keep forgetting that you don't have nothing to do with these fools from around here. Red is one of Darnell's old drug-selling friends." Monica continued, "He's probably right out there on the corner with him."

"On the corner?" Shemone asked in a shocked voice, hoping that what she suspected and feared, most of all, wasn't true.

"Mm-hmm, I've seen him out there myself, quite a few times. His head's too hard. He was doing fine and well," Monica said. "It's just like a man to go out and mess up a good thing. Hold on," she suddenly told her, clicking over to the other line before Shemone could respond.

Shemone wanted to hang up on Darnell's sister real bad by now.

"Hello?" Monica said as if she hadn't remembered who she was speaking with.

"Yes, it's still Shemone."

"Oh, I gotta go," Monica told her abruptly. "Girrl, do you know that I forgot that I had somebody else on the other line before I got on with you? I'll talk to you later," and just that quickly, she clicked over to resume her previous phone conversation.

Shemone hung up on her end, staring in disbelief at the phone for a while. His sister's antics were nothing compared to what she had just learned. Could it be that Darnell was out on the corner dealing drugs again? She doubted it, and she doubted that Monica would even relay the message that she'd tried to contact him. The phone rang not five minutes after she'd hung up. Shemone answered on the second ring, hoping it was Darnell. Maybe she was wrong. Maybe his sister had told him that she was looking for him.

56

The Dark Side

Yo, D., man, this is all good, you want another drink?" Red asked him. He took a swig for himself, straight from the bottle of bubbly champagne.

They had been standing outside the local liquor store, leaning against the side of Red's car door.

"Oh, hell yeah, you know that I'm not about to pass on another taste," Darnell sluggishly replied. He reached out for the bottle and took a swallow, using his hand to wipe away any of the pricey liquid that dripped from the corners of his mouth. Darnell had already had more than his fair share of alcohol earlier that Thursday afternoon, and here it was, now going on ten-thirty P.M. that evening. He couldn't remember the last time he'd gotten a restful night's sleep.

Lately, his days consisted of going to his mother's house to shower and change, and then back out on the streets to hang out again. It didn't matter that Darnell hadn't drunk this much since he couldn't even remember when. Besides, he and Red were becoming tighter than ever now that he was back in the neighborhood until one of the jobs he'd applied for came through. Darnell found that it didn't take much to make himself fit in with the crowd. The ways of street life easily coursed through his blood, by nature. It just didn't matter. Nothing mattered now that he didn't have Shemone in his life anymore.

Jailbird. That's what he was. Confined. Left with plenty of time to think about where he'd taken the right turn, and then gone wrong with his life. Right was his intention. Dealing drugs after high school, until he could save up enough to do something different. Wrong was getting caught, and being locked up, unable to do a thing about Terrance, and his death. Right was Shemone Waters. Real right. Shemone Waters, page 13 of the graduating class of Monroe High, 1992. He remembered those Final Four days like it was yesterday. There had always been a love for the overly smart, smooth-skinned brown girl with the Chinese hairdo.

He remembered feeling attracted to her mind and the ever-changing shape of her contoured body. Shemone intimidated him, just in the way that she used big words. She had a way with memorizing names and numbers. He, on the other hand, was the total opposite. He'd had to take both mathematics and English night school classes just to graduate. He'd barely made it out of high school. Darnell had never been book smart, but he could take things apart, and put them back together with little effort. And talk about funny—that was him, Mr. Comedian of the class. The jokes never stopped coming, just as long as Shemone Waters was laughing with him.

Wrong. The laughter lasted up until what she called her "grand acceptance announcement." Shemone told the Final Four group that she would be going away to Hampton University, in Virginia. Darnell knew right then that she would be meeting new people, and making new friends, leaving him behind. He never imagined that they'd come in con-

tact again under such horrible circumstances. But getting another chance at speaking to her, and potentially seeing her again, well, that definitely put him back on the right track, which brought him to the here and now. Shemone didn't want anything more to do with him, and that was all wrong. Wrong. Wrong. Wrong.

"That damned Hope," Darnell mumbled aloud.

"D., that shit is fucked up, what she did to you, man. You lost your girl over some real bullshit," Red told him, as if he needed reminding.

Darnell replied, "Nah, it was me, man. I should've never messed around with that chicken from the start. I should've known better." He swirled the champagne bottle around, but it was empty. He'd already finished it off.

"Yo, you seen her since?" Red asked.

"Did I?" Darnell chuckled. "Do you know that girl is still trying to get at me? Talk about desperate. It's wild what some women will do to get a man."

Red sat up on the hood of his car. "That shouldn't stop you from getting yours, though." He grinned, "I'm saying, a brother has needs. And if she's gonna put it all in your face—then, oh, well."

"I wouldn't touch that with a ten-foot pole," Darnell answered angrily. "She can count on that."

Pop approached, walking in their direction.

"Yo, here comes your boy," Red said. He spat on the sidewalk.

Pop came up to the car.

"Yo, whassup, Pop?" Darnell asked, greeting his friend.

"Yeah, whassup to you, too, D.," Pop said, looking over at Red, then quickly dismissing him with his eyes. "Can I holler at you for a minute, D.?"

"No problem," Darnell replied. He attempted to stand upright, steadying himself on the pavement. "Only I might have to hold on to you a little bit for balance."

"C'mon, I got your back, D.," Pop told him. He helped his friend by wrapping his arm around his shoulder, and taking him down the block. He lowered him down on a bench, a few cars away, where there wasn't an extra set of ears around. "Darnell, man, look at you."

Darnell attempted to look at himself in the midst of his drunken state. "What—what's wrong with me? I look okay," he slurred.

"You're pissy drunk, and is this where you wanna be? Out here with Red and his boys all the time? Man, this is wrong, it's not you anymore."

"This is me," Darnell said loudly. "Don't you get it, man? This is who I've been all along."

"Shemone doesn't believe that," Pop told him. "And neither do I."

Darnell looked down at the ground. "I don't need anybody feeling sorry for me," he told his friend.

Red walked down the block, over to where they were. "Yo, D., this man giving you a problem?" he asked.

"Ain't nobody speaking to you, this ain't your business, so go ahead with that," Pop told Red in a threatening tone of voice.

"Check this out. I bet I can make it my business," Red threatened back.

"Bring it on, then," Pop dared him.

"I've been looking for a reason to kick you and your punk goody-goody ass anyway."

"So now you got one, man," Pop told him. "You fake-ass *Alpo*."

Pop stepped forward.

Red stepped forward.

It was Darnell who forced himself forward, in between the two. Even in his drunken stupor, he'd remembered that Red and Pop had some kind of beef with each other. It was just too bad that he had not gotten the chance to get to the bottom of it. "Pop, go home, man," Darnell told him, putting his arm on his shoulder.

Pop snatched his body away, and replied, emphasizing his words, "No, you go home—man," he said.

Red watched Pop as he walked off, on his way back home. He still wasn't satisfied. Now he really had a reason to put something on his goody-goody ass.

Darnell's head was reeling. He knew that Pop was right. The streets weren't the place for him anymore. All he could go was downward from where he was, and somebody like Red could care less if he did.

57

NEW ADDITIONS

Shemone propped pillows up on the bed where Ohija was resting. "Girl, I am so thankful that you're all right and that you were able to come back home," she said to her.

"You and me both," Ohija replied. "If that dilation hadn't stopped, I'd still be in the hospital."

"I know, it's just not time yet for the twins to make their entrance into the world." Shemone added, "At least you're on complete bed rest. That doesn't sound so bad," she told her.

Ohija watched as her friend tucked and folded her inside the sheets like a beef burrito. Ohija felt like she could have been one with the dormant state she was ordered by her doctor to remain in. "It is that bad when bed rest is all that you do," she told Shemone, trying to loosen the edge on the sheet.

Shemone chuckled, realizing what she had done. "Oops, sorry," she told her, helping her out.

"I appreciate you helping me out today so that Ray could go back to work," Ohija told her. "Why don't you relax? Get something to drink, and take a sit down with me."

Shemone answered, "Something to drink? That depends on what you have."

Ohija chuckled as her friend went off to the kitchen to check her refrigerator.

There was a six-pack of cream soda. "Not you with soda," Shemone joked.

"Yes, me with soda," Ohija replied. "Ray bought it while I was in the hospital."

"That would explain it," Shemone replied, pulling the tab and pouring herself a full glass.

Ohija chuckled again. "Bring me some."

Shemone did. She walked back into the bedroom with the two soft drinks, then handed one to Ohija.

"Not bad," she told Shemone.

"Told you so."

Ohija let her know by saying, "But I still like my homemade juice blends from the juicer a whole lot better."

Shemone took a sip from her glass, then brought up the subject of Darnell, since that's who her mind was preoccupied with. "You know, I called Pop yesterday evening. He told me he hadn't seen Darnell himself, but had heard that Darnell was out there now." She continued, "I hope he doesn't think that I'm going looking for him this time. And you know what, Ohija?"

"What, girl?" Ohija asked her friend in a sympathetic tone of voice.

"I'm not sure."

"You're not sure of what?"

Shemone sat on the bed. "I'm not sure if Darnell really wanted to change."

"What do you mean?" Ohija asked.

"I don't know if he was doing it for me, or for himself. The lifestyle he lived, it suited him." Shemone added, "I wanted more out of his life for him."

"So does that mean that you're moving on? Without giving him the benefit of the doubt?" Ohija asked.

"I already gave him the benefit of the doubt." Shemone stirred her soda around using her finger and continued, "When I slept with him only weeks after he got out of jail. That was the benefit of the doubt. Ohija, I knew what his situation was. I was just hoping I could change him."

"Mmph," Ohija said aloud.

"I don't really have any other choice. I have to move on. I just hope that I still have my job at *Sister Soul*."

"Your columnist position? What happened?" she asked.

"I kind of gave my boss an ultimatum. I told them that either they give me a raise and a promotion or I'm leaving."

Ohija folded her arms over her chest. "That's an ultimatum, all right," she replied.

Shemone suddenly realized something since she was speaking about jobs. "Oh, that's right, I didn't get a chance to tell you. My mother got a job as a dance instructor, and Darnell got a job at Tayteck Electronics."

"Get outta here, congrats to them!" Ohija said in a surprised tone of voice.

"It is pretty fantastic, isn't it?" Shemone said to her. "Darnell doesn't even know he got the job. They called yesterday to let me know."

"That's progress, don't you think?" Ohija asked her. "I know Darnell would take that job if he knew about it. That's coming from the standpoint of me just being his friend." Ohija wasn't about to give up on him. Shemone was giving up on him as being her man, but someone still had to be there as his friend.

Shemone convinced herself. "I'm going to make sure that he knows before Monday, when he's scheduled to report in. Then I'm through with him."

"Okay," Ohija answered. She added, "You do know that matters of the heart are never that easy to end," she told her. Ohija hoped Shemone had thought her decision through.

"Probably so," Shemone replied, "but life does go on."

"I think I understand," Ohija said, trying to comfort her friend. "You just don't want to chance things with him anymore."

"Ohija, you know I thought I had my life all planned out. I was stable, you know?" Shemone said to her.

"Say no more," Ohija told her. "You just go on ahead and take your time with love, girl."

Shemone leaned over and rested her head on her friend's shoulder. "I know that bigger things have happened. You and Ray overcame his prostate cancer."

"We sure did," Ohija said. "He's back to work already, on light duty."

"Wow," was the only word Shemone could use to reply with.

58

SHIFTLESS

Darnell shifted his body on the couch to a more comfortable position. His body appreciated the rest after all the crazy late-night hanging out he'd been putting it through.

"Boy, you still in here sleeping at this time of day?" his mother, Louise, loudly asked him that Saturday morning. She plugged in the vacuum cleaner, and continued to mumble, but was drowned out by the sounds of the machine.

Darnell turned over on the couch, this time with his back facing his mother. He pulled the blanket over his head.

Louise kept on with her housework. Her mind was working. She vacuumed until there wasn't a speck on the rug, and until straight vacuum lines showed on the slightly worn, but now clean, beige carpeting.

Darnell could hear her again, now that she was finished and the vacuum was turned off.

"Just don't make no sense, for a man your age, to go back to things that you know are no good for you," Louise told him.

Monica entered the living room on her way to the kitchen to make her son something to eat. "Mama, what's wrong, what you fussing about now?" she asked, poking her mouth out.

"Your brother, your brother's what I'm fussing about," Louise answered.

"Hmph, figures," Monica replied. "He's got a bed. I don't know why he's out here in the living room, anyway. You need to put him out. He hasn't been staying here," she added.

"Yo, Monica, who asked you?" Darnell said, awakening from his half slumber. He sat up on the couch. His sister's snappy comments had waked him right up, and he didn't want his mother to think that he was lying around just being lazy.

"Nobody, and I can say what I want," Monica told him. "You ain't special."

"Darnell, please, do something useful with yourself today," his mother urged. Louise wasn't impressed with anything that Darnell had done since he'd come back to stay with her.

"Mama, I was just taking a little rest. I'm about to get up and get myself together now," he replied.

"Rest from what?" Monica interrupted from inside the kitchen. "You probably don't even work that much at that packing place," she told him.

"I work more than you do, Broom Hilda," Darnell quickly replied.

"Yeah, right," Monica answered with the baby bottle in her hand. "That's why Shemone called, and you didn't know," she teased.

"What, when?" Darnell asked her. "See how she is, Mama? She don't even give me my messages."

Louise sighed, and began to do her dusting. "Darnell, you gonna have to move from out of this living room. I'm trying to get my house clean. Monica, you give your brother his messages from now on because everybody knows you hit the roof when you don't get yours."

Darnell got up and wrapped his blanket around his waist. He'd fallen asleep in a T-shirt and underwear. "Did Shemone say what she wanted?" he asked his sister in an overinterested tone of voice.

Monica reluctantly answered, "Nope, sure didn't. She was trying to catch up with you for something—I don't know." She added in a sarcastic tone of voice, "She probably just wants you to come and get the rest of your junk out of her house."

Darnell sucked his teeth at his sister. He hoped that wasn't what Shemone wanted, for him to come and pick up something he'd left behind. He wasn't about to give up on his baby-girl just yet. Scratching his stomach, he went into the kitchen with an appetite. He glanced over at the empty stove and the empty black cast-iron pot. He opened the refrigerator, where there were only frozen foods, and cold drinks. "Mama," Darnell called out to his mother.

"What is it, boy?" Louise asked.

"You want me to cook everybody some breakfast?" he asked.

Louise didn't reply. She figured her son was playing around.

"Mama," he called out again, "I'm serious," he told her.

Louise shined the wooden souvenir piece that she'd gotten three years ago from Atlantic City. She set it down hard and marched into the kitchen. "Let me tell you and everybody else in this house something. There's no maid service here. I'm through catering to you grown children. Your little brother and me is really the only ones I have to cook a meal for these days." Louise's voice grew louder. "And that boy stays with his basketball practice all the time. He eats more on the outside than in. I don't know what y'all's excuse is."

"Yeah, I know, that's why I asked you if you wanted me to cook something," Darnell said with a smile.

Louise looked at the sincerity in her son's face. She thought to herself, This boy really would cook me something. She gave him a motherly kiss on the cheek. It was a sign of her gratitude. "Thank you, Darnell, but right now, all I need for you to do is listen. Both you and your sister," she told him. "Monica," Louise yelled.

"Yessss?" her daughter answered.

"Get in here."

"I'm trying to feed the baby, Ma," Monica complained.

"I don't care, bring him in here with you. I have something to say."

Monica trudged into the room with the little baby boy resting on her hip. She held his bottle in the other hand. "Yes, Mama?"

"My pressure is up now, because of you kids. Lord help you without me," Louise told them. "You and Darnell, I love you, and I want the best for you. But you-all have gotta go."

"What, go where, what are you talking about?" Monica asked. "Mama, you feeling all right today?" She had never heard her mother talk like this before.

Darnell looked on in astonishment as he stood in the kitchen. He couldn't believe what his ears had just heard, although he had planned on getting his own place as soon as he could, anyway. "Mama, you for real?"

"Yes, I am very for real," Louise told them both. "You have three weeks to get it together, and not a day more."

"But where would I go with a baby, Mama?" Monica asked. "Where am I supposed to go with your only grandchild?"

Louise shook her head and slowly replied, "I don't know, baby. Maybe a women's shelter if you have to, but you've got to learn to stand on your own two feet. You've got all these boyfriends, but none of them can help you with your own bills. The time has come for you to help yourself."

"A shelter?" Monica asked. "Why would I want to go to some dirty old place and live with a bunch of strangers?"

Darnell thought to himself. Putting him out was one thing. He was a man, and was supposed to carry his own weight. But his sister and the baby had to go, too? "Mama, you off the charts today," Darnell interrupted. "Why don't you go and lay down. Let us take care of you today. We'll bring you whatever you need," he said, thinking that she might be ill.

"What I need is my house back, and my sanity," Louise answered, going on the offensive. "I've tolerated a lot in the name of love. You-all got your stuff everywhere, you're inconsiderate, come in and outta here at all hours of the day and night. You have your friends calling whenever, and for whatever." Louise took a breath and went on with the list. "You expect me to baby-sit without asking. You want to be fed, and still have me around to answer all of your questions." She walked away, back into the living room, then returned. "It's just too much for any one person. I won't let you drive me to an early grave. All this worry and aggravation just ain't worth it to me."

"Mama, I don't know about this knucklehead, but I can change. I can get a job and help you out with the bills."

"Monica, you've been saying that for the longest. If you wanted a job, you would have had one by now. All you care about is being cute." Louise paused. "The truth is, you don't have a pot to piss in. At least your brother contributes."

Monica stood there holding her baby, Julius. The words stung, but they'd finally hit home with her.

"And that's another thing," Louise started in again. "The way you two go at each other. It's a shame. You're grown, and you-all are brother and sister. You need to be there for each other more." Louise pointed her finger at her eldest son. "Darnell, you're not saying anything, but I have something to say to you. I know you've been out of this house before, but this time there's no coming back for you." Louise went past him and opened the refrigerator to pour herself a glass of cold tea. "You're earning a clean, honest living now. I hope you know better than to go back to those streets again, boy. That kind of money is no longer welcome here."

"Mama, I haven't been doing anything, honest," Darnell said in a convincing tone of voice. He thought to himself that it felt refreshing to say it, and mean it.

"Not yet, but just make sure that you don't head anywhere in that direction." Louise continued, "I just hope you put that money you had to proper use."

Darnell was startled. "You mean you knew about my stash?"

"What stash?" nosy Monica asked in an overly interested tone of voice.

Louise and Darnell ignored her.

"How would I not know about everything and anything that goes on in my own house?" Louise took a drink from her glass. She drank as if she were refueling for the next load of sentences. "I see you got yourself a car, and I know you bought your girlfriend, Shemone, a nice ring. The ring was probably the best thing you could have done, money wise."

"No, it was the worse thing I could have done, Mama," Darnell replied. "Shemone doesn't want me anymore."

"I wouldn't want you either," Louise replied. "You need to stay consistent, off your mama's couch, and not out on those streets. That's probably what she wants. She's a strong woman, son. She's looking for a strong man."

Darnell kept quiet. He was that man inside.

"You are a man, Darnell." Louise's eyes began to tear up. "Be the person that I raised you to be. That's all that I'm going to say to both of you on the subject. I'm gonna be going to my room to lie down after all," Louise told them. "And I don't want to be disturbed by anyone, for any reason."

Monica slowly bounced Julius over her shoulders.

"He's asleep," Darnell told her from where he was.

Monica looked at her brother. "Thanks." She took the baby back into her room, laid him down in his crib, then came back out into the kitchen.

"She really means it, you know," Darnell told Monica.

"Yeah," Monica replied. "I don't know what I'm going to do," she told him.

"You know she's right about me and you, don't you?" Darnell said.

Monica went to the refrigerator and took out some ground beef. "Darnell, it's not like I hate you or nothing," she confessed.

"I don't hate you either." He did a double take. "You're cooking?" he asked. He never had seen his sister prepare a meal before. In fact, they'd never seen each other prepare a meal before.

"Not right now, but after this meat thaws, I will. Mama deserves a break." Monica added, "You know I do love you, because you are my brother."

"Yeah, I am," Darnell answered, not giving her much more information.

Monica waited to hear the words she was looking for. When she didn't hear them, she decided to ask him. "Well, aren't you going to say it back to me?"

"What, that I love you, too, sis?" Darnell joked. "You know I do." He went over and gave her a hug. "I gotta lot of love for you, girl. We'll help each other out."

"Glad I got somebody," Monica said with a laugh, hugging her brother back.

"You need to get on that Internet, like I did. See if you can find yourself some kind of program to get into. One that will give you somewhere to live and help you with getting yourself some training and a job."

"I don't know how to work that thing," Monica, said referring to James's computer.

"Well, I do, I'll help."

"Thanks," Monica said with a wide smile. "And you know what? You need to get on that phone and call your girlfriend, Shemone."

Darnell sighed. "I told you and Mama already. She doesn't want me anymore."

"I think she does."

"Oh, yeah? What would make you think that?"

"It was when she called."

Darnell chuckled. "That doesn't mean anything."

"That's what you think," Monica told him. "Feelings for you are still in her voice."

"You don't say," Darnell replied to his sister. He didn't want to think about it. He wanted to be about it. "C'mon let's get you on that computer while baby-boy is still sleeping and the food is thawing."

Monica followed her brother and smiled. She wasn't as afraid of the unknown as she'd thought, just knowing that Darnell was in her corner after all.

59

REVELATIONS

Shemone tapped her fingernails on her work desk, then stared at the phone. It was Sunday, and she still hadn't heard anything from Darnell. Pop hadn't called to say that he'd seen him either. Well, Shemone thought, she had to get in touch with him, at least to let him know that he'd gotten the job at Tayteck Electronics. Ohija was right, Darnell would not want to miss out on knowing that things had come through for him. She decided to try him at his mother's house again. Maybe this time, Monica would relay the message as she'd asked her to before. Or even better, maybe his mother, Miss Louise, would pick up. Shemone dialed his number and spoke into the phone. "Hello."

"Hello."

Wow. Sounded like Monica, Shemone thought to herself. As bad luck would have it.

"Shemone?" Monica asked.

Shemone was startled that Monica knew it was her. Monica did strike her as being slightly absentminded. "Yes, it's Shemone."

"I'm so glad that you called," Monica told her.

"Oh, really? He is okay, isn't he?" she asked.

"Yeah, girl, he's doing just fine."

Just fine? Shemone thought. Really. After hearing that, Shemone was, too. She could tell Monica the news, and get off the phone, because Mr. Darnell was doing just fine, and still wouldn't pick up the phone to call her. She didn't waste another minute. "Well, I was just calling so that you could let him know that he got the job at Tayteck Electronics. He starts first thing tomorrow morning at nine A.M."

"Get out!" Monica screamed excitedly. "Mama, Darnell got another job!"

Shemone heard Miss Louise giving her praises to the Lord, then she continued, "Yes, so—" she began to say, trying to end the phone call.

"So he can get on with his life and get back with you!" his sister blurted out loudly.

Shemone replied shortly, "Monica, I don't think so."

"He's still open for you, girl," she said.

Shemone didn't know exactly what that slang word "open" meant, but it sounded like Monica was trying to tell her that Darnell still cared for her. "And I'll always be open for him, too," she replied casually.

"So then what's the problem?" Monica asked her.

Obviously, she thought to herself, the slang word for "open" meant more than she'd thought. "Listen, I've got to go. I have work to do. Just make sure that he gets the message, okay?"

"Okay," Monica replied. In a last attempt, she asked, "Do you want me to tell him to call you?"

Shemone paused, and while the thought was somewhat appealing, she couldn't see herself giving in to it. "No, that won't be necessary," she answered. She hung up the phone, and rolled her chair in closer to her desk. Yep, yep, yep, yep, Shemone thought. Nothing like having a day free and clear, with no worries and nothing pressing to do.

She picked up the phone again, but this time called her mother. The phone rang several times before the machine picked up.

"Hi, this is Ruth, and I'm afraid I stepped out, but if you leave me a message with your name and number, I'll be sure to get back to you, okay? Have a pleasant day!" her machine chimed happily.

"Uh, yes, Mom, this is your daughter. I guess that you're not home, you're probably out teaching a dance class. I'll talk to you later." Just as Shemone was about to hang up she added, "Oh, and everything is fine with me, I just called to call." She didn't want Ruth to worry. She'd never heard her mother sound so upbeat before, kind of like she was on some kind of upper. Shemone went into the kitchen to fix herself a bite to eat. There was some leftover seafood salad and French bread from the night before that she had a taste for. Just then the phone rang.

"Good afternoon," Shemone said.

"Hello, Shemone? It's Marcello."

"Marcello?" Shemone repeated in a shocked tone of voice. She thought to herself, Please don't let this man be a stalker, before she said, "How did you get my home number?"

"From my caller ID. Your name came up on it. I must have missed your call," he told her.

Right, she'd called him and then hung up before rushing off to the hospital to go and see Ohija. "Yes, I had a bit of a family emergency," she said as she spooned some of the salad into a square wooden bowl. "So how are you?" she asked, trying to blow off what she'd done.

"I'm great, if you agree to go out with me for dinner. If you don't like me, I'll understand. You'll never have to see my ugly Italian mug face again," he promised.

Shemone couldn't help but chuckle. "Marcello, you're hardly ugly," she replied.

"So that's a yes, then?" he asked.

Shemone was about to tell him no. She was about to tell him that she wasn't doing the dating scene, and that she was strictly doing "her" at the moment. But she didn't. She'd already convinced herself that dinner with Marcello wouldn't hurt.

"Don't take too long flattering yourself, because I never pressure a lady," Marcello joked. "I'm a catch, too, you know."

There was that sexy accent again, she thought, laughing at what he'd said. "Fine, Serendipity's, Wednesday, at five-thirty P.M. I'll make the reservation," Shemone told him.

Marcello agreed. "Wednesday at five-thirty P.M. it is," he answered in a happy tone of voice. "It's a date."

Shemone thought to herself that well, so it was.

Pop walked down the poorly lit, desolate block on his way home Monday evening after completing an overtime shift at work. He'd had quite a day. Transit was making sure that he earned every penny. But in a few short months, it would all be worth it. He'd have the time he needed to qualify for his raise. Pop thought to himself that he wanted so much more for himself, his family, and his friend. He was troubled by what was going on with Darnell since he'd last seen him out in the streets.

Pop hadn't gotten around to calling Shemone to let her know that he'd seen him on the corner with Red last Thursday. That Red was some character. He'd never gotten past the fact that Pop had left working the streets and selling drugs to work a real job. And now it seemed as though Darnell was the one Red was trying to keep down. Pop knew that Red wanted to discourage his friend from taking the straight-and-narrow path. Fortunately, for himself, he had remained strong. He hoped Darnell would find that same kind of strength on his own.

The devil was busy, Pop said to himself. He'd thought Red right up, because he was walking his way, looking like he wanted to start some bullshit. He hadn't seen him since that last time they'd almost gotten into it, that day with Darnell. Pop slid his knapsack off his shoulder and undid the zipper, where he always kept his pocketknife for situations like this. If worse came to worse, he could defend himself.

"Well, well, well, look who's walking down my street," Red said loudly. "It's goody-goody," he told Pop.

Red wasn't by himself. There were two other guys with him, ones that Pop recognized as being the usual suspects. In other words, if you saw Red, you saw them with him. Pop didn't say anything at first. He knew that all he had was a knife. If it was just him and Red fighting without weapons, he'd whip his ass for sure. But to be out-numbered by the gang of them, with weapons, gave him little opportunity.

"What's the matter, you ain't got nothing to say now, goody-goody? That nine to five of yours must be working you too hard, kid. You can't even get a word out," Red said, determined to get a rise out of him.

Pop looked at him from the corner of his eye, but kept on walking. He didn't like the idea that he had his back to him, but it was a chance he'd have to take. Red and his punked-out crew didn't have a family like he did. Pop was walking past Red, maybe fifteen feet ahead of him, when a glass bottle was thrown. It just missed his head.

Pop turned around, angry. He thought to himself that nobody was gonna violate him. "Yo, fuck you, Red, just me and you," he yelled, turning to face him. He threw his hands up.

Red walked up to him in defense mode. His hands were up, too. "Yeah, okay," he told him. And as soon as Red got close enough to Pop, he reached inside his pants and pulled out a black .45-caliber gun. "Yeah, how about that, just you and me," he hollered out. Red took aim, and fired out a row of single gunshots. Bullets went flying wildly, and Pop was struck quickly, going down immediately. A pool of blood enveloped him where he lay on the concrete pavement.

Red wasn't satisfied, and was about to shoot again before one of his guys urged him to hurry and flee the scene before the police arrived. "Red, come on, man, the cops will be on their way soon, we gotta go!" he told Red.

Red grinned as he watched Pop squirm in pain. He kicked Pop as hard as he could before running off to join his group of boys, then they sped off down the street in his car.

Darnell whistled on his way to his mother's house from his new job at Tayteck Electronics on that same Monday evening. Monica had given him the message the instant he'd gotten in that Shemone had called.

Darnell took it as a sign. He'd made the right decision in keeping his life on track. His new job was everything he'd wished for, with lots of room to grow and spread his wings in the electronics field. They'd given him his own set of tools, a custom uniform with his name on it, and full access to the company van.

All he had to do was find a place. He had only three weeks left before he'd have to leave his mother's. Louise was keeping to her countdown, and Darnell understood why. Peace of mind, everybody was entitled to some, he thought to himself. He'd finally found some for himself, but still had constant thoughts of his baby-girl. Darnell hadn't seen anyone else, and hadn't planned to. What he did plan on was trying to get her back. He was going to return to her doorstep and grovel for forgiveness. He didn't care how long it took. And while she was deciding, trying to make up her mind whether she would or wouldn't, he'd stick to his goals, like Shemone had helped to teach him.

Darnell heard police sirens in the distance. He wondered what drama was going on now. Flashing red lights attached to a patrol car sped by, heading in the direction he was going. Darnell thought to himself that, in many ways, he was grateful. They weren't coming for him because of anything he might have gotten himself involved in with Red.

A familiar guy from his mother's building was suddenly running toward him, flailing his arms around. "Yo, Darnell, Pop's been shot, man!" The guy didn't wait. He raced back in the opposite direction, leading Darnell straight to his worst nightmare, the crime scene.

Darnell thought, This can't be real. He ran as fast as his legs would carry him. If Pop was dead, he'd never be able to forgive himself. When he arrived, the scene was crowded with onlookers. People stretched their necks out the windows of the surrounding projects, all wanting to know what had happened, and why. The location of the shooting had been taped off. Uniformed police officers, the same officers who had kept him locked down for all of those years, surrounded the area. A few feet away was an ambulance. Darnell pushed past the crowd, demanding his way to the front. "That's my family, that's my family," he kept yelling. The police officers ordered everyone to step aside and let him through.

"You're related to the victim?" one officer asked him.

"Yeah, I'm his brother," Darnell told him. He thought to himself that he and Pop were like blood brothers.

Inside the ambulance, Pop was being worked on.

Darnell stepped inside and took hold of his hand, which was all bloody from his gunshot wounds. "Pop, man, you can't die on me," he told him. "It's me, Darnell, you hear me? You can't die on me, man. You've got family who need you around."

The whites of Pop's eyes were the only things to be seen.

One of the paramedics abruptly announced, "We're losing him."

Just then, his screaming girlfriend, Monique, made her way up to the entrance of the ambulance. There wasn't an officer in the world who could stop her from getting through.

Darnell immediately jumped out of the van to hold her back, trying to calm her down. Pop's girlfriend would not stop screaming. "Monique, you've got to hold it together," he told her. "Pop needs us bad right now."

Monique did her best in trying to catch her breath. She demanded, "Did you have anything to do with this?," then began pounding on his chest. She asked him again, "Tell me, Darnell, was he with you?"

Darnell held on to her clenched fists, positive that Monique wanted to blame him for what had happened. All the while, in the background, he could hear the paramedics, speaking in medical lingo, desperately doing all they could to save his friend's life.

"He wasn't with me, Monique," Darnell shouted out. He shook her hard, not to hurt her, but to get through to her. Darnell said it again, "He wasn't with me."

Monique broke down, whimpering like a child in his arms.

Darnell summoned a close friend of Monique in the crowd, to tend to her while he went back to Pop, in the ambulance.

"You'll have to step aside," the ambulance worker told him as he hovered over his friend. "Will you be coming with us to the hospital?" he asked.

"You're damn right I am," Darnell told them all. "I'm not leaving my brother," he said, staring down at Pop. His friend's pupils were now visible, and he stared blankly at the interior roof of the ambulance with no verbal response. It freaked Darnell out to see his friend this way, suffering. He made a plea to him right then and there. "Pop, I'm here for you. Monique's losing it, I'm losing it. Things will never be the same. You've just got to pull through this, man!" Darnell squeezed down on Pop's hand. It was his way of letting him know that he wasn't ready to let him out of his life.

60

Shooting the Breeze

Shemone and Marcello met at Serendipity's on Wednesday evening. She was dressed smartly, in a navy below-the-knee V-necked dress that had a simple string belt around the waist.

Marcello didn't look too bad either. He was dressed in a black turtleneck sweater and black pants, which matched the color of his hair.

Shemone walked ahead of him once they were inside. "Waters, party of two, please," she told the woman seated at the front desk.

The hostess showed them to one of their best tables, not too close to the entrance or the kitchen.

Once seated, Shemone spoke again. "Have you ever eaten here before?" she asked a handsome Marcello.

"I have eaten almost everywhere," he answered with a wide smile.

His dark eyes and groomed, bushy eyebrows danced as he gazed at her. "You look terrific."

"Thank you," she replied, accepting the compliment. She thought to herself that she was not too surprised by his reply. Marcello seemed the type to frequent all kinds of restaurants.

"Would you like to order something to drink?" the waiter asked them both.

"We'll have a bottle of your finest champagne," Marcello ordered.

"Very good, sir," the waiter replied.

"Marcello, you don't have to be so extravagant," Shemone told him. "This is only an informal dinner."

"Maybe for you, it is," he said, "but when I'm out with a beautiful lady, it's always formal."

Shemone responded with a smile.

The waiter arrived with the champagne. He popped the bottle in front of them and poured the foamy liquid into their long-stemmed glasses.

Marcello picked up his glass, then told her, "In honor of you."

Shemone held her glass up, and toasted with him before they both took a taste.

"Is it to your satisfaction?" Marcello asked her.

"Yes," Shemone replied. "It's very good, thank you." The taste of the expensive champagne was concentrated. All of this attention. Hmph. If he kept this up, there was just no telling what would happen next, she thought to herself.

"Are you ready to look at the menu?" Marcello asked her. He quickly summoned the waiter and got their menus.

Shemone felt a sudden rush. She hadn't been out with such an assertive man since Darnell. Darnell was thug assertive. This man had class, and manners. She took another sip from her glass. A bigger one this time, just to ease the pain of the intrusive thought. She was reminiscing about Darnell during her dinner. "I think I want to get the broiled salmon with mustard sauce and dill," she told him.

Marcello nodded and placed the order, getting the same for himself as well as an order of au gratin potatoes and a mesclun salad tossed with a balsamic vinaigrette. He smiled again, happy that his dinner date was going well.

Shemone's mind began to wander, about Darnell again. She wondered if he'd gotten the message about his new job.

"I'm not boring you, am I?" Marcello asked. "If I am, I'll stand on this table right now and do a stripper dance to entertain you," he said.

Shemone snapped out of her thoughts as soon as he started speaking. "Marcello, be serious," she told him. She playfully hit his hands across the table. Shemone discovered that she liked saying his name: Marcello.

"I'm always being serious when I'm with you," Marcello answered flirtatiously, thinking to himself. He was intrigued. Marcello had dated plenty of black women before, but none like this. This one was, all together, a total package.

"So, how do you like being an automobile dealer?" she asked him. She wanted to know more about the business he was in. "Would you agree that you have the gift of gab?"

Marcello laughed. "I like being a dealer, but I don't interact with that many customers. I have people who work on the lots. I stay inside the office."

Shemone gave him a witty reply. "Oh, and count the money out, right?"

"Precisely." He laughed again.

The waiter arrived with their orders. She and Marcello enjoyed a quiet dinner, with interesting conversation. She'd learned that Marcello was really into name dropping, but didn't let it affect their meal.

Marcello walked her to her SUV after they left the restauraunt. "I see you keep her nice and clean," he told her, referring to her parked vehicle.

"How do you know that my car's a she?" Shemone asked.

"Because of her smooth lines," Marcello answered. "You look like a jaguar kind of woman," he told her. "I'd give you one if you wanted." He touched Shemone's brown skin as they stood on the curb.

She didn't stop him.

"I had a great evening," he told her.

"Yes, me, too," she replied. The champagne had her floating, but not drunk.

"Can we do it again sometime?" he asked.

"I think I'd like that," Shemone answered candidly. Her mind told her that there was no guarantee that she would.

Marcello moved in again, this time to kiss her softly on her lips.

She allowed him to, and found that his lips and tongue had rhythm. The texture was delicate, with no color.

"Good-bye for now," he told her. "Call me."

Shemone unlocked her vehicle, and stepped in. She replied, "I will." She drove off, back toward her apartment, knowingly. There wasn't going to be a second date.

The excitement of dinner was just too much for her. Shemone decided to dial Ohija on her cell phone on the way back home. "Ohija, girl, I just kissed a white man," she told her.

Ohija had just done her meditation from bed. "Seriously?" she asked in a taken-aback tone of voice. She didn't even know that her friend had had a date with anyone.

"I kid you not," Shemone answered. "His name is Marcello—"

Ohija interrupted in a whispered tone of voice. She didn't want Ray to hear, thinking it might get back to Darnell. "Let me guess, he's Italian?"

"Yes, girlfriend, I met him one afternoon while I was out cruising. Turns out he's got a dealership up in Utica. We went out for dinner, then I let him kiss me," Shemone said, trying to get the story out all at once.

"Scandalous, tell me the rest," Ohija said, wanting more detail as usual.

"Not too much to tell. He's very arrogant, and a huge name dropper," she told her.

"Really?" Ohija asked attentively.

"Really," Shemone replied. "I mean, he's white, I'm black, but that wasn't the problem. He was all that I'd bargained for and then some. He's handsome, mannerly, and knows what he wants out of life. Basically, he's got all the qualities that any sensible single woman would want in a man, but I'm still not interested. I knew that I wasn't during the middle of our conversation, and then finally," Shemone added, "after I kissed him."

"Hmmm, okay, somebody took a walk over the color line. It just might not be meant to be," Ohija told her, thinking to herself that for her, it honestly wasn't about race. But deep down she was still rooting for Darnell and the home team.

"Right," Shemone told her in an earnest tone of voice.

Ohija paused out of curiosity. "Did Darnell ever enter your mind during the date?"

"I didn't say that." Shemone confessed, answering her question, "I may have thought of him once, or twice."

Ohija smiled to herself, and thought, Yes, there's still a chance.

Shemone didn't expand any further on the subject. She asked about her friend's health and the babies. "So, the twins doing okay?"

"Yes, we're all doing okay over here," Ohija said.

"A little anxious over there, huh?" Shemone chuckled.

"Yes." Ohija laughed. "I feel like I should be doing something more." There was a pile of parenting magazines next to her on the bed. Reading them was about as exciting as it got.

Shemone told her, "I can come over tomorrow and beat you at backgammon if you like." She was trying to occupy some of her friend's time.

Ohija chuckled. "You mean you can come over and I can beat you," she answered back confidently.

"Oh, I meant to ask, how's Ray doing?" Shemone said.

"Ray's coming around," Ohija answered, slightly lowering her voice. She knew that he was just in the next room. "I think they secretly put the man on Viagra."

Shemone burst out laughing. "Why would you say that?"

"His sex drive has gone through the roof. Girl, you know we can't really indulge with my bed rest, but he can't seem to get enough of me taking care of him."

"So?" Shemone replied. "When was the last time you gave him some?"

"Last night, and he wants it every day," Ohija announced.

Shemone laughed again. "Well, you must have it going on then!"

"I must, right," Ohija said, joining in the laughter. "I'm not complaining. I love my husband, but what an adjustment."

"That's just what it is," Shemone agreed. "What about your meditation? How's that going?"

"Girl, I can't channel enough energy these days!"

"It's still helping though, right?"

"Of course," Ohija told her.

"Your mom's coming soon, right?" The call waiting on Shemone's cell phone beeped.

"Is that your other line?" Ohija asked her.

"Yes, but go ahead. They'll call me back if it's important," Shemone told her, thinking that Ohija deserved to have her ear for a change.

"Yeah, Moms will be here in a few more weeks. She'll be around for six whole months, until we get settled. You know, with me back to the boutique, and hopefully us closing on a house."

"I'm sure she'll be a big help," Shemone replied.

"Yes," Ohija replied. "Anyway, let me go. I need to call my sister up and have her fax me some paperwork," she told her.

"Okay, see you tomorrow," Shemone replied. She hung up the phone and checked the built-in caller ID on her cell phone. It was a private number. Whoever it was would have to call her back.

61

The Best of the Worst

The doctors had given it their all, working on Pop. The good news was that they'd managed to resuscitate him at a point when they'd thought they would lose him, enroute to Stratford Hospital. The bad news was that it was two days later, and he was on life support, with one bullet lodged in his head, and another one in his chest. At this point, things could go either way.

Darnell paced the floor of the hospital waiting room, as he had been for the past couple of days straight. His brain wouldn't allow him to stop thinking. He'd phoned Pop's mother and father in South Carolina. They hadn't taken the news well, which he'd expected. He'd told them what the doctors had told him. If Pop's condition didn't change within the next few days or so, they'd have to come in and make a decision as to whether or not they'd want to pull the plug on his life support. Immediate-family wise, Darnell, Monique, and his son were all Pop had until his parents could fly in. Monique did finally pull herself together, and hadn't left his bedside since she'd arrived at the hospital. Pop's son was safe at home with his maternal grandmother.

Darnell was trying really hard to keep himself together, but it was becoming more difficult by the minute. He'd tried to phone Shemone and let her know what had happened with Pop, but when he called her house, the machine wasn't on. And when he called her cell phone, he got nothing but voice mail. Darnell heaved a sigh of disappointment, and thought about what his mother had told him Shemone needed in her life: a strong man. Again, he thought that that was who he was. Darnell stopped short in front of Pop's room in the intensive-care unit. He took another breath before pushing the door open.

A lifeless-looking Monique sat next to Pop's bedside gazing at his friend, whose condition remained unchanged.

"Hey, Monique," Darnell said, "why don't you come on out for a little break? You eat anything?" he asked.

Monique lifted her head up slightly. "I don't wanna eat, thanks. I'm just not hungry," she replied.

Darnell persisted, "Well, you won't be of much use to him if you don't. At least come with me to get some juice. You need to get out of this room for a while."

"No, that's all right. I need to be here for Pop." Monique paused briefly. "Just in case he wakes up."

"The nurses will make sure Pop's well taken care of," Darnell told her, putting his hand out. He continued, "Pop's gonna want to see you looking your best when he does come around. You don't want him to have jokes on you, do you?"

Monique gave a half smile. She knew that Darnell was right. Pop would have jokes. Reluctantly, she rose from the chair and followed Darnell out into the hall, making sure to stop at the front desk. She told the nurse, "Take care of Aloysius Mason, I'll only be a few minutes."

Darnell pressed the elevator button. "How about a hot dog? I think I saw a man with a stand outside."

Monique nodded; her stomach made a growling noise as they rode down. "I guess I should eat something," she replied.

Darnell and Monique ate their food and drinks in the hospital guest lounge. Monique didn't have much to say.

"He's gonna be okay, you know. Pop's a fighter," Darnell said, trying to reassure her.

"Yeah, he is," Monique quietly replied. She was gently sipping her soda when something clicked, making her want to speak. "You know, word on the street is that Red was the shooter. They say he's on the run."

"Who told you that?" Darnell asked her.

"Somebody told somebody. You know how people are, nosy. They see stuff when it goes down. Sometimes they just don't want to get involved," she answered.

"Hmph," Darnell mumbled to himself. Gut instinct told him that Monique was on the money with this one. He should have known.

"Red is nothing but trouble, anyway. He never has liked Pop." She continued, "He even tried to come on to me before."

"Word?" Darnell replied. He was trying to sound as if what he'd just heard wasn't bothering him the way it was, but bombs exploded way down, within him. That muthafucker Red. That muthafucker Red was all that came to mind. There was something about that moment that made Darnell the most dangerous man alive.

Monique's mouth was finally in verbal motion, but he couldn't hear her words anymore. It was like watching a bad foreign movie. His thoughts rewound, back to the night when Pop was shot. He only heard the pitch of Monique's scream, the loudness and the never-ending length of it. He saw tears stream down her face, like the worst downpour of rain on earth, after seeing Pop in the back of that ambulance. Darnell also couldn't help but think about Pop's son. His life would be so different without a father. One of his best friends was in pain, lying helplessly in a bed upstairs with two holes in his body that he didn't deserve to have.

Monique tapped lightly on his arm. "Darnell, you all right?"

"Yeah, it's just been a long day, that's all," he answered, snapping out of his trance. "Listen, you think you'll be okay for a few hours? I have some stuff I need to take care of," he told her.

"Yeah, go on. I'll be here," Monique answered. "It's time I headed back upstairs, anyway."

Darnell tried to muster a smile, and kissed her on the cheek. He wrote his cell number down on a piece of paper he pulled from his pocket. "Call me if you need me."

"I will," Monique promised.

The automatic silver-and-glass hospital doors opened, and Darnell walked outside. There was a chill in the air. He walked swiftly to his parked car, got inside, and started the engine. He turned the radio up really loud. It didn't matter what song it was, it didn't matter what station. He opened the glove compartment, and checked to make sure the gun was where he had left it. Because yeah, he thought to himself, he had things to do.

62

AFTER HOURS

The hour was an ungodly 3:30 A.M. It was early Thursday morning, and the telephone was ringing. Shemone squinted through half-opened eyes in her darkened bedroom. She'd seen the clock, and reached for the phone. It was revelation. No good could possibly come from getting a call at this hour. "Hello," she said in a low tone of voice.

"Shemone, baby, it's Miss Louise," Darnell's mother said.

Shemone's heart pounded loudly in her chest. "Miss Louise, what is it? What's wrong?" she asked, immediately awakened from her sleep.

"It's Darnell. I'm worried about him," she said.

"Mama, just tell her," Monica said in the background.

"My brother better be all right," James added.

"Will somebody please tell me what's going on?" Shemone said loudly, sitting up in the bed and switching on the light.

"It's that boy that he hangs out with," Miss Louise tried to say before she broke into sobs.

Shemone was getting flashbacks, the way the news was coming at her. Not all at once, but in broken pieces. It was as if it was happening all over again. Terrance. Somebody was dead.

Monica took the phone away from her mother. She got right down to it in the best way that she could. "Pop got shot. They say it's

Red. Nobody's seen him or the guys that he was with, and Darnell never came home from work."

"Pop got shot?" Shemone repeated. "So, what, they think Darnell had something to do with it?" A lump formed in her throat. "He'd never do something like that to Pop," she said.

"No, we know that he didn't have anything to do with the shooting, that would be crazy," Monica replied.

Shemone cut her off. The picture was coming in clearer now. "Red, you think that he might have done something to Red?"

"Right," Monica replied.

"I'm on my way," Shemone told her. "Meet me downstairs in twenty minutes."

A slender, pretty young woman opened the building's front door. "Monica?" Shemone asked.

"Yeah," she answered, pulling Shemone in for a hug. "It's a shame we had to meet like this, but thanks for coming, girl." Monica had her hair pinned up with bobby pins. She was dressed in gray sweats and a T-shirt. She pushed the button to their floor as they rode up in silence.

"No thanks is neccessary, I want to help all that I can," Shemone replied.

Once they stepped off the elevator, they saw Miss Louise standing in front of the open apartment door. "I'm glad you two got up safe. I was just starting to come down," she told them.

"Mama, too much worrying ain't good. We're here now," Monica said.

"Welcome back, child," Miss Louise told Shemone. She opened her arms to give her a big hug.

Shemone hadn't paid it attention before, but it was easy to see where Darnell had gotten his dark eyes, long lashes, and straight white teeth.

His younger, handsome brother, James, sat in a chair in the living room.

"You must be James," Shemone said to him. "Hi."

"Hi," James replied shyly. James thought to himself, So this is the one. His big brother had been right on when he'd said she was the best-looking girl he'd ever had.

"You want some tea or coffee or something?" Miss Louise asked her.

"Chips or cookies?" Monica asked.

"No, just come and sit down with me. I want to know everything that you know," Shemone told everyone.

"We would, only we don't know that much," Monica replied. She took a seat on the couch.

Shemone asked them the question that was eating at her the most. "Is Pop . . ."

"Dead? No," Monica said, finishing her sentence. "He's in the ICU. We called, but they won't give us too much info because we're not the next of kin."

Shemone heaved a sigh of relief. At least Pop was still alive. "His girlfriend must be going out of her mind by now," she said.

"Red and them did it," James told her. "My friend's sister is the girlfriend of one of the guys he's running with. He called her from a pay phone, and told her that he was going out of town because they had something to do with shooting down this kid."

"Mmph," Shemone replied. "And Darnell went into work yesterday?"

"Yeah, sugar," Miss Louise replied, holding one of her hands up in testimony. "The Lord answered my prayers and got him a real decent job."

Shemone nodded; she was as proud of him as his own mother was for that. "And so Darnell hasn't called?"

"No," Monica replied.

"Have you tried to get him on his cell?" Shemone asked.

"I did, but I must have got the wrong number," Monica confessed. "I never had a reason to call him before."

Shemone nodded again. "Let me try him now," she replied. She pulled out her own phone, dialed the number, and waited. "Voice mail," she told them.

Miss Louise shook her head as if it was the end of the world.

"He must not have his cell on. I'll leave a message." Shemone said, concern in her voice, "Hi, Darnell, it's me, Shemone. I'm at your family's house and we're all concerned about you. We all care about you. We just want you to come home safe, or to at least let us know what's going on." Then she added, "I need for you to be okay, no matter what's going on with us."

Miss Louise smiled. She went over to Shemone and rested her hand on her shoulder. "He'll be all right, sugar, don't you worry none," she said.

"I just feel so damn helpless," Monica shouted.

"Watch your language in my house," her mother, Miss Louise, told her. "You gonna wake up that child if you keep it up."

"Sorry, Mama," Monica apologized. "There's got to be something we can do besides sitting here waiting."

And there was. Miss Louise spoke like an army drill sergeant. "James, you go in and get some rest. It don't make sense for you to stay up worrying."

"But, Mama, I ain't sleepy," he whined.

"Then just rest your eyes. You want to be able to see your brother clear tomorrow, don't you?"

"Yes," James replied with some enthusiasm. "Good night, everybody."

"Good night, James," Shemone told him. "Don't I get a kiss?"

James bopped over to her, looking like his big brother. He smiled, and laid a wet one right on her cheek.

"Looks like somebody's gonna have sweet dreams tonight," Monica teased. "Let me find out, you're plotting to get Darnell's girlfriend," she said.

James blushed and smiled, going off into his room.

"Monica," Miss Louise continued.

"Yes, Mama?"

"You call that hospital up again. See if you can find out anything."

Monica went to the phone and did as she was told.

"Miss Louise, what would you like for me to do?" Shemone asked.

"Child, just pray, just pray," Miss Louise told her, taking hold of her hand. She knew that faith was acting on the word of God. Her comfort was there. It already made everything all right.

Miss Louise had made up the couch really cozy for Shemone to sleep on. She persuaded her that it didn't make sense to be driving home so late at night, alone. Shemone tried, but couldn't sleep. She thought to herself that as soon as the sun came up, she'd be heading for the hospital to check on Pop, because Monica wasn't able to get any more information. Shemone switched on the ceramic lamp in the living room. She went into her purse and took out paper and a pen. Her mind was full of jumbled thoughts. She thought perhaps that writing them down would help to put them in perspective.

Darnell Williams, Shemone Waters. Uncertainty. Drama. Mistrust. Love. Family. Marriage. Uncertainty.
The end.

Shemone switched the light back off and lay down. She was able to rest for the next two hours, but was on the phone calling Ohija at 7:00 A.M. that Friday morning. "Ohija," she said into the phone, "did I wake you?"

"No, I was up going to the bathroom, girl, good morning. You and the sun keeping the same schedule, I see," Ohija told her.

"No, this is an emergency. Do you know if Darnell called Ray yesterday?" she asked in a serious tone of voice.

"I can find out. Why? What happened?" Ohija asked, concerned.

"Darnell's friend Pop got shot by a guy that Darnell was hanging out with. Pop's in the ICU, Darnell's nowhere to be found, and they say that the guy, Red, is on the run from the authorities, but we're not certain," she explained.

"Wha—at," Ohija replied. "Mmph. Mmph. Mmph, hold on," she told her.

Shemone could hear Ohija talking to Ray. She heard her explain the story to him just as she'd told her.

"Has he called, Ray?" Ohija asked her husband. Ray picked up the telephone.

"Shemone, it's Ray. So nobody knows where he is?" he asked her.

"No," she answered.

"You call him on his phone?" Ray asked.

"Yes."

"No answer?"

"No," Shemone replied.

Ray was just as worried about her. "And where are you?"

"At Darnell's mother's house. I stayed over last night."

Ray sighed heavily into the phone. "He hasn't called me, but if he does, you know you'll be the first person to know."

"Thanks, Ray, I appreciate it," Shemone told him.

"You try and take it easy. Is there anything we can do?" he asked.

"I'll let you know. For now, just keeping me posted helps," she assured him.

"You want to speak to Ohija?" he asked.

"No, just tell her that I'll call her later, after I find out something."

Good-byes were said and Shemone hung up. The appetizing smell of grits and sausage wafted in the air. "Miss Louise? That you in the kitchen?"

"Yes, sugar," she answered. "I'm an early bird. I'm fixing some breakfast for us to eat."

Shemone went into the kitchen where Miss Louise was. Thick, white, buttered grits in a heavy pot bubbled over a burner flame, and over another browned sausage sizzled sweetly in a pan.

"Hope you're hungry," Miss Louise said to her.

"Oh, I am," Shemone replied. "I just hope you don't mind if I eat and run. I need to get to the bottom of things today."

"I understand, sugar. I don't mind, just be careful," she warned. Miss Louise got out a serving spoon, and picked up a plate for Shemone.

"I will be," Shemone told her. It didn't seem as if she had any other choice. All she wanted was for Pop and Darnell to both be okay.

63

VISITING HOURS

Shemone drove further uptown, to Stratford Hospital, that morning. It was close to the Washington Heights area. Once she was inside, she rushed up to the desk, where a full-bodied Latina receptionist was sitting. "Good morning. My name is Shemone Waters, and I'm looking for a—" Shemone paused. She knew him as Pop, but Darnell's sister had called him Aloysius. "Aloysius Mason, please."

The receptionist began punching in the letters of his name, then suddenly stopped. She frowned, and with attitude, said, "Do you have a spelling for that?"

"I believe it's A-L-O-Y-S-I-U-S," Shemone answered quickly, thinking it was a blessing to have known. There was no telling how long she might have stood there wasting time and guessing.

The woman looked up from her computer screen. "Are you next of kin?"

Shemone answered, quick on her feet. "Yes. How else would I know how to spell that name of his?"

The receptionist smiled. "We only let one visitor up at a time. But his girlfriend finally left, something to do with her son, she told me." She handed Shemone a yellow pass wrapped in clear plastic. "He's in room 808, in the ICU unit."

"Thanks," Shemone replied. She walked off, then rode up on the elevator to see Pop. An arrow on the wall pointed to a room with his number on it. She pushed the door open and went inside. It was almost too much to take in at once, and she gasped at the sight of him, and all of the big machinery he was hooked up to. Shemone forced her feet over to his bedside. "Pop?" she called. "Can you hear me, Pop? It's Shemone."

Pop was unresponsive, still in a comalike state.

Just then a nurse entered the room to check Pop's vitals. The nurse monitored the machines, adjusted wires, and wrote down numbers.

"Excuse me, Nurse, how is he?" Shemone asked.

"Not very well, I'm afraid," she replied. "He's still in a coma, and not responding. The injuries he sustained seem to be having fatal results."

"So, then, now what?" Shemone asked. Her eyes were flooded with tears. It was all so unbelievable. Pop should have been awake and laughing, like he always had been.

"Authorization," the nurse told her. "We'll need the proper authorization from a family member to remove him from life support." The nurse eyed her. "I haven't seen you in here before, you are—"

"His sister, I'm the youngest," Shemone lied. "My parents will be up soon."

"Okay," the nurse replied before leaving the room. She added, "I'm so sorry."

Shemone picked up her bag and put it over her shoulder. "Pop, we're not giving up on you," she told him. And with that she left the room, too. Shemone got back into her SUV and drove to her apartment. If Darnell called the house, she wanted to be there.

Once Shemone was inside, she checked her messages. There were none. She threw herself down on her still-unmade bed, then thought. The caller-ID box. She went over to it and checked. Darnell had called yesterday from his cell phone. It looked to be a little after the time that Pop had gotten shot, and she'd missed his call. Thoughts of the worst kind filled her head. Darnell was probably so angry now. He'd already lost one best friend . . . What if he had gone after Red, looking for revenge? she thought to herself. There wasn't much she could do about it. She hoped that Darnell hadn't gone off and done anything crazy. Hurry up and wait, that was the plan for now. Shemone fell asleep where she was, her mind weary from thinking so much.

Shemone thought she was dreaming. The knocking on the door wouldn't stop, even after she'd sat up in bed. "Who is it?" she yelled out. "I'm coming," she told whoever it was. She threw on a robe, went to the door, and looked through the peephole. It was her mother, Ruth. "Mom, it's you." Shemone opened the door, then held on to her mother tightly.

Ruth thought her daughter sounded relieved that it was her. "Of course it's me, dear," Ruth replied. "I'm glad to see you, too." She chuckled. "I'm surprised you're not dressed. Did you forget that we were having lunch today?"

"Mom, Darnell is missing," she told her. It was the first time she'd mentioned his name to Ruth since the breakup.

Ruth saw a look of panic and fear on her daughter's face that she'd never seen before. As much as she wanted to say I told you so, he's nothing but a thug, a liar, and a thief, she didn't utter a negative word. That was the last thing Shemone needed now. Ruth put her purse down and walked Shemone over to the sofa. "He's missing how?" she asked in an interested tone of voice.

Shemone updated her mother on the past day's events.

"My, that is serious," Ruth replied. She tried to be helpful, at least for the sake of finding out that her daughter's ex-boyfriend was okay. "Shemone, I know that you may not want to, but perhaps it's time you got the police involved. Darnell's been missing for twenty-four hours, and their job is to protect and serve."

"But, Mom, you're not getting the whole picture," Shemone went on to explain. "I'm afraid that Darnell might have done something terrible, out of retaliation, to the guy who shot Pop."

"I see," Ruth replied. She wasn't the biggest fan of Darnell, but she was trying to be a fan of her daughter for once. Ruth tried to go the rational route. "You know that man, Shemone. You've known him since you were a teenager and have gotten to re-know him as an adult. Do you really think, in your heart of hearts, that he'd go and do something crazy like that?" she asked her.

Shemone could have pinched herself. Was this person her mother, Ruth Waters?

Ruth continued, "If Darnell hurts this Red person, he'll be going right back to jail. He'll lose his job, his family, and his friends, all over again. I don't think it's worth the risk for him."

"I don't think he went after Red," Shemone told her. "I'm hoping for the best, Mom. I always have when it comes to Darnell." She smiled and thought to herself, He'll always be my Final Four friend.

Ruth took her daughter in her arms. It wasn't a quick hug, and it wasn't strained.

64

Lost at Sea

Hurled his gun into the waters of the Chesapeake Bay, off Baltimore, Maryland? Yeah, Darnell thought, he couldn't believe he did it. It wasn't a choice, but a necessity if he wanted to safeguard himself and stay in the clear. Driving the straight three-and-a-half hour trip had become more of a mission, a mission to end the cycle of what could have been, his own self-destruction. It haunted Darnell, like a ghost in the night, all at once, when he'd first realized that Red was the shooter. The violent abruptness of it could have made him the person he'd vowed not to be. Drinking and driving, shootings, hospitals, and death. All flashbacks. None of which he wanted to be associated with anymore. In his mind, they all led to a dead end. School and education, work, home, family, and his woman. Those were the things that were important. Those were the things that no one could ever take away from him.

Now he was driving back home. He was going to go straight to his baby-girl to start pleading for that second chance. Darnell called Shemone before he reached the exit that let him off nearest her apartment.

"Hello," Shemone said in a long-winded tone. Everyone had been calling her but Darnell. She was seriously about to take her mother's advice and call the police, because at this point, Darnell was definitely a missing person.

"Baby-girl?" Darnell said into the phone.

"Darnell, is it really you?" Shemone asked. She quickly jumped up from on the sofa.

"Shemone, is it him?" Ruth, in the background, asked her daughter. She'd heard her say Darnell's name.

Shemone nodded an excited yes, it was him.

Ruth felt relieved for her daughter. It was at that moment that she knew that Shemone cared for this man much more than as just a friend. Undeniably, it was written all over her face. She still loves him, Ruth thought to herself.

"Where are you, is everything okay?" she asked. "I've been so worried. I went to see Pop."

"Is it okay if I come by? I really need to talk to you," he said.

Shemone evened her breathing and then answered, now that she knew that Darnell was okay, "Where are you?"

"I'm a few blocks away," he replied.

Shemone held the phone in close to her ear. "I'll see you when you get here," she told him.

"Okay," Darnell answered, and with that he hung up.

* * *

Shemone got herself together for Darnell's arrival. She put on jeans and a bright green sweater that complemented her red hair color. She didn't want Darnell to think that she was anywhere near the bottom of the barrel since they'd split up.

"You look nice," Ruth told her daughter as she entered the living room. "Should I be going?" she asked. Ruth thought to herself that she didn't want to be in the way of the two sorting things out if they could.

"No, Mom, you don't have to go anywhere. I'd like you to stay," Shemone said, thinking that there really was no reason for her mother to leave. Once she saw for herself that Darnell was okay, and saw to Pop, she'd be fine.

Ruth smiled and told her, "So I'll stay then."

The doorbell rang. "That's him," Shemone told her mother. She went to the door and opened it.

"Hey, baby-girl," Darnell said.

It reminded her of the very first time he'd come to visit her after leaving Pennington. "Hey, yourself," Shemone replied.

And just as before, he'd asked, "Can a brother at least get a hug?"

Shemone was so glad to set eyes on him that she did hug him. She thought, He's safe.

Darnell opened his arms and gave her the biggest embrace that he could.

Shemone broke away first. It was hardly a lovefest for her. She told him to come in, then directed him over to the couch where they could both sit. Ruth had disappeared into the back.

Darnell turned to face her, then spoke. "Shemone, I want us. I didn't realize how much I did until I had to be without you," he said. "You complete the person that I am, and I made a big mistake. I should have never slept with Hope, and I will never, ever betray your trust like that again," he told her in an earnest tone of voice. "I slept with her because I had a problem with me, not because of any problem with you." Darnell still wasn't finished. He continued, "I love you, and the only way for me to prove it is to start making up for the mistakes I made. The only way I can do that is if you give me one more chance."

Shemone could see Darnell's chest as it rose and fell from the rate at which he was breathing. She stared deep into his eyes, as far as she could, searching for truth. That's when she found it. She decided to give Darnell that chance. "Okay, Darnell," she told him. "I'll give us another chance."

"For real, baby-girl?" Darnell asked her.

"Yes, for real," she replied.

Darnell reached into his pocket. He produced the velvet box with her ring in it and took it out. "Shemone, will you be my wifey?" he asked her.

Shemone smiled and answered, "Yes, yes, I'll be your wifey," she said.

Darnell slid the ring onto her finger and then went in for the kiss.

It was the longest, deepest, and most meaningful one to date for them both.

Ruth entered the room and cleared her throat. She thought to herself that it wasn't her fault that the walls were thin. She'd overheard it all. She had to admit that she was impressed at how Mr. Thug had handled things. "You two kids all right out here?" she kidded.

Darnell pulled away after he'd heard her mother's voice. He gave Shemone another short kiss on the lips. "I love you," he told her again.

"I love you, too," Shemone said happily.

Darnell turned and looked at Ruth. "Hey, Miss Waters," he said with a smile.

Ruth took in the sight of the man her daughter had chosen to love. He wore rough blue jeans, a T-shirt, a bulky sweater, and, she didn't want to forget, that one diamond stud that sparkled in his ear. Ruth thought to herself that she supposed he was handsome-looking in a streety sense of the word. Although she didn't want to admit it, he'd brought her daughter back to her by breaking her heart. Luckily for him, he'd put the pieces back together. He and her daughter would make her a beautiful grandchild one day. Ruth's tone of voice was sincere. She told him, "Darnell, glad to have you back safely."

"Yeah, thanks," he replied in a shocked tone of voice. He thought, Shemone's mother is actually being nice to me.

"Darnell, Mom and I have been working things out between us," Shemone said.

"I'm glad. It's about time," he told them both.

"Yes," Ruth said. "We all should try and work things out. It's obvious that you make my daughter very happy. I'm through with trying to come between you two."

"So you're saying that you're through with being a pain in the you-know-what?" Darnell joked.

Shemone gasped, and used the heel of her foot to gently kick the back of Darnell's leg.

Ruth chuckled, to everyone's surprise. "You certainly aren't one to mince words, are you?" Then she added, "Yes, I do admit to being a pain in the ass."

Darnell burst out laughing, then Shemone joined in.

"Mmph, so then that means I can call you Mom?" Darnell asked Ruth.

"Don't push it," Ruth replied, smiling. She'd meant what she'd told him, but that didn't mean he could get crazy. Ruth suddenly noticed the diamond that was on her daughter's ring finger. From where she stood, it looked impressive. She got closer for a better inspection before finally giving it her approval. "Guess you can call me Mom," she said.

Darnell laughed again. "You're funny, Moms," he told her. Darnell took Shemone's hand in his. "Baby-girl, don't kill me, but I need to go and check on Pop," he said. "Monique is probably wondering where I disappeared to."

"Yes, that's a good question." Shemone asked, "Where did you disappear to?"

"I'll fill you in later; right now I've got to go," Darnell told her. He wanted to check on Pop. Monique hadn't called him, so he assumed everything was the same.

"I'm coming with you," Shemone answered. "I care what happens to Pop, too," she said.

"So then let's go," Darnell replied. He wanted his future wife-to-be by his side.

"Mom, you okay here by yourself?" Shemone asked.

"Of course I am," Ruth answered. "I'm about to leave in a bit, though. I'll just let myself out."

Shemone gave her mother a hug before she and Darnell left. "I'll call you later. If Ohija calls, please let her know that Darnell is okay, and that I'll call her tonight."

Darnell was already out the door. Ruth heard him say, "Yeah, Moms, we'll call you later."

Shemone and Darnell rode in his car to the hospital.

"So why don't you tell me now," Shemone said as she rested her head on the car headrest.

"Tell you what?" Darnell asked as he drove.

"Where you went, and what happened to you."

"Well," Darnell said, "I was coming home from my new job—"

Shemone interrupted him in the middle of his sentence. "Darnell, your job—"

"Relax, baby-girl. I still have it, and I love it. I handled my business. I called them and told them I had a family emergency and that I'd be in first thing tomorrow. My boss understood."

"Thank goodness. Now, you were saying?" she asked him.

Darnell stopped for a red light. "I was saying that when I found out that Pop was shot, I was hurting real bad."

"I know," Shemone said in a concerned voice. "Pop's like a brother to you."

"Yeah," he agreed. Darnell took off again once the light switched to green. "Then I saw the effects of it all, and him in the back of that ambulance, then in the hospital. Then Monique told me that Red was behind it."

"That's what your family told me. Oh my goodness," Shemone said, "your family." She dialed them on her cell phone. She told them that Darnell was okay, and put him on to reassure them. After he'd hung up, she asked him to please tell her the rest.

"So, yeah, Red, I found out, and at first all I wanted was revenge. I didn't care what the consequences were."

Shemone hung on his every word, shuddering at what he might be going to say next. She hoped that she was right, and that they wouldn't be getting married with him in a jail cell somewhere.

Darnell explained, "I had an unloaded gun in the glove compartment of my car. I never planned to use it. As a matter of fact, I was gonna get rid of it before the incident happened with Red. That's when I thought, I need bullets to go with it."

Shemone answered in a startled tone of voice, "I never knew you owned a gun."

"I know you didn't. You weren't supposed to. I didn't feel like you needed to know something like that. But from now on, no more guns," he told her.

"Okay," she replied, thinking to herself that that was one she was going to leave alone.

"Anyway, I was so filled with, like, rage that I just started driving." Darnell could laugh at it now. "I drove to Baltimore, Maryland, and threw my gun in the bay." Then he told her, "We should go and visit one day. It's kind of nice over there."

"So then you didn't do anything? All you did was get rid of your gun?" Shemone asked him.

"Mm-hmm, I had to," Darnell answered. "I'm a changed person. Because of me, and because of you."

"Darnell, I am so proud of you," she told him.

"Proud enough to let me come back home?" he asked.

"I think that we can work things out, with a few conditions," she replied.

Darnell smiled. "Just tell me, and I'm sticking to them," he said.

"First, no more cheating. I have to be able to trust you, or what we have won't work. Second, we have to make the love between us unconditional. That means that you agree that we're going to work through things together," she told him.

"Not a problem," Darnell answered. "And now that you mention it, I've got a few conditions of my own," he said.

Shemone was shocked. No, he did not. It was sexy. "What conditions?" she asked him.

"First, I'm gonna need for you to stick by your word. If you say you're not gonna doubt me, then don't. No more back and forth. Second, we agree on things together." Darnell's voice went up. "That means me and you." He paused for a few seconds. "I don't care if it's bills, places we go, or decisions we make, because this marriage shit, it's serious. We can't play games no more."

Shemone thought to herself that she was turned on, both mentally and physically. Succesful person. Educated. Good-looking. Funny as hell, but not perfect. Goodness. She felt appreciated. All those qualities she'd wanted in a man were right in front of her now in Darnell. "Okay, I understand, and you have my word," she promised.

Darnell stopped at the last light before the turn to the hospital. He leaned over and kissed his wife-to-be on the lips, sealing the deal of a lifetime. The only thing left to worry about now was Pop.

65

Outer Limits

A small-framed Asian woman sat at the front reception desk. It was a receptionist that neither Darnell, nor Shemone had seen before.

"May I help you?" she asked them in a soft, friendly tone of voice.

"Yeah, we need a pass to go see Aloysius Mason. He's in the ICU," Darnell said to her.

"Okay," the woman replied. She tapped at her computer. "You said that was Mason, right?"

Darnell and Shemone looked at each other at the same time, fearing the worst.

"Yes, Mason." Shemone spelled it out for her: "M-A-S-O-N."

The woman tapped some more. "I'm sorry, but there doesn't seem to be anyone in the ICU by that name," she said.

Darnell put his hands over his face.

"Let me just check one more thing." She tapped some more. "Here we are," she finally said to them.

"He's all right?" Darnell asked.

The woman reached down and handed each of them a visitor's pass, then said, "Room 705, on the second floor. He was moved to a regular room."

"Darnell, Pop came out of his coma!" Shemone shouted.

Darnell picked her up and swung her around.

"Let's go up," he told her in an excited voice. "Pop's waiting for us!"

* * *

Darnell knocked on the room door before he and Shemone went in.

"Come on in, D.," Pop's voice said. "Took your ass long enough to get here," he added.

Darnell laughed as they entered the room. He'd know those jokes anywhere.

"A man comes out of a coma, and still can't get no love," Pop told them.

Monique sat in a chair next to his bed. "Pop, I was here," she told him.

"Don't front, you were in the bathroom," Pop kidded.

Everyone laughed.

"Pop, we're so happy that you're okay," Shemone told him.

"I hope you two worked it out, or I might just slip back into the darkness," he joked.

Shemone held out her ring proudly.

"Damn, D., I didn't know you had it like that. That's a lot of dollars right there," Pop said.

"Man, that's from the money I put up before I got locked up," he explained.

"Now that's a rock!" Monique exclaimed, admiring Shemone's ring.

"Look at you now," Pop said. "See what you caused, Darnell? Now she's gonna want one."

"I deserve it," Monique replied with a smile.

"You do, boo, don't worry about it, you'll have your day," Pop vowed.

Monique smiled to herself. She knew that it wasn't too far off after all they'd been through.

"So how long are you going to be in here? Is everything back to normal?" Shemone asked Pop.

Monique answered, "It's a miracle. He's totally okay. The doctors just want to monitor him to be sure."

Shemone nodded. "That's right, you can't be too careful," she said.

"Pop, you have any of those out-of-body experiences like on *The X-Files?*" Darnell asked jokingly.

"Nah, nothing like that. But I appreciate living, man. I heard that you was on some revenge shit with Red and them punks. You had a lot of people shook."

"I almost was," Darnell told him. "Then I realized that it wasn't worth it. It wasn't worth losing everything that I had going for me."

"True, true," Pop agreed. "I'm glad you didn't do nothing crazy, too. You know they got caught, right?"

"Oh, yeah?" Darnell said.

"Red might be getting locked up in Rikers, serving five to ten for attempted murder, man," Pop told him, grinning.

"What about the guys he was with?" Darnell asked.

"I think they'll probably have to do some time, too, because they were accomplices to the crime and all. They might not serve as long."

"As long as they go away for something," Darnell said.

"How'd you find out?" Shemone asked Pop.

"People calling from around the way. Seems like they found out the telephone number as soon as I hit the recovery room." Pop told them, "I'm famous."

Darnell went over to Pop's window. He looked down at the view of trees and benches in the back. "Did you speak to your mother and father?"

"Hell, yeah, they were on their way. I think that's why I woke my ass up, so they wouldn't come up here pulling no plugs on me," he said.

Everyone in the room burst out in laughter. They were so loud that one of the nurses came inside.

"Okay, guests, you're going to have to leave now. Aloysius needs his rest," the nurse told them.

"Right," Darnell mocked, " 'Aloysius needs his rest.' We'll be back to see you tomorrow."

Monique gave Pop a kiss, Shemone gave him a hug, and Darnell slapped him five.

"Yeah, tomorrow, D.," Pop replied. He closed his eyes, and relaxed. He opened them again and thought to himself, Just checking.

* * *

"That was just like the first time," Darnell told Shemone, just after they'd made love that Friday night, back at home.

Her head was resting on Darnell's chest. "No, better," Shemone replied. "I absolutely think that it was better."

The hush of tranquility filled the room.

"Darnell?" Shemone said.

Darnell was almost out, on his way to sleep, but he wasn't quite there yet. "Yeah, I'm up," he answered.

"Since we're starting out new, I want us to be honest." She continued, "When we were separated, I kind of went out with someone else."

Darnell bit down on his lower lip, then replied, "What are you saying? You do something to make us even?" he asked. It got him to thinking. He'd slept with Hope, and she'd slept with who? All he wanted was for the whole situation to be over with already, but he'd brought it on himself.

"No, nothing like that. I just went out on a date, that's all," Shemone explained to him.

"A date?" he asked calmly.

"Yes, only one."

Darnell put his arms behind his head. "So, go ahead, what else?" he asked her.

Shemone got settled on her side of the bed and continued, "He's a white guy that I met while I was out one day."

"You don't say," Darnell replied. "That's real different."

"That's why I wanted to tell you, I just wanted you to know in case he calls here."

"So now I know," Darnell said. "I know, and I'm secure with the fact that I'm the only man you need in your life." He continued, "I know that you're all the woman I'll ever need," he said in a sexy, thugged-out tone of voice. He spooned her tightly, nuzzling the back of her neck. "So can I go to sleep now?"

"Yes. Sweet dreams," Shemone told him. She told Darnell "sweet dreams" because hers had already begun to come true.

* * *

Six months had passed, and when Shemone looked into the mirror these days, she liked what she saw, both inside and out. She had a few new titles to add to her credits. For one, she was a loved, newly wed wife. The all-cream-colored-inspired intimate wedding ceremony on the beach in the Caribbean with hers and Darnell's bare feet, was, simply, simple. The guest list was simple, too. It included Darnell's mom, sister, and brother, her mother, Ruth, Ben, yes, her mother's helper/new special friend, Ohija and Ray, and her two new healthy god-children, Ayanna and Zion. That covered the gamut of friends and family. It also didn't hurt to come back from the honeymoon to a raise, and her new position as the contributing editor of *Sister Soul Magazine*. She used the faith of her mate, and her confidence in herself, as a guide. Shemone could truly say that she was the woman she said she was.

Darnell looked in the rearview mirror of the Tayteck Electronics van he was driving. He caught a glimpse of his reflection. Something about him had changed, he thought. He was a married man now. Shemone and her fancy ass had carried him all the way to hot-ass Jamaica to make it happen. But it was worth it. He had gained new godchildren, friends like Ray, and the love of his life in Shemone. In thinking back, it was all worth it to him. Money was no longer such an issue. He'd learned how to make top dollar, and how to keep it. He was even looking into starting his own contracting business in the future. He also realized that money wasn't the end all be all in life. Having the vision was. Darnell could truly say that he was the man he said he was.